Approximate southern limit of Russian

HUNGRY STEPPE

Fort Raim
AkMechet
Syr Daria
Tashkent
Khokand

×
Oasis

Aral Sea

Tishkandi

KIZIL KUM

ST YURT

Samarkand

Khiva
Bokhara
Amu Daria (Oxus)

KARA KUM

Peshawar

Kabul

Herat

A F G H A N I S T A N

B A L U C H I S T A N

Teheran

R S I A

I N D I A

PERSIAN GULF

INDIAN OCEAN

Miles

0   100   200   300   400   500

W. Bromage

ALSO BY GEORGE MACDONALD FRASER

Flashman (1969)
Royal Flash (1970)
Flash for Freedom! (1972)
The Steel Bonnets (1972)
The General Danced at Dawn (1973)

FLASHMAN
at the
CHARGE

FLASHMAN
at the
CHARGE

GEORGE
MACDONALD
FRASER

 ALFRED A. KNOPF
NEW YORK 1973

THIS IS A BORZOI BOOK
PUBLISHED BY ALFRED A. KNOPF, INC.

Portions of this book originally appeared in *Playboy* Magazine.

Library of Congress Cataloging in Publication Data.

Fraser, George MacDonald, (date).   Flashman at the charge.
    I. Title.
PZ4.F8418F13   [PR6056.R287]   823'.9'14   73-7260
ISBN 0-394-48756-7

MANUFACTURED IN THE UNITED STATES OF AMERICA
FIRST AMERICAN EDITION

For "Ekaterin",
rummy champion of Samarkand

Explanatory Note

When the Flashman Papers, that vast personal memoir describing the adult career of the notorious bully of *Tom Brown's Schooldays*, came to light some years ago, it was at once evident that new and remarkable material was going to be added to Victorian history. In the first three packets of the memoirs, already published by permission of their owner, Mr Paget Morrison, Flashman described his early military career, his participation in the ill-fated First Afghan War, his involvement (with Bismarck and Lola Montez) in the Schleswig-Holstein Question, and his fugitive adventures as a slaver in West Africa, an abolitionist agent in the United States, and an erstwhile associate of Congressman Abraham Lincoln, Mr Disraeli, and others.

It will be seen from this that the great soldier's recollections were not all of a purely military nature, and those who regretted that these earlier papers contained no account of his major campaigns (Indian Mutiny, U.S. Civil War, etc.) will doubtless take satisfaction that in the present volume he deals with his experiences in the Crimea, as well as in other even more colourful —and possibly more important—theatres of conflict. That he adds much to the record of social and military history, illumines many curious byways, and confirms modern opinions of his own deplorable character, goes without saying, but his general accuracy where he deals with well-known events and personages, and his transparent honesty, at least as a memorialist, are evidence that the present volume is as trustworthy as those which preceded it.

As editor, I have only corrected his spelling and added the usual footnotes and appendices. The rest is Flashman.

G.M.F.

FLASHMAN
at the
CHARGE

SOUTH-WEST RUSSIA and CENTRAL ASIA 1854-55

Ekaterinoslav (Dnepropetrovsk)
+ STAROTORSK
Alexandrovsk (Zaporozhe)
Taganrog
Rostov
Don
Astrakhan
Odessa
Dnieper
CRIMEA
Kertch
Sevastopol
Danube
Varna
BLACK SEA
Constantinople
Volga
R U S
CASPIAN
Ural
O T T O M A N   E M P I R E

Odessa
To Starotorsk
0   Miles   50
Yenitchi
Sea of Azov
Arrow of Arabat
Sivache Lagoon
C R I M E A
Kertch
Eupatoria
Arabat
Calamity Bay
Alma
Sevastopol
Balaclava
B L A C K   S E A

I A

Approximate southern limit of Russian influence

HUNGRY STEPPE

Fort Raim

AkMechet

Syr Daria

× Oasis

Tashkent

Khokand

Aral Sea

KIZIL KUM

Tishkandi

UST YURT

Khiva

Amu Daria (Oxus)

Bokhara

Samarkand

KARA KUM

Peshawar

AFGHANISTAN

Kabul

SEA

Herat

BALUCHISTAN

Teheran

P E R S I A

I N D I A

PERSIAN GULF

INDIAN OCEAN

Miles

0   100   200   300   400   500

W. Bromage

&1   The moment after Lew Nolan wheeled his horse away and disappeared over the edge of the escarpment with Raglan's message tucked in his gauntlet, I knew I was for it. Raglan was still dithering away to himself, as usual, and I heard him cry: "No, Airey, stay a moment—send after him!" and Airey beckoned me from where I was trying to hide myself nonchalantly behind the other gallopers of the staff. I had had my bellyful that day, my luck had been stretched as long as a Jew's memory, and I knew for certain that another trip across the Balaclava plain would be disaster for old Flashy. I was right, too.

And I remember thinking, as I waited trembling for the order that would launch me after Lew towards the Light Brigade, where they sat at rest on the turf eight hundred feet below—this, I reflected bitterly, is what comes of hanging about pool halls and toad-eating Prince Albert. Both of which, you'll agree, are perfectly natural things for a fellow to do, if he likes playing billiards and has a knack of grovelling gracefully to royalty. But when you see what came of these apparently harmless diversions, you'll allow that there's just no security anywhere, however hard one tries. I should know, with my twenty-odd campaigns and wounds to match—not one of 'em did I go looking for, and the Crimea least of all. Yet there I was again, the reluctant Flashy, sabre on hip, bowels rumbling and whiskers bristling with pure terror, on the brink of the greatest cavalry carnage in the history of war. It's enough to make you weep.

You will wonder, if you've read my earlier memoirs (which I suppose are as fine a record of knavery, cowardice and fleeing for cover as you'll find outside the covers of Hansard), what fearful run of ill fortune got me to Balaclava at all. So I had better get things in their proper order, like a good memorialist, and before describing the events of that lunatic engagement, tell you of the confoundedly unlucky chain of trivial events that took me there.

It should convince you of the necessity of staying out of pool-rooms and shunning the society of royalty.

It was early in '54, and I had been at home some time, sniffing about, taking things very easy, and considering how I might lie low and enjoy a quiet life in England while my military colleagues braved shot and shell in Russia on behalf of the innocent defence-less Turk—not that there's any such thing, in my experience, which is limited to my encounter with a big fat Constantinople houri who tried to stab me in bed for my money-belt, and then had the effrontery to call the police when I thrashed her. I've never had a high opinion of Turks, and when I saw the war-clouds gathering on my return to England that year, the last thing I was prepared to do was offer my services against the Russian tyrant.

One of the difficulties of being a popular hero, though, is that it's difficult to wriggle out of sight when the bugle blows. I hadn't taken the field on England's behalf for about eight years, but neither had anyone else, much, and when the press starts to beat the drum and the public are clamouring for the foreigners' blood to be spilled—by someone other than themselves—they have a habit of looking round for their old champions. The laurels I had won so undeservedly in the Afghan business were still bright enough to catch attention, I decided, and it would be damned embarrassing if people in Town started saying: "Hollo, here's old Flash, just the chap to set upon Tsar Nicholas. Going back to the Cherrypickers, Flashy, are you? By Jove, pity the poor Rooskis when the Hero of Gandamack sets about 'em, eh, what?" As one of the former bright particular stars of the cavalry, who had covered himself with glory from Kabul to the Khyber, and been about the only man to charge in the right direction at Chillianwallah (a mistake, mind you), I wouldn't be able to say, "No, thank'ee, I think I'll sit out this time." Not and keep any credit, anyway. And credit's the thing, if you're as big a coward as I am, and want to enjoy life with an easy mind.

So I looked about for a way out, and found a deuced clever one —I rejoined the Army. That is to say, I went round to the Horse Guards, where my Uncle Bindley was still holding on in pursuit of his pension, and took up my colours again, which isn't difficult when you know the right people. But the smart thing was, I didn't ask for a cavalry posting, or a staff mount, or anything risky of that nature; instead I applied for the Board of Ordnance, for which I knew I was better qualified than most of its members, inasmuch as I knew which end of a gun the ball came out of. Let me once be installed there, in a comfortable office off Horse Guards, which I might well visit as often as once a fortnight, and Mars could go whistle for me.

And if anyone said, "What, Flash, you old blood-drinker, ain't you off to Turkey to carve up the Cossacks?", I'd look solemn and talk about the importance of administration and supply, and the need for having at home headquarters some experienced field men—the cleverer ones, of course—who would see what was required for the front. With my record for gallantry (totally false though it was) no one could doubt my sincerity.

Bindley naturally asked me what the deuce I knew about fire-arms, being a cavalryman, and I pointed out that that mattered a good deal less than the fact that I was related, on my mother's side, to Lord Paget, of the God's Anointed Pagets, who happened to be a member of the small arms select committee. He'd be ready enough, I thought, to give a billet as personal secretary, confidential civilian aide, and general tale-bearer, to a well-seasoned campaigner who was also a kinsman.

"Well-seasoned Haymarket Hussar," sniffs Bindley, who was from the common or Flashman side of our family, and hated being reminded of my highly-placed relatives. "I fancy rather more than that will be required."

"India and Afghanistan ain't in the Haymarket, uncle," says I, looking humble-offended, "and if it comes to fire-arms, well, I've handled enough of 'em, Brown Bess, Dreyse needles, Colts, Lancasters, Brunswicks, and so forth"—I'd handled them with considerable reluctance, but he didn't know that.

"H'm," says he, pretty sour. "This is a curiously humble ambition for one who was once the pride of the plungers. However, since you can hardly be less useful to the ordnance board than you would be if you returned to the wastrel existence you led in the 11th—before they removed you—I shall speak to his lordship."

I could see he was puzzled, and he sniffed some more about the mighty being fallen, but he didn't begin to guess at my real motive. For one thing, the war was still some time off, and the official talk was that it would probably be avoided, but I was taking no risks of being caught unprepared. When there's been a bad harvest, and workers are striking, and young chaps have developed a craze for growing moustaches and whiskers, just watch out.[1] The country was full of discontent and mischief, largely because England hadn't had a real war for forty years, and only a few of us knew what fighting was like. The rest were full of rage and stupidity, and all because some Papists and Turkish niggers had quarrelled about the nailing of a star to a door in Palestine. Mind you, nothing surprises me.

When I got home and announced my intention of joining the Board of Ordnance, my darling wife Elspeth was mortified beyond belief.

"Why, oh why, Harry, could you not have sought an appointment in the Hussars, or some other fashionable regiment? You looked so beautiful and dashing in those wonderful pink pantaloons! Sometimes I think they were what won my heart in the first place, the day you came to father's house. I suppose that in the Ordnance they wear some horrid drab overalls, and how can you take me riding in the Row dressed like ... like a common commissary person, or something?"

"Shan't wear uniform," says I. "Just civilian toggings, my dear. And you'll own my tailor's a good one, since you chose him yourself."

"That will be quite as bad," says she, "with all the other husbands in their fine uniforms—and you looked so well and dashing. Could you not be a Hussar again, my love—just for me?"

When Elspeth pouted those red lips, and heaved her remarkable bosom in a sigh, my thoughts always galloped bedwards, and she knew it. But I couldn't be weakened that way, as I explained.

"Can't be done. Cardigan won't have me back in the 11th, you may be sure; why, he kicked me out in '40."

"Because I was a ... a tradesman's daughter, he said. I know." For a moment I thought she would weep. "Well, I am not so now. Father ..."

"... bought a peerage just in time before he died, so you are a baron's daughter. Yes, my love, but that won't serve for Jim the Bear. I doubt if he fancies bought nobility much above no rank at all."

"Oh, how horridly you put it. Anyway, I am sure that is not so, because he danced twice with me last season, while you were away, at Lady Brown's assembly—yes, and at the cavalry ball. I distinctly remember, because I wore my gold ruffled dress and my hair à l'impératrice, and he said I looked like an Empress indeed. Was that not gallant? And he bows to me in the Park, and we have spoken several times. He seems a very kind old gentleman, and not at all gruff, as they say."

"Is he now?" says I. I didn't care for the sound of this; I knew Cardigan for as lecherous an old goat as ever tore off breeches. "Well, kind or not as he may seem, he's one to beware of, for your reputation's sake, and mine. Anyway, he won't have me back—and I don't fancy him much either, so that settles it."

She made a mouth at this. "Then I think you are both very stubborn and foolish. Oh, Harry, I am quite miserable about it; and poor little Havvy, too, would be so proud to have his father in one of the fine regiments, with a grand uniform. He will be *so* downcast."

Poor little Havvy, by the way, was our son and heir, a boisterous malcontent five-year-old who made the house hideous with his noise and was forever hitting his shuttlecocks about the place. I wasn't by any means sure that I was his father, for as I have explained before, my Elspeth hid a monstrously passionate nature under her beautifully innocent roses-and-cream exterior, and I suspected that she had been bounced about by half London during the fourteen years of our marriage. I'd been away a good deal, of course. But I'd never caught her out—mind you, that meant nothing, for she'd never caught *me*, and I had had more than would make a hand-rail round Hyde Park. But whatever we both suspected we kept to ourselves, and dealt very well. I loved her, you see, in a way which was not entirely carnal, and I think, I believe, I hope, that she worshipped me, although I've never made up my mind about that.

But I had my doubts about the paternity of little Havvy—so called because his names were Harry Albert Victor, and he couldn't say "Harry" properly, generally because his mouth was full. My chum Speedicut, I remember, who is a coarse brute, claimed to see a conclusive resemblance to me: when Havvy was a few weeks old, and Speed came to the nursery to see him getting his rations, he said the way the infant went after the nurse's tits proved beyond doubt whose son he was.

"Little Havvy," I told Elspeth, "is much too young to care a feather what uniform his father wears. But my present work is important, my love, and you would not have me shirk my duty. Perhaps, later, I may transfer"—I would, too, as soon as it looked safe—"and you will be able to lead your cavalryman to drums and balls and in the Row to your heart's content."

It cheered her up, like a sweet to a child; she was an astonishingly shallow creature in that way. More like a lovely flaxen-haired doll come to life than a woman with a human brain, I often thought. Still, that has its conveniences, too.

In any event, Bindley spoke for me to Lord Paget, who took me in tow, and so I joined the Board of Ordnance. And it was the greatest bore, for his lordship proved to be one of those meddling fools who insist on taking an interest in the work of committees to which they are appointed—as if a lord is ever expected to do anything but lend the light of his countenance and his title. He actually put me to work, and not being an engineer, or knowing more of stresses and moments than sufficed to get me in and out of bed, I was assigned to musketry testing at the Woolwich laboratory, which meant standing on firing-points while the marksmen of the Royal Small Arms Factory blazed away at the "eunuchs".[2] The fellows there were a very common lot, engineers and the like, full of nonsense about the virtues of the Minié as compared with the Long Enfield .577, and the Pritchard bullet, and the Aston backsight—there was tremendous work going on just then, of course, to find a new rifle for the army, and Molesworth's committee was being set up to make the choice. It was all one to me if they decided on arquebuses; after a month spent listening to them prosing about jamming ramrods, and getting oil on my trousers, I found myself sharing the view of old General Scarlett, who once told me:

"Splendid chaps the ordnance, but dammem, a powder monkey's a powder monkey, ain't he? Let 'em fill the cartridges and bore the guns, but don't expect *me* to know a .577 from a mortar! What concern is that of a gentleman—or a soldier, either? Hey? Hey?"

Indeed, I began to wonder how long I could stand it, and settled for spending as little time as I could on my duties, and devoting myself to the social life. Elspeth at thirty seemed to be developing an even greater appetite, if that were possible, for parties and dances and the opera and assemblies, and when I wasn't squiring her I was busy about the clubs and the Haymarket, getting back into my favourite swing of devilled bones, mulled port and low company, riding round Albert Gate by day and St John's Wood by night, racing, playing pool, carousing with Speed and the lads, and keeping the Cyprians busy. London is always lively, but there was a wild mood about in those days, and growing wilder as the weeks passed. It was all: when will the war break out? For soon it was seen that it must come, the press and the street-corner orators were baying for Russian blood, the Government talked interminably and did nothing, the Russian ambassador was sent packing, the Guards marched away to embark for the Mediterranean at an unconscionably early hour of the morning—Elspeth, full of bogus loyalty and snob curiosity, infuriated me by creeping out of bed at four to go and watch this charade, and came back at eight twittering about how splendid the Queen had looked in a dress of dark green merino as she cried farewell to her gallant fellows—and a few days later Palmerston and Graham got roaring tight at the Reform Club and made furious speeches in which they announced that we were going to set about the villain Nicholas and drum him through Siberia.[3]

I listened to a mob in Piccadilly singing about how British arms would "tame the frantic autocrat and smite the Russian slave," and consoled myself with the thought that I would be snug and safe down at Woolwich, doing less than my share to see that they got the right guns to do it with. And so I might, if I hadn't loafed out one evening to play pool with Speed in the Haymarket.

As I recall, I only went because Elspeth's entertainment for the evening was to consist of going to the theatre with a gaggle of her female friends to see some play by a Frenchman—it was patriotic to go to anything French just then, and besides the play was said to be risqué, so my charmer was bound to see it in order to be virtuously shocked.[4] I doubted whether it would ruffle *my* tender sensibilities, though—not enough to be interesting, anyway—so I went along with Speed.

We played a few games of sausage in the Piccadilly Rooms, and it was a dead bore, and then a chap named Cutts, a Dragoon whom I knew slightly, came by and offered us a match at billiards for a quid a hundred. I'd played with him before, and beat him, so we agreed, and set to.

I'm no pool-shark, but not a bad player, either, and unless there's a goodish sum riding, I don't much care whether I win or lose as a rule. But there are some smart-alecs at the table that I can't abide to be beat by, and Cutts was one of them. You know the sort—they roll their cues on the tables, and tell the bystanders that they play their best game off list cushions instead of rubber, and say "Mmph?" if you miss a shot they couldn't have got themselves in a hundred years. What made it worse, my eye was out, and Cutts' luck was dead in—he brought off middle-pocket jennies that Joe Bennet wouldn't have looked at, missed easy hazards and had his ball roll all round the table for a cannon, and when he tried long pots as often as not he got a pair of breeches. By the time he had taken a fiver apiece from us, I was sick of it.

"What, had enough?" cries he, cock-a-hoop. "Come on, Flash, where's your spirit? I'll play you any cramp game you like —shell-out, skittle pool, pyramids, caroline, doublet or go-back.[5] What d'ye say? Come on, Speed, you're game, I see."

So Speed, the ass, played him again, while I mooched about in no good humour, waiting for them to finish. And it chanced that my eye fell on a game that was going on at a corner table, and I stopped to watch.

It was a flat-catching affair, one of the regular sharks fleecing a novice, and I settled down to see what fun there would be when the sheep realized he was being sheared. I had noticed him while we were playing with Cutts—a proper-looking mamma's boy with a pale, delicate face and white hands, who looked as though he'd be more at home handing cucumber sandwiches to Aunt Jane than pushing a cue. He couldn't have been more than eighteen, but I'd noticed his clothes were beautifully cut, although hardly what you'd call pool-room fashion; more like Sunday in the country. But there was money about him, and all told he was the living answer to a billiard-rook's prayer.

They were playing pyramids, and the shark, a grinning specimen with ginger whiskers, was fattening his lamb for the kill.

You may not know the game, but there are fifteen colours, and you try to pocket them one after the other, like pool, usually for a stake of a bob a time. The lamb had put down eight of them, and the shark three, exclaiming loudly at his ill luck, and you could see the little chap was pretty pleased with himself.

"Only four balls left!" cries the shark. "Well, I'm done for; my luck's dead out, I can see. Tell you what, though; it's bound to change; I'll wager a sovereign on each of the last four."

You or I would know that this was the time to put up your cue and say good evening, before he started making the balls advance in column of route dressed from the front, and even the little greenhorn thought hard about it; but hang it, you could see him thinking, I've potted eight out of eleven—surely I'll get at least two of those remaining.

So he said very well, and I waited to see the shark slam the four balls away in as many shots. But he had weighed up his man's purse, and decided on a really good plucking, and after pocketing the first ball with a long double that made the green-horn's jaw drop, the shark made a miscue on his next stroke. Now when you foul at pyramids, one of the potted balls is put back on the table, so there were four still to go at. So it went on, the shark potting a ball and collecting a quid, and then fouling—damning his own clumsiness, of course—so that the ball was re-spotted again. It could go on all night, and the look of horror on the little greenhorn's face was a sight to see. He tried desperately to pot the balls himself, but somehow he always found himself making his shots from a stiff position against the cushion, or with the four colours all lying badly; he could make nothing of it. The shark took fifteen pounds off him before dropping the last ball—off three cushions, just for swank—and then dusted his fancy weskit, thanked the flat with a leer, and sauntered off whistling and calling the waiter for champagne.

The little gudgeon was standing woebegone, holding his limp purse. I thought of speeding him on his way with a taunt or two, and then I had a sudden bright idea.

"Cleaned out, Snooks?" says I. He started, eyed me suspiciously, and then stuck his purse in his pocket and turned to the door.

"Hold on," says I. "I'm not a Captain Sharp; you needn't run away. He rooked you properly, didn't he?"

He stopped, flushing. "I suppose he did. What is it to you?"

"Oh, nothing at all. I just thought you might care for a drink to drown your sorrows."

He gave me a wary look; you could see him thinking, here's another of them.

"I thank you, no," says he, and added: "I have no money left whatever."

"I'd be surprised if you had," says I, "but fortunately I have. Hey, waiter."

The boy was looking nonplussed, as though he wanted to go out into the street and weep over his lost fifteen quid, but at the same time not averse to some manly comfort from this cheery chap. Even Tom Hughes allowed I could charm when I wanted to, and in two minutes I had him looking into a brandy glass, and soon after that we were chatting away like old companions.

He was a foreigner, doing the tour, I gathered, in the care of some tutor from whom he had managed to slip away to have a peep at the flesh-pots of London. The depths of depravity for him, it seemed, was a billiard-room, so he had made for this one and been quickly inveigled and fleeced.

"At least it has been a lesson to me," says he, with that queer formal gravity which a man so often uses in speaking a language not his own. "But how am I to explain my empty purse to Dr Winter? What will he think?"

"Depends how coarse an imagination he's got," says I. "You needn't fret about him; he'll be so glad to get you back safe and sound, I doubt if he'll ask too many questions."

"That is true," says my lad, thoughtfully. "He will fear for his own position. Why, he has been a negligent guardian, has he not?"

"Dam' slack," says I. "The devil with him. Drink up, boy, and confusion to Dr Winter."

You may wonder why I was buying drink and being pleasant to this flat; it was just a whim I had dreamed up to be even with Cutts. I poured a little more into my new acquaintance, and got him quite merry, and then, with an eye on the table where Cutts was trimming up Speed, and gloating over it, I says to the youth:

"I tell you what, though, my son, it won't do for the sporting name of Old England if you creep back home without some credit. I can't put the fifteen sovs back in your pocket, but I'll tell you what—just do as I tell you, and I'll see that you win a game before you walk out of this hall."

"Ah, no—that, no," says he. "I have played enough; once is sufficient—besides, I tell you, I have no more money."

"Gammon," says I. "Who's talking about money? You'd like to win a match, wouldn't you?"

"Yes, but . . ." says he, and the wary look was back in his eye. I slapped him on the knee, jolly old Flash.

"Leave it to me," says I. "What, man, it's just in fun. I'll get you a game with a pal of mine, and you'll trim him up, see if you don't."

"But I am the sorriest player," cries he "How can I beat your friend?"

"You ain't as bad as you think you are," says I. "Depend on it. Now just sit there a moment."

I slipped over to one of the markers whom I knew well. "Joe," says I, "give me a shaved ball, will you?"

"What's that, cap'n?" says he. "There's no such thing in this 'ouse."

"Don't fudge me, Joe. I know better. Come on, man, it's just for a lark, I tell you. No money, no rooking."

He looked doubtful, but after a moment he went behind his counter and came back with a set of billiard pills. "Spot's the boy," says he. "But mind, Cap'n Flashman, no nonsense, on your honour."

"Trust me," says I, and went back to our table. "Now, Sam Snooks, just you pop those about for a moment." He was looking quite perky, I noticed, what with the booze and, I suspect, a fairly bouncy little spirit under his mama's boy exterior. He seemed to have forgotten his fleecing at any rate, and was staring about him at the fellows playing at nearby tables, some in flowery weskits and tall hats and enormous whiskers, others in the new fantastic coloured shirts that were coming in just then, with death's heads and frogs and serpents all over them; our little novice was drinking it all in, listening to the chatter and laughter, and watching the waiters weave in and out with their trays, and the markers calling off the breaks. I suppose it's something to see, if you're a bumpkin.

I went over to where Cutts was just demolishing Speed, and as the pink ball went away, I says:

"There's no holding you tonight, Cutts, old fellow. Just my luck, when my eye's out, to meet first you and then that little terror in the corner yonder."

"What, have you been browned again?" says he, looking round. "Oh, my stars, never by *that*, though, surely? Why, he's not out of leading-strings, by the looks of him."

"Think so?" says I. "He'll give you twenty in the hundred, any day."

Well, of course, that settled it, with a conceited pup like Cutts; nothing would do but he must come over, with his toadies in his wake, making great uproar and guffawing, and offer to make a game with my little greenhorn.

"Just for love, mind," says I, in case Joe the marker was watching, but Cutts wouldn't have it; insisted on a bob a point, and I had to promise to stand good for my man, who shied away as soon as cash was mentioned. He was pretty tipsy by now, or I doubt if I'd have got him to stay at the table, for he was a timid squirt, even in drink, and the bustling and cat-calling of the fellows made him nervous. I rolled him the plain ball, and away they went, Cutts chalking his cue with a flourish and winking to his pals.

You've probably never seen a shaved ball used—but then, you wouldn't know it if you had. The trick is simple; your sharp takes an ordinary ball beforehand, and gets a craftsman to peel away just the most delicate shaving of ivory from one side of it; some clumsy cheats try to do it by rubbing it with fine sand-paper, but that shows up like a whore in church. Then, in the game, he makes certain his opponent gets the shaved ball, and plays away. The flat never suspects a thing, for a carefully shaved ball can't be detected except with the very slowest of slow shots, when it will waver ever so slightly just before it stops. But of course, even with fast shots it goes off the true just a trifle, and in as fine a game as billiards or pool, where precision is everything, a trifle is enough.

It was for Cutts, anyhow. He missed cannons by a whisker, his winning hazards rattled in the jaws of the pocket and stayed out, his losers just wouldn't drop, and when he tried a jenny he often missed the red altogether. He swore blind and fumed, and I said, "My, my, damme, that was close, what?" and my little greenhorn plugged away—he was a truly shocking player, too—and slowly piled up the score. Cutts couldn't fathom it, for he knew he was hitting his shots well, but nothing would go right.

I helped him along by suggesting he was watching the wrong ball—a notion which is sure death, once it has been put in a player's mind—and he got wild and battered away recklessly, and my youngster finally ran out an easy winner, by thirty points.

I was interested to notice he got precious cocky at this. "Billiards is not a difficult game, after all," says he, and Cutts ground his teeth and began to count out his change. His fine chums, of course, were bantering him unmercifully—which was all I'd wanted in the first place.

"Better keep your cash to pay for lessons, Cutts, my boy," says I. "Here, Speed, take our young champion for a drink." And when they had gone off to the bar I grinned at Cutts. "I'd never have guessed it—with whiskers like yours."

"Guessed what, damn you, you funny flash man?" says he, and I held up the spot ball between finger and thumb.

"Never have guessed you'd had such a close *shave*," says I. "'Pon my soul, you ain't fit to play with rooks like our little friend. You'd better take up hoppity, with old ladies."

With a sudden oath he snatched the ball from me, set it on the cloth, and played it away. He leaned over, eyes goggling, as it came to rest, cursed foully, and then dashed it on to the floor.

"Shaved, by God! Curse you, Flashman—you've sharped me, you and that damned little diddler! Where is the little toad—I'll have him thrashed and flung out for this?"

"Hold your wind," says I, while his pals fell against each other and laughed till they cried. "He didn't know anything about it. And you ain't sharped—I've told you to keep your money, haven't I?" I gave him a mocking leer. "'Any cramp game you like,' eh? Skittle pool, go-back—but not billiards with little flats from the nursery." And I left him thoroughly taken down, and went off to find Speed.

You'll think this a very trivial revenge, no doubt, but then I'm a trivial chap—and I know the way under the skin of muffins like Cutts, I hope. What was it Hughes said—Flashman had a knack of knowing what hurt, and by a cutting word or look could bring tears to the eyes of people who would have laughed at a blow? Something like that; anyway, I'd taken the starch out of friend Cutts, and spoiled his evening, which was just nuts to me.

I took up with Speed and the greenhorn, who was now waxing voluble in the grip of booze, and off we went. I thought it would be capital sport to take him along to one of the accommodation houses in Haymarket, and get him paired off with a whore in a galloping wheelbarrow race, for it was certain he'd never been astride a female in his life, and it would have been splendid to see them bumping across the floor together on hands and knees towards the winning post. But we stopped off for punch on the way, and the little snirp got so fuddled he couldn't even walk. We helped him along, but he was maudlin, so we took off his trousers in an alley off Regent Street, painted his arse with blacking which we bought for a penny on the way, and then shouted, "Come on, peelers! Here's the scourge of A Division waiting to set about you! Come on and be damned to you!" And as soon as the bobbies hove in sight we cut, and left them to find our little friend, nose down in the gutter with his black bum sticking up in the air.

I went home well pleased that night, only wishing I could have been present when Dr Winter came face to face again with his erring pupil.

And that night's work changed my life, and preserved India for the British Crown—what do you think of that? It's true enough, though, as you'll see.

However, the fruits didn't appear for a few days after that, and in the meantime another thing happened which also has a place in my story. I renewed an old acquaintance, who was to play a considerable part in my affairs over the next few months—and that was full of consequence, too, for him, and me, and history.

I had spent the day keeping out of Paget's way at the Horse Guards, and chatting part of the time, I remember, with Colonel Colt, the American gun expert, who was there to give evidence before the select committee on firearms.[6] (I ought to remember our conversation, but I don't, so it was probably damned dull and technical.) Afterwards, however, I went up to Town to meet Elspeth in the Ride, and take her on to tea with one of her Mayfair women.

She was side-saddling it up the Ride, wearing her best mulberry rig and a plumed hat, and looking ten times as fetching as any female in view. But as I trotted up alongside, I near as not fell out of my saddle with surprise, for she had a companion with her, and who should it be but my Lord Haw-Haw himself, the Earl of Cardigan.

I don't suppose I had exchanged a word with him—indeed, I had hardly seen him, and then only at a distance—since he had packed me off to India fourteen years before. I had loathed the brute then, and time hadn't softened the sentiment; he was the swine who had kicked me out of the Cherrypickers for (irony of ironies) marrying Elspeth, and committed me to the horrors of the Afghan campaign.* And here he was, getting spoony round my wife, whom he had affected to despise once on a day for her lowly origins. And spooning to some tune, too, by the way he was leaning confidentially across from his saddle, his rangy old boozy face close to her blonde and beautiful one, and the little slut was laughing and looking radiant at his attentions.

She caught my eye and waved, and his lordship looked me over in his high-nosed damn-you way which I remembered so well. He would be in his mid-fifties by now, and it showed; the whiskers were greying, the gooseberry eyes were watery, and the legions of bottles he had consumed had cracked the veins in that fine nose of his. But he still rode straight as a lance, and if his voice was wheezy it had lost nothing of its plunger drawl.

"Haw-haw," says he, "it is Fwashman, I see. Where have you been, sir? Hiding away these many years, I dare say, with this lovely lady. Haw-haw. How-de-do, Fwashman? Do you know, my dear"—this to Elspeth, damn his impudence—"I decware that this fine fellow, your husband, has put on fwesh alarmingly since last I saw him. Haw-haw. Always was too heavy for a wight dwagoon, but now—pwepostewous! You feed him too well, my dear! Haw-haw!"

It was a damned lie, of course, no doubt designed to draw a comparison with his own fine figure—scrawny, some might have

* See Flashman.

thought it. I could have kicked his lordly backside, and given him a piece of my mind.

"Good day, milord," says I, with my best toady smile. "May I say how well your lordship is looking? In good health, I trust."

"Thank'ee," says he, and turning to Elspeth: "As I was saying, we have the vewy finest hunting at Deene. Spwendid sport, don't ye know, and specially wecommended for young wadies wike yourself. You must come to visit—you too, Fwashman. You wode pwetty well, as I wecollect. Haw-haw."

"You honour me with the recollection, milord," says I, wondering what would happen if I smashed him between the eyes. "But I—"

"Yaas," says he, turning languidly back to Elspeth. "No doubt your husband has many duties—in the ordnance, is it not, or some such thing? Haw-haw. But you must come down, my dear, with one of your fwiends, for a good wong stay, what? The faiwest bwossoms bwoom best in countwy air, don't ye know? Haw-haw." And the old scoundrel had the gall to lean over and pat her hand.

She, the little ninny, was all for it, giving him a dazzling smile and protesting he was too, too kind—this aged satyr who was old enough to be her father and had vice leering out of every wrinkle in his face. Of course, where climbing little snobs like Elspeth are concerned, there ain't such a thing as an ugly peer of the realm, but even she could surely have seen how grotesque his advances were. Of course, women love it.

"How splendid to see you two old friends together again, after such a long time, is it not, Lord Cardigan? Why, I declare I have never seen you in his lordship's company, Harry! Such a dreadfully long time it must have been!" Babbling, you see, like the idiot she was. I'm not sure she didn't say something about "comrades in arms". "You must call upon us, Lord Cardigan, now that you and Harry have met again. It will be so fine, will it not, Harry?"

"Yaas," says he. "I may call," with a look at me that said he would never dream of setting foot in any hovel of mine. "In the meantime, my dear, I shall wook to see you widing hereabouts. Haw-haw. I dewight to see a female who wides so gwacefully. Decidedwy you must come to Deene. Haw-haw." He took off his hat to her, bowing from the waist—and a Polish hussar couldn't have done it better, damn him. "Good day to you, Mrs Fwashman." He gave me the merest nod, and cantered off up the Ride, cool as you please.

"Is he not wonderfully condescending, Harry? Such elegant manners—but of course, it is natural in one of such noble breeding. I am sure if you spoke to him, my dear, he would be ready to give the most earnest consideration to finding a place for you —he is so kind, despite his high station. Why, he has promised me almost any favour I care to ask—Harry, whatever is the matter? Why are you swearing—oh, my love, no, people will hear! Oh!"

Of course, swearing and prosing were both lost on Elspeth; when I had vented my bile against Cardigan I tried to point out to her the folly of accepting the attentions of such a notorious roué, but she took this as mere jealousy on my part—not jealousy of a sexual kind, mark you, but supposedly rooted in the fact that here she was climbing in the social world, spooned over by peers, while I was labouring humbly in an office like any Cratchit, and could not abide to see her ascending so far above me. She even reminded me that she was a baron's daughter, at which I ground my teeth and hurled a boot through our bedroom window, she burst into tears, and ran from the room to take refuge in a broom cupboard, whence she refused to budge while I hammered on the panels. She was terrified of my brutal ways, she said, and feared for her life, so I had to go through the charade of forcing open the door and rogering her in the cupboard before peace was restored. (This was what she had wanted since the quarrel began, you see; very curious and wearing our domestic situation was, but strangely enjoyable, too, as I look back on it. I remember how I carried her to the bedroom afterwards, she nibbling at my ear with her arms round my neck, and at the sight of the broken window we collapsed giggling and kissing on the floor. Aye, married bliss. And like the fool I was I clean forgot to forbid her to talk to Cardigan again.)

But in the next few days I had other things to distract me from Elspeth's nonsense; my jape in the pool-room with the little greenhorn came home to roost, and in the most unexpected way. I received a summons from my Lord Raglan, of all people.

You will know all about him, no doubt. He was the ass who presided over the mess we made in the Crimea, and won deathless fame as the man who murdered the Light Brigade. He should have been a parson, or an Oxford don, or a waiter, for he was the kindliest, softest-voiced old stick who ever spared a fellow-creature's feelings—that was what was wrong with him, that he couldn't for the life of him say an unkind word, or set anyone down. And this was the man who was the heir to Wellington— as I sat in his office, looking across at his kindly old face, with its rumpled white hair and long nose, and found my eyes straying to the empty right sleeve tucked into his breast, he looked so pathetic and frail, I shuddered inwardly. Thank God, thinks I, that I won't be in *this* chap's campaign.

They had just made him Commander-in-Chief, after years spent bumbling about on the Board of Ordnance, and he was supposed to be taking matters in hand for the coming conflict. So you may guess that the matter on which he had sent for me was one of the gravest national import—Prince Albert, our saintly Bertie the Beauty, wanted a new aide-de-camp, or equerry, or toad-eater-extraordinary, and nothing would do but our new Commander must set all else aside to see the thing was done properly.

Mark you, I'd no time to waste marvelling over the fatuousness of this kind of mismanagement; it was nothing new in our army, anyway, and still isn't, from all I can see. Ask any commander to choose between toiling over the ammunition returns for a division fighting for its life, and taking the King's dog for a walk, and he'll be out there in a trice, bawling "Heel, Fido!" No, I was too much knocked aback to learn that I, Captain Harry Flashman, former Cherrypicker and erstwhile hero of the country, of no great social consequence and no enormous means or influence, should even be considered to breathe the lordly air of the court. Oh, I had my fighting reputation, but what's that, when London is bursting with pink-cheeked viscounts with cleft palates and long pedigrees? My great-great-great-grandpapa wasn't even a duke's bastard, so far as I know.

Raglan approached the thing in his usual roundabout way, by going through a personal history which his minions must have put together for him.

"I see you are thirty-one years old, Flashman," says he. "Well, well, I had thought you older—why, you must have been only—yes, nineteen, when you won your spurs at Kabul. Dear me! So young. And since then you have served in India, against the Sikhs, but have been on half-pay these six years, more or less. In that time, I believe, you have travelled widely?"

Usually at high speed, thinks I, and not in circumstances I'd care to tell your lordship about. Aloud I confessed to acquaintance with France, Germany, the United States, Madagascar, West Africa, and the East Indies.

"And I see you have languages—excellent French, German, Hindoostanee, Persian—bless my soul!—and Pushtu. Thanks of Parliament in '42, Queen's Medal—well, well, these are quite singular accomplishments, you know." And he laughed in his easy way. "And apart from Company service, you were formerly, as I apprehend, of the 11th Hussars. Under Lord Cardigan. A-ha. Well, now, Flashman, tell me, what took you to the Board of Ordnance?"

I was ready for that one, and spun him a tale about improving my military education, because no field officer could know too much, and so on, and so on. . . .

"Yes, that is very true, and I commend it in you. But you know, Flashman, while I never dissuade a young man from studying all aspects of his profession—which indeed, my own mentor, the Great Duke, impressed on us, his young men, as most necessary —still, I wonder if the Ordnance Board is *really* for you." And he looked knowing and quizzical, like someone smiling with a mouthful of salts. His voice took on a deprecatory whisper. "Oh, it is very well, but come, my boy, it cannot but seem—well, *beneath*, a little beneath, I think, a man whose career has been as, yes, brilliant as your own. I say nothing against the Ordnance—why, I was Master-General for many years—but for a young blade, well-connected, highly regarded . . . ?" He wrinkled his nose at me. "Is it not like a charger pulling a cart? Of course it is. Manufacturers and clerks may be admirably suited to dealing with barrels and locks and rivets and, oh, *dimensions*, and what not, but it is all so *mechanical*, don't you agree?"

Why couldn't the old fool mind his own business? I could see where this was leading—back to active service and being blown to bits in Turkey, devil a doubt. But who contradicts a Commander-in-Chief?

"I think it a most happy chance," he went on, "that only yesterday his Royal Highness Prince Albert"—he said it with reverence—"confided to me the task of finding a young officer for a post of considerable delicacy and importance. He must, of course, be well-born—your mother was Lady Alicia Paget, was she not? I remember the great pleasure I had in dancing with her, oh, how many years ago? Well, well, it is no matter. A quadrille, I fancy. However, station alone is not sufficient in this case, or I confess I should have looked to the Guards." Well, that was candid, damn him. "The officer selected must also have shown himself resourceful, valiant, and experienced in camp and battle. That is essential. He must be young, of equable disposition and good education, unblemished, I need not say, in personal reputation"—God knows how he'd come to pick on me, thinks I, but he went on: "— and yet a man who knows his world. But above all—what our good old Duke would call 'a man of his hands'." He beamed at me. "I believe your name must have occurred to me at once, had His Highness not mentioned it first. It seems our gracious Queen had recollected you to him." Well, well, thinks I, little Vicky remembers my whiskers after all these years. I recalled how she had mooned tearfully at me when she pinned my medal on, back in '42—they're all alike you know, can't resist a dashing boy with big shoulders and a trot-along look in his eye.

"So I may now confide in you," he went on, "what this most important duty consists in. You have not heard, I dare say, of Prince William of Celle? He is one of Her Majesty's European cousins, who has been visiting here some time, incognito, studying our English ways preparatory to pursuing a military career in the British Army. It is his family's wish that when our forces go overseas—as soon they must, I believe—he shall accompany us, as a member of my staff. But while he will be under my personal eye, as it were, it is most necessary that he should be in the immediate care of the kind of officer I have mentioned—one who will guide his youthful footsteps, guard his person, shield him from temptation, further his military education, and supervise his physical and spiritual welfare in every way." Raglan smiled.

"He is very young, and a most amiable prince in every way; he will require a firm and friendly hand from one who can win the trust and respect of an ardent and developing nature. Well, Flashman, I have no doubt that between us we can make something of him. Do you not agree?"

By God, you've come to the right shop, thinks I. Flashy and Co., wholesale moralists, ardent and developing natures supervised, spiritual instruction guaranteed, prayers and laundry two bob extra. How the deuce had they picked on me? The Queen, of course, but did Raglan know what kind of a fellow they had alighted on? Granted I was a hero, but I'd thought my randying about and boozing and general loose living were well known—by George, he must know! Maybe, secretly, he thought that was a qualification—I'm not sure he wasn't right. But the main point was, all my splendid schemes for avoiding shot and shell were out of court again; it was me for the staff, playing nursemaid to some little German pimp in the wilds of Turkey. Of all the hellish bad luck.

But of course I sat there jerking like a puppet, grinning foolishly —what else was there to do?

"I think we may congratulate ourselves," the old idiot went on, "and tomorrow I shall take you to the Palace to meet your new charge. I congratulate you, Captain, and"—he shook my hand with a noble smile—"I know you will be worthy of the trust imposed on you now, as you have been in the past. Good day to you, my dear sir. And now," I heard him say to his secretary as I bowed myself out, "there is this wretched war business. I suppose there is no word yet whether it has begun? Well, I do wish they would make up their minds."

You have already guessed, no doubt, the shock that was in store for me at the Palace next day. Raglan took me along, we went through the rigmarole of flunkeys with brushes that I remembered from my previous visit with Wellington, and we were ushered into a study where Prince Albert was waiting for us. There was a reverend creature and a couple of the usual court clowns in morning dress looking austere in the background—and there, at Albert's right hand, stood my little greenhorn of the billiard hall. The sight hit me like a ball in the leg—for a moment I stood stock still while I gaped at the lad and he gaped at me, but then he recovered, and so did I, and as I made my deep bow at Raglan's side I found myself wondering: have they got that blacking off his arse yet?

I was aware that Albert was speaking, in that heavy, German voice; he was still the cold, well-washed exquisite I had first met twelve years ago, with those frightful whiskers that looked as though someone had tried to pluck them and left off half-way through. He was addressing me, and indicating a side-table on which a shapeless black object was lying.

"'hat do you 'hink of the new hett for the Guards, Captain Flash-mann?" says he.

I knew it, of course; the funny papers had been full of it, and mocking H.R.H., who had invented it. He was always inflicting monstrosities of his own creation on the troops, which Horse Guards had to tell him tactfully were not quite what was needed. I looked at this latest device, a hideous forage cap with long flaps,[7] and said I was sure it must prove admirably serviceable, and have a very smart appearance, too. Capital, first-rate, couldn't be better, God knows how someone hadn't thought of it before.

He nodded smugly, and then says: "I un-erstend you were at Rugby School, Captain? Ah, but wait—a captain? That will hardly do, I think. A colonel, no?" And he looked at Raglan, who said the same notion had occurred to him. Well, thinks I, if that's how promotion goes, I'm all for it.

"At Rugby School," repeated Albert. "That is a great English school, Willy," says he to the greenhorn, "of the kind which turns younk boys like yourself into menn like Colonel Flash-mann here." Well, true enough, I'd found it a fair mixture of jail and knocking-shop; I stood there trying to look like a chap who says his prayers in a cold bath every day.

"Colonel Flash-mann is a famous soldier in England, Willy; although he is quite younk, he has vun—won—laurelss for brafery in India. You see? Well, he will be your friend and teacher, Willy; you are to mind all that he says, and obey him punctually and willingly, ass a soldier should. O-bedience is the first rule of an army, Willy, you understand?"

The lad spoke for the first time, darting a nervous look at me. "Yes, uncle Albert."

"Ver-ry good, then. You may shake hands with Colonel Flash-mann."

The lad came forward hesitantly, and held out his hand. "How do you do?" says he, and you could tell he had only lately learned the phrase.

"You address Colonel Flash-mann, as 'sir', Willy," says Albert. "He is your superior officer."

The kid blushed, and for the life of me I can't think how I had the nerve to say it, with a stiff-neck like Albert, but the favour I won with this boy was going to be important, after all—you can't have too many princely friends—and I thought a Flashy touch was in order. So I said:

"With your highness's permission, I think 'Harry' will do when we're off parade. Hullo, youngster."

The boy looked startled, and then smiled, the court clowns started to look outraged, Albert looked puzzled, but then he smiled, too, and Raglan hum-hummed approvingly. Albert said:

"There, now, Willy, you have an English comrade. You see? Very goot. You will find there are none better. And now, you will go with—with 'Harry' "—he gave a puffy smile, and the court clowns purred toadily,—"and he will instruct you in your duties."

2

I've been about courts a good deal in my misspent career, and by and large I bar royalty pretty strong. They may be harmless enough folk in themselves, but they attract a desperate gang of placemen and hangers-on, and in my experience, the closer you get to the throne, the nearer you may finish up to the firing-line. Why, I've been a Prince Consort myself, and had half the cutthroats of Europe trying to assassinate me,* and in my humbler capacities—as chief of staff to a White Rajah, military adviser and chief stud to that black she-devil Ranavalona, and irregular emissary to the court of King Gezo of Dahomey, long may he rot—I've usually been lucky to come away with a well-scarred skin. And my occasional attachments to the Court of St James's have been no exception; nurse-maiding little Willy was really the most harrowing job of the lot.

Mind you, the lad was amiable enough in himself, and he took to me from the first.

"You are a brick," he told me as soon as we were alone. "Is that not the word? When I saw you today, I was sure you would tell them of the billiard place, and I would be disgraced. But you said nothing—that was to be a true friend."

"Least said, soonest mended," says I. "But whatever did you run away for that night?—why, I'd have seen you home right enough. We couldn't think what had become of you."

"I do not know myself," says he. "I know that some ruffians set upon me in a dark place, and . . . stole some of my clothes." He blushed crimson, and burst out: "I resisted them fiercely, but they were too many for me! And then the police came, and Dr Winter had to be sent for, and—oh! there was such a fuss! But you were right—he was too fearful of his own situation to inform on me to their highnesses. However, I think it is by his insistence that a special guardian has been appointed for me."

* See *Royal Flash*.

He gave me his shy, happy smile. "What luck that it should be you!"

Lucky, is it, thinks I, we'll see about that. We'd be off to the war, if ever the damned thing got started—but when I thought about it, it stood to reason they wouldn't risk Little Willy's precious royal skin very far, and his bear-leader should be safe enough, too. All I said was:

"Well, I think Dr Winter's right; you need somebody and a half to look after you, for you ain't safe on your own hook. So look'ee here—I'm an easy chap, as anyone'll tell you, but I'll stand no shines, d'ye see? Do as I tell you, and we'll do famously, and have good fun, too. But no sliding off on your own again—or you'll find I'm no Dr Winter. Well?"

"*Very* well, sir—Harry," says he, prompt enough, but for all his nursery look, I'll swear he had a glitter in his eye.

We started off on the right foot, with a very pleasant round of tailors and gunsmiths and bootmakers and the rest, for the child hadn't a stick or stitch for a soldier, and I aimed to see him—and myself—bang up to the nines. The luxury of being toadied through all the best shops, and referring the bills to Her Majesty, was one I wasn't accustomed to, and you may believe I made the most of it. At my tactful suggestion to Raglan, we were both gazetted in the 17th, who were lancers—no great style as a regiment, perhaps, but I knew it would make Cardigan gnash his elderly teeth when he heard of it, and I'd been a lancer myself in my Indian days. Also, to my eye it was the flashiest rigout in the whole light cavalry, all blue and gold—the darker the better, when you've got the figure for it, which of course I had.

Anyway, young Willy clapped his hands when he saw himself in full fig, and ordered another four like it—no one spends like visiting royalty, you know. Then he had to be horsed, and armed, and given lashings of civilian rig, and found servants, and camp gear—and I spent a whole day on that alone. If we were going campaigning, I meant to make certain we did it with every conceivable luxury—wine at a sovereign the dozen, cigars at ten guineas the pound, preserved foods of the best, tip-top linen, quality spirits by the gallon, and all the rest of the stuff that you need if you're going to fight a war properly. Last of all I insisted on a lead box of biscuits—and Willy cried out with laughter.

"They are ship's biscuits—what should we need those for?"

"Insurance, my lad," says I. "Take 'em along, and it's odds you'll never need them. Leave 'em behind, and as sure as shooting you'll finish up living off blood-stained snow and dead mules." It's God's truth, too.

"It will be exciting!" cries he, gleefully. "I long to be off!"

"Just let's hope you don't find yourself longing to be back," says I, and nodded at the mountain of delicacies we had ordered. "That's all the excitement we want."

His face fell at that, so I cheered him up with a few tales of my own desperate deeds in Afghanistan and elsewhere, just to remind him that a cautious campaigner isn't necessarily a milksop. Then I took him the rounds, of clubs, and the Horse Guards, and the Park, presented him to anyone of consequence whom I felt it might be useful to toady—and, by George, I had no shortage of friends and fawners when the word got about who he was. I hadn't seen so many tuft-hunters since I came home from Afghanistan.

You may imagine how Elspeth took the news, when I notified her that Prince Albert had looked me up and given me a Highness to take in tow. She squealed with delight—and then went into a tremendous flurry about how we must give receptions and soirées in his honour, and Hollands would have to provide new curtains and carpet, and extra servants must be hired, and who should she invite, and what new clothes she must have—"for we shall be in *everyone's* eye now, and I shall be an object of general remark whenever I go out, and everyone will wish to call—oh, it will be famous!—and we shall be receiving all the time, and—"

"Calm yourself, my love," says I. "We shan't be receiving—we shall be being received. Get yourself a few new duds, by all means, if you've room for 'em, and then—wait for the pasteboards to land on the mat."

And they did, of course. There wasn't a hostess in Town but was suddenly crawling to Mrs Flashman's pretty feet, and she gloried in it. I'll say that for her, there wasn't an ounce of spite in her nature, and while she began to condescend most damnably, she didn't cut anyone—perhaps she realized, like me, that it never pays in the long run. I was pretty affable myself, just then, and pretended not to hear one or two of the more jealous remarks that were dropped—about how odd it was that Her Majesty hadn't chosen one of the purple brigade to squire her young cousin, not so much as Guardee even, but a plain Mr— and who the deuce were the Flashmans anyway?

But the Press played up all right; *The Times* was all approval that "a soldier, not a courtier, has been entrusted with the grave responsibility entailed in the martial instruction of the young prince. If war should come, as it surely must if Russian imperial despotism and insolence try our patience further, what better guardian and mentor of His Highness could be found than the Hector of Afghanistan? We may assert with confidence—*none*." (I could have asserted with confidence, any number, and good luck to 'em.)

Even *Punch*, which didn't have much to say for the Palace, as a rule, and loathed the Queen's great brood of foreign relations like poison, had a cartoon showing me frowning at little Willy under a signpost of which one arm said "Hyde Park" and the other "Honour and Duty", and saying: "What, my boy, do you want to be a stroller or a soldier? You can't be both if you march in step with me." Which delighted me, naturally, although Elspeth thought it didn't make me look handsome enough.

Little Willy, in the meantime, was taking to all this excitement like a Scotchman to drink. Under a natural shyness, he was a breezy little chap, quick, eager to please, and good-natured; he could be pretty cool with anyone over-familiar, but he could charm marvellously when he wanted—as he did with Elspeth when I took him home to tea. Mind you, the man who doesn't want to charm Elspeth is either a fool or a eunuch, and little Willy was neither, as I discovered on our second day together, as we were strolling up Haymarket—we'd been shopping for a pair of thunder-and-lightnings* which he admired. It was latish afternoon, and the tarts were beginning to parade; little Willy goggled at a couple of painted princesses swaying by in all their finery, ogling, and then he says to me in a reverent whisper:

"Harry—I say, Harry—those women—are they—"

"Whores," says I. "Never mind 'em. Now, to-morrow, Willy, we must visit the Artillery Mess, I think, and see the guns limbering up in—"

* Striped trousers.

"Harry," says he. "I want a whore."

"Eh?" says I. "You don't want anything of the sort, my lad." I couldn't believe my ears.

"I do, though," says he, and damme, he was gaping after them like a satyr, this well-brought-up, Christian little princeling. "I have never had a whore."

"I should hope not!" says I, quite scandalized. "Now, look here, young Willy, this won't answer at all. You're not to think of such things for a moment. I won't have this . . . this lewdness. Why, I'm surprised at you! What would—why, what would Her Majesty have to say to such talk? Or Dr Winter, eh?"

"I want a whore," says he, quite fierce. "I . . . I know it is wrong—but I don't care! Oh, you have no notion what it is like! Since I was quite small, they have never even let me talk to girls— at home I was not even allowed to play with my little cousins at kiss-in-the-ring, or anything! They would not let me go to dancing-classes, in case it should excite me! Dr Winter is always lecturing me about thoughts that pollute, and the fearful punishments awaiting fornicators when they are dead, and accusing me of having carnal thoughts! Of course I have, the old fool! Oh, Harry, I know it is sinful—but I don't care! I want one," says this remarkable youth dreamily, with a blissful look coming over his pure, chaste, boyish visage, "with long golden hair, and big, big, round—"

"Stop that this minute!" says I. "I never heard the like!"

"And she will wear black satin boots buttoning up to her thighs," he added, licking his lips.

I'm not often stumped, but this was too much. I know youth has hidden fires, but this fellow was positively ablaze. I tried to cry him down, and then to reason with him, for the thought of his cutting a dash through the London bordellos and trotting back to Buckingham Palace with the clap, or some harpy pursuing him for blackmail, made my blood run cold. But it was no good.

"If you say me nay," says he, quite determined, "I shall find one myself."

I couldn't budge him. So in the end I decided to let him have his way, and make sure there were no snags, and that it was done safe and quiet. I took him off to a very high-priced place I knew in St John's Wood, swore the old bawd to secrecy, and stated the randy little pig's requirements. She did him proud, too, with a strapping blonde wench—satin boots and all—and at the sight of her Willy moaned feverishly and pointed, quivering, like a setter. He was trying to clamber all over her almost before the door closed, and of course he made a fearful mess of it, thrashing away like a stoat in a sack, and getting nowhere. It made me quite sentimental to watch him—reminded me of my own ardent youth, when every coupling began with an eager stagger across the floor trying to disentangle one's breeches from one's ankles.

I had a brisk, swarthy little gypsy creature on the other couch, and we were finished and toasting each other in iced claret before Willy and his trollop had got properly buckled to. She was a knowing wench, however, and eventually had him galloping away like an archdeacon on holiday, and afterwards we settled down to a jolly supper of salmon and cold curry. But before we had reached the ices Willy was itching to be at grips with his girl again—where these young fellows get the fire from beats me. It was too soon for me, so while he walloped along I and the gypsy passed an improving few moments spying through a peephole into the next chamber, where a pair of elderly naval men were cavorting with three Chinese sluts. They were worse than Willy —it's those long voyages, I suppose.

When we finally took our leave, Willy was fit to be blown away by the first puff of wind, but pleased as punch with himself.

"You are a beautiful whore," says he to the blonde. "I am quite delighted with you, and shall visit you frequently." He did, too, and must have spent a fortune on her in tin, of which he had loads, of course. Being of a young and developing nature, as Raglan would have said, he tried as many other strumpets in the establishment as he could manage, but it was the blonde lass as often as not. He got quite spoony over her. Poor Willy.

So his military education progressed, and Raglan chided me for working him too hard. "His Highness appears quite pale," says he. "I fear you have him too much at the grindstone, Flashman. He must have some recreation as well, you know." I could have told him that what young Willy needed was a pair of locked iron drawers with the key at the bottom of the Serpentine, but I nodded wisely and said it was sometimes difficult to restrain a young spirit eager for instruction and experience. In fact, when it came to things like learning the rudiments of staff work and army procedure, Willy couldn't have been sharper; my only fear was that he might become really useful and find himself being actively employed when we went east.

For we were going, there was now no doubt. War was finally declared at the end of March, in spite of Aberdeen's dithering, and the mob bayed with delight from Shetland to Land's End. To hear them, all we had to do was march into Moscow when we felt like it, with the Frogs carrying our packs for us and the cowardly Russians skulking away before Britannia's flashing eyes. And mind you, I don't say that the British Army and the French together couldn't have done it—given a Wellington. They were sound at bottom, and the Russians weren't. I'll tell you something else, which military historians never realize: they call the Crimea a disaster, which it was, and a hideous botch-up by our staff and supply, which is also true, but what they don't know is that even with all these things in the balance against you, the difference between hellish catastrophe and brilliant success is sometimes no greater than the width of a sabre blade, but when all is over no one thinks of that. Win gloriously—and the clever dicks forget all about the rickety ambulances that never came, and the rations that were rotten, and the boots that didn't fit, and the generals who'd have been better employed hawking bedpans round the doors. Lose—and these are the only things they talk about.

But I'll confess I saw the worst coming before we'd even begun. The very day war was declared Willy and I reported ourselves to Raglan at Horse Guards, and it took me straight back to the Kabul cantonment—all work and fury and chatter, and no proper direction whatever. Old Elphy Bey had sat picking at his nails and saying: "We must certainly consider what is best to be done" while his staff men burst with impatience and spleen. You could see the germ of it here—Raglan's ante-room was jammed with all sorts of people, Lucan, and Hardinge, and old Scarlett, and Anderson of the Ordnance, and there were staff-scrapers and orderlies running everywhere and saluting and bustling, and mounds of paper growing on the tables, and great consulting of maps ("Where the devil *is* Turkey? " someone was saying. "Do they have much rain there, d'ye suppose? "), but in the inner sanctum all was peace and amiability. Raglan was talking about neck-stocks, if I remember rightly, and how they should fasten well up under the chin.

We were kept well up to the collar, though, in the next month before our stout and thick-headed commander finally took his leave for the scene of war—Willy and I were not of his advance party, which pleased me, for there's no greater fag than breaking in new ground. We were all day staffing at the Horse Guards, and Willy was either killing himself with kindness in St John's Wood by night, or attending functions about Town, of which there were a feverish number. It's always the same before the shooting begins—the hostesses go into a frenzy of gaiety, and all the spongers and civilians crawl out of the wainscoting braying with good fellowship because thank God they ain't going, and the young plungers and green striplings roister it up, and their fiancées let 'em pleasure them red in the face out of pity, because the poor brave boy is off to the cannon's mouth, and the dance goes on and the eyes grow brighter and the laughter shriller—and the older men in their dress uniforms look tired, and sip their punch by the fireplace and don't say much at all.

Elspeth, of course, was in her element, dancing all night, laughing with the young blades and flirting with the old ones—Cardigan was still roostering about her, I noticed, with every sign of the little trollop's encouragement. He'd got himself the Light Cavalry Brigade, which had sent a great groan through every hussar and lancer regiment in the army, and was even fuller of bounce than usual—his ridiculous lisp and growling "haw-haw" seemed to sound everywhere you went, and he was full of brag about how he and his beloved Cherrypickers would be the élite advanced force of the army.

"I believe they have given Wucan *nominal* charge of the cavalwy," I heard him tell a group of cronies at one party. "Well, I suppose they had to find him *something*, don't ye know, and he may vewwy well look to wemounts, I dare say. Haw-haw. I hope poor Waglan does not find him too gweat an incubus. Haw-haw."

This was Lucan, his own brother-in-law; they detested each other, which isn't to be wondered at, since they were both detestable, Cardigan particularly. But his mighty lordship wasn't having it all his own way, for the Press, who hated him, revived the old jibe about his Cherrypickers' tight pants, and *Punch* dedicated a poem to him called "Oh Pantaloons of Cherry", which sent him wild. It was all gammon, really, for the pants were no tighter than anyone else's—I wore 'em long enough, and should know —but it was good to see Jim the Bear roasting on the spit of popular amusement again. By God, I wish that spit had been a real one, with me to turn it.

It was a night in early May, I think, that Elspeth was bidden to some great drum in Mayfair to celebrate the first absolute fighting of the war, which had been reported a week or so earlier—our ships had bombarded Odessa, and broken half the windows in the place, so of course the fashionable crowd had to rave and riot in honour of the great victory.[8] I don't remember seeing Elspeth lovelier than she was that night, in a gown of some shimmering white satin stuff, and no jewels at all, but only flowers coiled in her golden hair. I would have had at her before she even set out, but she was all a-fuss tucking little Havvy into his cot—as though the nurse couldn't do it ten times better—and was fearful that I would disarrange her appearance. I fondled her, and promised I would put her through the drill when she came home, but she damped this by telling me that Marjorie had bidden her stay the night, although it was only a few streets away, because the dancing would go on until dawn, and she would be too fatigued to return.

So off she fluttered, blowing me a kiss, and I snarled away to the Horse Guards, where I had to burn the midnight oil over sapper transports; Raglan had set out for Turkey leaving most of the work behind him, and those of us who were left were kept at it until three each morning. By the time we had finished, even Willy was too done up to fancy his usual nightly exercise with his Venus, so we sent out for some grub—it was harry and grass,* I remember, which didn't improve my temper—and then he went home.

I was tired and cranky, but I couldn't think of sleep, somehow, so I went out and started to get drunk. I was full of apprehension about the coming campaign, and fed up with endless files and reports, and my head ached, and my shoes pinched, so I poured down the whistle-belly with brandy on top, and the inevitable result was that I finished up three parts tight in some cellar near Charing Cross. I thought of a whore, but didn't want one—and

* Haricot mutton and asparagus.

then it struck me: I wanted Elspeth, and nothing else. By God, there was I, on the brink of another war, slaving my innards into knots, while she was tripping about in a Mayfair ball-room, laughing and darting chase-me glances at party-saunterers and young gallants, having a fine time for hours on end, and she hadn't been able to spare me five minutes for a tumble! She was my wife, dammit, and it was too bad. I put away some more brandy while I considered the iniquity of this, and took a great drunken resolve—I would go round to Marjorie's at once, surprise my charmer when she came to bed, and make her see what she had been missing all evening. Aye, that was it—and it was romantic, too, the departing warrior tupping up the girl he was going to leave behind, and she full of love and wistful longing and be-damned. (Drink's a terrible thing.) Anyway, off I set west, with a full bottle in my pocket to see me through the walk, for it was after four, and there wasn't even a cab to be had.

By the time I got to Marjorie's place—a huge mansion fronting the Park, with every light ablaze—I was taking the width of the pavement and singing "Villikins and his Dinah".[9] The flunkeys at the door didn't mind me a jot, for the house must have been full of foxed chaps and bemused females, to judge by the racket they were making. I found what looked like a butler, inquired the direction of Mrs Flashman's chamber, and tramped up endless staircases, bouncing off the walls as I went. I found a lady's maid, too, who put me on the right road, banged on a door, fell inside, and found the place was empty.

It was a lady's bedroom, no error, but no lady, as yet. All the candles were burning, the bed was turned down, a fluffy little Paris night-rail which I recognized as one I'd bought my darling lay by the pillow, and her scent was in the air. I stood there sighing and lusting boozily; still dancing, hey? We'll have a pretty little hornpipe together by and by, though—aha, I would surprise her. That was it; I'd hide, and bound out lovingly when she came up. There was a big closet in one wall, full of clothes and linen and what-not, so I toddled in, like the drunken, love-sick ass I was—you'd wonder at it, wouldn't you, with all my experience?—settled down on something soft, took a last pull at my bottle—and fell fast asleep.

How long I snoozed I don't know; not long, I think, for I was still well fuddled when I came to. It was a slow business, in which I was conscious of a woman's voice humming "Allan Water", and then I believe I heard a little laugh. Ah, thinks I, Elspeth; time to get up, Flashy. And as I hauled myself ponderously to my feet, and stood swaying dizzily in the dark of the closet, I was hearing vague confused sounds from the room. A voice? Voices? Someone moving? A door closing? I can't be sure at all, but just as I blundered tipsily to the closet door, I heard a sharp exclamation which might have been anything from a laugh to a cry of astonishment. I stumbled out of the closet, blinking against the sudden glare of light, and my boisterous view halloo died on my lips.

It was a sight I'll never forget. Elspeth was standing by the bed, naked except for her long frilled pantaloons; her flowers were still twined in her hair. Her eyes were wide with shock, and her knuckles were against her lips, like a nymph surprised by Pan, or centaurs, or a boozed-up husband emerging from the wardrobe. I goggled at her lecherously for about half a second, and then realized that we were not alone.

Half way between the foot of the bed and the door stood the 7th Earl of Cardigan. His elegant Cherrypicker pants were about his knees, and the front tail of his shirt was clutched up before him in both hands. He was in the act of advancing towards my wife, and from the expression on his face—which was that of a starving, apoplectic glutton faced with a crackling roast—and from other visible signs, his intention was not simply to compare birthmarks. He stopped dead at sight of me, his mottled face paling and his eyes popping, Elspeth squealed in earnest, and for several seconds we all stood stock still, staring.

Cardigan recovered first, and looking back, I have to admire him. It was not an entirely new situation for me, you understand— I'd been in *his* shoes, so to speak, many a time, when husbands, traps, or bullies came thundering in unexpectedly. Reviewing Cardigan's dilemma, I'd have whipped up my britches, feinted towards the window to draw the outraged spouse, doubled back with a spring on to the bed, and then been through the door in a twinkling. But not Lord Haw-Haw; his bearing was magnificent. He dropped his shirt, drew up his pants, threw back his head, looked straight at me, rasped: "Good night to you!", turned about, and marched out, banging the door behind him.

Elspeth had sunk to the bed, making little sobbing sounds; I still stood swaying in disbelief, trying to get the booze out of my brain, wondering if this was some drunken nightmare. But it wasn't, and as I glared at that big-bosomed harlot on the bed, all those ugly suspicions of fourteen years came flooding back, only now they were certainties. And I had caught her in the act at last, all but in the grip of that lustful, evil old villain! I'd just been in the nick of time to thwart him, too, damn him. And whether it was the booze, or my own rotten nature, the emotion I felt was not rage so much as a vicious satisfaction that I had caught her out. Oh, the rage came later, and a black despair that sometimes wounds me like a knife even now, but God help me, I'm an actor, I suppose, and I'd never had a chance to play the outraged husband before.

"Well?" It came out of me in a strangled yelp. "Well? What? What? Hey?"

I must have looked terrific, I suppose, for she dropped her squeaking and shuddering like a shot, and hopped over t'other side of the bed like a jack rabbit.

"Harry!" she squealed. "What are you doing here?"

It must have been the booze. I had been on the point of striding —well, staggering—round the bed to seize her and thrash her black and blue, but at her question I stopped, God knows why.

"I was waiting for you! Curse you, you adultress!"

"In that cupboard?"

"Yes, blast it, in that cupboard. By God, you've gone too far, you vile little slut, you! I'll—"

"How could you!" So help me God, it's what she said. "How could you be so inconsiderate and unfeeling as to pry on me in this way? Oh! I was never so mortified! Never!"

"Mortified?" cries I. "With that randy old rip sporting his beef in your bedroom, and you simpering naked at him? You—you shameless Jezebel! You lewd woman! Caught in the act, by George! I'll teach you to cuckold me! Where's a cane? I'll beat the shame out of that wanton carcase, I'll—"

"It is not true!" she cried. "It is not true! Oh, how can you say such a thing!"

I was glaring round for something to thrash her with, but at this I stopped, amazed.

"Not true? Why, you infernal little liar, d'you think I can't see? Another second and you'd have been two-backed-beasting all over the place! And you dare—"

"It is not so!" She stamped her foot, her fists clenched. "You are quite in the wrong—I did not know he was there until an instant before you came out of that cupboard! He must have come in while I was disrobing—Oh!" And she shuddered. "I was taken quite unawares—"

"By God, you were! By me! D'you think I'm a fool? You've been teasing that dirty old bull this month past, and I find him all but mounting you, and you expect me to believe—" My head was swimming with drink, and I lost the words. "You've dishonoured me, damn you! You've—"

"Oh, Harry, it is not true! I vow it is not! He must have stolen in, without my hearing, and—"

"You're lying!" I shouted. "You were whoring with him!"

"Oh, that is untrue! It is unjust! How can you *think* such a thing? How can you *say* it?" There were tears in her eyes, as well there might be, and now her mouth trembled and drooped, and she turned her head away. "I can see," she sobbed, "that you merely wish to make this an excuse for a quarrel."

God knows what I said in reply to that; sounds of rupture, no doubt. I couldn't believe my ears, and then she was going on, sobbing away:

"You are wicked to say such a thing! Oh, you have no thought for my feelings! Oh, Harry, to have that evil old creature steal up on me—the shock of it—oh, I thought to have died of fear and shame! And then you—you!" And she burst into tears in earnest and flung herself down on the bed.

I didn't know what to say, or do. Her behaviour, the way she had faced me, the fury of her denial—it was all unreal. I couldn't credit it, after what I'd seen. I was full of rage and hate and disbelief and misery, but in drink and bewilderment I couldn't reason straight. I tried to remember what I'd heard in the closet —had it been a giggle or a muted shriek? Could she be telling the truth? Was it possible that Cardigan had sneaked in on her, torn down his breeches in an instant, and been sounding the charge when she turned and saw him? Or had she wheedled him in, whispering lewdly, and been stripping for action when I rolled out? All this, in a confused brandy-laden haze, passed through my mind—as you may be sure it has passed since, in sober moments.

I was lost, standing there half-drunk. That queer mixture of shock and rage and exultation, and the vicious desire to punish her brutally, had suddenly passed. With any of my other women, I'd not even have listened, but taken out my spite on them with a whip—except on Ranavalona, who was bigger and stronger than I. But I didn't *care* for the other women, you see. Brute and all that I am, I wanted to believe Elspeth.

Mind you, it was still touch and go whether I suddenly went for her or not; but for the booze I probably would have done. There was all the suspicion of the past, and the evidence of my eyes tonight. I stood, panting and glaring, and suddenly she swung up in a sitting position, like Andersen's mermaid, her eyes full of tears, and threw out her arms. "Oh, Harry! Comfort me!"

If you had seen her—aye. It's so easy, as none knows better than I, to sneer at the Pantaloons of this world, and the cheated wives, too, while the rakes and tarts make fools of them—"If only they knew, ho-ho!" Perhaps they do, or suspect, but would just rather not let on. I don't know why, but suddenly I was seated on the bed, with my arm round those white shoulders, while she sobbed and clung to me, calling me her "jo"—it was that funny Scotch word, which she hadn't used for years, since she had grown so grand, that made me believe her—almost.

"Oh, that you should think ill of me!" she sniffled. "Oh, I could die of shame!"

"Well," says I, breathing brandy everywhere, "there he was, wasn't he? By God! Well, I say!" I suddenly seized her by the shoulders at arms' length. "Do you—? No, by God! I saw him—and you—and—and—"

"Oh, you are cruel!" she cried. "Cruel, cruel!" And then her arms went round my neck, and she kissed me, and I was sure she was lying—almost sure.

She sobbed away a good deal, and protested, and I babbled a great amount, no doubt, and she swore her honesty, and I didn't know what to make of it. She might be true, but if she was a cheat and a liar and a whore, what then? Murder her? Thrash her? Divorce her? The first was lunatic, the second I couldn't do, not now, and the third was unthinkable. With the trusts that old swine Morrison had left to tie things up, she controlled all the cash, and the thought of being a known cuckold living on my pay —well, I'm fool enough for a deal, but not for that. Her voice was murmuring in my ear, and all that naked softness was in my arms, and her fondling touch was reminding me of what I'd come here for in the first place, so what the devil, thinks I, first things first, and if you don't pleasure her now till she faints, you'll look back from your grey-haired evenings and wish you had. So I did.

I still don't know—and what's more I don't care. But one thing only I was certain of that night—whoever was innocent, it wasn't James Brudenell, Earl of Cardigan. I swore then inwardly, with Elspeth moaning through her kiss, that I would get even with that one. The thought of that filthy old goat trying to board Elspeth—it brought me out in a sweat of fury and loathing. I'd kill him, somehow. I couldn't call him out—he'd hide behind the law, and refuse. Even worse, he might accept. And apart from the fact that I daren't face him, man to man, there would have been scandal for sure. But somehow, some day, I would find a way.

We went to sleep at last, with Elspeth murmuring in my ear about what a. mighty lover I was, recalling me in doting detail, and how I was at my finest after a quarrel. She was giggling drowsily about how we had made up our previous tiff, with me tumbling her in the broom closet at home, and what fun it had been, and how I'd said it was the most famous place for rogering, and then suddenly she asked, quite sharp:

"Harry—tonight—your great rage at my misfortune was not all a pretence, was it? You did not—you are sure?—have some ... some female in the cupboard?"

And damn my eyes, she absolutely got out to look. I don't suppose I've cried myself to sleep since I was an infant, but it was touch and go then.

3

While all these important events in my personal affairs were taking place—Willy and Elspeth and Cardigan and so forth—you may wonder how the war was progressing. The truth is, of course, that it wasn't, for it's a singular fact of the Great Conflict against Russia that no one—certainly no one on the Allied side—had any clear notion of how to go about it. You will think that's one of these smart remarks, but it's not; I was as close to the conduct of the war in the summer of '54 as anyone, and I can tell you truthfully that the official view of the whole thing was:

"Well, here we are, the French and ourselves, at war with Russia, in order to protect Turkey. Ve-ry good. What shall we do, then? Better attack Russia, eh? H'm, yes. (Pause). Big place, ain't it?"

So they decided to concentrate our army, and the Froggies, in Bulgaria, where they might help the Turks fight the Ruskis on the Danube. But the Turks flayed the life out of the Russians without anyone's help, and neither Raglan, who was now out in Varna in command of the allies, nor our chiefs at home, could think what we might usefully do next. I had secret hopes that the whole thing might be called off; Willy and I were still at home, for Raglan had sent word that for safety's sake his highness should not come out until the fighting started—there was so much fever about in Bulgaria, it would not be healthy for him.

But there was never any hope of a peace being patched up, not with the mood abroad in England that summer. They were savage—they had seen their army and navy sail away with drums beating and fifes tootling, and 'Rule Britannia' playing, and the press promising swift and condign punishment for the Muscovite tyrant, and street-corner orators raving about how British steel would strike oppression down, and they were like a crowd come to a prize-fight where the two pugs don't fight, but spar and weave

49

and never come to grips. They wanted blood, gallons of it, and to read of grape-shot smashing great lanes through Russian ranks, and stern and noble Britons skewering Cossacks, and Russian towns in flames—and they would be able to shake their heads over the losses of our gallant fellows, sacrificed to stern duty, and wolf down their kidneys and muffins in their warm breakfast rooms, saying: "Dreadful work this, but by George, England never shirked yet, whatever the price. Pass the marmalade, Amelia; I'm proud to be a Briton this day, let me tell you."[10]

And all they got that summer was—nothing. It drove them mad, and they raved at the Government, and the army, and each other, lusting for butchery, and suddenly there was a cry on every lip, a word that ran from tongue to tongue and was in every leading article—"Sevastopol!" God knows why, but suddenly that was the place. Why were we not attacking Sevastopol, to show the Russians what was what, eh? It struck me then, and still does, that attacking Sevastopol would be rather like an enemy of England investing Penzance, and then shouting towards London: "There, you insolent bastard, that'll teach you!" But because it was said to be a great base, and The Times was full of it, an assault on Sevastopol became the talk of the hour.

And the government dithered, the British and Russian armies rotted away in Bulgaria with dysentery and cholera, the public became hysterical, and Willy and I waited, with our traps packed, for word to sail.

It came one warm evening, with a summons to Richmond. Suddenly there was great bustle, and I had to ride post-haste to receive from His Grace the Duke of Newcastle despatches to be carried to Raglan without delay. I remember an English garden, and Gladstone practising croquet shots on the lawn, and dragon-flies buzzing among the flowers, and over on the terrace a group of men lounging and yawning—the members of the Cabinet, no less, just finished an arduous meeting at which most of 'em had dozed off—that's a fact, too, it's in the books.[11] And Newcastle's secretary, a dapper young chap with an ink smudge on the back of his hand, handing me a sealed packet with a "secret" label.

"The Centaur is waiting at Greenwich," says he. "You must be aboard tonight, and these are to Lord Raglan, from your hand into his, nothing staying. They contain the government's latest advices and instructions, and are of the first urgency."

"Very good," says I. "What's the word of mouth?" He hesitated, and I went on: "I'm on his staff, you know."

It was the practice of every staff galloper then—and for all I know, may still be—when he was given a written message, to ask if there were any verbal observations to add. (As you'll see later, it is a very vital practice.) He frowned, and then, bidding me wait, went into the house, and came out with that tall grey figure that everyone in England knew, and the mobs used to cheer and laugh at and say, what a hell of an old fellow he was: Palmerston.

"Flashman, ain't it?" says he, putting a hand on my shoulder. "Thought you had gone out with Raglan." I told him about Willy, and he chuckled. "Oh, aye, our aspiring Frederick the Great. Well, you may take him with you, for depend upon it, the war is now *under way*. You have the despatches? Well, now, I think you may tell his lordship, when he has digested them— I daresay Newcastle has made it plain enough—that the capture of Sevastopol is held by Her Majesty's Government as being an enterprise that cannot but be seen as signally advancing the success of Allied arms. Hum? But that it will be a damned serious business to undertake. You see?"

I nodded, looking knowing, and he grunted and squinted across the lawn, watching Gladstone trying to knock a ball through a hoop. He missed, and Pam grunted again. "Off you go then, Flashman," says he. "Good luck to you. Come and see me when you return. My respects to his lordship." And as I saluted and departed, he hobbled stiffly out on to the lawn, and I watched him say something to Gladstone, and take his mallet from him. And that was all.

We sailed that night, myself after a hasty but passionate farewell with Elspeth, and Willy after a frantic foray to St John's Wood for a final gallop at his blonde. I was beginning to feel that old queasy rumbling in my belly that comes with any departure, and it wasn't improved by Willy's chatter as we stood on deck, watching the forest of shipping slip by in the dusk, and the lights twinkling on the banks.

"Off to the war!" exclaims the little idiot. "Isn't it capital,

51

Harry? Of course, it is nothing new to you, but for me, it is the most exciting thing I have ever known! Did you not feel, setting out on your first campaign, like some knight in the old time, going out to win a great name, oh, for the honour of your house and the love of your fair lady?"

I hadn't, in fact—and if I had, it wouldn't have been for a whore in St John's Wood. So I just grunted, à la Pam, and let him prattle.

It was a voyage, like any other, but faster and pleasanter than most, and I won't bore you with it. In fact, I won't deal at any great length at all with those things which other Crimean writers go on about—the fearful state of the army at Varna, the boozing and whoring at Scutari, the way the Varna sickness and the cholera swept through our forces in that long boiling summer, the mismanagement of an untrained commissariat and inexperienced regimental officers, the endless bickering among commanders— like Cardigan for instance. He had left England for Paris within two days of our encounter in Elspeth's bedroom, and on arrival in Bulgaria had killed a hundred horses with an ill-judged patrol in the direction of the distant Russians. All this—the misery and the sickness and the bad leadership and the rest—you can read if you wish elsewhere; Billy Russell of *The Times* gives as good a picture as any, although you have to be wary of him. He was a good fellow, Billy, and we got on well, but he always had an eye cocked towards his readers, and the worse he could make out a case, the better they liked it. He set half England in a passion against Raglan, you remember, because Raglan wouldn't let the army grow beards. "I like an Englishman to look like an Englishman," says Raglan, "and beards are *foreign*, and breed vermin. Also, depend upon it, they will lead to filthy habits." He was dead right about the vermin, but Russell wouldn't have it; he claimed this was just stiff-necked parade-ground nonsense and red tape on Raglan's part, and wrote as much. (You may note that Billy Russell himself had a beard like a quickset hedge, and I reckon he took Raglan's order as a personal insult.)

In any event, this memorial isn't about the history of the war, but about me, so I'll confine myself to that all-important subject, and let the war take its chance, just the way the government did.

We got to Varna, and the stink was hellish. The streets were filthy, there were stretcher-parties everywhere, ferrying fever cases from the camps outside town to the sewers they called hospitals, there was no order about anything, and I thought, well, we'll make our quarters on board until we can find decent lodgings at leisure. So leaving Willy, I went off to report myself to Raglan.

He was full of affability and good nature, as always, shook hands warmly, called for refreshment for me, inquired at great length about Willy's health and spirits, and then settled down to read the despatches I'd brought. It was close and warm in his office, even with the verandah doors wide and a nigger working a fan; Raglan was sweating in his shirt-sleeves, and as I drank my whistle-belly at a side-table and studied him, I could see that even a couple of months out east had aged him. His hair was snow-white, the lines on his face were deeper than ever, the flesh was all fallen in on his skinny wrist—he was an old man, and he looked and sounded it. And his face grew tireder as he read; when he had done he summoned George Brown, who had the Light Division, and was his bosom pal. Brown read the despatch, and they looked at each other.

"It is to be Sevastopol," says Raglan. "The government's direction seems quite clear to me."

"Provided," says Brown, "both you and the French commander believe the matter can be carried through successfully. In effect, they leave the decision to you, and to St Arnaud."

"Hardly," says Raglan, and picked up a paper. "Newcastle includes a personal aide memoire in which he emphasizes the wishes of the Ministers—it is all Sevastopol, you see."

"What do we know about Sevastopol—its defences, its garrison? How many men can the Russians oppose to us if we invade Crimea?"

"Well, my dear Sir George," says Raglan, "we know very little, you see. There are no reconnaissance reports, but we believe the defences to be strong. On the other hand, I know St Arnaud thinks it unlikely there can be more than 70,000 Russians mustered in the Crimean peninsula."

"About our own numbers," says Brown.

"Precisely, but that is only conjecture. There may be fewer, there may well be more. It is all so uncertain." He sighed, and kneaded his brow with his left hand, rather abstracted. "I cannot say for sure that they might not field 100,000 men, you know. There has been no blockade, and nothing to prevent their troop movements."

"And we would have to invade across the Black Sea, make a foothold, perhaps face odds of four to three, invest Sevastopol, reduce it speedily—or else carry on a siege through a Russian winter—and all this while relying solely on our fleet for supply, while the Russians may send into the Crimea what strength they choose."

"Exactly, Sir George. Meanwhile, only one fourth of our siege equipment has arrived. Nor is the army in the best of health, and I believe the French to be rather worse."

I listened to this with mounting horror—not so much at what they were saying, but how they said it. Perfectly calmly, reasonably, and without visible emotion, they were rehearsing a formula which even I, ignorant staff-walloper that I was, could see was one for disaster. But I could only keep mum, clutching my pot of beer and listening.

"I should welcome your observations, my dear Sir George," says Raglan.

Brown's face was a study. He was an old Scotch war horse this, and nobody's fool, but he knew Raglan, and he knew something of the politics of power and warfare. He put the despatch back on the table.

"As to the enterprise of Sevastopol which the ministers appear to be suggesting," says he, "I ask myself how our old master the Duke would have seen it. I believe he would have turned it down flat—there is not enough information about the Crimea and the Russians, and our armies are reduced to the point where we have no leeway to work on. He would not have taken the terrible responsibility of launching such a campaign."[12]

You could see the relief spreading over Raglan's old face like water.

"I concur exactly in what you say, Sir George," says he, "in which case—"

"On the other hand," says Brown, "I judge from this despatch that the government are determined on Sevastopol. They have made up their minds at home. Now, if you decline to accept the responsibility, what will they do? In my opinion, they will recall you; in fine, if you will not do the job, they'll send out someone who will."

Raglan's face lengthened, and I saw an almost pettish set to his mouth as he said:

"Dear me, that is to be very precise, Sir George. Do you really think so?"

"I do, sir. As I see it, things have reached a pass where they will have action, whatever it may be." He was breathing heavy, I noticed. "And I believe that with them, one place is as good as another."

Raglan sighed. "It may be as you say; it may be. Sevastopol. Sevastopol. I wonder why? Why that, rather than the Danube or the Caucasus?" He glanced round, as though he expected to see the answer on the wall, and noticed me. "Ah, Colonel Flashman, perhaps you can enlighten us a little in this. Are you aware of any factor in affairs at home that may have determined the government on this especial venture?"

I told him what I knew—that the Press was yelping Sevastopol right and left, and that everyone had it on the brain.

"Do they know where it *is*?" says Brown.

I wasn't too sure myself where it was, but I said I supposed they did. Raglan tapped his lip, looking at the despatch as though he hoped it would go away.

"Did you see anyone when the despatch was delivered to you —Newcastle, or Argyll, perhaps?"

"I saw Lord Palmerston, sir. He remarked that the government were confident that the occupation of Sevastopol would be an excellent thing, but that it would be a damned serious business. Those were his words, sir."

Brown gave a bark of disgust, and Raglan laughed. "We may agree with him, I think. Well, we must see what our Gallic allies think, I suppose, before we can reach a fruitful conclusion."

So they did—all the chattering Frogs of the day, with St Arnaud, the little mountebank from the Foreign Legion, who had once earned his living on the stage and looked like an ice-cream vendor, with his perky moustache, at their head. He had the feverish look of a dying man—which he was—and Canrobert, with his long hair and ridiculous curling moustaches, wasn't one to inspire confidence either. Not that they were worse than our own crew—the ass Cambridge, and Evans snorting and growling, and old England burbling, and Raglan sitting at the table head, like a vicar at a prize-giving, being polite and expressing gratified pleasure at every opinion, no matter what it was.

And there was no lack of opinions. Raglan thought an invasion might well come off—given luck—Brown was dead against it, but at first the Frogs were all for it, and St Arnaud said we should be in Sevastopol by Christmas, death of his life and sacred blue. Our navy people opposed the thing, and Raglan got peevish, and then the Frogs began to have their doubts, and everything fell into confusion. They had another meeting, at which I wasn't present, and then the word came out: the Frogs and Raglan were in agreement again, Brown was over-ruled and the navy with him, we were to go to the Crimea.

"I dare say the sea air will do us good and raise everyone's spirits," says Raglan, and by God, he didn't raise mine. I've wondered since, if I could have done anything about it, and decided I could. But what? If Otto Bismarck had been in my boots and uniform, I daresay he could have steered them away, as even a junior man can, if he goes about it right. But I've never meddled if I could avoid it, where great affairs are concerned; it's too chancy. Mind you, if I could have seen ahead I'd have sneaked into Raglan's tent one night and brained the old fool, but I didn't know, you see.

So there was tremendous sound and fury for the next month, with everyone preparing for the great invasion. Willy and I had established ourselves snugly in a cottage outside the town, and with all our provisions and gear we did comfortably enough, but being staff men we couldn't shirk too much, although Raglan worked Willy lightly, and was forever encouraging him to go riding and shooting and taking it easy. For the rest, it was touch and go, so far as I could see, whether the army, which was still full of fever and confusion, would ever be well enough to crawl on the transports, but as you know, the thing was done in the end. I've written about it at length elsewhere—the fearful havoc of embarking, with ships full of spewing soldiers rocking at anchor for days on end, the weeping women who were ordered to stay behind (although my little pal, Fan Duberly,[13] sneaked aboard disguised as a washerwoman), the horses fighting and smashing in their cramped stalls, the hideous stink, the cholera corpses floating in the bay, Billy Russell standing on the quay with his note-book damning Lord Lucan's eyes—"I have *my* duty, too, my lord, which is to inform my readers, and if you don't like what you're doing being reported, why then, don't do it! And that's my advice to you!" Of course he was daft and Irish, was Billy, but so was Lucan, and they stood and cussed each other like Mississippi pilots.

I had my work cut out latterly in bagging a berth on the *Caradoc*, which was Raglan's flagship, and managed to get not a bad billet for Willy and myself and Lew Nolan, who was galloper to Airey, the new chief of staff. He was another Irish, with a touch of dago or something, this Nolan, a cavalry maniac who held everybody in contempt, and let 'em feel it, too, although he was a long way junior. Mind you, he came no snuff with me, because I was a better horseman, and he knew it. We three bunked in together, while major-generals and the like had to make do with hammocks—I played Willy's royalty for all it was worth, you may be sure. And then, heigh-ho, we were off on our balmy cruise across the Black Sea, a huge fleet of sixty thousand soldiers, only half of 'em rotten with sickness, British, Frogs, Turks, a few Bashi-bazooks, not enough heavy guns to fire more than a salute or two, and old General Scarlett sitting on top of a crate of hens learning the words of command for manoeuvring a cavalry brigade, closing his book on his finger, shutting his boozy old eyes, and shouting, "Walk, march, trot. Damme, what comes next?"

The only thing was—no one knew where we were going. We ploughed about the Black Sea, while Raglan and the Frogs wondered where we should land, and sailed up and down the Russian coast looking for a likely spot. We found one, and Raglan stood there smiling and saying what a capital beach it was. "Do you smell the lavender?" says he. "Ah, Prince William, you may think you are back in Kew Gardens."

Well, it may have smelled like it at first, but by the time we had spent five days crawling ashore, with everyone spewing and soiling themselves in the pouring rain, and great piles of stores and guns and rubbish growing on the beach, and the sea getting fouler and fouler with the dirt of sixty thousand men—well, you may imagine what it was like. The army's health was perhaps a little better than it had been on the voyage, but not much, and when we finally set off down the coast, and I watched the heavy, plodding tread of the infantry, and saw the stretched looked of the cavalry mounts—I thought, how far will this crowd go, on a few handfuls of pork and biscuit, no tents, devil a bottle of jallop, and the cholera, the invisible dragon, humming in the air as they marched?

Mind you, from a distance it looked well. When that whole army was formed up, it stretched four miles by four, a great glittering host from the Zouaves on the beach, in their red caps and blue coats, to the shakos of the 44th on the far horizon of the plain—and they were a sight of omen to me, for the last time I'd seen them they'd been standing back to back in the bloodied snow of Gandamack, with the Ghazi knives whittling 'em down, and Souter with the flag wrapped round his belly. I never see those 44th facings but I think of the army of Afghanistan dying in the ice-hills, and shudder.

I was privileged, if that is the word, to give the word that started the whole march, for Raglan sent me and Willy to gallop first to the rear guard and then to the advance guard with the order to march. In fact, I let Willy deliver the second message, for the advance guard was led by none other than Cardigan, and it was more than I could bear to look at the swine. We cantered through the army, and the fleeting pictures are in my mind still —the little French canteen tarts sitting laughing on the gun limbers, the scarlet stillness of the Guards, rank on rank, the bearded French faces with their kepis, and Bosquet balancing his belly above a horse too small for him, the sing-song chatter of the Highlanders in their dark green tartans, the sombre jackets of the Light Division, the red yokel faces burning in the heat, the smell of sweat and oil and hot serge, the creak of leather and the jingle of bits, the glittering points of the lances where the 17th sat waiting—and Willy burst out in excitement: "Our regiment, Harry! See how grand they look! What noble fellows they are!" —Billy Russell sitting athwart his mule and shouting "What is it, Flash? Are we off at last?", and I turned away to talk to him while Willy galloped ahead to where the long pink and blue line of the 11th marked the van of the army.

"I haven't seen our friends so close before," says Billy. "Look yonder." And following his pointing finger, far out to the left flank, with the sun behind them, I saw the long silent line of horsemen on the crest, the lances like twigs in the hands of pygmies.

"Cossacks," says Billy. We'd seen 'em before, of course, the first night, scouting our landing, and I'd thought then, it's well seen you ain't Ghazis, my lads, or you'd pitch our whole force back into the sea before we're right ashore. And as the advance was sounded, and the whole great army lumbered forward into the heat haze, with a band lilting "Garryowen", and the chargers of the 17th snorting and fidgeting at the sound, I saw to my horror that Willy, having delivered his message, was not riding back towards me, but was moving off at a smart gallop towards the left flank.

I cut out at once, to head him off, but he was light and his horse was fast, and he was a good three hundred yards clear of the left flank before I came up with him. He was cantering on, his eyes fixed on the distant ridge—and it was none so distant now; as I came up roaring at him, he turned and pointed: "Look, Harry—the enemy!"

"You little duffer, what are you about?" cries I. "D'you want to get your head blown off?"

"They are some way off," says he, laughing, and indeed they were—but close enough to be able to see the blue and white stripes of the lances, and make out the shaggy fur caps. They sat immovable while we stared at them, and I felt the sweat turn icy on my spine in spite of the heat. These were the famous savages of Tartary, watching, waiting—and God knew how many of them there might be, in great hordes advancing on our pathetic little army, as it tootled along with its gay colours by the sea. I pulled Willy's bridle round.

"Out of this, my lad," says I, "and don't stray again without my leave, d'ye hear?"

"Why, it is safe enough. None of them is advancing, or even looking like it. What a bore it is! If this were—oh, the Middle Ages, one of them would ride out and challenge us, and we could have a set-to while the army watched!" He was actually sitting there, with his eyes shining, and his hand twitching at his sabre-hilt, *wanting* a fight! A fine credit to me he was, you'll agree. And before I could rebuke him, there was the boom of gunfire, beyond the ridge, and boom-boom-boom, and the whistle of shot ahead, and a little cloud of pink-panted Hussars broke away and went dashing over towards the ridge, sabres out. There was cries and orders, and a troop of horse artillery came thundering out towards us, and I had to shout at Willy to get him trotting back towards the army, while the horse artillery unlimbered, and wheeled their pieces, and crashed their reply to the Russian guns.

He wanted to stay, but I wouldn't have it. "Gallopers can get killed," says I, "but not sitting with their mouths open staring at a peep-show." To tell truth, the sound of those bloody guns had set my innards quaking again, in the old style. "Now—gallop!" says I.

"Oh, very well," says he. "But you need not be so careful of me, you know—I don't mean to go astray just yet." And seeing my expression, he burst out laughing: "My word, what a cautious old stick you are, Harry—you are getting as bad as Dr Winter!"

And I wish I were with Dr Winter this minute, thinks I, whatever the old whoreson's doing. But I was to remember what Willy had said—and in the next day or so, too, when the army had rolled on down the coast, choking with heat by day and shivering by the fires at night, and we had come at last to the long slope that runs down to a red-banked river with great bluffs and gullies beyond. Just a little Russian creek, and today in any English parish church you may see its name on stone memorials, on old tattered flags in cathedrals, in the metalwork of badges, and on the nameplates of grimy back streets beside the factories. Alma.

You have seen the fine oil-paintings, I dare say—the perfect lines of guardsmen and Highlanders fronting up the hill towards the Russian batteries, with here and there a chap lying looking thoughtful with his hat on the ground beside him, and in the distance fine silvery clouds of cannon smoke, and the colours to the fore, and fellows in cocked hats waving their swords. I dare say some people saw and remember the Battle of the Alma like that, but Flashy is not among them. And I was in the middle of it, too, all on account of a commander who hadn't the sense to realize that generals ought to stay in the rear, directing matters.

It was bloody lunacy, from the start, and bloody carnage, too. You may know what the position was—the Russians, forty thousand strong, on the bluffs south of the Alma, with artillery positions dug on the forward slopes above the river, and our chaps, with the Frogs on the right, advancing over the river and up the slopes to drive the Ruskis out. If Menschikoff had known his work, or our troops had had less blind courage, they'd have massacred the whole allied army there and then. But the Russians fought as badly and stupidly as they nearly always do, and by sheer blind luck on Raglan's part, and idiot bravery among our fellows, the thing went otherwise.

You may read detailed accounts of the slaughter, if you wish, in any military history, but you may take my word for it that the battle was for all practical purposes divided into four parts, as follows. One, Flashy observes preliminary bombardment from his post in the middle of Raglan's staff, consoling himself that there are about twenty thousand other fellows between him and the enemy. Two, Flashy is engaged in what seem like hours of frantic galloping behind the lines of the Frog battalions on the right, keeping as far from the firing as he decently can, and inquiring on Lord Raglan's behalf why the hell the Frogs are not driving the seaward flank of the Russian position before them? Three, Flashy is involved in the battle with Lord Raglan. Four, Flashy reaps the fruits of allied victory, and bitter they were.

It was supposed to begin, you see, with the Frogs turning the Ruskis' flank, and then our chaps would roll over the river and finish the job. So for hours we sat there, sweating in the heat, and watching the powder-puff clouds of smoke popping out of the Russian batteries, and peppering our men in the left and centre. But the Frogs made nothing of their part of the business, and Nolan and I were to and fro like shuttlecocks to St Arnaud; he was looking like death, and jabbering like fury, while a bare half-mile away his little blue-coats were swarming up the ridges, and being battered, and the smoke was rolling back over the river in long grey wreaths.

"Tell milor it will take a little longer," he kept saying, and back we would gallop to Raglan. "We shall never beat the French at this rate," says he, and when he was reminded that the enemy were the Russians, not the French, he would correct himself hurriedly, and glance round to see that no Frog gallopers were near to overhear. And at last, seeing our silent columns being pounded by the Russian shot as they lay waiting for the advance, he gave the word, and the long red lines began rolling down the slope to the river.

There was a great reek of black smoke drifting along the banks from a burning hamlet right before us, and the white discharge of the Russian batteries rolled down in great clouds to meet it. The huge wavering lines of infantry vanished into it, and through gaps we could see them plunging into the river, their pieces above their heads, while the crash-crash-crash of the Russian guns reverberated down from the bluffs, and the tiny white spots of musket-fire began to snap like fire-crackers along the lips of the Russian trenches. And then the ragged lines of our infantry appeared beyond the smoke, clambering up the foot of the bluffs, and we could see the shot ploughing through them, tearing up the ground, and our guns were thundering in reply, throwing great fountains of earth up round the Russian batteries. Willy beside me was squirming in his saddle, yelling his head off with excitement, the little fool; it made no odds, for the din was deafening.

And Raglan looked round, and seeing the boy, smiled, and beckoned to me. He had to shout. "Keep him close, Flashman!" cries he. "We are going across the river presently," which was the worst news I had heard in weeks. Our attack was coming to a standstill; as the Russian firing redoubled, you could see our men milling anywhere at the foot of the bluffs, and the ground already thick with still bodies, in little heaps where the cannon had caught them, or singly where they had gone down before the muskets.

Then Nolan comes galloping up, full of zeal and gallantry, damn him, and shouted a message from the Frogs, and I saw Raglan shake his head, and then he trotted off towards the river, with the rest of us dutifully tailing on behind. Willy had his sabre out, God knows why, for all we had to worry about just then was the Russian shot, which was bad enough. We spurred down to the river, myself keeping Willy at the tail of the group, and I saw Airey throw aside his plumed hat just as we took the water. There were bodies floating in the stream, which was churned up with mud, and the smoke was billowing down and catching at our throats, making the horses rear and plunge—I had to grip Willy's bridle to prevent his being thrown. On our left men of the 2nd

Division were crowded on the bank, waiting to go forward; they were retching and coughing in the smoke, and the small shot and balls were whizzing and whining by in a hideously frightening way. I just kept my head down, praying feverishly, as is my wont, and then I saw one of the other gallopers, just ahead of me, go reeling out of his saddle with the blood spouting from his sleeve. He staggered up, clutching at my stirrup, and bawling, "I am perfectly well, my lord, I assure you!" and then he rolled away, and someone else jumped down to see to him.

Raglan halted, cool as you like, glancing right and left, and then summoned two of the gallopers and sent them pounding away along the bank to find Evans and Brown, whose divisions were being smashed to pieces at the foot of the bluffs. Then he says, "Come along, gentlemen. We shall find a vantage point," and cantered up the gully that opened up before us just there in the bluff-face. For a wonder it seemed empty, all the Ruskis being on the heights to either side, and the smoke was hanging above our heads in such clouds you couldn't see more than twenty yards up the hill. A hell of a fine position for a general to be in, you may think, and Raglan must have thought so, too, for suddenly he spurred his horse at the hill to the left, and we all ploughed up behind him, scrambling on the shale and rough tufts, through the reeking smoke, until suddenly we were through it, and on the top of a little knoll at the bluff foot.

I'll never forget that sight. Ahead and to our left rose the bluffs, bare steep hillside for five hundred feet. We could see the Russian positions clear as day, the plumes of musket smoke spouting down from the trenches, and the bearded faces behind them. Directly to our left was a huge redoubt, packed with enemy guns and infantry; there were other great batteries above and beyond. In front of the big redoubt the ground was thick with the bodies of our men, but they were still swarming up from the river, under a hail of firing. And beyond, along the bluffs, they were still advancing, a great sprawling mass of scarlet coats and white cross belts, clawing their way up, falling, scattering, re-forming and pressing on. For a mile, as far as one could see, they were surging up, over that hellish slope with the dead scattered before them towards the smoking positions of the enemy.

Better here than there, thinks I, until I realized that we were sitting up in full view, unprotected, with the Ruski infantry not a hundred yards away. We were absolutely ahead of our own infantry, thanks to that fool Raglan—and he was sitting there, with his blue coat flapping round him, and his plumed hat on his head, as calm as if it were a review, clinging to his saddle with his knees alone, while he steadied his glass with his single arm. There was so much shot whistling overhead, you couldn't be sure whether they were firing on us with intent or not.

And then right up on the crest, above the batteries, we saw the Russian infantry coming down the slope—a great brown mass, packed like sardines, rank after rank of them. They came clumping slowly, inexorably down towards the batteries, obviously intent on rolling into our infantry below. They looked unstoppable, and Raglan whistled through his teeth as he watched them.

"Too good to miss, by George!" cries he, and turning, caught my eye. "Down with you, Flashman! Guns, at once!" and you may understand that I didn't need telling twice. "Stay there!" shouts I to Willy, and then had my charger down that slope like a jack-rabbit. There were gun-teams labouring and splashing up the bank, and I bawled to them to make haste to the ridge. The horses were lashed up the muddy slope, the guns swinging wildly behind them; one of our gallopers got them positioned, with the gunners hauling them round by main force, and as I came back up the hill—none too swiftly—the first salvoes were screaming away to crash into the flank of the Russian columns.

It was havoc all along the bluffs, and smoking hell on that little hill. There were infantry pouring past us now, sweating, panting, smoke-blackened faces, and bayonets thrust out ahead as they surged by and upwards towards the Russian positions. They were shrieking and bawling like madmen, heedless apparently of the bloody holes torn in their ranks by the Russian firing; I saw two of them suddenly turn into pulp as a fusillade struck them, and another lying screaming with a thigh shot away. I looked for Raglan, and saw him with a couple of gallopers preparing to descend the hill; I looked for Willy, and there he was, his hat gone, shouting like a madman at the passing infantry.

And then, by God, he whirled up his sabre, and went flying along with them, across the face of the slope towards the nearest battery. His horse stumbled and recovered, and he waved his sword and huzza'd. "Come back, you German lunatic!" I yelled, and Raglan must have heard me, for he checked his horse and turned. Even with the shot flying and the screaming and the thunder of the guns, with the fate of the battle in his hands, those ears which were normally deaf to sense caught my words. He saw me, he saw Willy, careering away along the bluffs among the infantry, and he sang out: "After him, Flashman!"

Probably, addressed to any other man in the army, that order would have evoked an immediate response. The Eye of the Chief, and all that. But I took one look along that shell-swept slope, with the bodies thick on it, and that young idiot riding through the blood and bullets, and I thought, by God, let him go for me. I hesitated, and Raglan shouted again, angrily, so I set my charger towards him, cupping a hand behind my ear, and yelling: "What's that, my lord?" He shouted and pointed again, stabbing with his finger, and then a shot mercifully ploughed up the ground between us, and as the dirt showered over me I took the opportunity to roll nimbly out of the saddle.

I clambered up again, like a man dazed, and rot him, he was still there, and looking thoroughly agitated. "The Prince, Flashman!" he bawls, and then one of the gallopers plucked at his coat, and pointed to the right, and off they went, leaving me clutching at my horse's head, and Willy a hundred yards away, in the thick of the advancing infantry, setting his horse to the breastwork of the battery. It baulked, and he reeled in the saddle, his sabre falling, and then he pitched straight back, losing his grip, and went down before the feet of the infantry. I saw him roll a yard or two, and then he lay still, as the advance passed over him.

Christ, I thought, he's done for, and as our fellows surged into the battery, and the firing from above slackened, I picked my way cautiously along, through those dreadful heaps of dead and dying and wounded, with the stink of blood and powder everywhere, and the chorus of shrieks and moans of agony in my ears. I dropped on one knee beside the little blue-clad figure among the crimson; he was lying face down. I turned him over, and vomited. He had half a face—one glazed eye, and brow, and cheek, and on the other side, just a gory mash, with his brains running out of it.

I don't know how long I crouched there, staring at him, horror-struck. Above me, I could hear all hell of firing and shouting still going on as the battle surged up the slope, and I shook with fear at it. I wasn't going near that again, not for a pension, but as I forced myself to look at what was left of Willy, I found myself babbling aloud: "Jesus, what'll Raglan say? I've lost Willy—my God, what will they say?" And I began cursing and sobbing—not for Willy, but out of shock and for the folly and ill-luck that had brought me to this slaughterhouse and had killed this brainless brat, this pathetic princeling who thought war was great sport, and had been entrusted to my safe-keeping. By God, his death could be the ruin of me! So I swore and wept, crouched beside his corpse.

"Of all the fearful sights I have seen on this day, none has so wrung my heart as this." That's what Airey told Raglan, when he described how he had found me with Willy's body above the Alma. "Poor Flashman, I believe his heart is broken. But to see the bravest blade on your staff, an officer whose courage is a byword in the army, weeping like a child beside his fallen comrade—it is a terrible thing. He would have given his own life a hundred times, I know, to preserve that boy."

I was listening outside the tent-flap, you see, stricken dumb with manly grief. Well, I thought, that's none so bad; crying with funk and shock has its uses, provided its mistaken for noble tears. Raglan couldn't blame me, after all; I hadn't shot the poor little fool, or been able to stop him throwing his life away. Anyway, Raglan had a victory to satisfy him, and even the loss of a royal galloper couldn't sour that, you'd think. Aye, but it could.

He was all stern reproach when finally I stood in front of him, covered in dust, played out with fear, and doing my damndest to look contrite—which wasn't difficult.

"What," says he, in a voice like a church bell, "will you tell her majesty?"

"My lord," says I. "I am sorry, but it was no fault—"

He held up his one fine hand. "Here is no question of fault, Flashman. You had a sacred duty—a trust, given into your hands by your own sovereign, to preserve that precious life. You have failed, utterly. I ask again, what will you tell the Queen?"

Only a bloody fool like Raglan would ask a question like that, but I did my best to wriggle clear.

"What could I have done, my lord? You sent me for the guns, and—"

"And you had returned. Your first thought thereafter should have been for your sacred charge. Well, sir, what have you to say? Myself, in the midst of battle, had to point to where honour should have taken you at once; And yet you paused; I saw you, and—"

"My lord!" cries I, full of indignation. "That is unjust! I did not fully understand, in the confusion, what your order was, I—"

"Did you need to understand?" says he, all quivering sorrow. "I do not question your courage, Flashman; it is not in doubt." Not with me, either, I thought, "But I cannot but charge you, heavily though it weighs on my heart to do so, with failing in that... that instinct for your first duty, which should have been not to me, or to the army even, but to that poor boy whose shattered body lies in the ambulance. His soul, we may be confident, is with God." He came up to me, and his eyes were full of tears, the maudlin old hypocrite. "I can guess at your own grief; it has moved not only Airey, but myself. And I can well believe that you wish that you, too, could have found an honourable grave on the field, as William of Celle has done. Better, perhaps, had you done so." He sighed, thinking about it, and no doubt deciding that he'd be a deal happier, when he saw the Queen again, to be able to say: 'Oh, Flashy's kicked the bucket, by the way, but your precious Willy is all right.' Well, fearful and miserable as I was, I wasn't that far gone, myself.

He prosed on a bit, about duty and honour and my own failure, and what a hell of a blot I'd put on my copybook. No thought, you'll notice, for the blot *he'd* earned, with those thousands of dead piled up above the Alma, the incompetent buffoon.

"I doubt not you will carry this burden all your life," says he, with gloomy satisfaction. "How it will be received at home— I cannot say. For the moment, we must all look to our duty in the campaign ahead. There, it may be, reparation lies." He was still thinking about Flashy filling a pit, I could see. "I pity you, Flashman, and because I pity you, I shall not send you home. You may continue on my staff, and I trust that your future conduct will enable me to think that this lapse—irreparable though its consequences are—was but one terrible error of judgment, one sudden dereliction of duty, which will never—nay, *can* never— be repeated. But for the moment, I cannot admit you again to that full fellowship of the spirit in which members of my staff are wont to be embraced."

Well, I could stand that. He rummaged on his table, and picked up some things. "These are the personal effects of your . . . your dead comrade. Take them, and let them be an awful reminder to you of duty *undone*, of trust neglected, and of honour—no, I will not say aught of honour to one whose courage, at least, I believe to be beyond reproach." He looked at the things; one of them was a locket which Willy had worn round his neck. Raglan snapped it open, and gave a little gulp. He held it out to me, his face all noble and working. "Look on that fair, pure face," cries he, "and feel the remorse you deserve. More than anything I can say, it will strike to your soul—the face of a boy's sweetheart, chaste, trusting, and innocent. Think of that poor, sweet creature who, thanks to your neglect, will soon be draining the bitterest cup of sorrow."

I doubted it myself, as I looked at the locket. Last time I'd seen her, the poor sweet creature had been wearing nothing but black satin boots. Only Willy in this wide world would have thought of wearing the picture of a St John's Wood whore round his neck; he had been truly wild about her, the randy little rascal. Well, if I'd had my way, he'd still have been thumping her every night, instead of lying on a stretcher with only half his head. But I wonder if the preaching Raglan, or any of the pious hypocrites who were his relatives, would have called him back to life on those terms? Poor little Willy.

4

Well, if I was in disgrace, I was also in good health, and that's what matters. I might have been one of the three thousand dead, or of the shattered wounded lying shrieking through the dusk along that awful line of bluffs. There seemed to be no medical provision—among the British, anyway—and scores of our folk just lay writhing where they fell, or died in the arms of mates hauling and carrying them down to the beach hospitals. The Russian wounded lay in piles by the hundred round our bivouacs, crying and moaning all through the night—I can hear their sobbing "*Pajalsta! pajalsta!*" still. The camp ground was littered with spent shot and rubbish and broken gear among the pools of congealed blood—my stars, wouldn't I just like to take one of our Ministers, or street-corner orators, or blood-lusting, break-fast-scoffing papas, over such a place as the Alma hills—not to let him *see*, because he'd just tut-tut and look anguished and have a good pray and not care a damn—but to shoot him in the belly with a soft-nosed bullet and let him die screaming where he belonged. That's all they deserve.

Not that I cared a fig for dead or wounded that night. I had worries enough on my own account, for in brooding about the injustice of Raglan's reproaches, I convinced myself that I'd be broke in the end. The loss of that mealy little German pimp swelled out of all proportion in my imagination, with the Queen calling me a murderer and Albert accusing me of high treason, and *The Times* trumpeting for my impeachment. It was only when I realized that the army might have other things to think about that I cheered up.

I was feeling as lonely as the policeman at Herne Bay[14] when I loafed into Billy Russell's tent, and found him scribbling away by a storm lantern, with Lew Nolan perched on an ammunition box, holding forth as usual.

"Two brigades of cavalry!" Nolan was saying. "Two brigades,

enough to have pursued and routed the whole pack of 'em! And what do they do? Sit on their backsides, because Lucan's too damned scared to order a bag of oats without a written order from Raglan. Lord Lucan? Bah! Lord bloody Look-on, more like."

"Hm'm," says Billy, writing away, and glanced up. "Here, Flash—you'll know. Were the Highlanders first into the redoubt? I say yes, but Lew says not.[15] Stevens ain't sure, and I can't find Campbell anywhere. What d'ye say?"

I said I didn't know, and Nolan cried what the devil did it matter, anyway, they were only infantry. Billy, seeing he would get no peace from him, threw down his pen, yawned, and says to me:

"You look well used up, Flash. Are you all right? What's the matter, old fellow?"

I told him Willy was lost, and he said aye, that was a pity, a nice lad, and I told him what Raglan had said to me, and at this Nolan forgot his horses for a minute, and burst out:

"By God, isn't that of a piece? He's lost the best part of five brigades, and he rounds on one unfortunate galloper because some silly little ass who shouldn't have been here at all, at all, gets himself blown up by the Russians! If he was so blasted concerned for him, what did he let him near the field for in the first place? And if you was to wet-nurse him, why did he have you galloping your arse off all day? The man's a fool! Aye, and a bad general, what's worse—there's a Russian army clear away, thanks to him and those idle Frogs, and we could have cut 'em to bits on this very spot! I tell you, Billy, this fellow'll have to go."

"Come, Lew, he's won his fight," says Russell, stroking his beard. "It's too bad he's set on you, Flash—but I'd lose no sleep over it. Depend upon it, he's only voicing his own fears of what may be said to *him*—but he's a decent old stick, and bears no grudges. He'll have forgotten about it in a day or so."

"You think so?" says I, brightening.

"I should hope so!" cries Nolan. "Mother of God, if he hasn't more to think about, he should have. Here's him and Lucan between 'em have let a great chance slip, but by the time Billy here has finished tellin' the British public about how the matchless Guards and stern Caledonians swept the Muscovite horde aside on their bayonet points—"

"I like that," says Billy, winking at me. "I like it, Lew; go on, you're inspiring."

"Ah, bah, the old fool'll be thinking he's another Wellington," says Lew. "Aye, you can laugh, Russell—tell your readers what I've said about Lucan, though—I dare ye! That'd startle 'em!"

This talk cheered me up, for after all, it was what Russell thought—and wrote—that counted, and he never even mentioned Willy's death in his despatches to *The Times*. I heard that Raglan later referred to it, at a meeting with his generals, and Cardigan, the dirty swine, said privately that he wondered why the Prince's safety had been entrusted to a common galloper. But Lucan took the other side, and said only a fool would blame me for the death of another staff officer, and de Lacy Evans said Raglan should think himself lucky it was Willy he had lost and not me. Sound chaps, some of those generals.

And Nolan was right—Raglan and everyone else had enough to occupy them, after the Alma. The clever men were for driving on hard to Sevastopol, a bare twenty miles away, and with our cavalry in good fettle we could obviously have taken it. But the Frogs were too tired, or too sick, or too Froggy, if you ask me, and days were wasted, and the Ruskis managed to bolt the door in time.

What was worse, the carnage at Alma, and the cholera, had thinned the army horribly, there was no proper transport, and by the time we had lumbered on to Sevastopol peninsula we couldn't have robbed a hen-roost. But the siege had to be laid, and Raglan, looking wearier all the time, was thrashing himself to be cheerful and enthusiastic, with his army wasting, and winter coming, and the Frogs groaning at him. Oh, he was brave and determined and ready to take on all the odds—the worst kind of general imaginable. Give me a clever coward every time (which, of course, is why I'm such a dam' fine general myself).

So the siege was laid, the French and ourselves sitting down on the muddy, rain-sodden gullied plateau before Sevastopol, the dismalest place on earth, with no proper quarters but a few poor huts and tents, and everything to be carted up from Balaclava on the coast eight miles away. Soon the camp, and the road to it, was a stinking quagmire; everyone looked and felt filthy, the rations were poor, the work of preparing the siege was cruel hard (for the men, anyway), and all the bounce there had been in the army after Alma evaporated in the dank, feverish rain by day and the biting cold by night. Soon half of us were lousy, and the other half had fever or dysentery or cholera or all three—as some wag said, who'd holiday at Brighton if he could come to sunny Sevastopol instead?

I didn't take any part in the siege operations myself, not because I was out of favour with Raglan, but for the excellent reason that like so many of the army I spent several weeks on the flat of my back with what was thought at first to be cholera, but was in fact a foul case of dysentery and wind, brought on by my own hoggish excesses. On the march south after the Alma I had been galloping a message from Airey to our advance guard, and had come on a bunch of our cavalry who had bushwacked a Russian baggage train and were busily looting it.[16] Like a good officer, I joined in, and bagged as much champagne as I could carry, and a couple of fur cloaks as well. The cloaks were splendid, but the champagne must have carried the germ of the Siberian pox or something, for within a day I was blown up like a sheep on weeds, and spewing and skittering damnably. They sent me down to a seedy little house in Balaclava, not far from where Billy Russell was established, and there I lay sweating and rumbling, and wishing I were dead. Part of it I don't remember, so I suppose I must have been delirious, but my orderly looked after me well, and since I still had all the late Willy's gear and provisions—not that I ate much, until the last week—I did tolerably well. Better at least than any other sick man in the army; they were being carted down to Balaclava in droves, rotten with cholera and fever, lying in the streets as often as not.

Lew Nolan came down to see me when I was mending, and gave me all the gossip—about how my old friend Fan Duberly was on hand, living on a ship in the bay, and how Cardigan's yacht had arrived, and his noble lordship, pleading a weak chest, had deserted his Light Brigade for the comforts of life aboard, where he slept soft and stuffed his guts with the best. There were rumours, too, Lew told me, of Russian troops moving up in huge strength from the east, and he thought that if Raglan didn't look alive, he'd find himself bottled up in the Sevastopol peninsula. But most of Lew's talk was a great harangue against Lucan and

Cardigan; to him, they were the clowns who had mishandled our cavalry so damnably and were preventing it earning the laurels which Lew thought it deserved. He was a dead bore on the subject, but I'll not say he was wrong—we were both to find out all about that shortly.

For now, although I couldn't guess it, as I lay pampering myself with a little preserved jellied chicken and Rhine wine—of which Willy's store-chest yielded a fine abundance—that terrible day was approaching, that awful thunderclap of a day when the world turned upside down in a welter of powder-smoke and cannon-shot and steel, which no one who lived through it will ever forget. Myself least of all. I never thought that anything could make Alma or the Kabul retreat seem like a charabanc picnic, but *that* day did, and I was through it, dawn to dusk, as no other man was. It was sheer bad luck that it was the very day I returned to duty. Damn that Russian champagne; if it had kept me in bed just one day longer, what I'd have been spared. Mind you, we'd have lost India, for what that's worth.

I had been up a day or two, riding a little up to the Balaclava Plain, and wondering if I was fit enough to look up Fan Duberly, and take up again the attempted seduction which had been so maddeningly frustrated in Wiltshire six years before. She'd ripened nicely, by what Lew said, and I hadn't bestrode anything but a saddle since I'd left England—even the Turks didn't fancy the Crim Tartar women, and anyway, I'd been ill. But I'd convalesced as long as I dared, and old Colin Campbell, who commanded in Balaclava, had dropped me a sour hint that I ought to be back with Raglan in the main camp up on the plateau. So on the evening of October 24 I got my orderly to assemble my gear, left Willy's provisions with Russell, and loafed up to headquarters.

Whether I'd exerted myself too quickly, or it was the sound of the Russian bands in Sevastopol, playing their hellish doleful music, that kept me awake, I was taken damned ill in the night. My bowels were in a fearful state, I was blown out like a boiler, and I was unwise enough to treat myself with brandy, on the principle that if your guts are bad they won't feel any worse for your being foxed. They do, though, and when my orderly suddenly tumbled me out before dawn, I felt as though I were about to give birth. I told him to go to the devil, but he insisted that Raglan wanted me, p.d.q., so I huddled into my clothes in the cold, shivering and rumbling, and went to see what was up.

They were in a great sweat at Raglan's post; word had come from Lucan's cavalry that our advanced posts were signalling enemy in sight to the eastward, and gallopers were being sent off in all directions, with Raglan dictating messages over his shoulder while he and Airey pored over their maps.

"My dear Flashman," says Raglan, when his eye lit on me, "why, you look positively unwell. I think you would be better in your berth." He was all benevolent concern this morning—which was like him, of course. "Don't you think he looks ill, Airey?" Airey agreed that I did, but muttered something about needing every staff rider we could muster, so Raglan tut-tutted and said he much regretted it, but he had a message for Campbell at Balaclava, and it would be a great kindness if I would bear it. (He really did talk like that, most of the time; consideration fairly oozed out of him.) I wondered if I should plead my belly, so to speak, but finding him in such a good mood, with the Willy business apparently forgotten, I gave him my brave, suffering smile, and pocketed his message, fool that I was.

I felt damned shaky as I hauled myself into the saddle, and resolved to take my time over the broken country that lay between headquarters and Balaclava. Indeed, I had to stop several times, and try to vomit, but it was no go, and I cantered on over the filthy road with its litter of old stretchers and broken equipment, until I came out on to the open ground some time after sunrise.

After the downpour of the night before, it was dawning into a beautiful clear morning, the kind of day when, if your innards aren't heaving and squeaking, you feel like a fine gallop with the wind in your face. Before me the Balaclava Plain rolled away like a great grey-green blanket, and as I halted to have another unsuccessful retch, the scene that met my eyes was like a galloping field day. On the left of the plain, where it sloped up to the long line of the Causeway Heights, our cavalry were deployed in full strength, more than a thousand horsemen, like so many brilliant little puppets in the sunny distance, trotting in their squadrons, wheeling and reforming. About a mile away, nearest to me, I could easily distinguish the Light Brigade—the pink trousers of the Cherrypickers, the scarlet of Light Dragoons, and the blue tunics and twinkling lance-points of the 17th. The trumpets were tootling on the breeze, the words of command drifted across to me as clear as a bell, and even beyond the Lights I could see, closer in under the Causeway, and retiring slowly in my direction, the squadrons of the Heavy Brigade—the grey horses with their scarlet riders, the dark green of the Skins, and the hundreds of tiny glittering slivers of the sabres. It was for all the world like a green nursery carpet, with tiny toy soldiers deployed upon it, and as pretty as these pictures of reviews and parades that you see in the galleries.

Until you looked beyond, to where Causeway Heights faded into the haze of the eastern dawn, and you could see why our cavalry were retiring. The far slopes were black with scurrying ant-like figures—Russian infantry pouring up to the gun redoubts which we had established along the three miles of the Causeway; the thunder of cannon rolled continuously across the plain, the flashes of the Russian guns stabbing away at the redoubts, and the sparkle of their muskets was all along the far end of the Causeway. They were swarming over the gun emplacements, engulfing our Turkish gunners, and their artillery was pounding away towards our retreating cavalry, pushing it along under the shadow of the Heights.

I took all this in, and looked off across the plain to my right, where it sloped up into a crest protecting the Balaclava road. Along the crest there was a long line of scarlet figures, with dark green blobs where their legs should be—Campbell's Highlanders, at a safe distance, thank God, from the Russian guns, which were now ranging nicely on the Heavy Brigade under the Heights. I could see the shot plumping just short of the horses, and hear the urgent bark of commands: a troop of the Skins scattered as a great column of earth leaped up among them, and then they reformed, trotting back under the lee of the Causeway.

Well, there was a mile of empty, unscathed plain between me and the Highlanders, so I galloped down towards them, keeping a wary eye on the distant artillery skirmish to my left. But before I'd got halfway to the crest I came on their outlying picket breakfasting round a fire in a little hollow, and who should I see but little Fanny Duberly, presiding over a frying-pan with half a dozen grinning Highlanders round her. She squealed at the sight of me, waving and shoving her pan aside; I swung down out of my saddle, bad belly and all, and would have embraced her, but she caught my hands at arms' length. And then it was Harry and Fanny, and where have you sprung from, and all that nonsense and chatter, while she laughed and I beamed at her. She had grown prettier, I think, with her fair hair and blue eyes, and looking damned fetching in her neat riding habit. I longed to give her tits a squeeze, but couldn't, with all those leering Highlanders nudging each other.

She had ridden up, she said, with Henry, her husband, who was in attendance on Lord Raglan, although I hadn't seen him.

"Will there be a great battle to-day, Harry?" says she. "I am so glad Henry will be safely out of it, if there is. See yonder" —and she pointed across the plain towards the Heights— "where the Russians are coming. Is it not exciting? Why do the cavalry not charge them, Harry? Are you going to join them? Oh, I hope you will take care! Have you had any breakfast? My dear, you look so tired. Come and sit down, and share some of our haggis!"

If anything could have made me sick, it would have been that, but I explained that I hadn't time to tattle, but must find Campbell. I promised to see her again, as soon as the present business was by, and advised her to clear off down to Balaclava as fast as she could go—it was astonishing, really, to see her picnicking there, as fresh as a May morning, and not much more than a mile away the Russian forces pounding away round the redoubts, and doubtless ready to sweep right ahead over the plain when they had regrouped.

The sergeant of Highlanders said Campbell was somewhere off with the Heavy Brigade, which was bad news, since it meant I must approach the firing, but there was nothing for it, so I galloped off north again, through the extended deployment of the Lights, who were now sitting at rest, watching the Heavies re-forming. George Paget hailed me; he was sitting with one ankle cocked up on his saddle, puffing his cheroot, as usual.

"Have you come from Raglan?" cries he. "Where the hell are the infantry, do you know? We shall be sadly mauled at this rate, unless he moves soon. Look at the Heavies yonder; why don't Lucan shift 'em back faster, out of harm's way?" And indeed they were retiring slowly, it seemed to me, right under the shadow of the Heights, with the Russian fire still kicking up the clods round them as they came. I ventured forward a little way: I could see Lucan, and his staff, but no sign of Campbell, so I asked Morris, of the 17th, and he said Campbell had gone back across the plain, towards Balaclava, a few minutes since.

Well, that was better, since it would take me down to the Highlanders' position, away from where the firing was. And yet, it suddenly seemed very secure in my present situation, with the blue tunics and lances of the 17th all round me, and the familiar stench of horse-flesh and leather, and the bits jingling and the fellows patting their horses' necks and muttering to steady them against the rumble of the guns; there were troop horse artillery close by, banging back at the Russians, but it was still rather like a field day, with the plain all unmarked, and the uniforms bright and gay in the sunlight. I didn't want to leave 'em—but there were the Highlanders drawn up near the crest across the plain southward: I must just deliver my message as quickly as might be, and then be off back to head-quarters.

So I turned my back to the Heights, and set off again through the ranks of the 17th and the Cherrypickers, and was halfway down the plain to the Highlanders on the crest when here came a little knot of riders moving up towards the cavalry. And who should it be but my bold Lord Cardigan, with Squire Brough and his other toadies, all in great spirits after a fine comfortable boozy night on his yacht, no doubt.

I hadn't seen the man face to face since that night in Elspeth's bedroom, and my bile rose up even at the thought of the bastard, so I cut him dead. When Brough hailed me, and asked what was the news I reined up, not even looking in Cardigan's direction, and told Brough the Ruskis were over-running the far end of the Heights, and our horse were falling back.

"Ya-as," says Cardigan to his toadies, "it is the usual foolishness. There are the Wussians, so our cavalry move in the other diwection. Haw-haw. You, there, Fwashman, what does Word Waglan pwopose to do?"

I continued to ignore him. "Well, Squire," says I to Brough, "I must be off; can't stand gossiping with yachtsmen, you know," and I wheeled away, leaving them gaping, and an indignant "Haw-haw" sounding behind me.

But I hadn't time to feel too satisfied, for in that moment there was a new thunderous cannonade from the Russians, much closer now; the whistle of shot sounded overhead, there was a great babble of shouting and orders from the cavalry behind me, the calls of the Lights and Heavies sounded, and the whole mass of our horse began to move off westward, retiring again. The cannonading grew, as the Russians turned their guns southward, I saw columns of earth ploughed up to the east of the Highlanders' position, and with my heart in my mouth I buried my head in the horse's mane and fairly flew across the turf. The shot was still falling short, thank God, but as I reached the crest a ball came skipping and rolling almost up to my horse's hooves, and lay there, black and smoking, as I tore up to the Highlanders' flank.

"Where is Sir Colin?" cries I, dismounting, and they pointed to where he was pacing down between the ranks in my direction. I went forward, and delivered my message.

"Oot o' date," says he, when he had read it. "Ye don't look weel, Flashman. Bide a minute. I've a note here for Lord Raglan." And he turned to one of his officers, but at that moment the shouting across the plain redoubled, there was the thunderous plumping of shot falling just beyond the Highland position, and Campbell paused to look across the plain towards the Causeway Heights.

"Aye," says he, "there it is."

I looked towards the Heights, and my heart came up into my throat.

Our cavalry was now away to the left, at the Sevastopol end of the plain, but on the Heights to the right, near the captured redoubts, the whole ridge seemed to have come alive. Even as we watched, the movement resolved itself into a great mass of cavalry—Russian cavalry, wheeling silently down the side of the Heights in our direction. They've told me since that there were only four squadrons, but they looked more like four brigades, blue uniforms and grey, with their sabres out, preparing to descend the long slope from the Heights that ran down towards our position.

It was plain as a pikestaff what they were after, and if I could have sprouted wings in that moment I'd have been fluttering towards the sea like a damned gull. Directly behind us the road to Balaclava lay open; our own cavalry were out of the hunt, too far off to the left; there was nothing between that horde of Russians and the Balaclava base—the supply line of the whole British army —but Campbell's few hundred Highlanders, a rabble of Turks on our flank, and Flashy, full of wind and horror.

Campbell stared for a moment, that granite face of his set; then he pulled at his dreary moustache and roared an order. The ranks opened and moved and closed again, and now across our ridge there was a double line of Highlanders, perhaps a furlong from end to end, kneeling down a yard or so on the seaward side of the crest. Campbell looked along them from our stance at the right-hand extremity of the line, bidding the officers dress them. While they were doing it, there was a tremendous caterwauling from the distant flank, and there were the Turks, all order gone, breaking away from their positions in the face of the impending Russian charge, flinging down their arms and tearing headlong for the sea road behind us.

"Dross," says Campbell.

I was watching the Turks, and suddenly, to their rear, riding towards us, and then checking and wheeling away southward, I recognized the fair hair and riding fig of Fanny Duberly. She was flying along as she passed our far flank, going like a little jockey—she could ride, that girl.

"Damn all society women," says Campbell. And it occurred to me, even through the misery of my stomach and my rising fear, that Balaclava Plain that morning was more like the Row—Fanny Duberly out riding, and Cardigan ambling about haw-hawing.

I looked towards the Russians; they were rumbling down the slope now, a bare half-mile away; Campbell shouted again, and the long scarlet double rank moved foward a few paces, with a great swishing of their kilts and clatter of gear, and halted on the crest, the front rank kneeling and the second standing behind them. Campbell glanced across at the advancing mass of the Russian horse, measuring the distance.

"Ninety-third!" he shouted. "There is no retreat from here! Ye must stand!"

He had no need to tell *me*; I couldn't have moved if I had wanted to. I could only gape at that wall of horsemen, galloping now, and then back at the two frail, scarlet lines that in a moment must be swept away into bloody rabble with the hooves smashing down on them and the sabres swinging; it was the finish, I knew, and nothing to do but wait trembling for it to happen. I found myself staring at the nearest kneeling Highlander, a huge, swarthy fellow with his teeth bared under a black moustache; I remember noticing the hair matting the back of his right hand as it gripped his musket. Beyond him there was a boy, gazing at the advancing squadrons with his mouth open; his lip was trembling.

"Haud yer fire until I give the wurr-rd!" says Campbell, and then quite deliberately he stepped a little out before the front rank and drew his broadsword, laying the great glittering blade across his chest. Christ, I thought, that's a futile thing to do—the ground was trembling under our feet now, and the great quadruple rank of horsemen was a bare two hundred yards away, sweeping down at the charge, sabres gleaming, yelling and shouting as they bore down on us, a sea of flaring horse heads and bearded faces above them.

"Present!" shouts Campbell, and moved past me in behind the front rank. He stopped behind the boy with the trembling lip. "Ye never saw the like o' that comin' doon the Gallowgate," says he. "Steady now, Ninety-third! Wait for my command!"

They were a hundred yards away now, that thundering tide of men and horses, the hooves crashing like artillery on the turf. The double bank of muskets with their fixed bayonets covered them; the locks were back, the fingers hanging on the triggers; Campbell was smiling sourly beneath his moustache, the madman; he glanced to his left along the silent lines—give the word, damn you, you damned old fool, I wanted to shout, for they were a bare fifty yards off, in a split second they would be into us, he had left it too late—

"Fire!" he bellowed, and like one huge bark of thunder the front-rank volley crashed out, the smoke billowed back in our faces, and beyond it the foremost horsemen seemed to surge up in a great wave; there was a split-second of screaming confusion, with beasts plunging and rearing, a hideous chorus of yells from the riders, and the great line crashed down on the turf before us, the men behind careering into the fallen horses and riders, trying to jump them or pull clear, trampling them, hurtling over them in a smashing tangle of limbs and bodies.

"Fire!" roars Campbell above the din, and the pieces of the standing rank crashed together into the press; it seemed to shudder at the impact, and behind it the Russian ranks wheeled and stumbled in confusion, men screaming and going down, horses lashing out blindly, sabres gleaming and flying. As the smoke cleared there was a great tangled bloody bank of stricken men and beasts wallowing within a few yards of the kneeling Highlanders—they'll tell you, some of our historians, that Campbell fired before they reached close range, but here's one who can testify that one Russian, with a fur-crested helmet and pale blue tunic rolled right to within a foot of us; the swarthy Highlander nearest me didn't have to advance a step to plunge his bayonet into the Russian's body.

A great yell went up from the Ninety-third; the front rank seemed to leap forward, but Campbell was before them, bawling them back. "Damn your eagerness!" cries he. "Stand fast! Reload!"

They dropped back, snarling like dogs, and Campbell turned and calmly surveyed the wreckage of the Russian ranks. There were beasts thrashing about everywhere and men crawling blindly away, the din of screaming and groaning was fearful, and a great reek that you could literally see was steaming up from them. Behind, the greater part of the Russian squadrons was turning, reforming, and for a moment I thought they were coming again, but they moved off back towards the Heights, closing their ranks as they went.

"Good," says Campbell, and his sword grated back into its scabbard.

"Ye niver saw a sight like that goin' back up the Gallowgate, Sir Colin," pipes a voice from somewhere, and they began to laugh and cheer, and yell their heathenish slogans, shaking their muskets, and Campbell grinned and pulled at his moustache again. He saw me—I hadn't stirred a yard since the charge began, I'd been so petrified—and walked across.

"I'll add a line to my message for Lord Raglan," says he, and looks at me. "Ye've mair colour in yer cheeks now, Flashman. Field exercises wi' the Ninety-third must agree wi' ye."

And so, with those kilted devils still holding their ranks, and the Russians dying and moaning before them, I waited while he dictated his message to one of his aides. Now that the terror was past, my belly was aching horribly and I felt thoroughly ill again, but not so ill that I wasn't able to note (and admire) the carriage of the retreating Russian cavalry. In charging, I had noticed how they had opened their ranks at the canter and then closed them at the gallop, which isn't easy; now they were doing the same thing as they retired towards the heights, and I thought, these fellows ain't so slovenly as we thought. I remember thinking they'd perhaps startle Jim the Bear and his Light Brigade—but most of all, from that moment of aftermath, I can still see vividly that tangled pile of Russian dead, and sprawled out before them the body of an officer, a big grey-bearded man with the front of his blue tunic soaked in blood, lying on his back with one knee bent up, and his horse standing above him, nuzzling at the dead face.

Campbell put a folded paper into my hand and stood, shading his eyes with a hand under his bonnet-rim, as he watched the Russian horse canter up the Causeway Heights.

"Poor management," says he. "They'll no' come this way again. In the meantime, I've said to Lord Raglan that in my opeenion the main Russian advance will now be directed north of the Causeway, and will doubtless be wi' artillery and horse against our cavalry. What it is doin' sittin' yonder, I cannae—but, hollo! Is that Scarlett movin'? Hand me that glass, Cattenach. See yonder."

The Russian cavalry were now topping the Causeway ridge, vanishing from our view, but on the plain farther left, perhaps half a mile from us, there was movement in the ranks of our Heavy Brigade: a sudden uniform twinkle of metal as the squadrons nearest to us turned.

"They're coming this way," says someone, and Campbell snapped his glass shut.

"Behind the fair," says he, glumly—I never saw him impatient yet. Where other men would get angry and swear, Campbell simply got more melancholy. "Flashman—on your way to

Lord Raglan, I'll be obliged if you'll present my compliments to General Scarlett, or Lord Lucan, whichever comes first in your road, and tell them that in my opeenion they'll do well to hold the ground they have, and prepare for acteevity on the northern flank. Away wi' ye, sir."

I needed no urging. The farther I could get from that plain, the better I'd be suited, for I was certain Campbell was right. Having captured the eastern end of the Causeway Heights, and run their cavalry over the central ridge facing us, it was beyond doubt that the Russians would be moving up the valley north of the Heights, advancing on the plateau position which we occupied before Sevastopol. God knew what Raglan proposed to do about that, but in the meantime he was holding our cavalry on the southern plain—to no good purpose. They hadn't budged an inch to take the retreating Russian cavalry in flank, as they might have done, and now, after the need for their support had passed, the Heavies were moving down slowly towards Campbell's position.

I rode through their ranks—Dragoon Guards and a few Skins, riding in open order, eyeing me curiously as I galloped through —"That's Flashman, ain't it?" cries someone, but I didn't pause. Ahead of me I could see the little knot of coloured figures, red and blue, of Scarlett and his staff; as I reined up, they were cheering and laughing, and old Scarlett waved his hat to me.

"Ho-ho, Flashman!" cries he. "Were you down there with the Sawnies? Capital work, what? That's a bloody nose for Ivan, I say. Ain't it, though, Elliot? Dam' fine, dam' fine! And where are you off to, Flashman, my son?"

"Message to Lord Raglan, sir," says I. "But Sir Colin Campbell also presents his compliments, and advises that you should move no nearer to Balaclava at present."

"Does he, though? Beatson, halt the Dragoons, will you? Now then, why not? Lord Lucan has ordered us to support the Turks, you know, in case of Russian movement towards Balaclava."

"Sir Colin expects no further movement there, sir. He bids you look to your northern flank," and I pointed to the Causeway Heights, only a few hundred yards away. "Anyway, sir, there are no longer any Turks to support. Most of 'em are probably on the beach by now."

"That's true, bigod!" Scarlett exploded in laughter. He was a fat, cheery old Falstaff, mopping his bald head with a hideously-coloured scarf, and then dabbing the sweat from his red cheeks. "What d'ye think, Elliot? No point in goin' down to Campbell that I can see; he and his red-shanks don't need support, that's certain."

"True, sir. But there is no sign of Russian movement to our north, as yet."

"No," said Scarlett, "that's so. But I trust Campbell's judgment, ye know; clever fella. If he smells Ruskis to our north, beyond the Heights, well, I dunno. I trust an old hound any day, what?" He sniffed and mopped himself again, tugging at his puffy white whiskers. "Tell you what, Elliot, I think we'll just hold on here, and see what breaks cover, hey? What d'ye say to that, Beatson? Flashman? No harm in waitin', is there?"

He could dig trenches for all I cared; I was already measuring the remaining distance across the plain westward; once in the gullies I'd be out of harm's way, and could pick my way to Raglan's head-quarters at my leisure. North of us, the ground sloping up to the heights through an old vineyard was empty; so was the crest beyond, but the thump of cannon from behind it seemed to be growing closer to my nervous imagination. There was an incessant whine and thump of shot; Beatson was scanning the ridge anxiously through his glass.

"Campbell's right, sir," says he. "They must be up there in the north valley in strength."

"How d'ye know?" says Scarlett, goggling.

"The firing, sir. Listen to it—that's not just cannon. There— you hear? That's Whistling Dick! If they have mortars with 'em, they're not skirmishing!"

"By God!" says Scarlett. "Well I'm damned! I can't tell one from another, but if you say so, Beatson, I—"

"Look yonder!" It was one of his young gallopers, up in his stirrups with excitement, pointing. "The ridge, sir! Look at 'em come!"

We looked, and for the second time that day I forgot my gurgling aching belly in a freezing wave of fear. Slowly topping the crest, in a great wave of colour and dancing steel, was a long rank of Russian horsemen, and behind them another, and then another, moving at a walk. They came over the ridge as if they were in review, extended line after extended line, and then slowly closed up, halting on the near slope of the ridge, looking down at us. God knows how far their line ran from flank to flank, but there were thousands of them, hanging over us like an ocean roller frozen in the act of breaking, a huge body of blue and silver hussars on the left, and to the right the grey and white of their dragoons.

"By God!" cries Scarlett. "By God! Those are Russians—damn 'em!"

"Left about!" Beatson was yelling. "Greys, stand fast! Cunningham, close 'em up! Inniskillings—close order! Connor, Flynn, keep 'em there! Curzon, get those squadrons of the Fifth up here, lively now!"

Scarlett was sitting gaping at the ridge, damning his eyes and the Russians alternately until Beatson jerked at his sleeve.

"Sir! We must prepare to receive them! When they take the brake off they'll roll down—"

"Receive 'em?" says Scarlett, coming back to earth. "What's that, Beatson? Damned if I do!" He reared up in his stirrups, glaring along to the left, where the Greys' advanced squadrons were being dressed to face the Russian force. "What? What? Connor, what are you about there?" He was gesticulating to the right now, waving his hat. "Keep your damned Irishmen steady there! Wild devils, those! Where's Curzon, hey?"

"Sir, they have the slope of us!" Beatson was gripping Scarlett by the sleeve, rattling urgently in his ear. "They outflank us, too—I reckon that line's three times the length of ours, and when they charge they can sweep round and take us flank, both sides, and front! They'll swallow us, sir, if we break— we must try to hold fast!"

"Hold fast nothin'!" says Scarlett, grinning all over his great red cheeks. "I didn't come all this way to have some dam' Cossack open the ball! Look at 'em, there, the saucy bastards! What? What? Well, they're there, and we're here, and I'm goin' to chase the scoundrels all the way to Moscow! What, Elliot? Here, you, Flashman, come to my side, sir!"

You may gather my emotions at hearing this; I won't attempt to describe them. I stared at this purpling old lunatic in bewilderment, and tried to say something about my message to Raglan, but the impetuous buffoon grabbed at my bridle and hauled me along as he took post in front of his squadrons.

"You shall tell Lord Raglan presently that I have engaged a force of enemy cavalry on my front an' dispersed 'em!" bawls he. "Beatson, Elliot, see those lines dressed! Where are the Royals, hey? Steady, there, Greys! Steady now! Inniskillings, look to that dressing, Flynn! Keep close to me, Flashman, d'ye hear? Like enough I'll have somethin' to add to his lordship. Where the devil's Curzon, then? Damn the boy, if it's not women it's somethin' else! Trumpeter, where are you? Come to my left side! Got your tootler, have you? Capital, splendid!"

It was unbelievable, this roaring fat old man, waving his hat like some buffer at a cricket match, while Beatson tried to shout sense into him.

"You cannot move from here, sir! It is all uphill! We must hold our ground—there's no other hope!" He pointed up hill frantically. "Look, they're moving sir! We must hold fast!"

And sure enough, up on the heights a quarter of a mile away, the great Russian line was beginning to advance, shoulder to shoulder, blue and silver and grey, with their sabres at the present; it was a sight to send you squealing for cover, but there I was, trapped at this idiot's elbow, with the squadrons of the Greys hemming us in behind.

"You cannot advance, sir!" shouts Beatson again.

"Can't I, by God!" roars Scarlett, throwing away his hat. "You just watch me!" He lugged out his sabre and waved it. "Ready, Greys? Ready, old Skins? Remember Waterloo, you fellas, what? Trumpeter—sound the . . . the thing, whatever it is! Oh, the devil! Come on, Flashman! Tally-ho!"

And he dug in his heels, gave one final yell of "Come on, you fellas!" and set his horse at the hill like a madman. There was a huge, crashing shout from behind, the squadrons leaped forward, my horse reared, and I found myself galloping along, almost up Scarlett's dock, with Beatson at my elbow shouting, "Oh, what the blazes—charge! Trumpeter, charge! charge! charge!"

They were all stark, raving mad, of course. When I think of them—and me, God help me—tearing up that hill, and that overwhelming force lurching down towards us, gathering speed with every step, I realize that there's no end to human folly, or human luck, either. It was ridiculous, it was nonsense, that old red-faced pantaloon, who'd never fired a shot or swung a sabre in action before, and was fit for nothing but whipping off hounds, urging his charger up that hill, with the whole Heavy Brigade at his heels, and poor old suffering Flashy jammed in between, with nothing to do but hope to God that by the time the two irresistible forces met, I'd be somewhere back in the mob behind.

And the brutes were enjoying it, too! Those crazy Ulstermen were whooping like Apaches, and the Greys, as they thundered forward, began to make that hideous droning noise deep in their throats; I let them come up on my flanks, their front rank hemming me in with glaring faces and glittering blades on either side; Scarlett was yards ahead, brandishing his sabre and shouting, the Russian mass was at the gallop, sweeping towards us like a great blue wave, and then in an instant we were surging into them, men yelling, horses screaming, steel clashing all round, and I was clinging like a limpet to my horse's right side, Cheyenne fashion, left hand in the mane and right clutching my Adams revolver. I wasn't breaking surface in that melee if I could help it. There were Greys all round me, yelling and cursing, slashing with their sabres at the hairy blue coats—"Give 'em the point! The point!" yelled a voice, and I saw a Greys trooper dashing the hilt of his sword into a bearded face and then driving his point into the falling man's body. I let fly at a Russian in the press, and the shot took him in the neck, I think; then I was dashed aside and swept away in the whirl of fighting, keeping my head ducked low, squeezing my trigger whenever I saw a blue or grey tunic, and praying feverishly that no chance slash would sweep me from the saddle.

I suppose it lasted five or ten minutes; I don't know. It seemed only a few seconds, and then the whole mass was struggling up the hill, myself roaring and blaspheming with the best of them; my revolver was empty, my hat was gone, so I dragged out my sabre, bawling with pretended fury, and seeing nothing but grey horses, gathered that I was safe.

"Come on!" I roared. "Come on! Into the bastards! Cut 'em to bits!" I made my horse rear and waved my sword, and as a stricken Russian came blundering through the mob I lunged at him, full force, missed, and finished up skewering a fallen horse.

The wrench nearly took me out of my saddle, but I wasn't letting that sabre go, not for anything, and as I tugged it free there was a tremendous cheering set up—"Huzza! huzza! huzza"—and suddenly there were no Russians among us, Scarlett, twenty yards away, was standing in his stirrups waving a blood-stained sabre and yelling his head off, the Greys were shaking their hats and their fists, and the rout of that great mass of enemy cavalry was trailing away towards the crest.

"They're beat!" cries Scarlett. "They're beat! Well done, you fellas! What, Beatson? Hey, Elliot? Can't charge uphill, hey? Damn 'em, damn 'em, we did it! Hurrah!"

Now it is a solemn fact, but I'll swear I didn't see above a dozen corpses on the ground around me as the Greys reordered their squadrons, and the Skins closed in on the right, with the Royals coming up behind. I still don't understand it—why the Russians, with the hill behind 'em, didn't sweep us all away, with great slaughter. Or why, breaking as they did, they weren't cut to pieces by our sabres. Except that I remember one or two of the Greys complaining that they hadn't been able to make their cuts tell; they just bounced off the Russian tunics. Anyway, the Ruskis broke, thank heaven, and away beneath us, to our left, the Light Brigade were setting up a tremendous cheer, and it was echoing along the ridge to our left, and on the greater heights beyond.

"Well done!" shouts Scarlett. "Well done, you Greys! Well done, Flashman, you are a gallant fellow! What? Hey? That'll show that damned Nicholas, what? Now then, Flashman, off with you to Lord Raglan—tell him we've . . . well, set about these chaps and driven 'em off, you see, and that I shall hold my position, what, until further orders. You understand? Capital!" He shook with laughter, and hauled out his coloured scarf for another mop at his streaming face. "Tell ye what, Flashman; I don't know much about fightin', but it strikes me that this Russian business is like huntin' in Ireland—confused and primitive, what, but damned interestin'!"

I reported his words to Raglan, exactly as he spoke them, and the whole staff laughed with delight, the idiots. Of course, they were safe enough, snug on the top of the Sapoune Ridge, which lay at the western end of Causeway Heights, and I promise you

I had taken my time getting there. I'd ridden like hell on my spent horse from the Causeway, across the north-west corner of the plain, when Scarlett dismissed me, but once into the safety of the gullies, with the noise of Russian gunfire safely in the distance, I had dismounted to get my breath, quiet my trembling heart-strings, and try to ease my wind-gripped bowels, again without success. I was a pretty bedraggled figure, I suppose, by the time I came to the top of Sapoune, but at least I had a bloody sabre, artlessly displayed—Lew Nolan's eyes narrowed and he swore enviously at the sight: he wasn't to know it had come from a dead Russian horse.

Raglan was beaming, as well he might be, and demanded details of the action I had seen. So I gave 'em, fairly offhand, saying I thought the Highlanders had behaved pretty well—"Yes, and if we had just followed up with cavalry we might have regained the whole Causeway by now!" pipes Nolan, at which Airey told him to be silent, and Raglan looked fairly stuffy. As for the Heavies—well, they had seen all that, but I said it had been warm work, and Ivan had got his bellyful, from what I could see.

"Gad, Flashy, you have all the luck!" cries Lew, slapping his thigh, and Raglan clapped me on the shoulder.

"Well done, Flashman," says he. "Two actions today, and you have been in the thick of both. I fear you have been neglecting your staff duties in your eagerness to be at the enemy, eh?" And he gave me his quizzical beam, the old fool. "Well, we shall say no more about that."

I looked confused, and went red, and muttered something about not being able to abide these damned Ruskis, and they all laughed again, and said that was old Flashy, and the young gallopers, the pink-cheeked lads, looked at me with awe. If it hadn't been for my aching belly, I'd have been ready to enjoy myself, now that the horror of the morning was past, and the cold sweat of reaction hadn't had a chance to set in. I'd come through again, I told myself—twice, no less, and with new laurels. For although we were too close to events just then to know what would be said later—well, how many chaps have you heard of who stood with the Thin Red Line *and* took part in the Charge of the Heavy Brigade? None, 'cos I'm the only one, damned unwilling and full of shakes, but still, I've dined out on it for years. That—and the other thing that was to follow.

But in the meantime, I was just thanking my stars for safety, and rubbing my inflamed guts. (Someone said later that Flashman was more anxious about his bowels than he was about the Russians, and had taken part in all the charges to try to ease his wind.) I sat there with the staff, gulping and massaging, happy to be out of the battle, and taking a quiet interest while Lord Raglan and his team of idiots continued to direct the fortunes of the day.

Now, of that morning at Balaclava I've told you what I remember, as faithfully as I can, and if it doesn't tally with what you read elsewhere, I can't help it. Maybe I'm wrong, or maybe the military historians are: you must make your own choice. For example, I've read since that there were Turks on both flanks of Campbell's Highlanders, whereas I remember 'em only on the left flank; again, my impression of the Heavy Brigade action is that it began and ended in a flash, but I gather it must have taken Scarlett some little time to turn and dress his squadrons. I don't remember that. It's certain that Lucan was on hand when the charge began, and I've been told he actually gave the word to advance—well, I never even saw him. So there you are; it just shows that no one can see everything.[17]

I mention this because, while my impressions of the early morning are fairly vague, and consist of a series of coloured and horrid pictures, I'm in no doubt about what took place in the late forenoon. That is etched forever; I can shut my eyes and see it all, and feel the griping pain ebbing and clawing at my guts—perhaps that sharpened my senses, who knows? Anyway, I have it all clear; not only what happened, but what caused it to happen. I know, better than anyone else who ever lived, why the Light Brigade was launched on its famous charge, because I was the man responsible, and it wasn't wholly an accident. That's not to say I'm to *blame*—if blame there is, it belongs to Raglan, the kind, honourable, vain old man. Not to Lucan, or to Cardigan, or to Nolan, or to Airey, or even to my humble self: we just played our little parts. But blame? I can't even hold it against Raglan, not now. Of course, your historians and critics and hypocrites are full of virtuous zeal to find out who was "at fault", and wag their heads and say "Ah, you see," and tell him what should have been done, from the safety of their studies and lecture-rooms—but I was there, you see, and while I could have wrung Raglan's neck, or blown him from the muzzle of a gun, at the time—well, it's all by now, and we either survived it or we didn't. Proving someone guilty won't bring the six hundred to life again—most of 'em would be dead by now anyway. And they wouldn't blame anyone. What did that trooper of the 17th say afterwards: "We're ready to go in again." Good luck to him, I say; once was enough for me —but, don't you understand, nobody else has the right to talk of blame, or blunders? Just us, the living and the dead. It was *our* indaba. Mind you, I could kick Raglan's arse for him, and my own.

I sat up there on the Sapoune crest, feeling bloody sick and tired, refusing the sandwiches that Billy Russell offered me, and listening to Lew Nolan's muttered tirade about the misconduct of the battle so far. I hadn't much patience with him—*he* hadn't been risking his neck along with Campbell and Scarlett, although he no doubt wished he had—but in my shaken state I wasn't ready to argue. Anyway, he was fulminating against Lucan and Cardigan and Raglan mostly, which was all right by me.

"If Cardigan had taken in the Lights, when the Heavies were breaking up the Ruskis, we'd have smashed 'em all by this," says he. "But he wouldn't budge, damn him—he's as bad as Lucan. Won't budge without orders, delivered in the proper form, with nice salutes, and 'Yes, m'lord' an' 'if your lordship pleases'. Christ—cavalry leaders! Cromwell'd turn in his grave, bad cess to him. And look at Raglan yonder—does he know what to do? He'd got two brigades o' the best horsemen in Europe, itchin' to use their sabres, an' in front of 'em a Russian army that's shakin' in its boots after the maulin' Campbell an' Scarlett have given 'em—but he sits there sendin' messages to the infantry! The infantry, bigod, that're still gettin' out of their beds somewhere. Jaysus, it makes me sick!"

He was in a fine taking, but I didn't mind him much. At the same time, looking down on the panorama beneath us, I could see there was something in what he said. I'm not Hannibal, but I've picked up a wrinkle or two in my time, about ground and movement, and it looked to me as though Raglan had it in his grasp to do the Russians some no-good, and maybe even hand them a splendid licking, if he felt like it. Not that I cared, you understand;

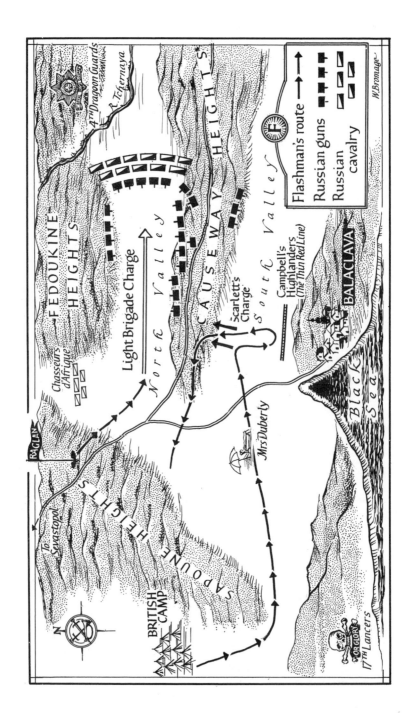

FEDOUKINE HEIGHTS

4ᵀᴴ Dragoon Guards

R. Tchernaya

Chasseurs d'Afrique

RAGLAN

To Sevastopol

N

BRITISH CAMP

SAPOUNE HEIGHTS

Mrs Duberly

Light Brigade Charge

North Valley

CAUSEWAY HEIGHTS

Scarlett's Charge

South Valley

Campbell's Highlanders
(The Thin Red Line)

BALACLAVA

Black Sea

17ᵀᴴ Lancers

F

Flashman's route
Russian guns
Russian cavalry

W. Bromage

I'd had enough, and was all for a quiet life for everybody. But anyway, this is how the land lay.

The Sapoune, on which we stood, is a great bluff rising hundreds of feet above the plain. Looking east from it, you see below you a shallow valley, perhaps two miles long and half a mile broad; to the north, there is a little clump of heights on which the Russians had established guns to command that side of the valley. On the south the valley is bounded by the long spine of the Causeway Heights, running east from the Sapoune for two or three miles. The far end of the valley was fairly hazy, even with the strong sunlight, but you could see the Russians there as thick as fleas on a dog's back—guns, infantry, cavalry, everything except Tsar Nick himself, tiny puppets in the distance, just holding their ground. They had guns on the Causeway, too, pointing north; as I watched I saw the nearest team of them unlimbering just beside the spot where the Heavies' charge had ended.

So there it was, plain as a pool table—a fine empty valley with the main force of the Russians at the far end of it, and us at the near end, but with Ruskis on the heights to either side, guns and sharpshooters both—you could see the grey uniforms of their infantry moving among their cannon down on the Causeway, not a mile and a half away.

Directly beneath where I stood, at the near end of the valley, our cavalry had taken up station just north of the Causeway, the Heavies slightly nearer the Sapoune and to the right, the Lights just ahead of them and slightly left. They looked as though you could have lobbed a stone into the middle of them—I could easily make out Cardigan, threading his way behind the ranks of the 17th, and Lucan with his gallopers, and old Scarlett, with his bright scarf thrown over one shoulder of his coat—they were all sitting out there waiting, tiny figures in blue and scarlet and green, with here and there a plumed hat, and an occasional bandage: I noticed one trooper of the Skins binding a stocking on to the forefoot of his charger, the little dark-green figure crouched down at the horse's hooves. The distant pipe of voices drifted up from the plain, and from the far end of the Causeway a popping of musketry; for the rest it was all calm and still, and it was this tranquillity that was driving Lew to a frenzy, the blood-thirsty young imbecile.

Well, thinks I, there they all are, doing nothing and taking no harm; let 'em be, and let's go home. For it was plain to see the Ruskis were going to make no advance up the valley towards the Sapoune; they'd had their fill for the day, and were content to hold the far end of the valley and the heights either side. But Raglan and Airey were forever turning their glasses on the Causeway, at the Russian artillery and infantry moving among the redoubts they'd captured from the Turks; I gathered both our infantry and cavalry down in the plain should have been moving to push them out, but nothing was happening, and Raglan was getting the frets.

"Why does not Lord Lucan move?" I heard him say once, and again: "He has the order; what delays him now?" Knowing Look-on, I could guess he was huffing and puffing and laying the blame on someone else. Raglan kept sending gallopers down— Lew among them—to tell Lucan, and the infantry commanders, to get on with it, but they seemed maddeningly obtuse about his orders, and wanted to wait for our infantry to come up, and it was this delay that was fretting Raglan and sending Lew half-crazy.

"Why doesn't Raglan *make* 'em move, dammit?" says he, coming over to Billy Russell and me after reporting back to Raglan. "It's too bad! If he would give 'em one clear simple command, to push in an' sweep those fellows off the Causeway —oh, my God! An' he won't listen to me—I'm a young pup green behind the ears. The cavalry alone could do it in five minutes—it's about time Cardigan earned his general's pay, anyway!"

I approved heartily of that, myself. Every time I heard Cardigan's name mentioned, or saw his hateful boozy vulture face, I remembered that vile scene in Elspeth's bedroom, and felt my fury boiling up. Several times it had occurred to me on the campaign that it would be a capital thing if he could be induced into action where he might well be hit between the legs and so have his brains blown out, but he'd not looked like taking a scratch so far. And there seemed scant chance of it today; I heard Raglan snapping his glass shut with impatience, and saying to Airey: "I despair almost of moving our horse. It looks as though we shall have to rely on Cambridge alone—whenever his infantry come up! Oh, this is vexing! We shall accomplish nothing against the Causeway positions at this rate!"

And just at that moment someone sang out: "My lord! See

there—the guns are moving! The guns in the second redoubt—the Cossacks are getting them out!"

Sure enough, there were Russian horsemen limbering up away down the Causeway crest, tugging at a little toy cannon in the captured Turkish emplacement. They had tackles on it, and were obviously intent on carrying it off to the main Russian army. Raglan stared at it through his glass, his face working.

"Airey!" cries he. "This is intolerable! What is Lucan thinking of—why, these fellows will clear the guns away before our advance begins!"

"He is waiting for Cambridge, I suppose, my lord," says Airey, and Raglan swore, for once, and continued to gaze fretfully down on the Causeway.

Lew was writhing with impatience in his saddle. "Oh, Christ!" he moaned softly. "Send in Cardigan, man—never mind the bloody infantry. Send in the Lights!"

Good idea, thinks I—let Jim the Bear skirmish into the redoubts, and get a Cossack lance where it'll do most good. So you may say it was out of pure malice towards Cardigan that I piped up—taking care that my back was to Raglan, but talking loud enough for him to hear:

"There goes our record—Wellington never lost a gun, you know."

I've heard since, from a galloper who was at Raglan's side, that it was those words, invoking the comparison with his God Wellington, that stung him into action—that he started like a man shot, that his face worked, and he jerked at his bridle convulsively. Maybe he'd have made up his mind without my help —but I'll be honest and say that I doubt it. He'd have waited for the infantry. As it was he went pale and then red, and snapped out:

"Airey—another message to Lord Lucan! We can delay no longer—he must move without the infantry. Tell him—ah, he is to advance the cavalry rapidly to the front, to prevent the enemy carrying off the guns—ah, to follow the enemy and prevent them. Yes. Yes. He may take troop horse artillery, at his discretion. There—that will do. You have it, Airey? Read it back, if you please."

I see it so clearly still—Airey's head bent over the paper,

jabbing at the words with his pencil, as he read back (more or less in Raglan's words, certainly in the same sense), Nolan's face alight with joy beside me—"At last, at last, thank God!" he was muttering—and Raglan sitting, nodding carefully. Then he cried out: "Good. It is to be acted on at once—make that clear!"

"Ah, that's me darlin'!" whispers Lew, and nudged me. "Well done, Flashy, me boy—you've got him movin'!"

"Send it immediately," Raglan was telling Airey. "Oh, and notify Lord Lucan that there are French cavalry on his left. Surely that should suffice." And he opened his glass again, looking down at Causeway Heights. "Send the fastest galloper."

I had a moment's apprehension at that—having started the ball, I'd no wish to be involved—but Raglan added: "Where is Nolan?—yes, Nolan," and Lew, beside himself with excitement, wheeled his horse beside Airey, grabbed at the paper, tucked it in his gauntlet, smacked down his forage cap, threw Raglan the fastest of salutes, and would have been off like a shot, but Raglan stayed him, repeating that the message was of the utmost importance, that it was to be delivered with all haste to Lucan personally, and that it was vital to act at once, before the Ruskis could make off with our guns.[18] All unnecessary repetition of course, and Lew was in a fever, going pink with impatience.

"Away, then!" cries Raglan at last, and Lew was over the brow in a twinkling, with a flurry of dust—showy devil—and Raglan shouting after him: "At once, Nolan—tell Lord Lucan at once, you understand."

That's how they sent Nolan off—that and no more, on my oath. And so I come to the point with which I began this memoir, with Raglan having a second thought, and shouting to Airey to send after him, and Airey looking round, and myself retiring modestly, you remember, and Airey spotting me and gesturing me violently up beside him.

Well, you know what I thought, of the unreasoning premonition that I had, that this would be the ultimate terror of that memorable day in which I had, much against my will, already been charged at by, and charged against, overwhelming hordes of Russians. There was nothing, really, to be agitated about, up there on the heights—I was merely to be sent after Nolan, with some addition or correction. But I felt the finger of doom on me, I don't know why, as I scrambled aboard a fresh horse with Raglan and Airey clamouring at me.

"Flashman," says Raglan, "Nolan must make it clear to Lord Lucan—he is to behave defensively, and attempt nothing against his better judgment. Do you understand me?"

Well, I understood the words, but what the hell Lucan was expected to make of them, I couldn't see. Told to advance, to attack the enemy, and yet to act defensively. But it was nothing to me; I repeated the order, word for word, making sure Airey could hear me, and then went over the bluff after Lew.

It was as steep as hell's half acre, like a seaside sandcliff shot across by grassy ridges. At any other time I'd have picked my way down nice and leisurely, but with Raglan and the rest looking down, and in full view of our cavalry in the plain, I'd no choice but to go hell-for-leather. Besides, I wasn't going to let that cocky little pimp Nolan distance *me*—I may not be proud of much, but I fancied myself against any galloper in the army, and was determined to overtake him before he reached Lucan. So down I went, with the game little mare under me skipping like a mountain goat, sliding on her haunches, careering headlong, and myself clinging on with my knees aching and my hands on the mane, jolting and swaying wildly, and in the tail of my eye Lew's red cap jerking crazily on the escarpment below.

I *was* the better horseman. He wasn't twenty yards out on the level when I touched the bottom and went after him like a bolt, yelling to him to hold on. He heard me, and reined up, cursing, and demanding to know what was the matter. "On with you!" cries I, as I came alongside, and as we galloped I shouted my message.

He couldn't make it out, but had to pluck the note from his glove and squint at it while he rode. "What the hell does it mean in the first place?" cries he. "It says here, 'advance rapidly to the front'. Well, God love us, the guns ain't in front; they're in flank front if they're anywhere."

"Search me," I shouted. "But he says Look-on is to act defensively, and undertake nothing against his better judgment. So there!"

"Defensive?" cries Lew. "Defensive be damned! He must have said offensive—how the hell could he attack defensively? And this order says nothin' about Lucan's better judgment. For one thing, he's got no more judgment than Mulligan's bull pup!"

"Well, that's what Raglan said!" I shouted. "You're bound to deliver it."

"Ah, damn them all, what a set of old women!" He dug in his spurs, head down, shouting across to me as we raced towards the rear squadrons of the Heavies. "They don't know their minds from one minute to the next. I tell ye, Flash, that ould ninny Raglan will hinder the cavalry at all costs—an' Lucan's not a whit better. What do they think horse-soldiers are for? Well, Lucan shall have his order, and be damned to them!"

I eased up as we shot through the ranks of the Greys, letting him go ahead; he went streaking through the Heavies, and across the intervening space towards the Lights. I'd no wish to be dragged into the discussion that would inevitably ensue with Lucan, who had to have every order explained to him three times at least. But I supposed I ought to be on hand, so I cantered easily up to the 4th Lights, and there was George Paget again, wanting to know what was up.

"You're advancing shortly," says I, and "Damned high time, too," says he. "Got a cheroot, Flash?—I haven't a weed to my name."

I gave him one, and he squinted at me. "You're looking peaky," says he. "Anything wrong?"

"Bowels," says I. "Damn all Russian champagne. Where's Lord Look-on?"

He pointed, and I saw Lucan out ahead of the Lights, with some galloper beside him, and Nolan just reining up. Lew was saluting, and handing him the paper, and while Lucan pored over it I looked about me.

It was drowsy and close down here on the plain after the breezy heights of the Sapoune; hardly a breath of wind, and the flies buzzing round the horses' heads, and the heavy smell of dung and leather. I suddenly realized I was damned tired, and my belly wouldn't lie quiet again; I grunted in reply to George's questions, and took stock of the Brigade, squirming uncomfortably in my saddle—there were the Cherrypickers in front, all very spruce in blue and pink with their pelisses trailing; to their right the mortarboard helmets and blue tunics of the 17th, with their lances at rest and the little red point plumes hanging limp; to their right again, not far from where Lucan was sitting, the 13th Lights, with the great Lord Cardigan himself out to the fore, sitting very aloof and alone and affecting not to notice Lucan and Nolan, who weren't above twenty yards from him.

Suddenly I was aware of Lucan's voice raised, and trotted away from George in that direction; it looked as though Lew would need some help in getting the message into his lordship's thick skull. I saw Lucan look in my direction, and just at that moment, as I was passing the 17th, someone called out:

"Hollo, there's old Flashy! Now we'll see some fun! What's the row, Flash?"

This sort of thing happens when one is generally admired; I replied with a nonchalant wave of the hand, and sang out: "Tally-ho, you fellows! You'll have all the fun you want presently," at which they laughed, and I saw Tubby Morris grinning across at me.

And then I heard Lucan's voice, clear as a bugle. "Guns, sir? What guns, may I ask? I can see no guns."

He was looking up the valley, his hand shading his eyes, and when I looked, by God, you couldn't see the redoubt where the Ruskis had been limbering up to haul the guns away—just the long slope of Causeway Heights, and the Russian infantry uncomfortably close.

"Where, sir?" cries Lucan. "What guns do you mean?"

I could see Lew's face working; he was scarlet with fury, and his hand was shaking as he came up by Lucan's shoulder, pointing along the line of the Causeway.

"There, my lord—there, you see, are the guns! *There's* your enemy!"

He brayed it out, as though he was addressing a dirty trooper, and Lucan stiffened as though he'd been hit. He looked as though he would lose his temper, but then he commanded himself, and Lew wheeled abruptly away and cantered off, making straight for me where I was sitting to the right of the 17th. He was shaking with passion, and as he drew abreast of me he rasped out:

"The bloody fool! Does he want to sit on his great fat arse all day and every day?"

"Lew," says I, pretty sharp, "did you tell him he was to act defensively and at his own discretion?"

"Tell him?" says he, baring his teeth in a savage grin. "By Christ, I told him three times over! As if that bastard needs telling to act defensively—he's capable of nothing else! Well, he's got his bloody orders—now let's see how he carries them out!"

And with that he went over to Tubby Morris, and I thought, well, that's that—now for the Sapoune, home and beauty, and let 'em chase to their hearts content down here. And I was just wheeling my horse, when from behind me I heard Lucan's voice.

"Colonel Flashman!" He was sitting with Cardigan, before the 13th Lights. "Come over here, if you please!"

Now what, thinks I, and my belly gave a great windy twinge as I trotted over towards them. Lucan was snapping at him impatiently, as I drew alongside:

"I know, I know, but there it is. Lord Raglan's order is quite positive, and we must obey it."

"Oh, vewy well," says Cardigan, damned ill-humoured; his voice was a mere croak, no doubt with his roupy chest, or over-boozing on his yacht. He flicked a glance at me, and looked away, sniffing; Lucan addressed me.

"You will accompany Lord Cardigan," says he. "In the event that communication is needed, he must have a galloper."

I stared horrified, hardly taking in Cardigan's comment: "I envisage no necessity for Colonel Fwashman's pwesence, or for communication with your lordship."

"Indeed, sir," says I, "Lord Raglan will need me . . . I dare not wait any longer . . . with your lordship's permission, I—"

"You will do as I say!" barks Lucan. "Upon my word, I have never met such insolence from mere gallopers before this day! First Nolan, and now you! Do as you are told, sir, and let us have none of this shirking!"

And with that he wheeled away, leaving me terrified, enraged, and baffled. What could I do? I couldn't disobey—it just wasn't possible. He had said I must ride with Cardigan, to those damned redoubts, chasing Raglan's bloody guns—my God, after what I had been through already! In an instant, by pure chance, I'd been snatched from security and thrust into the melting-pot again —it wouldn't do. I turned to Cardigan—the last man I'd have appealed to, in any circumstances, except an extremity like this.

"My lord," says I. "This is preposterous—unreasonable! Lord Raglan will need me! Will you speak to his lordship—he must be made to see—"

"If there is one thing," says Cardigan, in that croaking drawl, "of which I am tolewably certain in this uncertain world, it is the total impossibiwity of making my Word Wucan see anything at all. He makes it cwear, furthermore, that there is no discussion of his orders." He looked me up and down. "You heard him, sir. Take station behind me, and to my weft. Bewieve me, I do not welcome your pwesence here any more than you do yourself."

At that moment, up came George Paget, my cheroot clamped between his teeth.

"We are to advance, Lord George," says Cardigan. "I shall need close support, do you hear?—your vewy best support, Lord George. Haw-haw. You understand me?"

George took the cheroot from his mouth, looked at it, stuck it back, and then said, very stiff: "As always, my lord, you shall have my support."

"Haw-haw. Vewy well," says Cardigan, and they turned aside, leaving me stricken, and nicely hoist with my own petard, you'll agree. Why hadn't I kept my mouth shut in Raglan's presence? I could have been safe and comfy up on the Sapoune—but no, I'd had to try to vent my spite, to get Cardigan in the way of a bullet, and the result was I would be facing the bullets alongside him. Oh, a skirmish round gun redoubts is a small enough thing by military standards—unless you happen to be taking part in it, and I reckoned I'd used up two of my nine lives today already. To make matters worse, my stomach was beginning to churn and heave most horribly again; I sat there, with my back to the Light Brigade, nursing it miserably, while behind me the orders rattled out, and the squadrons reformed; I took a glance round and saw the 17th were now directly behind me, two little clumps of lances, with the Cherrypickers in behind. And here came Cardigan, trotting out in front, glancing back at the silent squadrons.

He paused, facing them, and there was no sound now but the restless thump of hooves, and the creak and jingle of the gear. All was still, five regiments of cavalry, looking down the valley, with Flashy out in front, wishing he were dead and suddenly aware that dreadful things were happening under his belt. I moved, gasping gently to myself, stirring on my saddle, and suddenly, without the slightest volition on my part, there was the most crashing discharge of wind, like the report of a mortar. My horse started; Cardigan jumped in his saddle, glaring at me, and from the ranks of the 17th a voice muttered: "Christ, as if Russian artillery wasn't bad enough!" Someone giggled, and another voice said: "We've 'ad Whistlin' Dick—now we got Trumpetin' Harry an' all!"

"Silence!" cries Cardigan, looking like thunder, and the murmur in the ranks died away. And then, God help me, in spite of my straining efforts to contain myself, there was another fearful bang beneath me, echoing off the saddle, and I thought Cardigan would explode with fury.

I could not merely sit there. "I beg your pardon, my lord," says I, "I am not well—"

"Be silent!" snaps he, and he must have been in a highly nervous condition himself, otherwise he would never have added, in a hoarse whisper:

"Can you not contain yourself, you disgusting fellow?"

"My lord," whispers I, "I cannot help it—it is the feverish wind, you see—" and I interrupted myself yet again, thunderously. He let out a fearful oath, under his breath, and wheeled his charger, his hand raised; he croaked out "Bwigade will advance —first squadron, 17th—walk-march—twot!" and behind us the squadrons stirred and moved forward, seven hundred cavalry, one of them palsied with fear but in spite of that feeling a mighty relief internally—it was what I had needed all day, of course, like these sheep that stuff themselves on some windy weed, and have to be pierced to get them right again.

And that was how it began. Ahead of me I could see the short turf of the valley turning to plough, and beyond that the haze at the valley end, a mile and more away, and only a few hundred yards off, on either side, the enclosing slopes, with the small figures of Russian infantry clearly visible. You could even see their artillerymen wheeling the guns round, and scurrying among the limbers—we were well within range, but they were watching, waiting to see what we would do next. I forced myself to look straight ahead down the valley; there were guns there in plenty, and squadrons of Cossacks flanking them; their lance points and sabres caught the sun and threw it back in a thousand sudden gleams of light. Would they try a charge when we wheeled right towards the redoubts? Would Cardigan deploy the 4th Lights? Would he put the 17th forward as a screen when we made our flank movement? If I stuck close by him, would I be all right? Oh, God, how had I landed in this fix again—three times in a day? It wasn't fair—it was unnatural, and then my innards spoke again, resoundingly, and perhaps the Russian gunners heard it, for far down the Causeway on the right a plume of smoke blossomed out as though in reply, there was the crash of the discharge and the shot went screaming overhead, and then from all along the Causeway burst out a positive salvo of firing; there was an orange flash and a huge bang a hundred paces ahead, and a fount of earth was hurled up and came pattering down before us, while behind there was the crash of exploding shells, and a new barrage opening up from the hills on the left.

Suddenly it was, as Lord Tennyson tells us, like the very jaws of hell; I realized that, without noticing, I had started to canter, babbling gently to myself, and in front Cardigan was cantering too, but not as fast as I was (one celebrated account remarks that, "In his eagerness to be first at grips with the foe, Flashman was seen to forge ahead; ah, we can guess the fierce spirit that burned in that manly breast"—I don't know about that, but I'm here to inform you that it was nothing to the fierce spirit that burned in my manly bowels). There was a crash-crash-crash of flaming bursts across the front, and the scream of shell splinters whistling by; Cardigan shouted "Steady!", but his own charger was pacing away now, and behind me the clatter and jingle was being drowned by the rising drum of hooves, from a slow canter to a fast one, and then to a slow gallop, and I tried to rein in that little mare, smothering my own panic, and snarling fiercely to myself: "Wheel, wheel, for God's sake! Why doesn't the stupid bastard wheel?" For we were level with the first Russian redoubt; their guns were levelled straight at us, not four hundred yards away, the ground ahead was being torn up by shot, and then from behind me there was a frantic shout.

I turned in the saddle, and there was Nolan, his sabre out,

charging across behind me, shouting hoarsely, "Wheel, my lord! Not that way! Wheel—to the redoubts!" His voice was all but drowned in the tumult of explosion, and then he was streaking past Cardigan, reining his beast back on its haunches, his face livid as he turned to face the brigade. He flourished his sabre, and shouted again, and a shell seemed to explode dead in front of Cardigan's horse; for a moment I lost Nolan in the smoke, and then I saw him, face contorted in agony, his tunic torn open and gushing blood from shoulder to waist. He shrieked horribly, and his horse came bounding back towards us, swerving past Cardigan with Lew toppling forward on to the neck of his mount. As I stared back, horrified, I saw him careering into the gap between the Lancers and the 13th Light, and then they had swallowed him, and the squadrons came surging down towards me.

I turned to look for Cardigan; he was thirty yards ahead, tugging like damnation to hold his charger in, with the shot crashing all about him. "Stop!" I screamed. "Stop! For Christ's sake, man, rein in!" For now I saw what Lew had seen—the fool was never going to wheel, he was taking the Light Brigade straight into the heart of the Russian army, towards those massive batteries at the valley foot, that were already belching at us, while the cannon on either side were raking us from the flanks, trapping us in a terrible enfilade that must smash the whole command to pieces.

"Stop, damn you!" I yelled again, and was in the act of wheeling to shout at the squadrons behind when the earth seemed to open beneath me in a sheet of orange flame; I reeled in the saddle, deafened, the horse staggered, went down, and re-covered, with myself clinging for dear life, and then I was grasping nothing but loose reins. The bridle was half gone, my brute had a livid gash spouting blood along her neck; she screamed and hurtled madly forward, and I seized the mane to prevent myself being thrown from the saddle.

Suddenly I was level with Cardigan; we bawled at each other, he waving his sabre, and now there were blue tunics level with me, either side, and the lance points of the 17th were thrusting forward, with the men crouched low in the saddles. It was an inferno of bursting shell and whistling fragments, of orange flame and choking smoke; a trooper alongside me was plucked from his saddle as though by an invisible hand, and I found myself drenched in a shower of blood. My little mare went surging ahead, crazy with pain; we were outdistancing Cardigan now—and even in that hell of death and gunfire, I remember, my stomach was asserting itself again, and I rode yelling with panic and farting furiously at the same time. I couldn't hold my horse at all; it was all I could do to stay aboard as we raced onwards, and as I stared wildly ahead I saw that we were a bare few hundred yards from the Russian batteries. The great black muzzles were staring me in the face, smoke wreathing up around them, but even as I saw the flame belching from them I couldn't hear the crash of their discharge—it was all lost in the fearful continuous reverberating cannonade that surrounded us. There was no stopping my mad career, and I found myself roaring pleas for mercy to the distant Russian gunners, crying stop, stop, for God's sake, cease fire, damn you, and let me alone. I could see them plainly, crouching at their breeches, working furiously to reload and pour another torrent of death at us through the smoke; I raged and swore mindlessly at them, and dragged out my sabre, thinking, by heaven, if you finish me I'll do my damndest to take one of you with me, you filthy Russian scum. ("And then", wrote that fatuous ass of a correspondent, "was seen with what nobility and power the gallant Flashman rode. Charging ahead even of his valiant chief, the death cry of the illustrious Nolan in his ears, his eye flashing terribly as he swung the sabre that had stemmed the horde at Jallalabad, he hurtled against the foe.") Well, yes, you might put it that way, but my nobility and power was concentrated, in a moment of inspiration, in trying to swerve that maddened beast out of the fixed lines of the guns; I had just sense enough left for that. I tugged at the mane with my free hand, she swerved and stumbled, recovered, reared, and had me half out of the saddle; my innards were seized with a fresh spasm, and if I were a fanciful man I'd swear I blew myself back astride of her. The ground shook beneath us with another exploding shell, knocking us sideways; I clung on, sobbing, and as the smoke cleared Cardigan came thundering by, sabre thrust out ahead of his charger's ears, and I heard him hoarsely shouting:

"Steady them! Hold them in! Cwose up and hold in!"

I tried to yell to him to halt, that he was going the wrong way, but my voice seemed to have gone. I turned in the saddle to shout or signal the men behind, and my God, what a sight it was! Half a dozen riderless horses at my very tail, crazy with fear, and behind them a score—God knows there didn't seem to be any more—of the 17th Lancers, some with hats gone, some streaked with blood, strung out any old how, glaring like madmen and tearing along. Empty saddles, shattered squadrons, all order gone, men and beasts going down by the second, the ground furrowing and spouting earth even as you watched—and still they came on, the lances of the 17th, and behind the sabres of the 11th—just a fleeting instant's thought I had, even in that inferno, remembering the brilliant Cherrypickers in splendid review, and there they were tearing forward like a horde of hell-bound spectres.

I had only a moment to look back—my mare was galloping like a thing demented, and as I steadied, there was Cardigan, waving his sabre and standing in his stirrups; the guns were only a hundred yards away, almost hidden in a great billowing bank of smoke, a bank which kept glaring red as though some Lucifer were opening furnace doors deep inside it. There was no turning, no holding back, and even in that deafening thunder I could hear the sudden chorus of yells behind me as the torn remnant of the Light Brigade gathered itself for the final mad charge into the battery. I dug in my heels, yelling nonsense and brandishing my sabre, shot into the smoke with one final rip from my bowels and a prayer that my gallant little mare wouldn't career headlong into a gun-muzzle, staggered at the fearful concussion of a gun exploding within a yard of me—and then we were through, into the open space behind the guns, leaping the limbers and ammunition boxes with the Russians scattering to let us through, and Cardigan a bare two yards away, reining his beast back almost on its haunches.

And then for a moment everything seemed to happen very slowly. I can see it all so distinctly: immediately to my left, and close enough to toss a biscuit, there was a squadron of Cossacks, with their lances couched, but all immobile, staring as though in amazement. Almost under my mare's hooves there was a Russian gunner, clutching a rammer, sprawling to get out of the way— he was stripped to the waist, I remember, and had a medal round his neck on a string—ahead of me, perhaps fifty yards off, was a brilliant little group of mounted men who could only be staff officers, and right beside me, still stiff and upright as a lance at rest, was Cardigan—by God, I thought, you're through *that* without a scratch on you, damn you! And so, it crossed my mind, was I—for the moment. And then everything jerked into crazy speed again, as the Light Brigade came careering out of the smoke, and the whole battery was suddenly a melee of rearing beasts, yelling maniacs, cracking pieces and flashing steel.

I was in the final moments of Little Big Horn, and the horror of Chillianwallah, which are among my nastiest recollections still, but for sheer murderous fury I recall nothing like the mad few minutes when the battered rabble of the Light Brigade rode over that Russian battery. It was as though they had gone mad— which, in a sense, they had. They slashed those Russian gun-crews apart, sabring, lancing, pounding them down under-hoof—I saw a corporal of the 17th drive his lance point four feet through a gunner's body and then leap from the saddle to tear at the fellow with his hands, Cardigan exchanging cuts with a mounted officer, troopers wrestling with Cossacks in the saddle, one of our Hussars on foot, whirling his sabre round his head and driving into a crowd of half a dozen, a Russian with his arm off at the elbow and a trooper still sabring him about the head—and then a Cossack came lumbering at me, roaring, with his lance couched to drive me through, but he was a handless clown, and missed me by a yard. I howled and slashed him back-handed as he blundered by, and then I was buffeted clean out of the saddle and went rolling away, weaponless, beneath a gun limber.

If I hadn't been scared witless I dare say I'd have stayed where I was, meditating, getting rid of some more wind, and generally taking a detached view, but in my panic I came scurrying out again, and there was George Paget, of all people, leaning from his saddle to grab my arm and swing me towards a riderless horse. I scrambled up, and George shouted:

"Come on, Flash, you old savage—we can't lose *you*! I'll want another of your cheroots presently![19] Close here, 4th Lights! Clo-o-o-se!"

There was a swirl of troopers round us, glaring smoke-blackened, bloody faces, a volley of commands, someone thrust a sabre into my hand, and George was crying:

"What a bloody pickle! We must cut our way home! Follow me!" and off we pounded, gasping and blinded, at his heels. I must have been near stupid with panic, for all I could think was: one more rush, just one more, and we'll be out of this hell-hole and back into the valley—God knows that was a horrifying prospect enough, but at least we were riding in the right direction, and providence or something had been on my side so far, and if only my luck would hold I might come through and reach the Sapoune and the camp beyond it and my bed and a ship and London and never, never go near a bloody uniform again—

"Halt!" bawls George, and I thought, I don't care, this is one gallant cavalryman who isn't halting for anything, I've had enough, and if I'm the only man who goes streaking back up that valley, leaving his comrades in the lurch, to hell with it. I put my head down and my heels in, thrust out my sabre to discourage any fool who got in the way, and charged ahead for all I was worth.

I heard George bawling behind me: "Halt! No, Flash, no!" and thought, carry on, George, and be damned to you. I fairly flew over the turf, the shouting died behind me, and I raised my head and looked—straight at what appeared to be the entire Russian army, drawn up in review order. There were great hideous ranks of the brutes, with Cossacks dead ahead, not twenty yards off— I had only a fleeting glimpse of amazed, bearded faces, there wasn't a hope of stopping, and then with a blasphemous yell of despair I plunged into them, horse, sabre and all.

"Picture, if you can bear it, reader"—as that idiot journalist put it—"the agony of Lord George Paget and his gallant remnant, in that moment. They had fought like heroes in the battery, Lord George himself had plucked the noble Flashman from bloody hand-to-hand conflict, they had rallied and ridden on through the battery, Lord George had given the halt, preparatory to wheeling about and charging back into the battery and the valley beyond, where ultimate safety lay—picture then, their anguish, when that great heart, too full to think of safety, or of aught but the cruel destruction of so many of his comrades, chose instead to launch himself *alone* against the embattled ranks of Muscovy! Sabre aloft, proud defiance on his lips, he chose the course that honour pointed, and rode like some champion of old to find death on the sabres of his enemies."

Well, I've always said, if you get the Press on your side you're half way there. I've never bothered to correct that glowing tribute, until now; it seems almost a shame to do it at last. I don't remember which journal it appeared in—*Bell's Sporting Life*, for all I know—but I don't doubt it caused many a manly tear to start, and many a fair bosom to heave when they read it. In the meantime, I was doing a bit in the manly tear and bosom-heaving line myself, with my horse foundering under me, my sabre flying from my hand, and my sorely-tried carcase sprawling on the turf while all those peasant horsemen shied back, growling and gaping, and then closed in again, staring down at me in that dull, astonished way that Russians have. I just lay there, gasping like a salmon on the bank, waiting for the lance-points to come skewering down on me, and babbling weakly:

"*Kamerad! Ami! Sarte! Amigo!* Oh God, what's the Russian for 'friend'?"

5

Being a prisoner of war has its advantages, or used to. If you were a British officer, taken by a civilized foe, you could expect to be rather better treated than your adversary would treat his own people; he would use you as a guest, entertain you, be friendly, and' not bother overmuch about confining you. He might ask your parole not to try to escape, but not usually—since you would be exchanged for one of his own people at the first opportunity there wasn't much point in running off.

Mind you, I think we British fared rather better than most. They respected us, and knew we didn't make war in a beastly fashion, like these Balkan fellows, so they treated us accordingly. But a Russian taken by the Poles, or an Austrian by the Eyetyes, or even a Confederate by the Yankees—well, he might not come off quite so comfortably. I'm told it's all changing now, and that war's no longer a gentleman's game (as though it ever was), and that among the "new professionals" a prisoner's a prisoner so damned well cage him up. I don't know: we treated each other decently, and weren't one jot more incompetent than this Sandhurst-and-Shop crowd. Look at that young pup Kitchener —what that fellow needs is a woman or two.

At all events, no one has ever treated me better, by and large, than the Russians did, although I don't think it was kindness, but ignorance. From the moment I measured my length among those Cossacks, I found myself being regarded with something like awe. It wasn't just the Light Brigade fiasco, which had impressed them tremendously, but a genuine uncertainty where the English were concerned—they seemed to look on us as though we were men from the moon, or made of dynamite and so liable to go off if scratched. The truth is, they're such a dull, wary lot of peasants —the ordinary folk and soldiers, that is—that they go in fear of anything strange until someone tells 'em what to do about it.

In those days, of course, most of them were slaves—except for the Cossacks—and behaved as such.

I'll have more to say about this, but for the moment it's enough to note that the Cossacks kept away from me, glowering, until one of their officers jumped down, helped me to my feet, and accepted my surrender. I doubt if he understood a word I said, for I was too shocked and confused to be coherent, even if I'd spoken Russian, which I didn't much, at that time. He led me through the crowd, and once I had realized that they weren't going to do me violence, and that I was safely out of that hellish maelstrom, I set myself to collect my wits and consider what should be done.

They stuck me in a tent, with two massive Cossacks at the entrance—Black Sea Cossacks, as I learned later, with those stringy long-haired caps, and scarlet lances—and there I sat, listening to the growing chatter outside, and every now and then an officer would stick his face in, and regard me, and then withdraw. I was still feeling fearfully sick and giddy, and my right ear seemed to have gone deaf with the cannonading, but as I leaned against the pole, shuddering, one thought kept crowding gloriously into my mind: I was alive, and in one piece. I'd survived, God knew how, the shattering of the Light Brigade, to say nothing of the earlier actions of the day—it seemed like a year since I'd stood with Campbell's Highlanders, though it was a bare five hours ago. You've come through again, my boy, I kept thinking; you're going to live. That being the case, head up, look alive and keep your eyes open.

Presently in came a little dapper chap in a fine white uniform, black boots, and a helmet with a crowned eagle. "Lanskey," says he, in good French—which most educated Russians spoke, by the way—"Major, Cuirassiers of the Guard. Whom have I the pleasure of addressing?"

"Flashman," says I, "Colonel, 17th Lancers."

"Enchanted," says he, bowing. "May I request that you accompany me to General Liprandi, who is most anxious to make the acquaintance of such a distinguished and gallant officer?"

Well, he couldn't have said fairer; I bucked up at once, and he led me out, through a curious throng of officers and staff hangers-on, into a great tent where about a dozen senior officers were waiting, with a genial-looking, dark-whiskered fellow in a splendid sable coat, whom I took to be Liprandi, seated behind a table. They stopped talking at once; a dozen pairs of eager eyes fixed on me as Lanskey presented me, and I stood up tall, ragged and muck-smeared though I was, and just stared over Liprandi's head, clicking my heels.

He came round the table, right up to me, and said, also in excellent French: "Your pardon, colonel. Permit me." And to my astonishment he stuck his nose up close to my lips, sniffing.

"What the devil?" cries I, stepping back.

"A thousand pardons, sir," says he. "It is true, gentlemen," turning to his staff. "Not a suspicion of liquor." And they all began to buzz again, staring at me.

"You are perfectly sober," says Liprandi. "And so, as I have ascertained, are your troopers who have been taken prisoner. I confess, I am astonished.[20] Will you perhaps enlighten us, colonel, what was the explanation of that . . . that extraordinary action by your light cavalry an hour ago? Believe me," he went on, "I seek no military intelligence from you—no advantage of information. But it is beyond precedent—beyond understanding. Why, in God's name, did you do it?"

Now, I didn't know, at that time, precisely what we had done. I guessed we must have lost three-quarters of the Light Brigade, by a hideous mistake, but I couldn't know that I'd just taken part in the most famous cavalry action ever fought, one that was to sound round the world, and that even eye-witnesses could scarcely believe. The Russians were amazed; it seemed to them we must have been drunk, or drugged, or mad—they weren't to guess that it had been a ghastly accident. And I wasn't going to enlighten them. So I said:

"Ah, well, you know, it was just to teach you fellows to keep your distance."

At this they exclaimed, and shook their heads and swore, and Liprandi looked bewildered, and kept muttering: "Five hundred sabres! To what end?", and they crowded round, plying me with questions—all very friendly, mind, so that I began to get my bounce back, and played it off as though it were just another day's work. What they couldn't fathom was how we'd held together all the way to the guns, and hadn't broken or turned back, even with four saddles empty out of five, so I just told 'em, "We're British cavalry," simple as that, and looked them in the eye. It was true, too, even if no one had less right to say it than I.

At that they stamped and swore again, incredulously, and one huge chap with a beard began to weep, and insisted on embracing me, stinking of garlic as he was, and Liprandi called for brandy, and demanded of me what we, in English, called our light cavalry, and when I told him they all raised their glasses and shouted together: "Thee Light Brigedde!" and dashed down their glasses and ground them underfoot, and embraced me again, laughing and shouting and patting me on the head, while I, the unworthy recipient, looked pretty bluff and offhand and said, no, dammit all, it was nothing, just our usual form, don't you know. (I should have felt shame, doubtless, at the thought that I, old windy Harry, was getting the plaudits and the glory, but you know me. Anyway, I'd been there, hadn't I, all the way; should I be disqualified, just because I was babbling scared?)

After that it was all booze and good fellowship, and when I'd been washed and given a change of clothes Liprandi gave me a slap-up dinner with his staff, and the champagne flowed—French, you may be certain; these Russians know how to go to war— and they were all full of attention and admiration and a thousand questions, but every now and then they would fall silent and look at me in that strange way that every survivor of the charge has come to recognize: respectfully, and almost with reverence, but with a hint of suspicion, as though you weren't quite canny.

Indeed their hospitality was so fine, that night, that I began to feel regretful at the thought that I'd probably be exchanged in the next day or two, and would find myself back in that lousy, fever-ridden camp under Sevastopol—it's a curious thing, but my belly, which had been in such wicked condition all day, felt right as rain after that dinner. We all got gloriously tight, drinking healths, and the bearded garlic giant and Lanskey carried me to bed, and we all fell on the floor, roaring and laughing. As I crawled on to my blankets I had only a moment's blurred recollection of the sound of cannonade, and ranks of Highlanders, and Scarlett's gaudy scarf, and the headlong gallop down the Sapoune, and Cardigan cantering slowly and erect, and those belching guns, all whirling together in a great smoky confusion. And it all seemed past and unimportant as I slid away into unconsciousness and slept like a winter hedgehog.

They didn't exchange me. They kept me for a couple of weeks, confined in a cottage at Yalta, with two musketmen on the door and a Russian colonel of Horse Pioneers to walk the little garden with me for exercise, and then I was visited by Radziwill, a very decent chap on Liprandi's staff who spoke English and knew London well. He was terribly apologetic, explaining that there wasn't a suitable exchange, since I was a staff man, and a pretty rare catch. I didn't believe this; we'd taken senior Russian officers every bit as important as I, at the Alma, and I wondered exactly why they wanted to keep me prisoner, but there was no way of finding out, of course. Not that it concerned me much—I didn't mind a holiday in Russia, being treated as an honoured guest rather than a prisoner, for Radziwill hastened to reassure me that what they intended to do was send me across the Crimea to Kertch, and then by boat to mainland Russia, where I'd be safely tucked away on a country estate. The advantage of this was that I would be so far out of harm's way that escape would be impossible —I tried to look serious and knowing when he said this, as though I'd been contemplating running off to rejoin the bloody battle again—and I could lead a nice easy life without over-many restrictions, until the war was over, which couldn't be long, anyway.

I've learned to make the best of things, so I accepted without demur, packed up my few traps, which consisted of my cleaned and mended Lancer blues and a few shirts and things which Radziwill gave me, and prepared to go where I was taken. I was quite looking forward to it—fool that I was.

Before I went, Radziwill—no doubt meaning to be kind, but in fact just being an infernal nuisance—arranged for me to visit those survivors of the Light Brigade who'd been taken prisoner, and were in confinement down near Yalta. I didn't want to see them, much, but I couldn't refuse.

There were about thirty of them in a big stuffy shed, and not above six of them unwounded. The others were in cots, with bandaged heads and slings, some with limbs off, lying like wax dummies, one or two plainly just waiting to die, and all of them looking desperate hangdog. The moment I went inside I wished

I hadn't come—it's this kind of thing, the stale smell of blood, the wasted faces, the hushed voices, the awful hopeless tiredness, that makes you understand what a hellish thing war is. Worse than a battle-field, worse than the blood and the mud and the smoke and the steel, is the dank misery of a hospital of wounded men—and this place was a good deal better than most. Russians ain't clean, by any means, but the ward they'd made for our fellows was better than our own medical folk could have arranged at Balaclava.

Would you believe it, when I came in they raised a cheer? The pale faces lit up, those that could struggled upright in bed, and their non-com, who wasn't wounded, threw me a salute.

"Ryan, sir," says he. "Troop sergeant-major, Eighth 'Ussars. Sorry to see you're took, sir—but glad to see you well."

I thanked him, and shook hands, and then went round, giving a word here and there, as you're bound to do, and feeling sick at the sight of the pain and disfigurement—it could have been me, lying there with a leg off, or my face stitched like a football.

"Not takin' any 'arm, sir, as you see," says Ryan. "The grub ain't much, but it fills. You're bein' treated proper yourself, sir, if I may make so bold? That's good, that is; I'm glad to 'ear that. You'll be gettin' exchanged, I reckon? No—well, blow me! Who'd ha' thought that? I reckon they doesn't want to let you go, though—why, when we heard t'other day as you'd been took, old Dick there—that's 'im, sir, wi' the sabre-cut— 'e says: 'That's good noos for the Ruskis; ole Flashy's worth a squadron any day' —beggin' yer pardon, sir."

"That's mighty kind of friend Dick," says I, "but I fear I'm not worth very much at present, you know."

They laughed—such a thin laugh—and growled and said "Garn!", and Ryan dropped his voice, glancing towards where Lanskey loitered by the door, and says softly:

"I knows better, sir. An' there's 'arf a dozen of us sound enough 'ere to be worth twenty o' these Ruski chaps. If you was to say the word, sir, I reckon we could break our way out of 'ere, grab a few sabres, an' cut our way back to th'Army! It can't be above twenty mile to Sevasto-pool! We could do it, sir! The boys is game fer it, an'—"

"Silence, Ryan!" says I. "I won't hear of it." This was one of these dangerous bastards, I could see, full of duty and desperate notions. "What, break away and leave our wounded comrades? No, no, that would never do—I'm surprised at you."

He flushed. "I'm sorry, sir; I was just—"

"I know, my boy." I put a hand on his shoulder. "You want to do your duty, as a soldier should. But, you see, it can't be. And you can take pride in what you have done already—all of you can." I thought a few patriotic words wouldn't do any harm. "You are stout fellows, all of you. England is proud of you." And will let you go to the poor-house, in time, or sell laces at street corners, I thought to myself.

"Ole Jim the Bear'll be proud, an' all," pipes up one chap with a bandage swathing his head and eye, and I saw the blood-stained Cherrypicker pants at the foot of his cot. "They do say as 'is Lordship got out the battery, sir. Dryden there was picked up by the Ruskis in the valley, an' 'e saw Lord Cardigan goin' back arterwards—says 'e 'ad a bloody sabre, too, but wasn't hurt 'isself."

That was bad news; I could have borne the loss of Cardigan any day.

"Good ole Jim!"

"Ain't 'e the one, though!"

"'E's a good ole commander, an' a gentleman, even if 'e is an 11th 'Ussar!" says Ryan, and they all laughed, and looked shy at me, because they knew I'd been a Cherrypicker, once.

There was a very pale, thin young face in the cot nearest the door, and as I was turning away, he croaked out, in a little whisper:

"Colonel Flashman, sir—Troop sarn't major was sayin'—it never 'appened afore—cavalry, chargin' a battery wi' no support, an' takin' it. Never 'appened nowheres, in any war, sir. Is that right, sir?"

I didn't know, but I'd certainly never heard of it. So I said: "I believe that's right. I think it may be."

He smiled. "That's good, then. Thank'ee, sir." And he lay back, with his eyelids twitching, breathing very quietly.

"Well," says I. "Good-bye, Ryan. Good-bye, all of you. Ah—keep your spirits up. We'll all be going home soon."

"When the Ruskis is beat," cries someone, and Ryan says:

"Three cheers for the Colonel!" and they all cheered, feebly, and shouted "Good old Flash Harry!" and the man with the patched eye began to sing, and they all took it up, and as I drove off with Lanskey I heard the words of the old Light Brigade canter fading behind me:

> In the place of water we'll drink ale,
> An' pay no reck'ning on the nail,
> No man for debt shall go to jail,
> While he can Garryowen hail.

I've heard it from Afghanistan to Whitehall, from the African veldt to drunken hunting parties in Rutland; heard it sounded on penny whistles by children and roared out in full-throated chorus by Custer's 7th on the day of Greasy Grass—and there were survivors of the Light Brigade singing on that day, too—but it always sounds bitter on my ears, because I think of those brave, deluded, pathetic bloody fools in that Russian shed, with their mangled bodies and lost limbs, all for a shilling a day and a pauper's grave—and yet they thought Cardigan, who'd have flogged 'em for a rusty spur and would see them murdered under the Russian guns because he hadn't wit and manhood enough to tell Lucan to take his order to hell—they thought he was "a good old commander", and they even cheered *me*, who'd have turned tail on them at the click of a bolt. Mind you, I'm harmless, by comparison—I don't send 'em off, stuffed with lies and rubbish, to get killed and maimed for nothing except a politician's vanity or a manufacturer's profit. Oh, I'll sham it with the best in public, and sport my tinware, but I know what I am, and there's no room for honest pride in me, you see. But if there was—just for a little bit, along with the disgust and hatred and selfishness—I'd keep it for them, those seven hundred British sabres.

It must be the drink talking. That's the worst of it; whenever I think back to Balaclava, there's nothing for it but the booze. It's not that I feel guilt or regret or shame—they don't *count* beside feeling alive, anyway, even if I were capable of them. It's just that I don't really understand Balaclava, even now. Oh, I can understand, without sharing, most kinds of courage—that which springs from rage, or fear, or greed or even love. I've had a bit of them myself—anyone can show brave if his children or his woman are threatened. (Mind you, if the hosts of Midian were assailing my little nest, offering to ravish my loved one, my line would be to say to her, look, you jolly 'em along, old girl, and look your best, while I circle round to a convenient rock with my rifle.) But are these emotions, that come of anger or terror or desire, really bravery at all? I doubt it, myself—but what happened in the North Valley, under those Russian guns, *all for nothing*, that's bravery, and you may take the word of a true-blue coward for it. It's beyond my ken, anyway, thank God, so I'll say no more of it, or of Balaclava, which as far as my Russian adventure is concerned, was really just an unpleasant prelude. Enough's enough; Lord Tennyson may have the floor for me.

The journey from Yalta through the woody hills to Kertch was not noteworthy; once you've seen a corner of the Crimea you've seen it all, and it's not really Russia. From Kertch, where a singularly surly and uncommunicative French-speaking civilian took me in charge (with a couple of dragoons to remind me what I was), we went by sloop across the Azov Sea to Taganrog, a dirty little port, and joined the party of an imperial courier whose journey lay the same way as ours. Ah-ha, thinks I, we'll travel in style, which shows how mistaken one can be.

We travelled in two *telegues*, which are just boxes on wheels, with a plank at the front for the driver, and straw or cushions for the passengers. The courier was evidently in no hurry, for we crawled along at an abominably slow pace, although *telegues* can travel at a tremendous clip when they want to, with a bell clanging in front, and everyone scattering out of their way. It always puzzled me, when I later saw the shocking condition of Russian roads, with their ruts and pot-holes, how the highways over which the *telegues* travelled were always smooth and level. The secret was this: *telegues* were used only by couriers and officials of importance, and before they came to a stretch of road, every peasant in the area was turned out to sand and level it.

So as we lumbered along, the courier in state in the first *telegue*, and Flashy with his escort in the second, there were always peasants standing by the roadside, men and women, in their belted smocks and ragged puttees, silent, unmoving, staring as we rolled by. This dull brooding watchfulness got on my nerves, especially at the post stations, where they used to assemble in silent groups to stare at us—they were so different from the Crim Tartars I had seen, who are lively, tall, well-made men, even if their women are seedy. The steppe Russians were much smaller, and ape-like by comparison.

Of course, what I didn't realize then was that these people were slaves—real bound, European white slaves, which isn't easy to understand until you see it. This wasn't always so; it seems that Boris Godunov—whom most of you will know as a big fellow who takes about an hour and a half to die noisily in an opera—imposed serfdom on the Russian peasants, which meant that they became the property of the nobles and land-owners, who could buy and sell them, hire them out, starve them, lash them, imprison them, take their goods, beasts and womenfolk whenever they chose—in fact, do anything short of maiming them permanently or killing them. They did those things, too, of course, for I saw them, but it was officially unlawful.

The serfs were just like the nigger slaves in the States—worse off, if anything, for they didn't seem to realize they were slaves. They looked on themselves as being attached to the soil ("we belong to the master, but the land is ours", was a saying among them) and traditionally they had bits of land to work for their own benefit—three days on their patch each week, three on the master's, was supposed to be the rule, but wherever I went it seemed to be six on the master's and one for themselves, if they were lucky.

It may not seem possible to you that in Europe just forty years ago white folk could be used like this, that they could be flogged with rods and whips up to ten times a day, or knouted (which is something infintely worse), or banished to Siberia for years at their landlord's whim; all he had to do was pay the cost of their transportation. They could be made to wear spiked collars, the women could be kept in harems, the men could be drafted off to the army so that the owners could steal their wives without embarrassment, their children could be sold off—and in return for this they were meant to be grateful to their lords, and literally crawl in front of them, calling them "father", touching their heads on the ground, and kissing their boots. I've watched them do it—just like political candidates at home. I've seen a lot of human sorrow and misery in my time, but the lot of the Russian serf was the most appalling I've ever struck.

Of course, it's all changed now; they freed the serfs in '61, just a few years after I was there, and now, I'm told, they are worse off than ever. Russia depended on slavery, you see, and when they freed them they upset the balance, and there was tremendous starvation and the economy went to blazes—well, in the old days the landlords had at least kept the serfs alive, for their own benefit, but after emancipation, why should they? And it was all nonsense, anyway; the Russians will always be slaves—so will most of the rest of mankind, of course, but it tends to be more obvious among the Ruskis.

For one thing, they look so damned slavish. I remember the first time I really noticed serfs, the first day's drive out of Taganrog. It was at a little village post-station, where some official was thrashing a peasant—don't know why—and this dull clown was just standing and letting himself be caned by a fellow half his size, hardly even wincing under the blows. There was a little crowd of serfs looking on, ugly, dirty-looking rascals in hairy blue smocks and rough trousers, with their women and a few ragged brats—and they were just watching, like cowed, stupid brutes. And when the little official finally broke his cane, and kicked the peasant and screamed at him to be off, the fellow just lumbered away, with the others trailing after him. It was as though they had no feeling whatever.

Oh, it was a cheery place, all right, this great empire of Russia as I first saw it in the autumn of '54—a great ill-worked wilderness ruled by a small landed aristocracy with their feet on the necks of a huge human-animal population, with Cossack devils keeping order when required. It was a brutal, backward place, for the rulers were ever fearful of the serfs, and held back everything educational or progressive—even the railway was discouraged, in case it should prove to be revolutionary—and with discontent everywhere, especially among those serfs who had managed to better themselves a little, and murmurings of revolt, the iron hand of government was pressing ever harder. The "white terror", as they called the secret police, were everywhere; the whole population was on their books, and everyone had to have his "billet", his "ticket to live"—without it you were nobody, you did not exist. Even the nobility feared the police, and it was from a landlord that I heard the Russian saying about being in jail—"Only there shall we sleep sound, for only there are we safe."[21]

The land we travelled through was a fit place for such people—indeed, you have to see it to understand why they are what they are. I've seen big countries before—the American plains on the old wagon-trails west of St Louis, with the whispering grasses waving away and away to the very edge of the world, or the Saskatchewan prairies in grasshopper time, dun and empty under the biggest sky on earth. But Russia is bigger: there is no sky, only empty space overhead, and no horizon, only a distant haze, and endless miles of sun-scorched rank grass and emptiness. The few miserable hamlets, each with its rickety church, only seemed to emphasize the loneliness of that huge plain, imprisoning by its very emptiness—there are no hills for a man to climb into or to catch his imagination, nowhere to *go*: no wonder it binds its people to it.

It appalled me, as we rolled along, with nothing to do but strain your eyes for the next village, soaked by the rain or sweating in the sun, or sometimes huddling against the first wintry gusts that swept the steppes—they seemed to have all weathers together, and all bad. For amusement, of course, you could try to determine which stink was more offensive—the garlic chewed by the driver or the grease of his axles—or watch the shuttlecocks of the wind-witch plant being blown to and fro. I've known dreary, depressing journeys, but that was the limit; I'd sooner walk through Wales.

The truth is, I was beginning to find Russia a frightening place, with its brooding, brutish people and countryside to match; one began to lose the sense of space and time. The only reliefs were provided by our halts at the way-stations—poor, flea-ridden places with atrocious accommodation and worse food. You'd been able to get decent beef in the Crimea for a penny a pound, but here it was *stchee* and *borsch*, which are cabbage soups, horse-meat porridge, and sweet flour tarts, which were the only palatable things available. That, and their tea, kept me alive; the tea is good, provided you can get "caravan tea", which is Chinese, and the best. The wine they may put back in the *moujiks** for me.

So my spirits continued to droop, but what shook them worst was an incident on the last morning of our journey when we had halted at a large village only thirty versts [twenty miles] from Starotorsk, the estate to which I was being sent. It wasn't so different, really, from the peasant-thrashing I'd already seen, yet it, and the man involved, branded on my mind the knowledge of what a fearful, barbarous, sickeningly cruel land this Russia was.

The village lay on what seemed to be an important cross-roads; there was a river, I remember, and a military camp, and uniforms coming and going from the municipal building where my civilian took me to report my arrival—everything has to be reported to someone or other in Russia, in this case the local registrar, a surly, bull-necked brute in a grey tunic, who pawed over the papers, eyeing me nastily the while.

These Russian civil servants are a bad lot—pompous, stupid and rude at the best. They come in various grades, each with a military title—so that General or Colonel So-and-so turns out to be someone who neglects the parish sanitation or keeps inaccurate records of livestock. The brutes even wear medals, and are immensely puffed-up, and unless you bribe them lavishly they will cause you all the trouble they can.

I was waiting patiently, being eyed curiously by the officials and officers with whom the municipal hall was packed, and the registrar picked his teeth, scowling, and then launched into a great tirade in Russian—I gather it was addressed against all Englishmen in general and me in particular. He made it clear to my escort, and everyone else, that he considered it a gross waste of board and lodging that I should be housed at all—he'd have had me in the salt-mines for a stinking foreigner who had defiled the holy soil of Mother Russia—and so forth, until he got quite worked up, banging his desk and shouting and glaring, so that the noise and talk in the room died away as everyone stopped to listen.

It was just jack-in-office unpleasantness, and I had no choice but to ignore it. But someone else didn't. One of the officers who had been standing to one side, chatting, suddenly strolled forward in front of the registrar's table, paused to drop his cigarette

* Peasants.

122

and set a foot on it, and then without warning lashed the registrar full across the face with his riding crop. The fellow shrieked and fell back in his chair, flinging up his hands to ward another blow; the officer said something in a soft, icy voice, and the trembling hands came down, revealing the livid whip-mark on the coarse bearded face.

There wasn't a sound in the room, except for the registrar's whimpering, as the officer leisurely raised his crop again, and with the utmost deliberation slashed him across the face a second time, laying the bearded cheek open, while the creature screamed but didn't dare move or protect himself. A third slash sent man and chair over, the officer looked at his whip as though it had been in the gutter, dropped it on the floor, and then turned to me.

"This offal," says he, and to my amazement he spoke in English, "requires correction. With your permission, I shall reinforce the lesson." He looked at the blubbering, bleeding registrar crawling out of the wreck of his chair, and rapped out a string of words in that level, chilly whisper; the stricken man changed course and came wriggling across to my feet, babbling and snuffling at my ankles in a most disgusting fashion, while the officer lit another cigarette and looked on.

"He will lick your boots," says he, "and I have told him that if he bleeds on them, I shall have him knouted. You wish to kick him in the face?"

As you know, I'm something in the bullying line myself, and given a moment I dare say I'd have accepted; it isn't every day you have the opportunity. But I was too amazed—aye, and alarmed, too, at the cold, deliberate brutality I'd seen, and the registrar seized the opportunity to scramble away, followed by a shattering kick from my protector.

"Scum—but rather wiser scum," says he. "He will not insult a gentleman again. A cigarette, colonel?" And he held out a gold case of those paper abominations I'd tried at Sevastopol, but hadn't liked. I let him light one for me; it tasted like dung soaked in treacle.

"Captain Count Nicholas Pavlovitch Ignatieff,"[22] says he, in that cold, soft voice, "at your service." And as our eyes met through the cigarette smoke I thought, hollo, this is another of those momentous encounters. You didn't have to look at this chap twice to remember him forever. It was the eyes, as it so often is—I thought in that moment of Bismarck, and Charity Spring, and Akbar Khan; it had been the eyes with them, too. But this fellow's were different from anything yet: one was blue, but the other had a divided iris, half-blue, half-brown, and the oddly fascinating effect of this was that you didn't know where to look, but kept shifting from one to the other.

For the rest, he had gingerish, curling hair and a square, masterful face that was no way impaired by a badly-broken nose. He looked tough, and immensely self-assured; it was in his glance, in the abrupt way he moved, in the slant of the long cigarette between his fingers, in the rakish tilt of his peaked cap, in the immaculate white tunic of the Imperial Guards. He was the kind who knew exactly what was what, where everything was, and precisely who was who—especially himself. He was probably a devil with women, admired by his superiors, hated by his rivals, and abjectly feared by his subordinates. One word summed him up: bastard.

"I caught your name, in that beast's outburst," says he. He was studying me calmly, as a doctor regards a specimen. "You are the officer of Balaclava, I think. Going to Starotorsk, to be lodged with Colonel Count Pencherjevsky. He already has another English officer—under his care." I tried to meet his eye and not keep glancing at the registrar, who had hauled himself up at a nearby table, and was shakily trying to staunch his gashed face: no one moved a finger to help him. For some reason, I found my cigarette trembling between my fingers; it was foolish, with this outwardly elegant, precise, not unfriendly young gentleman doing no more than make civil conversation. But I'd just seen him at work, and knew the kind of soulless, animal cruelty behind the suave mask. I know my villains, and this Captain Count Ignatieff was a bad one; you could feel the savage strength of the man like an electric wave.

"I will not detain you, colonel," says he, in that same cold murmur, and there was all the immeasurable arrogance of the Russian nobleman in the way he didn't look or beckon for my civilian escort, but simply turned his head the merest fraction, and the fellow came scurrying out of the silent crowd.

"We may meet at Starotorsk," says Ignatieff, and with the slightest bow to me he turned away, and my escort was hustling me respectfully out to the *telegue*, as though he couldn't get away fast enough. I was all for it; the less time you spend near folk like that, the better.

It left me shaken, that little encounter. Some people are just terrible, in the true sense of the word—I knew now, I thought, how Tsar Ivan had earned that nickname: it implies something far beyond the lip-licking cruelty of your ordinary torturer. Satan, if there is one, is probably a Russian; no one else could have the necessary soulless brutality; it is just part of life to them.

I asked my civilian who Ignatieff was, and got an unwilling mumble in reply. Russians don't like to talk about their superiors at any time; it isn't safe, and I gathered that Ignatieff was so important, and so high-born—mere captain though he was—that you just didn't mention him at all. So I consoled myself that I'd probably seen the last of him (ha!) and took stock of the scenery instead. After a few miles the bare steppe was giving way to large, well-cultivated fields, with beasts and peasants labouring away, the road improved, and presently, on an eminence ahead of us there was a great, rambling timbered mansion with double wings, and extensive outbuildings, all walled and gated, and the thin smoke of a village just visible beyond. We bowled up a fine gravel drive between well-kept lawns with willow trees on their borders, past the arched entrance of a large courtyard, and on to a broad carriage sweep before the house, where a pretty white fountain played.

Well, thinks I, cheering up a bit, this will do. Civilization in the midst of barbarism, and very fine, too. Pleasant grounds, genteel accommodation, salubrious outlook, company's own water no doubt, to suit overworked military man in need of rest and recreation. Flashy, my son, this will answer admirably until they sign the peace. The only note out of harmony was the Cossack guard lounging near the front steps, to remind me that I was a prisoner after all.

A steward emerged, bowing, and my civilian explained that he would conduct me to my apartment, and thereafter I would doubtless meet Count Pencherjevsky. I was led into a cool, light-panelled hall, and if anything was needed to restore my flagging spirits it was the fine furs on the well-polished floor, the comfortable leather furniture, the flowers on the table, the cosy air of civilian peace, and the delightful little blonde who had just descended the stairs. She was so unexpected, I must have goggled at her like poor Willy in the presence of his St John's Wood whore.

And she was worth a long stare. About middle height, perhaps eighteen or nineteen, plump-bosomed, tiny in the waist, with a saucy little upturned nose, pink, dimpled cheeks and a cloud of silvery-blonde hair, she was fit to make your mouth water—especially if you hadn't had a woman in two months, and had just finished a long, dusty journey through southern Russia, gaping at misshapen peasants. I stripped, seized, and mounted her in a twinkling of my mind's eye, as she tripped past, I bowing my most military bow, and she disregarding me beyond a quick, startled glance from slanting grey eyes. May it be a long war, thinks I, watching her bouncing out of sight, and then my attention was taken by the major-domo, muttering the eternal "*Pajalsta, excellence,*" and leading me up the broad, creaky staircase, along a turning passage, and finally halting at a broad door. He knocked, and an English voice called:

"Come in—no, hang it all—*khadee-tyeh!*"

I grinned at the friendly familiar sound, and strode in, saying: "Hollo, yourself, whoever you are," and putting out my hand. A man of about my own age, who had been reading on the bed, looked up in surprise, swung his legs to the ground, stood up, and then sank back on the bed again, gaping as though I were a ghost. He shook his head, stuttering, and then got out:

"Flashman! Good heavens!"

I stopped short. The face was familiar, somehow, but I didn't know from where. And then the years rolled away, and I saw a boy's face under a tile hat, and heard a boy's voice saying: "I'm sorry, Flashman." Yes, it was him all right—Scud East of Rugby.

6

For a long moment we just stared at each other, and then we both found our voices in the same phrase: "What on earth are you doing here?" And then we stopped, uncertainly, until I said:

"I was captured at Balaclava, three weeks back."

"They took me at Silistria, three months ago. I've been here five weeks and two days."

And then we stared at each other some more, and finally I said:

"Well, you certainly know how to make a fellow at home. Ain't you going to offer me a chair, even?"

He jumped up at that, colouring and apologizing—still the same raw Scud, I could see. He was taller and thinner than I remembered; his brown hair was receding, too, but he still had that quick, awkward nervousness I remembered.

"I'm so taken aback," he stuttered, pulling up a chair for me. "Why—why, I am *glad* to see you, Flashman! Here, give me your hand, old fellow! There! Well—well—my, what a mountainous size you've grown, to be sure! You always were a big ... er, a tall chap, of course, but ... I say, isn't this a queer fix, us meeting again like this ... after so long! Let's see, it must be fourteen, no fifteen, years since ... since ... ah ..."

"Since Arnold kicked me out for being pissy drunk?"

He coloured again. "I was going to say, since we said goodbye."

"Aye. Well, ne'er mind. What's your rank, Scud? Major, eh? I'm a colonel."

"Yes," says he. "I see that." He gave me an odd, almost shy grin. "You've done well—everyone knows about you—all the fellows from Rugby talk about you, when one meets 'em, you know ..."

"Do they, though? Not with any great love, I'll be bound, eh, young Scud?"

"Oh, come!" cries he. "What d'you mean? Oh, stuff! We were

all boys then, and boys never get on too well, 'specially when some are bigger and older and . . . why, that's all done with years ago! Why—everyone's proud of you, Flashman! Brooke and Green—and young Brooke—he's in the Navy, you know." He paused. "The Doctor would have been proudest of all, I'm sure."

Aye, he probably would, thinks I, the damned old hypocrite.

". . . everyone knows about Afghanistan, and India, and all that," he ran on. "I was out there myself, you know, in the Sikh campaign, when you were winning another set of laurels. All I got was a shot wound, a hole in my ribs, and a broken arm."[23] He laughed ruefully. "Not much to show, I'm afraid—and then I bought out of the 101st, and—but heavens, how I'm rattling on! Oh, it is good to see you, old fellow! This is the best, most famous thing! Let me have a good look at you! By George, those are some whiskers, though!"

I couldn't be sure if he meant it, or not. God knows, Scud East had no cause to love me, and the sight of him had so taken me back to that last black day at Rugby that I'd momentarily forgotten we were men now, and things had changed—perhaps even his memories of me. For he *did* seem pleased to see me, now that he'd got over his surprise—of course, that could just be acting on his part, or making the best of a bad job, or just Christian decency. I found myself weighing him up; I'd knocked him about a good deal, in happier days, and it came as a satisfaction to realize that I could probably still do it now, if it came to the pinch; he was still smaller and thinner than I. At that, I'd never detested him as much as his manly-mealy little pal, Brown; he'd had more game in him than the others, had East, and now—well, if he was disposed to be civil, and let bygones be bygones . . . We were bound to be stuck together for some months at least.

All this in a second's consideration—and you may think, what a mean and calculating nature, or what a guilty conscience. Never you mind; I know my own nature hasn't changed in eighty years, so why should anyone else's? And I never forget an injury—I've done too many of 'em.

So I didn't quite enter into his joyous spirit of reunion, but was civil enough, and after he had got over his sham-ecstasies at meeting his dear old school-fellow again, I said:

"What about this place, then—and this fellow Pencherjevsky?"

He hesitated a moment, glanced towards the wall, got up, and as he walked over to it, said loudly: "Oh, it is as you see it—a splendid place. They've treated me well—very well indeed." And then he beckoned me to go over beside him, at the same time laying a finger on his lips. I went, wondering, and followed his pointing finger to a curious protuberance in the ornate carving of the panelling beside the stove. It looked as though a small funnel had been sunk into the carving, and covered with a fine metal grille, painted to match the surrounding wood.

"I say, old fellow," says East, "what d'you say to a walk? The Count has splendid gardens, and we are free of them, you know."

I took the hint, and we descended the stairs to the hall, and out on to the lawns. The lounging Cossack looked at us, but made no move to follow. As soon as we were at a safe distance, I asked:

"What on earth was it?"

"Speaking-tube, carefully concealed," says he. "I looked out for it as soon as I arrived—there's one in the next room, too, where you'll be. I fancy our Russian hosts like to be certain we're not up to mischief."

"Well, I'm damned! The deceitful brutes! Is that any way to treat gentlemen? And how the deuce did you know to look for it?"

"Oh, just caution," says he, offhand, but then he thought for a moment, and went on: "I know a little about such things, you see. When I was taken at Silistria, although I was officially with the Bashi-Bazouk people, I was more on the political side, really. I think the Russians know it, too. When they brought me up this way I was most carefully examined at first by some very shrewd gentlemen from their staff—I speak some Russian, you see. Oh, yes, my mother's family married in this direction, a few generations ago, and we had a sort of great-aunt who taught me enough to whet my interest. Anyway, on top of their suspicions of me, that accomplishment is enough to make 'em pay very close heed to H. East, Esq."

"It's an accomplishment you can pass on to me as fast as you like," says I. "But d'you mean they think you're a spy?"

"Oh, no, just worth watching—and listening to. They're the

most suspicious folk in the world, you know; trust no one, not even each other. And for all they're supposed to be thick-headed barbarians, they have some clever jokers among 'em."

Something made me ask: "D'you know a chap called Ignatieff—Count Ignatieff?"

"Do I not!" says he. "He was one of the fellows who ran the rule over me when I came up here. That's Captain Swing with blue blood, that one—why, d'you know him?"

I told him what had happened earlier in the day, and he whistled. "He was there to have a look and a word with you, you may depend on it. We must watch what we say, Flashman—not that our consciences aren't clear, but we may have some information that would be useful to them." He glanced about. "And we won't feed their suspicions by talking too much where they can't hear us. Another five minutes, and we'd better get back to the room. If we want to be private there, at any time, we'll hang a coat over their confounded tube—you may believe me, that works. But before we go in, I'll tell you, as quickly as I may, those things that are better said in the open air."

It struck me, he was a cool, assured hand, this East—of course, he had been all that as a boy, too.

"Count Pencherjevsky—an ogre, loud-mouthed, brutal, and a tyrant. He's a Cossack, who rose to command a hussar regiment in the army, won the Tsar's special favour, and retired here, away from his own tribal land. He rules his estate like a despot, treats his serfs abominably, and will surely have his throat cut one day. I can't abide him, and keep out of his way, although I sometimes dine with the family, for appearance's sake. But he's been decent enough, I'll admit; gives me the run of the place, a horse to ride, that sort of thing."

"Ain't they worried you might ride for it?" says I.

"Where to? We're two hundred miles north of the Crimea here, with nothing but naked country in between. Besides, the Count has a dozen or so of his old Cossacks in his service—they're all the guard anyone needs. Kubans, who could ride down anything on four legs. I saw them bring back four serfs who ran away, soon after I got here—they'd succeeded in travelling twenty miles before the Cossacks caught them. Those devils brought them back tied by the ankles and dragged behind their ponies—

the whole way!" He shuddered. "They were flayed to death in the first few miles!"

I felt my stomach give one of its little heaves. "But, anyway, those were serfs," says I. "They wouldn't do that sort of thing to—"

"Wouldn't they, though?" says he. "Well, perhaps not. But this ain't England, you know, or France, or even India. This is Russia—and these land-owners are no more accountable than . . . than a baron in the Middle Ages. Oh, I dare say he'd think twice about mishandling *us*—still, I'd think twice about getting on his wrong side. But, I say, I think we'd best go back, and treat 'em to some harmless conversation—if anyone's bothering to listen."

As we strolled back, I asked him a question which had been exercising me somewhat. "Who's the fair beauty I saw when I arrived?"

He went red as a poppy, and I thought, o-ho, what have we here, eh? Young Scud with lecherous notions—or pure Christian passion, I wonder which?

"That would be Valentina," says he, "the Count's daughter. She and her Aunt Sara—and an old deaf woman who is a cousin of sorts—are his only family. He is a widower." He cleared his throat nervously. "One sees very little of them, though—as I said, I seldom dine with the family. Valentina . . . ah . . . is married."

I found this vastly amusing—it was my guess that young Scud had gone wild about the little bundle—small blame to him—and like the holy little humbug he was, preferred to avoid her rather than court temptation. One of Arnold's shining young knights, he was. Well, lusty old Sir Lancelot Flashy had galloped into the lists now—too bad she had a husband, of course, but at least she'd be saddle-broken. At that, I'd have to see what her father was like, and how the land lay generally. One has to be careful about these things.

I met the family at dinner that afternoon, and a most fascinating occasion it turned out to be. Pencherjevsky was worth travelling a long way to see in himself—the first sight of him, standing at his table head, justified East's description of ogre, and made me think of Jack and the Beanstalk, and smelling the blood of

Englishmen, which was an unhappy notion, when you considered it.

He must have been well over six and a half feet tall, and even so, he was broad enough to appear squat. His head and face were just a mass of brown hair, trained to his shoulders and in a splendid beard that rippled down his chest. His eyes were fine, under huge shaggy brows, and the voice that came out of his beard was one of your thunderous Russian basses. He spoke French well, by the way, and you would never have guessed from the glossy colour of his hair, and the ease with which he moved his huge bulk, that he was over sixty. An enormous man, in every sense, not least in his welcome.

"The Colonel Flashman," he boomed. "Be happy in this house. As an enemy, I say, forget the quarrel for a season; as a soldier, I say, welcome, brother." He shook my hand in what was probably only the top joints of his enormous fingers, and crushed it till it cracked. "Aye—you look like a soldier, sir. I am told you fought in the disgraceful affair at Balaclava, where our cavalry were chased like the rabble they are. I salute you, and every good sabre who rode with you. Chased like rabbits, those *tuts** and *moujiks* on horseback. Aye, you would not have chased my Kubans so—or Vigenstein's Hussars²⁴ when I had command of them—no, by the great God!" He glowered down at me, rumbling, as though he would break into "Fee-fi-fo-fum" at any moment, and then released my hand and waved towards the two women seated at the table.

"My daughter Valla, my sister-in-law, Madam Sara." I bowed, and they inclined their heads and looked at me with that bold, appraising stare which Russian women use—they're not bashful or missish, those ladies. Valentina, or Valla, as her father called her, smiled and tossed her silver-blonde head—she was a plumply pert little piece, sure enough, but I spared a glance for Aunt Sara as well. She'd be a few years older than I, about thirty-five, perhaps, with dark, close-bound hair and one of those strong, masterful, chiselled faces—handsome, but not beautiful. She'd have a moustache in a few years, but she was well-built and tall, carrying her bounties before her.

For all that Pencherjevsky looked like Goliath, he had good

* Renegades.

taste—or whoever ordered his table and domestic arrangements had. The big dining-room, like all the apartments in the house, had a beautiful wood-tiled floor, there was a chandelier, and any amount of brocade and flowered silk about the furnishings. (Pencherjevsky himself, by the way, was dressed in silk: most Russian gentlemen wear formal clothes as we do, more or less, but he affected a magnificent shimmering green tunic, clasped at the waist by a silver-buckled belt, and silk trousers of the same colour tucked into soft leather boots—a most striking costume, and comfortable too, I should imagine.)

The food was good, to my relief—a fine soup being followed by fried fish, a ragout of beef, and side-dishes of poultry and game of every variety, with little sweet cakes and excellent coffee. The wine was indifferent, but drinkable. Between the vittles, the four fine bosoms displayed across the table, and Pencherjevsky's conversation, it was a most enjoyable meal.

He questioned me about Balaclava, most minutely, and when I had satisfied his curiosity, astonished me by rapidly sketching how the Russian cavalry should have been handled, with the aid of cutlery, which he clashed about on the table to demonstrate. He knew his business, no doubt of it, but he was full of admiration for our behaviour, and Scarlett's particularly.

"Great God, there is an English Cossack!" says he. "Uphill, eh? I like him! I like him! Let him be captured, dear Lord, and sent to Starotorsk, so that I can keep him forever, and talk, and fight old battles, and shout at each other like good companions!"

"And get drunk nightly, and be carried to bed!" says Miss Valla, pertly—they enter into talk with the men, you know, these Russian ladies, with a freedom that would horrify our own polite society. And they drink, too—I noticed that both of them went glass for glass with us, without becoming more than a trifle merry.

"That, too, *golubashka*," says Pencherjevsky. "Can he drink, then, this Scarlett? Of course, of course he must! All good horse-soldiers can, eh, colonel? Not like your Sasha, though," says he to Valla, with a great wink at me. "Can you imagine, colonel, I have a son-in-law who cannot drink? He fell down at his wedding, on this very floor—yes, over there, by God!—after what? A glass or two of vodka! Saint Nicholas! Aye, me—how I must have offended the Father God, to have a son-in-law who cannot drink, and does not get me grandchildren."

At this Valla gave a most unladylike snort, and tossed her head, and Aunt Sara, who said very little as a rule, I discovered, set down her glass and observed tartly that Sasha could hardly get children while he was away fighting in the Crimea.

"Fighting?" cries Pencherjevsky, boisterously. "Fighting—in the horse artillery? Whoever saw one of them coming home on a stretcher? I would have had him in the Bug Lancers, or even the Moscow Dragoons, but—body of St Sofia!—he doesn't *ride* well! A fine son-in-law for a Zaporozhiyan *hetman*,* that!"

"Well, dear father!" snaps Valla. "If he had ridden well, and been in the lancers or the dragoons, it is odds the English cavalry would have cut him into little pieces—since you were not there to direct operations!"

"Small loss that would have been," grumbles he, and then leaned over, laughing, and rumpled her blonde hair. "There, little one, he is your man—such as he is. God send him safe home."

I tell you all this to give you some notion of a Russian country gentleman at home, with his family—although I'll own that a Cossack may not be typical. No doubt he wasn't to East's delicate stomach—and I gather he didn't care for East too much, either—but I found myself liking Pencherjevsky. He was gross, loud, boisterous—boorish, if you like, but he was worth ten of your proper gentlemen, to me at any rate. I got roaring drunk with him, that evening, after the ladies had retired—they were fairly tipsy, themselves, and arguing at the tops of their voices about dresses as they withdrew to their drawing-room—and he sang Russian hunting songs in that glorious organ voice, and laughed himself sick trying to learn the words of "The British Grenadiers". I flatter myself he took to me enormously—folk often do, of course, particularly the coarser spirits—for he swore I was a credit to my regiment and my country, and God should send the Tsar a few like me.

"Then we should sweep you English bastards into the sea!" he roared. "A few of your Scarletts and Flashmans and Carragans—that is the name, no?—that is all we need!"

But drunk as he was, when he finally rose from the table he

* Leader.

was careful to turn in the direction of the church, and cross himself devoutly, before stumbling to guide me up the stairs.

I was to see a different side to Pencherjevsky—and to all of them for that matter—in the winter that followed, but for the first few weeks of my sojourn at Starotorsk I thoroughly enjoyed myself, and felt absolutely at home. It was so much better than I had expected, the Count was so amiable in his bear-like, thundering way, his ladies were civil (for I'd decided to go warily before attempting a more intimate acquaintance with Valla) and easy with me, and East and I were allowed such freedom, that it was like a month of week-ends at an English country-house, without any of the stuffiness. You could come and go as you pleased, treat the place as your own, attend at meal-times or feed in your chamber, whichever suited—it was Liberty Hall, no error. I divided my days between working really hard at my Russian, going for walks or rides with Valla and Sara or East, prosing with the Count in the evenings, playing cards with the family—they have a form of whist called "biritsch" which has caught on in England this last few years, and we played that most evenings —and generally taking life easy. My interest in Russian they found especially flattering, for they are immensely proud and sensitive about their country, and I made even better progress than usual. I soon spoke and understood it better than East— "He has a Cossack somewhere in his family!" Pencherjevsky would bawl. "Let him add a beard to those foolish English whiskers and he can ride with the Kubans—eh, colonel?"

All mighty pleasant—until you discovered that the civility and good nature were no deeper than a May frost, the thin covering on totally alien beings. For all their apparent civilization, and even good taste, the barbarian was just under the surface, and liable to come raging out. It was easy to forget this, until some word or incident reminded you—that this pleasant house and estate were like a medieval castle, under feudal law; that this jovial, hospitable giant, who talked so knowledgably of cavalry tactics and the hunting field, and played chess like a master, was also as dangerous and cruel as a cannibal chief; that his ladies, chattering cheerfully about French dressmaking or flower arrangement, were in some respects rather less feminine than Dahomey Amazons.

One such incident I'll never forget. There was an evening when the four of us were in the salon, Pencherjevsky and I playing chess—he had handicapped himself by starting without queen or castle, to make a game of it—and the women at some two-handed game of cards across the room. Aunt Sara was quiet, as usual, and Valla prattling gaily, and squeaking with vexation when she lost. I wasn't paying much attention, for I was happy with the Count's brandy, and looked like beating him for once, too, but when I heard them talking about settling the wager I glanced across, and almost fell from my chair.

Valla's maid and the housekeeper had come into the room. The maid—a serf girl—was kneeling by the card table, and the housekeeper was carefully shearing off her long red hair with a pair of scissors. Aunt Sara was watching idly; Valla wasn't even noticing until the house-keeper handed her the tresses.

"Ah, how pretty!" says she, and shrugged, and tossed them over to Aunt Sara, who stroked them, and said:

"Shall I keep them for a wig, or sell them? Thirty roubles in Moscow or St Petersburg." And she held them up in the light, considering.

"More than Vera is worth now, at any rate," says Valla, carelessly. Then she jumped up, ran across to Pencherjevsky, and put her arms round his shaggy neck from behind, blowing in his ear. "Father, may I have fifty roubles for a new maid?"

"What's that?" says he, deep in the game. "Wait, child, wait; I have this English rascal trapped, if only ..."

"Just fifty roubles, father. See, I cannot keep Vera now."

He looked up, saw the maid, who was still kneeling, cropped like a convict, and guffawed. "She doesn't need hair to hang up your dresses and fetch your shoes, does she? Learn to count your aces, you silly girl."

"Oh, father! You know she will not do now! Only fifty roubles —please—from my kind little *batiushka!*"*

"Ah, plague take you, can a man not have peace? Fifty roubles, then, to be let alone. And next time, bet something that I will not have to replace out of my purse." He pinched her cheek. "Check, colonel."

I've a strong stomach, as you know, but I'll admit that turned

* Father.

it—not the disfigurement of a pretty girl, you understand, although I didn't hold with that, much, but the cheerful unconcern with which they did it—those two cultured ladies, in that elegant room, as though they had been gaming for sweets or counters. And now Valla was leaning on her father's shoulder, gaily urging him on to victory, and Sara was running the hair idly through her hands, while the kneeling girl bowed her pathetically shorn head to the floor and then followed the housekeeper from the room. Well, thinks I, they'd be a rage in London society, these two. You may have noticed, by the way, that the cost of a maid was fifty roubles, of which her hair was worth thirty.

Of course, they didn't think of her as human. I've told you something of the serfs already, and most of that I learned first-hand on the Pencherjevsky estate, where they were treated as something worse than cattle. The more fortunate of them lived in the outbuildings and were employed about the house, but most of them were down in the village, a filthy, straggling place of log huts, called *isbas*, with entrances so low you had to stoop to go in. They were foul, verminous hovels, consisting of just one room, with a huge bed bearing many pillows, a big stove, and a "holy corner" in which there were poor, garish pictures of their saints.

Their food was truly fearful—rye bread for the most part, and cabbage soup with a lump of fat in it, salt cabbage, garlic stew, coarse porridge, and for delicacies, sometimes a little cucumber or beetroot. And those were the well-fed ones. Their drink was as bad—bread fermented in alcohol which they call *qvass* ("it's black, it's thick, and it makes you drunk," as they said), and on special occasions vodka, which is just poison. They'll sell their souls for brandy, but seldom get it.

Such conditions of squalor, half the year in stifling heat, half in unimaginable cold, and all spent in back-breaking labour, are probably enough to explain why they were such an oppressed, dirty, brutish, useless people—just like the Irish, really, but without the gaiety. Even the Mississippi niggers were happier—there was never a smile on the face of your serf, just patient, morose misery.

And yet that wasn't the half of their trouble. I remember the court that Pencherjevsky used to hold in a barn at the back of the house, and those cringing creatures crawling on their bellies along the floor to kiss the edge of his coat, while he pronounced sentence on them for their offences. You may not believe them, but they're true, and I noted them at the time.

There was the local dog-killer—every Russian village is plagued in winter by packs of wild dogs, who are a real danger to life, and this fellow had to chase and club them to death—he got a few kopecks for each pelt. But he had been shirking his job, it seemed.

"Forty strokes of the cudgel," says Pencherjevsky. And then he added: "Siberia," at which a great wail went up from the crowd trembling at the far end of the barn. One of the Cossacks just lashed at them with his *nagaika*,* and the wail died.

There was an iron collar for a woman whose son had run off, and floggings, either with the cudgel or the whip, for several who had neglected their labouring in Pencherjevsky's fields. There was Siberia for a youth employed to clean windows at the house, who had started work too early and disturbed Valla, and for one of the maids who had dropped a dish. You will say, "Ah, here's Flashy pulling the long bow", but I'm not, and if you don't believe me, ask any professor of Russian history.[25]

But here's the point—if you'd suggested to Pencherjevsky or his ladies, or even to the serfs, that such punishments were cruel, they'd have thought you were mad. It seemed the most natural thing in the world to them—why, I've seen a man cudgelled by the Cossacks in Pencherjevsky's courtyard—tied to a post half-naked in the freezing weather, and smashed with heavy rods until he was a moaning lump of bruised and broken flesh, with half his ribs cracked—and through it all Valla was standing not ten yards away, never even glancing in his direction, but discussing a new sledge-harness with one of the grooms.

Pencherjevsky absolutely believed that his *moujiks* were well off. "Have I not given them a stone church, with a blue dome and gilt stars? How many villages can show the like, eh?" And when those he had condemned to years of exile in Siberia were driven off in a little coffle under the *nagaikas* of the Cossacks—they would be taken to the nearest town, to join other unfortunates,

* Cossack whip.

138

and they would all *walk* the whole way—he was there to give them his blessing, and they would embrace his knees, crying: "*Izvenete, batiushka, veno vat,*"* and he would nod and say "*Horrosho,*"† while the housekeeper gave them bundles of dainties from the "*Sudarinia*‡ Valla". God knows what they were —cucumber rinds, probably.

"From me they have strict justice, under the law," says this amazing gorilla. "And they love me for it. Has anyone ever seen the knout, or the *butuks,*§ used on my estate? No, and never shall. If I correct them, it is because without correction they will become idle and shiftless, and ruin me—and themselves. For without me, where are they? These poor souls, they believe the world rests on three whales swimming in the Eternal Sea! What are you to do with such folk? I will meet with the best, the wisest of them, the spokesman of their *gromada,*¶ driving his *droshky.*‖ 'Ha, Ivan,' I will say, 'your axles squeal; why do you not grease them?' And he ponders, and replies, 'Only a thief is afraid to make a noise, *batiushka.*' So the axles remain ungreased—unless I cudgel his foolish head, or have the Cossacks whip and salt his back for him. And he respects me"—he would thump his great fist on his thigh as he said it—"because he knows I am a bread and salt man, and go with my neck open, as he does.[26] And I am just—to the inch."

And you may say he was: when he flogged his *dvornik*** for insolence, and the fellow collapsed before the prescribed punishment was finished, they sent him to the local quack—and when he was better, gave him the remaining strokes. "Who would trust me again, if I excused him a single blow?" says Pencherjevsky.

Now, I don't recite all these barbarities to shock or excite your pity, or to pose as one of those holy hypocrites who pretend to be in a great sweat about man's inhumanity to man. I've seen too much of it, and know it happens wherever strong folk have absolute power over spiritless creatures. I merely tell you truly what I saw—as for my own view, well, I'm all for keeping the peasants in order, and if hammering 'em does good, and makes life better for

---

* Pardon, father, I am guilty.   † Very well.
‡ Lady.   § Press for crushing feet.
¶ Village assembly.   ‖ Gig.   ** Porter.

the rest of us, you won't find me leaping between the tyrant and his victim crying "Stay, cruel despot!" But I would observe that much of the cruelty I saw in Russia was pure senseless brutishness—I doubt if they even enjoyed it much. They just knew no better.

I wondered sometimes why the serfs, dull, ignorant, superstitious clods though they were, endured it. The truth, as I learned it from Pencherjevsky, was that they didn't, always. In the thirty years just ending when I was in Russia, there had been peasant revolts once every fortnight, in one part of the country or another, and as often as not it had taken the military to put them down. Or rather, it had taken the Cossacks, for the Russian army was a useless thing, as we'd seen in the Crimea. You can't make soldiers out of slaves. But the Cossacks were free, independent tribesmen; they had land, and paid little tax, had their own tribal laws, drank themselves stupid, and served the Tsar from boyhood till they were fifty because they loved to ride and fight and loot—and they liked nothing better than to use their *nagaikas* on the serfs, which was just nuts to them.

Pencherjevsky wasn't worried about revolution among his own *moujiks* because, as I say, he regarded himself as a good master. Also he had Cossacks of his own to strike terror into any malcontents. "And I never commit the great folly," says he. "I never touch a serf-woman—or allow one to be used or sold as a concubine." (Whether he said it for my benefit or not, it was bad news, for I hadn't had a female in ages, and some of the peasants —like Valla's maid—were not half bad-looking once they were washed.) "These uprisings on other estates—look into them, and I'll wager every time the master has ravished some serf wench, or stolen a *moujik's* wife, or sent a young fellow into the army so that he can enjoy his sweetheart. They don't like it, I tell you— and I don't blame them! If a lord wants a woman, let him marry one, or buy one from far afield—but let him slake his lust on one of his own serf-women, and he'll wake up one fine morning with a split head and his roof on fire. And serve him right!"

I gathered he was unusual in this view: most landlords just used the serf-wenches the way American owners used their nigger girls, and pupped 'em all over the place. But Pencherjevsky had his own code, and believed his *moujiks* thought the better of him for it, and were content. I wondered if he wasn't gammoning himself.

Because I paid attention, toady-like, to his proses, and was eager in studying his language, he assumed I was interested in his appalling country and its ways, and was at pains to educate me, as he saw it. From him I learned of the peculiar laws governing the serfs—how they might be free if they could run away for ten years, how some of them were allowed to leave the estates and work in the towns, provided they sent a proportion of earnings to their master; how some of these serfs became vastly rich—richer than their masters, sometimes, and worth millions—but still could not buy their freedom unless he wished. Some serfs even owned serfs. It was an idiotic system, of course, but the landowners were all for it, and even the humanitarian ones believed that if it were changed, and political reforms allowed, the country would dissolve in anarchy. I daresay they were right, but myself I believe it will happen anyway; it was starting even then, as Pencherjevsky admitted.

"The agitators are never idle," says he. "You have heard of the pernicious German-Jew, Marx?" (I didn't like to tell him Marx had been at my wedding, as an uninvited guest.*) "He vomits his venom over Europe—aye, he and other vile rascals like him would spread their poison even to our country if they could.[27] Praise God the *moujiks* are unlettered folk—but they can hear, and our cities crawl with revolutionary criminals of the lowest stamp. What do they understand of Russia, these filth? What do they seek to do but ruin her? And yet countries like your own give harbour to such creatures, to brew their potions of hate against us! Aye, and against you, too, if you could only see it! You think to encourage them, for the downfall of your enemies, but you will reap the wild wind also, Colonel Flashman!"

"Well, you know, Count," says I, "we let chaps say what they like, pretty well, always have done. We don't have any *kabala*,† like you—don't seem to need it, for some reason. Probably because we have factories, and so on, and everyone's kept busy, don't you know? I don't doubt all you say is true—but it suits us, you see. And our *moujiks* are, well, different from yours." I

* See *Royal Flash*.   † Slavery.

wondered, even as I said it, if they were; remembering that hospital at Yalta, I doubted it. But I couldn't help adding: "Would your *moujiks* have ridden into the battery at Balaclava?"

At this he roared with laughter, and called me an evil English rascal, and clapped me on the back. We were mighty close, he and I, really, when I look back—but of course, he never really knew me.

So you see what kind of man he was, and what kind of a place it was. Most of the time, I liked it—it was a fine easy life until, as I say, you got an unpleasant reminder of what an alien, brooding hostile land it was. It was frightening then, and I had to struggle to make myself remember that England and London and Elspeth still existed, that far away to the south Cardigan was still croaking "Haw-haw" and Raglan was fussing in the mud at Sevastopol. I would look out of my window sometimes, at the snow-frosted garden, and beyond it the vast, white, endless plain, streaked only by the dark field-borders, and it seemed the old world was just a dream. It was easy then, to get the Russian melancholy, which sinks into the bones, and is born of a knowledge of helplessness far from home.

The thing that bored me most, needless to say, was being without a woman. I tried my hand with Valla, when we got to know each other and I had decided she wasn't liable to run squealing to her father. By George, she didn't need to. I gave her bottom a squeeze, and she laughed at me and told me she was a respectable married woman; taking this as an invitation I embraced her, at which she wriggled and giggled, puss-like, and then hit me an atrocious clout in the groin with her clenched fist, and ran off, laughing. I walked with a crouch for days, and decided that these Russian ladies must be treated with respect.

East felt the boredom of captivity in that white wilderness more than I, and spent long hours in his room, writing. One day when he was out I had a turn through his papers, and discovered he was writing his impressions, in the form of an endless letter to his odious friend Brown, who was apparently farming in New Zealand. There was some stuff about me in it, which I read with interest:

". . . I don't know what to think of Flashman. He is very well liked by all in the house, the Count especially, and I fear that little

Valla admires him, too—it would be hard not to, I suppose, for he is such a big, handsome fellow. (Good for you, Scud; carry on.) I say I fear—because sometimes I see him looking at her, with such an ardent expression, and I remember the kind of brute he was at Rugby, and my heart sinks for her fair innocence. Oh, I trust I am wrong! I tell myself that he has changed—how else did the mean, cowardly, spiteful, bullying toady (steady, now, young East) become the truly brave and valiant soldier that he now undoubtedly is? But I *do* fear, just the same; I know he does not pray, and that he swears, and has evil thoughts, and that the cruel side of his nature is still there. Oh, my poor little Valla— but there, old fellow, I mustn't let my dark suspicions run away with me. I must think well of him, and trust that my prayers will help to keep him true, and that he will prove, despite my doubts, to be an upright, Christian gentleman at last."

You know, the advantage to being a wicked bastard is that everyone pesters the Lord on your behalf; if volume of prayers from my saintly enemies means anything, I'll be saved when the Archbishop of Canterbury is damned. It's a comforting thought.

So time passed, and Christmas came and went, and I was slipping into a long, bored tranquil snooze as the months went by. And I was getting soft, and thoroughly off guard, and all the time hell was preparing to break loose.

It was shortly before "the old wives' winter", as the Russians call February, that Valla's husband came home for a week's furlough. He was an amiable, studious little chap, who got on well with East, but the Count plainly didn't like him, and once he had given us the news from Sevastopol—which was that the siege was still going on, and getting nowhere, which didn't surprise me—old Pencherjevsky just ignored him, and retired moodily to his study and took to drink. He had me in to help him, too, and I caught him giving me odd, thoughtful looks, which was disconcerting, and growling to himself before topping up another bumper of brandy, and drinking sneering toasts to "the blessed happy couple", as he called them.

Then, exactly a week after Valla's husband had gone back— with no very fond leave-taking from his little spouse, it seemed to me—I was sitting yawning in the salon over a Russian novel, when Aunt Sara came in, and asked if I was bored. I was mildly surprised, for she seldom said much, or addressed one directly. She looked me up and down, with no expression on that fine horse face, and then said abruptly:

"What you need is a Russian steam-bath. It is the sovereign remedy against our long winters. I have told the servants to make it ready. Come."

I was idle enough to be game for anything, so I put on my *tulup*,* and followed her to one of the farthest outbuildings, beyond the house enclosure; it was snowing like hell, but a party of the servants had a great fire going under a huge grille out in the snow, and Aunt Sara took me inside to show me how the thing worked. It was a big log structure, divided down the middle by a high partition, and in the half where we stood was a raised wooden slab, like a butcher's block, surrounded by a trench in the floor. Presently the serfs came in, carrying on metal stretchers great glowing stones which they laid in the trench; the heat was terrific, and Aunt Sara explained to me that you lay on the slab, naked, while the minions outside poured cold water through openings at the base of the wall, which exploded into steam when it touched the stones.

"This side is for men-folk," says she. "Women are through there"—and she pointed to a gap in the partition. "Your clothes go in the sealed closet on the wall, and when you are ready you lie motionless on the slab, and allow the steam to envelope you." She gave me her bored stare. "The door is bolted from within." And off she went, to the other side of the partition.

Well, it was something new, so I undressed and lay on the slab, Aunt Sara called out presently from beyond the partition, and the water came in like Niagara. It hissed and splashed on the stones, and in a twinkling the place was like London fog, choking, scalding, and blotting you in, and you lay there gasping while it sweated into you, turning you scarlet. It was hellish hot and clammy, but not unpleasant, and I lay soaking in it; by and by they pumped in more water, the steam gushed up again, and I was turning over drowsily on my face when Aunt Sara's voice spoke unexpectedly at my elbow.

"Lie still," says she, and peering through the mist, I saw that she was wrapped in a clinging sheet, with her long, dark hair

* Sheepskin coat.

144

hanging in wet strands on either side of that strong, impassive face. I suddenly choked with what East would have called dark thoughts; she was carrying a bunch of long birch twigs, and as she laid a hot, wet hand on my shoulder she muttered huskily: "This is the true benefit of the baths; do not move."

And then, in that steam-heat, she began to birch me, very lightly at first, up the backs of my legs and to my shoulders, and then back again, harder and harder all the time, until I began to yelp. More steam came belching up, and she turned me over and began work on my chest and stomach. I was fairly interested by now, for mildly painful though it was, it was distinctly stimulating.

"Now, for me," says she, and motioned me to get up and take the birches. "Russian ladies often use nettles," says she, and for once her voice was unsteady. "I prefer the birch—it is stronger." And in a twinkling she was out of her sheet and face down on the slab. I was having a good gloat down at that long, strong, naked body, when the damned serfs blotted everything out with steam again, so I lashed away through the murk, belabouring her vigorously; she began to moan and gasp, and I went at it like a man possessed, laying on so that the twigs snapped, and as the steam cleared again she rolled over on her back, mouth open and eyes staring, and reached out to seize hold of me, pumping away at me and gasping:

"Now! Now! For me! *Pajalsta!* I must have! Now! *Pajalsta!*"

Now, I can recognize a saucy little flirt when I see one, so I gave her a few last thrashes and leaped aboard, nearly bursting. God, it must have been months—so in my perversity, I had to tease her, until she dragged me down, sobbing and scratching at my back, and we whaled away on that wet slab, with the steam thundering round us, and she writhed and grappled fit to dislocate herself, until I began to fear we would slither off on to the hot stones. And when I lay there, utterly done, she slipped away and doused me with a bucket of cold water—what with one thing and another, I wonder I survived that bath.

Mind you, I felt better for it; barbarians they may be, but the Russians have some excellent institutions, and I remain grateful to Sara—undoubtedly my favourite aunt.

I supposed, in my vanity, that she had just proposed our steam-bath romp to help pass the winter, but there was another reason, as I discovered the following day. It was a bizarre, unbelievable thing, really, to people like you and me, but in feudal Russia— well, I shall tell you.

It was after the noon meal that Pencherjevsky invited me to go riding with him. This wasn't unusual, but his manner was; he was curt and silent as we rode—if it had been anyone but this hulking tyrant, I'd have said he was nervous. We rode some distance from the house, and were pacing our beasts through the silent snow-fields, when he suddenly began to talk—about the Cossacks, of all things. He rambled most oddly at first, about how they rode with bent knees, like jockeys (which I'd noticed anyway), and how you could tell a Ural Cossack from the Black Sea variety because one wore a sheepskin cap and the other the long string-haired bonnet. And how the flower of the flock were his own people, the Zaporozhiyan Cossacks, or Kubans, who had been moved east to new lands near Azov by the Empress generations ago, but *he*, Pencherjevsky, had come back to the old stamping-ground, and here he would stay, by God, and his family after him forever.

"The old days are gone," says he, and I see him so clearly still, that huge bulk in his sheepskin *tulup*, hunched in his saddle, glowering with moody, unseeing eyes across the white wilderness, with the blood-red disc of the winter sun behind him. "The day of the great Cossack, when we thumbed our noses at Tsar and Sultan alike, and carried our lives and liberty on our lance-points. We owed loyalty to none but our comrades and the *hetman* we elected to lead us—I was such a one. Now it is a new Russia, and instead of the *hetman* we have rulers from Moscow to govern the tribe. So be it. I make my place here, in my forefathers' land, I have my good estate, my *moujiks*, my land—the inheritance for the son I never sired." He looked at me. "I would have had one like you, a tall lancer fit to ride at the head of his own *sotnia*.* You have a son, eh? A sturdy fellow? Good. I could wish it were not so—that you had no wife in England, no son, nothing to bind you or call you home. I would say to you then: 'Stay with us here. Be as a son to me. Be a husband to my daughter, and get yourself a son, and me a grandson, who will follow

* Company, band.

146

after us, and hold our land here, in this new Russia, this empire born of storm, where only a man who is a man can hope to plant himself and his seed and endure.' That is what I would say."

Well, it was flattering, no question, although I might have pointed out to him that Valla had a husband already, and even if I'd been free and willing . . . but it occurred to me that he probably wasn't the man to let a little thing like that stand in the way. Morrison may not have been much of a father-in-law, but this chap would have been less comfortable still.

"As it is," he growled on, "I have a son-in-law—you saw what kind of a thing he is. God knows how any daughter of mine could . . . but there. I have doted on her, and indulged her, for her dear mother's sake—aye, and because I love her. And if he was the last man I would have chosen for her—well, she cared for him, and I thought, their sons will have my blood, they may be Cossacks, horse-and-lance men, grandchildren to be proud of. But I have no grandsons—*he* gets me none!"

And he growled and spat and then swung round to face me. For a moment he wrestled with his tongue, and couldn't speak, and then it came out in a torrent.

"There must be a *man* to follow me here! I am too old now, there are no children left in me, or I would marry again. Valla, my lovely child, is my one hope—but she is tied to this . . . this empty thing, and I see her going childless to her grave. Unless . . ." He was gnawing at his lip, and his face was terrific. "Unless . . . she can bear me a grandson. It is all I have to live for! To see a Pencherjevsky who will take up this inheritance when I am gone—be his father who he will, so long as he is a man! It cannot be her husband, so . . . If it is an offence against God, against the Church, against the law—I am a Cossack, and we were here before God or the Church or the law! I do not care! I will see a male grandchild of mine to carry my line, my name, my land—and if I burn in hell for it, I shall count it worth the cost! At least a Pencherjevsky shall rule here—what I have built will not be squandered piecemeal among the rabble of that fellow's knock-kneed relatives! A man shall get my Valla a son!"

I'm not slow on the uptake, even with a bearded baboon nearly seven feet tall roaring at my face from a few inches away, and what I understood from this extraordinary outburst simply took my breath away. I'm all for family, you understand, but I doubt if I have the dynastic instinct as strong as all that.

"You are such a man," says he, and suddenly he edged his horse even closer, and crushed my arm in his enormous paw. "You can get sons—you have done so," he croaked, his livid face beside mine. "You have a child in England—and Sara has proved you also. When the war is over, you will leave here, and go to England, far away. No one will ever know—but you and I!"

I found my voice, and said something about Valla.

"She is my daughter," says he, and his voice rasped like an iron file. "She knows what this means to the house of Pencherjevsky. She obeys." And for the first time he smiled, a dreadful, crooked grin through his beard. "From what Sara tells me, she may be happy to obey. As for you, it will be no hardship. And"—he took me by the shoulder, rocking me in the saddle—"it may be worth much or little, but hereafter you may call Pencherjevsky from the other side of hell, and he will come to your side!"

If it was an extraordinary proposition, I won't pretend it was unwelcome. Spooky, of course, but immensely flattering, after all. And you only had to imagine, for a split second, what Pencherjevsky's reaction would have been to a polite refusal—I say no more.

"It will be a boy," says he, "I know it. And if by chance it is a girl—then she shall have a *man* for a husband, if I have to rake the world for him!"

An impetuous fellow, this Count—it never occurred to him that it might be his little Valla who was barren, and not her husband. However, that was not for me to say, so I kept mum, and left all the arrangements to papa.

He did it perfectly, no doubt with the connivance of that lustful slut Sara—there was a lady who took pleasure in her experimental work, all right. I sallied forth at midnight, and feeling not unlike a prize bull at the agricultural show—"'ere 'e is, ladies'n' gennlemen, Flashman Buttercup the Twenty-first of Horny Bottom Farm"—tip-toed out of the corridor where my room and East's lay, and set off on the long promenade to the other wing. It was ghostly in that creaky old house, with not a soul about, but true love spurred me on, and sure enough Valla's door was ajar, with a little sliver of light lancing across the passage floor.

I popped in—and she was kneeling beside the bed, praying! I didn't know whether it was for forgiveness for the sin of adultery, or for the sin to be committed successfully, and I didn't stop to ask. There's no point in talking, or hanging back shuffling on these occasions, and saying: "Ah . . . well, shall we . . .?" On the other hand, one doesn't go roaring and ramping at respectable married women, so I stooped and kissed her very gently, drew off her nightdress, and eased her on to the bed. I felt her plump little body trembling under my hands, so I kissed her long and carefully, fondling her and murmuring nonsense in her ear, and then her arms went round my neck.

Frankly, I think the Count had under-estimated her horse artillery husband, for she had learned a great deal from somewhere. I'd been prepared for her to be reluctant, or to need some jollying along, but she entered into the spirit of the thing like a tipsy widow, and it was from no sense of duty or giving the house of Pencherjevsky its money's worth that I stayed until past four o'clock. I do love a bouncy blonde with a hearty appetite, and when I finally crawled back to my own chilly bed it was with the sense of an honest night's work well done.

But if a job is worth doing, it's worth doing well, and since there seemed to be an unspoken understanding that the treatment should be continued, I made frequent forays to Valla's room in the ensuing nights. And so far as I'm a judge, the little baggage revelled in being a dutiful daughter—they're a damned randy lot, these Russians. Something to do with the cold weather, I dare say. A curious thing was, I soon began to feel as though we were truly married, and no doubt this had something to do with the purpose behind our night games; yet during the day we remained on the same easy terms as before, and if Sara grudged her niece the pleasuring she was getting, she never let on. Pencherjevsky said nothing, but from time to time I would catch him eyeing us with sly satisfaction, fingering his beard at the table head.

East suspected something, I'm certain. His manner to me became nervous, and he avoided the family's society even more than before, but he didn't dare say anything. Too scared of finding his suspicions well grounded, I suppose.

The only fly in the ointment that I could see was the possibility that during the months ahead it might become apparent that I was labouring in vain; however, I was ready to face Pencherjevsky's disappointment when and if it came. Valla's yawns at breakfast were proof that I was doing my share manfully. And then something happened which made the whole speculation pointless.

From time to time in the first winter months there had been other guests at the big house of Starotorsk: military ones. The nearest township—where I'd encountered Ignatieff—was an important army head-quarters, a sort of staging post for the Crimea, but as there was no decent accommodation in the place, the more important wayfarers were in the habit of putting up with Pencherjevsky. On these occasions East and I were politely kept in our rooms, with a Cossack posted in the corridor, and our meals sent up on trays, but we saw some of the comings and goings from our windows—Liprandi, for example, and a grandee with a large military staff whom East said was Prince Worontzoff. After one such visit it was obvious to both of us that some sort of military conference had been held in the Count's library—you could *smell* it the next morning, and there was a big map easel leaned up in a corner that hadn't been there before.

"We should keep our eyes and ears open," says East to me later. "Do you know—if we could have got out of our rooms when that confabulation was going on, we might have crept into the old gallery up yonder, and heard all kinds of useful intelligence."

This was a sort of screened minstrel's gallery that overlooked the library; you got into it by a little door off the main landing. But it was no welcome suggestion to me, as you can guess, who am all for lying low.

"Rot!" says I. "We ain't spies—and if we were, and the whole Russian general staff were to blab their plans within earshot, what could we do with the knowledge?"

"Who knows—" says he, looking keen. "That Cossack they put to watch our doors sleeps half the night—did you know? Reeking of brandy. We could get out, I daresay—I tell you what,

Flashman, if another high ranker comes this way, I think we're bound to try and overhear him, if we can. It's our duty."

"Duty?" says I, alarmed. "Duty to eavesdrop? What kind of company have you been keeping lately? I can't see Raglan, or any other honourable man, thinking much of that sort of conduct." The high moral line, you see; deuced handy sometimes. "Why, we're as good as guests in this place."

"We're prisoners," says he, "and we haven't given any parole. Any information we can come by is a legitimate prize of war—and if we heard anything big enough it might even be worth trying a run for it. We're not that far from the Crimea."

This was appalling. Wherever you go, however snug you may have made yourself, there is always one of these duty-bound, energetic bastards trying to make trouble. The thought of spying on the Russians, and then lighting out in the snow some dark night, with Pencherjevsky's Cossacks after us—my imagination was in full flight in a trice, while Scud stood chewing his lip, muttering his thoughtful lunacies. I didn't argue—it would have looked bad, as though I weren't as eager to strike a blow for Britannia as he was. And it wasn't even worth talking about—we weren't going to get the chance to spy, or escape, or do anything foolish. I'd have given a thousand to one on that—which, as it turned out, would have been very unwise odds to offer.

However, after that small discussion the weeks had slipped by without any other important Russians visiting the place, and then came my diversion with Valla, and East's ridiculous daydream went clean out of my mind. And then, about ten days after I had started galloping her, a couple of Ruski staff captains jingled into the courtyard one morning, to be followed by a large horse-sled, and shortly afterwards comes the Count's major-domo to East and me, presenting his apologies, and chivvying us off to our rooms.

We took the precaution of muffling the hidden speaking-tube, and kept a good watch from East's window that day. We saw more sleds arrive, and from the distant hum of voices in the house and the sound of tramping on the stairs we realized there must be a fair-sized party in the place. East was all excited, but what really stirred him was when a sled arrived late in the afternoon, and Pencherjevsky himself was in the yard to meet it—attired as we'd never seen him before, in full dress uniform.

"This is important," says East, his eyes alight. "Depend upon it, that's some really big wig. Gad! I'd give a year's pay to hear what passes below tonight." He was white with excitement. "Flashman, I'm going to have a shot at it!"

"You're crazy," says I. "With a Cossack mooching about the passage all night? You say he sleeps—he can wake up, too, can't he?"

"I'll chance that," says he, and for all I could try—appeals to his common sense, to his position as a guest, to his honour as an officer (I think I even invoked Arnold and religion) he remained set.

"Well, don't count on me," I told him. "It ain't worth it—they won't be saying anything worth a damn—it ain't safe, and by thunder, it's downright ungentlemanly. So now!"

To my surprise, he patted my arm. "I respect what you say, old fellow," says he. "But—I can't help it. I may be wrong, but I see my duty differently, don't you understand? I know it's St Paul's to a pub it'll be a fool's errand, but—well, you never know. And I'm not like you—I haven't done much for Queen and country. I'd like to try."

Well, there was nothing for it but to get my head under the bed-clothes that night and snore like hell, to let the world know that Flashy wasn't up to mischief. Neither, it transpired, was the bold East: he reported next day that the Cossack had stayed awake all night, so his expedition had to be called off. But the sleds stayed there all day, and the next, and they kept us cooped up all the time, and the Cossack remained vigilant, to East's mounting frenzy.

"Three days!" says he. "Who can it be, down there? I tell you, it must be some important meeting! I *know* it! And we have to sit here, like mice in a cage, when if we could only get out for an hour, we might find out something that would—oh, I don't know, but it might be vital to the war! It's enough to drive a chap out of his wits!"

"It already has," says I. "You haven't been shut up like this before, have you? Well, I've been a prisoner more times than I care to think of, and I can tell you, after a while you don't reason straight any longer. That's what's wrong with you. Also, you're tired out; get to sleep tonight, and forget this nonsense."

He fretted away, though, and I was almost out of patience with him by dinner-time, when who should come up with the servants bearing dinner, but Valla. She had just dropped in to see us, she said, and was very bright, and played a three-handed card game with us, which was a trying one for East, I could see. He was jumpy as a cat with her at the best of times, blushing and falling over his feet, and now in addition he was fighting to keep from asking her what was afoot downstairs, and who the visitors were. She prattled on, till about nine, and then took her leave, and as I held the door for her she gave me a glance and a turn of her pretty blonde head that said, as plain as words: "It's been three nights now. Well?" I went back to my room next door, full of wicked notions, and leaving East yawning and brooding.

If I hadn't been such a lustful brute, no doubt prudence would have kept me abed that night. But at midnight I was peeping out, and there was the Cossack, slumped on his stool, head back and mouth open, reeking like Davis's cellar. Valla's work, thinks I, the charming little wretch. I slipped past him, and he never even stirred, and I padded out of the pool of lamplight round him and reached the big landing.

All was still up here, but there was a dim light down in the hall, and through the banisters I could see two white-tunicked and helmeted sentries on the big double doors of the library, with their sabres drawn, and an orderly officer pacing idly about smoking a cigarette. It struck me that it wasn't safe to be gallivanting about this house in the dark—they might think I was on the East tack, spying—so I flitted on, and two minutes later was stallioning away like billy-o with my modest flower of the steppes—by jingo, she was in a fine state of passion, I remember. We had one violent bout, and then some warm wine from her little spirit lamp, and talked softly and dozed and played, and then went to it again, very slowly and wonderfully, and I can see that lovely white shape in the flickering light even now, and smell the perfume of that silver hair, and—dear me, how we old soldiers do run on.

"You must not linger too long, sweetheart," says she, at last. "Even drunk Cossacks don't sleep forever," and giggled, nibbling at my chin. So I kissed her a long good-night, with endearments, resumed my night-shirt, squeezed her bouncers again for luck, and toddled out into the cold, along her corridor, down the little stairs to the landing—and froze in icy shock against the wall on the second step, my heart going like a hammer.

There was someone on the landing. I could hear him, and then see him by the dim light from the far corridor where my room lay. He was crouched by the archway, listening, a man in a night-shirt, like myself. With a wrenching inward sigh, I realized that it could only be East.

The fool had stayed awake, seen the Cossack asleep, and was now bent on his crack-brained patriotic mischief. I hissed very gently, had the satisfaction of seeing him try to leap through the wall, and then was at his side, shushing him for all I was worth. He seized me, gurgling.

"You! Flashman!" He let out a shuddering breath. "What—? You've been . . . why didn't you tell me?" I wondered what the blazes this meant, until he whispered fiercely: "Good man! Have you heard anything? Are they still there?"

The madman seemed to think I'd been on his eavesdropping lay. Well, at least I'd be spared recriminations for fornicating with his adored object. I shook my head, he bit his lip, and then the maniac breathed in my ear: "Come, then, quickly! Into the gallery—they're still down there!" And while I was peeping, terrified, into the dimness through the banisters, where the white sentries were still on guard, he suddenly flitted from my side across the landing. I daren't even try a loud whisper to call him back; he was fumbling with the catch of the little door in the far shadows, and I was just hesitating before bolting for bed and safety, when from our corridor sounded a cavernous yawn. Panicking, I shot across like a whippet, clutching vainly at East as he slipped through the low aperture into the gallery. Come back, come back, you mad bastard, my lips were saying, but no sound emerged, which was just as well, for with the opening of the little gallery door the clear tones of someone in the library echoed up to us. And light was filtering up through the fine screen which concealed the gallery from the floor below. If our Cossack guard was waking, and took a turn to the landing, he'd see the dim glow from the open gallery door. Gibbering silently to myself, half-way inside the little opening, I crept forward, edging the door delicately shut behind me.

East was flat on the dusty gallery floor, his feet towards me; it stank like a church in the confined space between the carved wooden screen on the one hand and the wall on the other. My head was no more than a foot from the screen; thank God it was a nearly solid affair, with only occasional carved apertures. I lay panting and terrified, hearing the voice down in the library saying in Russian:

". . . so there would be no need to vary the orders at present. The establishment is large enough, and would not be affected."

I remember those words because they were the first I heard, but for the next few moments I was too occupied with scrabbling at East's feet, and indicating to him in dumb show that the sooner we were out of this the better, to pay any heed to what they were talking about. But damn him, he wouldn't budge, but kept gesturing me to lie still and listen. So I did, and some first-rate military intelligence we overheard, too—about the appointment of a commissary-general for the Omsk region, and whether the fellow who commanded Orianburg oughtn't to be retired. Horse Guards would give their buttocks to know this, thinks I furiously, and I had just determined to slide out and leave East alone to his dangerous and useless foolery, when I became conscious of a rather tired, hoarse, but well-bred voice speaking in the library, and one word that he used froze me where I lay, ears straining:

"So that is the conclusion of our agenda? Good. We are grateful to you, gentlemen. You have laboured well, and we are well pleased with the reports you have laid before us. There is Item Seven, of course," and the voice paused. "Late as it is, perhaps Count Ignatieff would favour us with a résumé of the essential points again."

Ignatieff. My icy bully of the registrar's office. For no reason I felt my pulse begin to run even harder. Cautiously I turned my head, and put an eye to the nearest aperture.

Down beneath us, Pencherjevsky's fine long table was agleam with candles and littered with papers. There were five men round it. At the far end, facing us, Ignatieff was standing, very spruce and masterful in his white uniform; behind him there was the huge easel, covered with maps. On the side to his left was a stout, white-whiskered fellow in a blue uniform coat frosted with decorations—a marshal if ever I saw one. Opposite him, on Ignatieff's right, was a tall, bald, beak-nosed civilian, with his chin resting on his folded hands. At the end nearest us was a high-backed chair whose wings concealed the occupant, but I guessed he was the last speaker, for an aide seated at his side was saying:

"Is it necessary, majesty? It is approved, after all, and I fear your majesty is over-tired already. Perhaps tomorrow . . ."

"Let it be tonight," says the hidden chap, and his voice was dog-weary. "I am not as certain of my tomorrows as I once was. And the matter is of the first urgency. Pray proceed, Count."

As the aide bowed I was aware of East craning to squint back at me. His face was a study and his lips silently framed the words: "Tsar? The Tsar?"

Well, who else would they call majesty?[28] I didn't know, but I was all ears and eyes now as Ignatieff bowed, and half-turned to the map behind him. That soft, metallic voice rang upwards from the library panelling.

"Item Seven, the plan known as the expedition of the Indus. By your majesty's leave."

I thought I must have misheard. Indus—that was in Northern India! What the devil did they have to do with that?

"Clause the first," says Ignatieff. "That with the attention of the allied Powers, notably Great Britain, occupied in their invasion of your majesty's Crimean province, the opportunity arises to further the policy of eastward pacification and civilization in those unsettled countries beyond our eastern and southern borders. Clause the second, that the surest way of fulfilling this policy, and at the same time striking a vital blow at the enemy, is to destroy, by native rebellion aided by armed force, the British position on the Indian continent. Clause the third, that the time for armed invasion by your majesty's imperial forces is now ripe, and will be undertaken forthwith. Hence, the Indus expedition."

I think I had stopped breathing; I couldn't believe what I was hearing.

"Clause the fourth," says Ignatieff. "The invasion is to be made by an imperial force of thirty thousand men, of whom ten thousand will be Cossack cavalry. General Duhamel," and he bowed towards the bald chap, "your majesty's agent in Teheran, believes that it would be assisted if Persia could be provoked into war against Britain's ally, Turkey. Clause the fifth—"

"Never mind the clauses,'" says Duhamel. "That advice has been withdrawn. Persia will remain neutral, but hostile to British interest—as she always has been."

Ignatieff bowed again. "With your majesty's leave. It is so agreed, and likewise approved that the Afghan and Sikh powers should be enlisted against the British, in our imperial invasion. They will understand—as will the natives of India—that our expedition is not one of conquest, but to overthrow the English and liberate India." He paused. "We shall thus be liberating the people who are the source of Britain's wealth."

He picked up a pointer and tapped the map, which was of Central Asia and Northern India. "We have considered five possible routes which the invasion might take. First, the three desert routes—Ust-Yurt–Khiva–Herat, or Raim–Bokhara, or Raim–Syr Daria–Tashkent. These, although preferred by General Khruleff"—at this the stout, whiskered fellow stirred in his seat —"have been abandoned because they run through the unsettled areas where we are still engaged in pacifying the Tajiks, Uzbeks and Khokandians, under the brigand leaders Yakub Beg and Izzat Kutebar. Although stinging reverses have been administered to these lawless bandits, and their stronghold of Ak Mechet occupied, they may still be strong enough to hinder the expedition's advance. The less fighting there is to do before we cross the Indian frontier the better."

Ignatieff lowered his pointer on the map. "So the southern routes, beneath the Caspian, are preferred—either through Tabriz and Teheran, or by Herat. An immediate choice is not necessary. The point is that infantry and artillery may be moved with ease across the South Caspian to Herat, while the cavalry move through Persia. Once we are in Persia, the British will have warning of our attempt, but by then it will be too late—far too late. We shall proceed through Kandahar and Kabul, assisted by the hatred which the Afghans owe the British, and so—to India.

"There are, by reliable report, twenty-five thousand British troops in India, and three hundred thousand native soldiers.

These latter present no problem—once a successful invasion is launched, the majority of them will desert, or join in the rebellion which our presence will inspire. It is doubtful if, six months after we cross the Khyber, a single British soldier, civilian, or settlement will remain on the continent. It will have been liberated, and restored to its people. They will require our assistance, and armed presence, for an indefinite period, to guard against counter-invasion."

At this I heard East mutter, "I'll bet they will." I could feel him quivering with excitement; myself, I was trying to digest the immensity of the thing. Of course, it had been a fear in India since I could remember—the Great Bear coming over the passes, but no one truly believed they'd ever have the nerve or the ability to try it. But now, here it was—simple, direct, and certain. Not the least of the coincidences of our remarkable eavesdrop was that I, who knew as much about Afghan affairs from first hand, and our weakness on the north Indian frontier, as any man living, should be one of the listeners. As I took it in, I could see it happening; yes, they could do it all right.

"That, your majesty," Ignatieff was saying, "is an essential sketch of our purpose. We have all studied the plans in detail, as has your highness, and unless some new points have arisen from my résumé, your majesty will no doubt wish to confirm the royal assent already given." He said it with deference, trying to hide his eagerness—your promoter anxious to get the official seal.

"Thank you, Count." It was the weak voice again. "We have it clear. Gentlemen?" There was a pause. "It is a weighty matter. No such attempt has ever been made before. But we are confident —are we not?"

Khruleff nodded slowly. "It has always been possible. Now it is a certainty. In a stroke, we clear the British from India, and extend your majesty's imperial . . . influence from the North Cape to the isle of Ceylon. No Tsar in history has achieved such an advance for our country. The troops are ample, the planning exact, the conditions ideal. The pick of Britain's army, and of her navy, are diverted in the Crimea, and it is certain that no assistance could be rendered in India within a year. By then— we shall have supplanted England in southern Asia."[29]

"And it can begin without delay?" says the Tsar's voice.

"'Immediately, majesty. By the southern route, we can be at the Khyber, with every man, gun, and item of equipment, seven months from this night." Ignatieff was almost striking an attitude, his tawny head thrown back, one hand on the table. They waited, silently, and I heard the Tsar sigh.

"So be it, then. Forgive us, gentlemen, for desiring to hear it in summary again, but it is a matter for second, and third thoughts, even after the resolve has been given." He coughed, wearily. "All is approved, then—and the other items, with the exception of—yes, Item Ten. It can be referred to Omsk for further study. You have our leave, gentlemen."

At this there was a scrape of chairs, and East was kicking at me, and jabbing a finger at the door behind us. I'd been so spellbound by our enormous discovery, I'd almost forgotten where we were—but, by gad, it was time we were no longer here. I edged back to the door, East crowding behind me, and then we heard Ignatieff's voice again.

"Majesty, with permission. In connection with Item Seven—the Indian expedition—mention was made of possible diversionary schemes, to prevent by all means any premature discovery of our intentions. I mentioned, but did not elaborate, a plan for possibly deluding the enemy with a false scent."

At this we stopped, crouched by the door. He went on:

"Plans have been prepared, but in no considerable detail, for a spurious expedition through your Alaskan province, aimed at the British North American possessions. It was thought that if these could be brought to the attention of the British Government, in a suitably accidental manner, they would divert the enemy's attention from the eastern theatre entirely."

"I don't like it," says Khruleff's voice. "I have seen the plan, majesty; it is over-elaborate and unnecessary."

"There are," says Ignatieff, quite unabashed, "two British officers, at present confined in this house—prisoners from the Crimea whom I had brought here expressly for the purpose. It should not be beyond our wits to ensure that they discovered the false North American plan; thereafter they would obviously attempt to escape, to warn their government of it."

"And then?" says Duhamel.

"They would succeed, of course. It is no distance to the Crimea—it could be arranged without their suspecting they were mere tools of our purpose. And their government would at least be distracted."

"Too clever," says Khruleff. "Playing at spies."

"With submission, majesty," says Ignatieff, "there would be no difficulty. I have selected these two men with care—they are ideal for our purpose. One is an agent of intelligence, taken at Silistria—a clever, dangerous fellow. Show him the hint of a design against his country, and he would fasten on it like a hawk. The other is a very different sort—a great, coarse bully of a man, all brawn and little brain; he has spent his time here lechering after every female he could find." I felt East stiffen beside me, as we listened to this infernal impudence. "But he would be necessary—for even if we permitted, and assisted, their escape here, and saw that they reached the Crimea in safety, they would still have to rejoin their army at Sevastopol, and we could hardly issue orders to our forces in Crimea to let them pass through. This second fellow is the kind of resourceful villain who would find a way."

There was a silence, and then Duhamel says: "I must agree with Khruleff, majesty. It is not necessary, and might even be dangerous. The British are not fools; they smell a rat as soon as anyone. These false plans, these clever stratagems—they can excite suspicion and recoil on the plotter. Our Indus scheme is soundly based; it needs no pretty folly of this kind."

"So." The Tsar's voice was a hoarse murmur. "The opinion is against you, Count. Let your British officers sleep undisturbed. But we thank you for your zeal in the matter, even so. And now, gentlemen, we have worked long enough—"

East was bundling me on to the dark landing before the voice had finished speaking. We closed the door gently, and tip-toed across towards our passage even as we heard the library doors opening down in the hall. I peeped round the corner; the Cossack was snoring away again, and we scuttled silently past him and into East's room. I sank down, shaking, on to his bed, while he fumbled at the candle, muttering furiously till he got it lit. His face was as white as a sheet—but he remembered to muffle the mouth of the hidden speaking-tube with his pillow.

"My God, Flashman," says he, when he had got his wind back. We were staring helplessly at each other. "What are we to do?"

"What can we do?" says I.

"We did hear aright—didn't we?" says he. "They're going for India—while our back's turned? A Russian army over the Khyber—a rebellion! Good God—is the thing possible?"

I thought of '42, and the Afghans—and what they could do with a Russian army to help them. "Aye," says I. "It's possible all right."

"I *knew* we were right to watch and listen!" cries he. "I knew it! But I never dreamed—this is the most appalling thing!" He slapped his hands and paced about. "Look—we've got to do something! We've got to get away—somehow! They must have news of this at Sevastopol. Raglan's there; he's the commander —if we could get this to him, and London, there'd be time— to try to prepare, at least. Send troops out—increase the north-west garrisons—perhaps even an expedition into Persia, or Afghanistan—"

"There isn't time," says I. "You heard them—seven months from tonight they'll be on the edge of the Punjab with thirty thousand men, and God knows how many Afghans ready to join in for a slap at us and the loot of India. It would take a month to get word to England, twice as long again to assemble an army —if that's possible, which I doubt—and then it's four months to India—"

"But that's in time—just in time!" cries he. "If only we can get away—at once!"

"Well, we can't," says I. "The thing's not possible."

"We've got to make it possible!" says he, feverishly. "Look— look at this, will you?" And he snatched a book from his bureau: it was some kind of geography or guide, in Russian script—that hideous lettering that always made me think of black magic recipes for conjuring the Devil. "See here; this map. Now, I've pieced this together over the past few months, just by listening and using my wits, and I've a fair notion where we are, although Starotorsk ain't shown on this map; too small. But I reckon we're about here, in this empty space—perhaps fifty miles from Ekaterinoslav, and thirty from Alexandrovsk, see? It startled me, I tell you; I'd thought we were miles farther inland."

"So did I," says I. "You're sure you're right?—they must have brought me a hell of a long way round, then."

"Of course—that's their way! They'll never do anything straight, I tell you. Confuse, disturb, upset—that's their book of common prayer! But don't you see—we're not much above a hundred miles from the north end of the Crimea—maybe only a couple of hundred from Raglan at Sevastopol!"

"With a couple of Russian armies in between," I pointed out. "Anyway, how could we get away from here?"

"Steal a sled at night—horses. If we went fast enough, we could get changes at the post stations on the way, as long as we kept ahead of pursuit. Don't you see, man—it must be possible!" His eyes were shining fiercely. "*Ignatieff was planning for us to do this very thing!* My God, why did they turn him down! Think of it—if he had had his way, they'd be *helping* us to escape with their bogus information, never dreaming we had the *real* plans! Of all the cursed luck!"

"Well, they did turn him down," says I. "And it's no go. You talk of stealing a sled—how far d'you think we'd get, with Pencherjevsky's Cossacks on our tail? You can't hide sleigh-tracks, you know—not on land as flat as your hat. Even if you could, they know exactly where we'd go—there's only one route"—and I pointed at his map—"through the neck of the Crimean peninsula at—what's it called? Armyansk. They'd overhaul us long before we got there."

"No, they wouldn't," says he, grinning—the same sly, fag grin of fifteen years ago. "Because we won't go that way. There's another road to the Crimea—I got it from this book, but they'd never dream we knew of it. Look, now, old Flashy friend, and learn the advantages of studying geography. See how the Crimean peninsula is joined to mainland Russia—just a narrow isthmus, eh? Now look east a little way along the coast—what d'ye see?"

"A town called Yenitchi," says I. "But if you're thinking of pinching a boat, you're mad—"

"Boat nothing," says he. "What d'ye see in the sea, south of Yenitchi?"

"A streak of fly-dung," says I, impatiently. "Now, Scud—"

"That's what it looks like," says he triumphantly. "But it ain't. That, my boy, is the Arrow of Arabat—a causeway, not more than half a mile across, without even a road on it, that runs from Yenitchi a clear sixty miles *through* the sea of Azov to Arabat in the Crimea—and from there it's a bare hundred miles across to Sevastopol! Don't you see, man? No one ever uses it, according to this book, except a few dromedary caravans in summer. Why, the Russians hardly know it exists, even! All we need is one night of snow, here, to cover our traces, and while they're chasing us towards the isthmus, we're tearing down to Yenitchi, along the causeway to Arabat, and then westward ho to Sevastopol—"

"Through the bloody Russian army!" cries I.

"Through whoever you please! Can't you see—no one will be looking for us there! They've no telegraph, anyway, in this benighted country—we both speak enough Russian to pass! Heavens, we speak it better than most *moujiks*, I'll swear. It's the way, Flashman—the only way!"

I didn't like this one bit. Don't misunderstand me—I'm as true-blue a Briton as the next man, and I'm not unwilling to serve the old place in return for my pay, provided it don't entail too much discomfort or expense. But I draw the line where my hide is concerned—among the many things I'm not prepared to do for my country is die, especially at the end of a rope trailing from a Cossack's saddle, or with his lance up my innards. The thought of abandoning this snug retreat, where I was feeding full, drinking well, and rogering my captivity happily away, and going careering off through the snow-fast Russian wilderness, with those devils howling after me—and all so that we could report this crazy scheme to Raglan! It was mad. Anyway, what did I care for India? I'd sooner we had it than the Russians, of course, and if the intelligence could have been conveyed *safely* to Raglan (who'd have promptly forgotten it, or sent an army to Greenland by mistake, like as not) I'd have done it like a shot. But I draw the line at risks that aren't necessary to my own well-being. *That's* why I'm eighty years old today, while Scud East has been mouldering underground at Cawnpore this forty-odd years.

But I couldn't say this to him, of course. So I looked profound, and anxious, and shook my head. "Can't be done, Scud. Look now; you don't know much about this Arrow causeway, except what's in that book. Who's to say it's open in winter—or that it's still there? Might have been washed away. Who knows what guards they may have at either end? How do we get through the Crimea to Sevastopol? I've done a bit of travelling in disguise, you know, in Afghanistan and Germany...and, oh, lots of places, and it's a sight harder than you'd think. And in Russia—where everyone has to show his damned ticket every few miles—we'd never manage it. But"—I stilled his protest with a stern finger—"I'd chance that, of course, if it wasn't an absolute certainty that we'd be nabbed before we'd got halfway to this Yenitchi place. Even if we got clear away from here—which would be next to impossible—they would ride us down in a few hours. It's hopeless, you see."

"I know that!" he cried. "I can count, too! But I tell you we've got to *try!* It's a chance in a million that we've found out this infernal piece of Russian treachery! We must try to use it, to warn Raglan and the people at home! What have we got to lose, except our lives?"

D'you know, when a man talks like that to me, I feel downright insulted. Why other, unnamed lives, or the East India Company's dividend, or the credit of Lord Aberdeen, or the honour of British arms, should be held *by me* to be of greater consequence than my own shrinking skin, I've always been at a loss to understand.

"You're missing the point," I told him. "Of course, one doesn't think twice about one's neck when it's a question of duty"—I don't, anyway—"but one has to be sure where one's duty lies. Maybe I've seen more rough work than you have, Scud, and I've learned there's no point in suicide—not when one can wait and watch and think. If we sit tight, who knows what chance may arise that ain't apparent now? But if we go off half-cock, and get killed or something—well, *that* won't get the news to Raglan. Here's something: now that Ignatieff don't need us any more, they may even exchange us. Then the laugh would be on them, eh?"

At this he cried out that time was vital, and we daren't wait. I replied that we daren't go until we saw a reasonable chance (if I knew anything, we'd wait a long time for one), and so we bandied it to and fro and got no forrarder, and finally went to bed, played out.

When I thought the thing over, alone (and got into a fine

sweat at the recollection of the fearful risk we'd run, crouching in that musty gallery) I could see East's point. Here we were, by an amazing fluke, in possession of information which any decent soldier would have gone through hell to get to his chiefs. And Scud East was a decent soldier, by anyone's lights but mine. My task, plainly, was to prevent his doing anything rash—in other words, anything at all—and yet appear to be in as big a sweat as he was himself. Not too difficult, for one of my talents.

In the next few days we mulled over a dozen notions for escaping, each more lunatic than the last. It was quite interesting, really, to see at what point in some particular idiocy poor Scud would start to boggle; I remember the look of respectful horror which crept into his eyes when I regretted absently that we hadn't dropped from the gallery that night and cut all their throats, the Tsar's included—"too late, now, of course, since they've all gone," says I. "Pity, though; if we'd finished 'em off, that would have scotched their little scheme. And I haven't had a decent set-to since Balaclava. Aye, well."

Scud began to worry me, though; he was working himself up into a fever of anxiety and impatience where he might do something foolish. "We must try!" he kept insisting. "If we can think of no alternative soon, we're bound to make a run for it some night! I'll go mad if we don't, I tell you! How can you just sit there?—oh, no, I'm sorry, Flashman; I know this must be torturing you too! Forgive me, old fellow. I haven't got your steady nerve."

He hadn't got Valla to refresh him, either, which might have had a calming effect. I thought of suggesting that he take a steam-bath with Aunt Sara, to settle his nerves, but he might have enjoyed it too much, and then gone mad repenting. So I tried to look anxious and frustrated, while he chewed his nails and fretted horribly, and a week passed, in which he must have lost a stone. Worrying about India, stab me. And then the worst happened: we got our opportunity, and in circumstances which even I couldn't refuse.

It came after a day in which Pencherjevsky lost his temper, a rare thing, and most memorable. I was in the salon when I heard him bawling at the front door, and came out to find him standing in the hallway, fulminating at two fellows outside on the steps. One looked like a clergyman; the other was a lean, ugly little fellow dressed like a clerk.

"... effrontery, to seek to thrust yourself between me and my people!" Pencherjevsky was roaring. "Merciful God, how do I keep my hands from you? Have you no souls to cure, you priest fellow, and you, Blank, no pen-pushing or pimping to occupy you? Ah, but no—you have your agitating, have you not, you seditious scum! Well, agitate elsewhere, before I have my Cossacks take their whips to you! Get out of my sight and off my land—both of you!"

He was grotesque in his rage, towering like some bearded old-world god—I'd have been in the next county before him, but these two stood their ground, jeopardizing their health.

"We are no serfs of yours!" cries the fellow Blank. "You do not order us," and Pencherjevsky gave a strangled roar and started forward, but the priest came between.

"Lord Count! A moment!" He was game, that one. "Hear me, I implore. You are a just man, and surely it is little enough to ask. The woman is old, and if she cannot pay the soul-tax on her grandsons, you know what will happen. The officials will block her stove, and she will be driven out—to what? To die in the cold, or to starve, and the little ones with her. It is a matter of only one hundred and seventy silver kopecks—I do not ask you to pay for her, but let me find the money, and my friend here. We will be glad to pay! Surely you will let us—be merciful!"

"Look you," says Pencherjevsky, holding himself in. "Do I care for a handful of kopecks? No! Not if it was a hundred and seventy thousand roubles, either! But you come to me with a pitiful tale of this old crone, who cannot pay the tax on her brats —do I not know her son—worthless bastard!—is a *koulak** in Odessa, and could pay it for her, fifty times over! Well, let him! But if he will not, then it is for the government to enforce the law —no man hindering! No, not even me! Suppose I pay, or permit you to pay, on her behalf, what would happen then? I shall tell you. Next year, and every year thereafter, you would have all the *moujiks* from here to Rostov bawling at my door: 'We cannot pay the soul-tax,[30] *batiushka*; pay for us, as you paid for so-and-so.' And where does that end?"

* A peasant with money, a usurer.

"But—" the priest was beginning, but Pencherjevsky cut him short.

"You would tell me that you will pay for them all? Aye, Master Blank there would pay—with the filthy money sent by his Communist friends in Germany! So that he could creep among my *moujiks*, sowing sedition, preaching revolution! I know him! So get him hence, priest, out of my sight, before I forget myself!"

"And the old woman, then? Have a little pity, Count!"

"I have explained!" roars Pencherjevsky. "By God, as though I owe you that much! Get out, both of you!"

He advanced, hands clenched, and the two of them went scuttling down the steps. But the fellow Blank[31] had to have a last word:

"You filthy tyrant! You dig your own grave! You and your kind think you can live forever, by oppression and torture and theft—you sow dragon's teeth with your cruelty, and they will grow to tear you! You will see, you fiend!"

Pencherjevsky went mad. He flung his cap on the ground, foaming, and then ran bawling for his whip, his Cossacks, his sabre, while the two malcontents scampered off for their lives, Blank screaming threats and abuse over his shoulder. I listened with interest as the Count raved and stormed:

"After them! I'll have that filthy creature knouted, God help me! Run him down, and don't leave an inch of hide on his carcase!"

Within a few moments a group of his Cossacks were in the saddle and thundering out of the gate, while he stormed about the hall, raging still:

"The dog! The insolent garbage! To beard *me*, at my own door! The priest's a meddling fool—but that Blank! Anarchist swine! He'll be less impudent when my fellows have cut the buttocks off him!"

He stalked away, finally, still cursing, and about an hour later the Cossacks came back, and their leader stumped up the steps to report. Pencherjevsky had simmered down a good deal by this time; he had ordered a brew of punch, and invited East and myself to join him, and we were sipping at the scalding stuff by the hall fire when the Cossack came in, an old, stout, white-whiskered scoundrel with his belt at the last hole.[32] He was grinning, and had his *nagaika* in his hand.

"Well?" growled Pencherjevsky. "Did you catch that brute and teach him manners?"

"Aye, *batiushka*," says the Cossack, well pleased. "He's dead. Thirty cuts—and, pouf! He was a weakling, though."

"Dead, you say?" Pencherjevsky set down his cup abruptly, frowning. Then he shrugged: "Well, good riddance! No one'll mourn his loss. One anarchist more or less will not trouble the prefect."

"The fellow Blank escaped," continued the Cossack. "I'm sorry, *batiushka*—"

"Blank escaped!" Pencherjevsky's voice came out in a hoarse scream; his eyes dilating. "You mean—it was the *priest* you killed! The holy man!" He stared in disbelief, crossing himself. "*Slava Bogu!** The priest!"

"Priest? Do I know?" says the Cossack. "Was it wrong, *batiushka*?"

"Wrong, animal? A priest! And you ... you flogged him to death!" The Count looked as though he would have a seizure. He gulped, and clawed at his beard, and then he blundered past the Cossack, up the stairs, and we heard his door crash behind him.

"My God!" says East. The Cossack looked at us in wonder, and then shrugged, as his kind will, and stalked off. We just stood, looking at each other.

"What will this mean?" says East.

"Search me," I said. "They butcher each other so easily in this place—I don't know. I'd think flogging a priest to death is a trifle over the score, though—even for Russia. Old man Pencherjevsky'll have some explaining to do, I'd say—shouldn't wonder if they kick him out of the Moscow Carlton Club."

"My God, Flashman!" says East again. "What a country!"

We didn't see the Count at dinner, nor Valla, and Aunt Sara was uncommunicative. But you could see in her face, and the servants', and feel in the very air of the house, that Starotorsk was a place appalled. For once East forgot to talk about escaping, and we went to bed early, saying good-night in whispers.

* Glory to God!

I didn't rest too easy, though. My stove was leaking, and making the room stuffy, and the general depression must have infected me, for when I dozed I dreamed badly. I got my old nightmare of drowning in the pipe at Jotunberg, probably with the stove fumes,[33] and then it changed to that underground cell in Afghanistan, where my old flame, Narreeman, was trying to qualify me for the Harem Handicap, and then someone started shooting outside the cell, and shrieking, and suddenly I was awake, lathered with sweat, and the shooting was real, and from beneath me in the house there was an appalling crash and the roar of Pencherjevsky's voice, and a pattering of feet, and by that time I was out of bed and into my breeches, struggling with my boots as I threw open the door.

East was in the passage, half-dressed like myself, running for the landing. I reached it on his very heels, crying: "What's happening? What the devil is it?", when there was a terrible shriek from Valla's passage, and Pencherjevsky was bounding up the stairs, bawling over his shoulder to the Cossacks whom I could see in the hall below:

"Hold them there! Hold the door! My child, Valentina! Where are you?"

"Here, father!" And she came hurrying in her night-gown, hair all disordered, eyes starting with terror. "Father, they are everywhere—in the garden! I saw them—oh!"

There was a crash of musket-fire from beyond the front door, splinters flew in the hall, and one of the Cossacks sang out and staggered, clutching his leg. The other were at the hall windows, there was a smashing of glass, and the sound of baying, screaming voices from outside. Pencherjevsky swore, clasped Valla to him with one enormous arm, saw us, and bawled above the shooting:

"That damned priest! They have risen—the serfs have risen! They're attacking the house!"

⤳7

I've been in a good few sieges in my time, from full-dress affairs like Cawnpore, Lucknow, and the Pekin nonsense a few years ago, to more domestic squabbles such as Kabul residency in '41. But I can't think of one worse managed than the *moujiks'* attack on Starotorsk. I gathered afterwards that several thousand of them, whipped on by Blank's fiery oratory, had just up and marched on the house to avenge their priest's death, seizing what weapons were handiest, and making no attempt at concealment or concerted attack to take the place on all sides at once. They just stamped up the road, roaring, the Cossacks in their little barrack saw them, knocked a few over with rifle fire, and then retired to the main house just as the mob surged into the drive and threw themselves at the front door. And there it was, touch and go, with the *moujiks* beating on the panels, smashing in the downstairs windows on that side to clamber in, waving their trowels and torches and yelling for Pencherjevsky's blood.[34]

As he stood there, clasping Valla and glaring round like a mad thing, I doubt if he fully understood it himself—that his beloved slaves were out to string him from the nearest limb, with his family on either side of him. It was like the sun falling out of the sky for him. But he knew deadly danger when he saw it, and his one thought was for his daughter. He seized me by the arm.

"The back way—to the stables! Quickly! Get her away, both of you! We shall hold them here—the fools, the ingrate clods!" He practically flung her into my arms. "Take a sled and horses, and drive like the wind to the Arianski house—on the Alexandrovsk road! There she will be safe. But hasten, in God's name!"

I'd have been off at the run, but East, the posturing ass, had to thrust in:

"One of us will stay, sir! Or let a Cossack escort your daughter —it is not fitting that British officers should—"

"You numskull!" bawled Pencherjevsky, seizing him and thrusting him violently towards the back corridor. "Go! They will be in, or round the house, while you stand prating! This is no affair of yours—and I command here!" There was a tearing crash from the front door, several pistol shots amid the clamour of the mob and the shouting of the Cossacks, and over the banisters I saw the door cave in, and a torrent of ragged figures pouring in, driving the Cossacks back towards the foot of the stairs. The smoky glare of their torches turned the place suddenly into a struggling hell, as the Cossacks swung their sabres and *nagaikas* to force them back.

"Get her away!" Pencherjevsky encircled both me and Valla for an instant in his bear-like hug, his great, bearded face within an inch of my own, and there were tears in his glaring eyes. "You know what is to do, my son! See to her—and to that other life! God be with you!"

And he bundled us into the corridor, and then rushed to the head of the stairs. I had a glimpse of his towering bulk, with the smoky glare beneath him, and then the chorus of yells and screams from the hall redoubled, there was a rushing of feet, a splintering of timber—and East and I were doubling down the back-stairs at speed, Valla sobbing against my chest as I swept her along.

We tore through the kitchen, East pausing to grab some loaves and bottles, while I hurried out into the yard. It was dead still in the moonlight; nothing but the soft stamp of the beasts in their stalls, and the distant tumult muffled on the other side of the house. I was into the coach-building in a flash, bundled Valla into the biggest sled, and was leading round the first of the horses when East joined me, his arms full.

I don't know the record for harnessing a three-horse sled, but I'll swear we broke it; I wrenched home the last buckle while East scuttled across the snow to unbar the gate. I jumped into the driver's seat and tugged the reins, the horses whinnied and reared and then danced forward, any old how—it's deuced difficult, tooling a sled—and with me swearing at the beasts and East swinging up as we slid past, we scraped through the gateway on to the open road beyond.

There was a bang to our left, and a shot whistled overhead,

causing me to duck and the horses to swerve alarmingly. They were rounding the house wall, a bare thirty yards away, a confused, roaring rabble, torches waving, running to head us off. East seized the whip from its mount and lashed at the beasts, and with a bound that nearly overturned us they tore away, down the road, with the mob cursing at our tail, waving their fists, and one last shot singing wide as we distanced them.

We didn't let up for a mile, though, by which time I had the beasts under control, and we were able to pull up on a gentle rise and look back. It was like a Christmas scene, a great white blanket glittering in the full moon, and the dark house rising up from it, with the red dots of torch-light dancing among the outbuildings, and the thin sound of voices echoing through the frosty air, and the stars twinkling in the purple sky. Very bonny, I suppose— and then East clutched my arm.

"My God! Look yonder!"

There was a dull glow at one corner of the house; it grew into an orange flame, licking upwards with a shower of sparks; the torches seemed to dance more madly than ever, and from the sled behind there was a sudden shrieking sob, and Valla was trying to struggle out—my God, she still had nothing on but her night-dress, and as she half fell out it ripped and sent her tumbling into the snow.

I threw the reins to East, jumped down, and bundled her quickly back into the sled. There were furs there, any amount of them, and I swaddled her in them before the cold could get at her. "Father! Father!" she was moaning, and then she fainted dead away, and I laid her down on the back seat and went forward to East, handing him up one of the furs—for we had nothing but our shirts and breeches and boots, and the cold was crippling.

"Let's get on," says I, wrapping up myself, with my teeth chattering. "The sooner we're out of here, the better. Come on, man, what ails you?"

He was sitting staring ahead, his mouth open, and when he swung round to me, he was positively laughing.

"Flashman!" he cried. "This is our chance! Heaven-sent! The sled—the horses—and a clear start! We're away—old fellow, and no one to stop us!"

It shows you what a hectic scramble it had been, with not a

moment's pause to collect one's wits from the shock of waking until now, but for a second I didn't see what he was driving at. And then it struck me—escape. We could light out for Yenitchi, and East's causeway, and not a living soul would know we had gone. One couldn't be sure, of course, but I doubted whether any civilized being would survive what was happening at Starotorsk; it might be days before the police or the army came on the scene and realized that there were three persons not accounted for. And by then we could be in Sevastopol—always assuming we got through the Russian army. I didn't like it, but I didn't much care for the Alexandrovsk road, either, wherever that was—God knew how far the insurrection would spread, and to be caught up in it, with Pencherjevsky's daughter in tow, would be asking to be torn limb from limb.

Even as the thoughts rushed through my mind, I was glancing at the stars, picking out the Plough and judging our line south. That way, even if we hit the coast fifty versts either side of Yenitchi, we at least stood a decent chance of finding our road to it in the end, for we had time on our side.

"Right," says I. "Let's be off. We're sure to hit some farm or station where we can change horses. We'll drive in turns, and—"

"We must take Valla with us," cries he, and even in that ghostly light I'll swear he was blushing. "We cannot abandon her —God knows what kind of villages these will be we shall pass through—we could not leave her, not knowing what...I mean, if we can reach the camp at Sevastopol, she will be truly safe... and...and..."

And he would be able to press his suit, no doubt, the poor skirt-smitten ninny, if he ever plucked up courage enough. I wonder what he'd have thought if he'd known I had been pupping his little Ukrainian angel for weeks. And there she was, in the sled, with not a stitch to her name.

"You're right!" I cried. "We must take her. You are a noble fellow, Scud! Off we go, then, and I'll take the ribbons as soon as you're tired."

I jumped in the back, and off we swept, over the snowy plain, and far behind us the red glow mounted to the night sky. I peered back at it, wondering if Pencherjevsky was dead yet, and what had happened to Aunt Sara. Whatever it was, I found myself hoping that for her, at least, it had been quick. And then I busied myself putting the sled in some order.

They are splendid things, these three-horse sleighs, less like a coach than a little room on runners. They are completely enclosed with a great hood, lashed down all round, with flaps which can be secured on all the window spaces, so that when they are down the whole thing is quite snug, and if you have furs enough, and a bottle or two, you can be as warm as toast. I made sure everything was secure, set out the bread, and a leg of ham, which East had thoughtfully picked up, on the front seat, and counted the bottles—three of brandy, one of white wine. Valla seemed to be still unconscious; she was wrapped in a mountain of furs between the seats, and when I opened the rear window-flap for light to examine her, sure enough, she was in that uneasy shocked sleep that folk sometimes go into when they've been terribly scared. The shaft of moonlight shone on her silvery hair, and on one white tit peeping out saucily from the furs—I had to make sure her heart was beating, of course, but beyond that I didn't disturb her—for the moment. Fine sledges these: the driver is quite walled off.

So there we were; I huddled in my fur, took a pull at the brandy, and then crawled out under the side flap on to the mounting of the runner; the wind hit me like a knife, with the snow furrowing up round my legs from the runner-blades. We were fairly scudding along as I pulled myself up on to the driving seat beside East and gave him a swig at the brandy.

He was chattering with cold, even in his fur wrap, so I tied it more securely round him, and asked how we were going. He reckoned, if we could strike a village and get a good direction, we might make Yenitchi in five or six hours—always allowing for changes of horses on the way. But he was sure we wouldn't be able to stand the cold of driving for more than half an hour at a time. So I took the ribbons and he crept back perilously into the sled—one thing I was sure of: Valla would be safe with him.

It it hadn't been for the biting cold, I'd have enjoyed that moonlight drive. The snow was firm and flat, so that it didn't ball in the horses' hooves, and the runners hissed across the snow —it was strange, to be moving at that speed with so little noise. Ahead were the three tossing manes, with the vapour streaming back in the icy air, and beyond that—nothing. A white sheet to the black horizon, a magnificent silver moon, and that reassuring Pole star dead astern when I looked back.

I was about frozen, though, when I spotted lights to starboard after about twenty minutes, and swerved away to find a tumble-down little village, populated by the usual half-human peasants. After consultation with East, I decided to ask the distance and direction to Osipenke; East was carrying a rough table of places and directions in his head, out of the book he had studied, and from the peasants' scared answers—for they were in awe of any strangers—we were able to calculate our proper course, and swerve away south-west.

East had taken over the reins. Valla had come to while he was in the sled—I wondered if he'd been chancing his arm, but probably not—and had had mild hysterics, about her father, and Aunt Sara, who had been sitting up with a sick Cossack woman in the barracks, and had presumably been cut off there.

"The poor little lamb," says East, as he took the reins. "It tore my heart to see her grief, Flashman—so I have given her a little laudanum from a phial which ... which I carry always with me. She should sleep for several hours; it will be best so."

I could have kicked him, for if there's one thing I'd fancy myself good at, it's comforting a bereaved and naked blonde under a fur rug. But he had put her to sleep, no error, and she was snoring like a walrus. So I had to amuse myself with bread and ham, and try to snatch a nap myself.

We made good progress, and after a couple of hours found a way-station, by great good luck, on what must have been the Mariupol road. We got three new nags, and bowled away famously, but what with lack of sleep it was getting to be hard work now, and a couple of hours after sun-rise we pulled up in the first wood we'd seen—a straggly little affair of stunted bushes, really—and decided to rest ourselves and the horses. Valla was still out to the wide, and East and I took a seat apiece and slept like the dead.

I woke first, and when I put my head out the sky was already dimming in the late afternoon. It was bleak and grey, and freezing starvation, and looking through the twisted branches at the pale, endless waste, I felt a shiver running through me that had nothing to do with cold. Not far away there were two or three of those funny little mounds called *koorgans*, which I believe are the barrows of long-forgotten barbarian peoples; they looked eery and uncanny in the failing light, like monstrous snowmen. The stillness was awful; you could feel it, not even a breath of wind, but just the cold and the weight of emptiness hanging over the steppe. It was unnerving, and suddenly I could hear Kit Carson's strained quiet voice in the dread silence of the wagon road west of Leavenworth: "Nary a sight nor sound anywhere—not even a sniff o' danger. *That's what frets me.*"

It fretted me, too, at this minute; I roused East, and then we made all fast, and I took the reins and off we slid silently south-west, past those lonely *koorgans*, into the icy wilderness. I had a bottle, and some bread, but nothing could warm me; I was scared, but didn't know of what—just the silence and the unknown, I suppose. And then from somewhere far off to my right I heard it —that thin, dismal sound that is the terror of the empty steppe, unmistakable and terrifying, drifting through the vast distance: the eldritch cry of the wolf.

The horses heard it too, and whinnied, bounding forward in fear with a stumble of hooves, until we were flying at our uttermost speed. My imagination was flying even faster; I remembered Pencherjevsky's story of the woman who had thrown her children out when those fearful monsters got on the track of her sled, and had been executed for it, and countless other tales of sleds run down by famished packs and their occupants literally eaten alive. I daren't look back for fear of what I might see loping over the snow behind me.

The cry was not repeated, and after a few more miles I breathed easier; there was a twinkle of light dead ahead, and when we reached it, we found it was a *moujik's* cabin, and the man himself at the door, axe in hand, glowering at us. We asked him the nearest town, and could have cried with relief when he said Yenitchi: it was only forty versts away—a couple of hours' driving, if the beasts held up and weren't pressed too hard. East took the reins, I climbed in behind—Valla was sleeping still, uneasily, and mumbling incoherently—and we set off on what I prayed was the last stage of our mainland journey.

For rather more than an hour nothing happened; we drove on

through the silence, I took another turn, and then I halted not far from another clump of *koorgans* to let East climb into the driver's seat again. I had my foot on the runner, and he was just chuckling to the horses, when it came again—that bloodchilling wail, far closer this time, and off to the left. The horses shrieked, and the sled shot forward so fast that for a moment I was dragged along, clinging to the side by main strength, until I managed to drag myself inboard, tumbling on to the back seat. Valla was stirring, muttering sleepily, but I'd no time for her; I thrust out my head, staring fearfully across the snow, trying to pierce the dusk, but there was nothing to be seen. East was letting the horses go, and the sled was swaying with the speed—and then it came again, closer still, like the sound of a lost soul falling to hell. I heard East shouting to the horses, cracking his whip; I clutched the side, feeling the sweat pouring off me in spite of the cold.

Still nothing, as we fairly flew along; there was another cluster of *koorgans* just visible in the mirk a quarter of a mile or so to our left. As I watched them—was that something moving beyond them? My heart flew to my mouth—no, they stood bleak and lonely, and I found I was panting with fear as I dashed the sweat from my eyes and peered again. Silence, save for the muffled thump of the hooves and the hissing of the runners—and there *was* something flitting between the last two *koorgans*, a low, long dark shape rushing over the snow, and another behind it, and another, speeding out now into the open, and swerving towards us.

"Jesus!" I shrieked. "Wolves!"

East yelled something I couldn't hear, and the sled rocked horribly as he bore on his offside rein; then we righted, and as I gazed over the side, the hellish baying broke out almost directly behind us. There they were—five of them, gliding in our wake; I could see the leader toss up his hideous snout as he let go his evil wail, and then they put their heads down and came after us in dead silence.

I've seen horror in my time, human, animal, and natural, but I don't know much worse than that memory—those dim grey shapes bounding behind us, creeping inexorably closer, until I could make out the flat, wicked heads and the snow spurting up under their loping paws. I must have been petrified, for God knows how long I just stared at them—and then my wits came back, and I seized the nearest rug and flung it out to the side, as far as I could.

As one beast they swerved, and were on it in a twinkling, tearing it among them. Only for a second, and then they were after us again—probably all the fiercer for being fooled. I grabbed another rug and hurled it, and this time they never even broke stride, but shot past it, closing in on the sled until they were a bare twenty paces behind, and I could see their open jaws— I've never been able to look an Alsatian in the face since—and delude myself that I could even make out their glittering eyes. I'd have given my right arm, then, for the feel of my faithful old Adams in my grip—"You wouldn't run so fast with a forty-four bullet in you, damn you!" I yelled at them—and they came streaking up, while the horses screamed with fear and tore ahead, widening the gap for about ten blessed seconds. I was cursing and scrabbling in the back looking for something else to throw—a bottle, that was no use, but by George, if I smashed one at the bottom it might serve as a weapon when the last moment came and they were ravening over the tailboard—in desperation I seized a loaf (we'd finished the ham) and hurled it at the nearest of them, and I am here to tell you that wolves don't eat bread —they don't even bloody well look at it, for that matter. I heard East roaring something, and cracking his whip like a madman, and God help me, I *could* see the eyes behind us now, glaring in those viciously pointed heads, with their open jaws and gleaming teeth, and the vapour panting out between them. The leader was a bare five yards behind, bounding along like some hound of hell; I grabbed another rug, balled it, prayed, and flung it at him, and for one joyous moment it enveloped him; he stumbled, recovered, and came on again, and East sang out from the box to hold tight. The sled rocked, and we were shooting along between high snow banks on either side, with those five devils barely a leap from us—and suddenly they were falling back, slackening their lope, and I couldn't believe my eyes, and then a cabin flashed by on the right, and then another, with beautiful, wonderful light in its windows, and the five awful shapes were fading into the gloom, and we were gliding up a street, between rows of cottages on either side, and as East brought the sled slowly to a halt I collapsed, half-done, on the seat. Valla, I remember, muttered something and turned over in her rugs.

You would not think much of Yenitchi, I dare say, or its single mean street, but to me Piccadilly itself couldn't have looked better. It was five minutes before I crawled out, and East and I faced the curious stares of the folk coming out of the cabins; the horses were hanging in their traces, and we had no difficulty in convincing them that we needed a change. There was a post-station at the end of the street, beside a bridge, and a drunk postmaster who, after much swearing and cajoling, was induced to produce a couple of fairly flea-bitten brutes; East wondered if we should rest for a few hours, and go on with our own nags refreshed, but I said no—let's be off while the going's good. So when we had got some few items of bread and sausage and cheese from the postmaster's wife, and a couple of female garments for Valla to wear when she woke up, we put the new beasts to and prepared to take the road again.

It was a dismal prospect. Beyond the bridge, which spanned a frozen canal, we could see the Arrow of Arabat, a long, bleak tongue of snow-covered land running south like a huge railway embankment into the Azov Sea. The sea proper, which was frozen —at least as far out as we could see—lay to the left; on the right of the causeway lies a stinking inland lagoon, called the Sivache, which is many miles wide in places, but narrows down as you proceed along the Arrow, until it peters away altogether where the causeway reaches Arabat, on the eastern end of the Crimea. The lagoon seems to be too foul to freeze entirely, even in a Russian winter, and the stench from it would poison an elephant.

We were just preparing to set off, when Valla woke up, and after we had told her where she was, and reassured her that all was well, and she had wept a little, and I'd helped her out discreetly to answer a call of nature—well, she'd been asleep for the best of twenty-four hours—we decided after all to have a caulk before setting out again. East and I were both pretty done, but I wouldn't allow more than two hours' rest—having got this far, I'd no wish to linger. We had some food, and now Valla was beginning to come to properly, and wanted to know where we were taking her.

"We're going back to our own army," I told her. "We must

take you with us—we can't leave you here, and you'll be well cared for. I believe your father is all right—we saw him and his Cossacks escaping as we drove away—and I know he would wish us to see you safe, and there's nowhere better than where we're going, d'you see?"

It served, after a deal of questioning and answering; whether she was still under the influence of the laudanum or not, I wasn't certain, but she seemed content enough, in a sleepy sort of way, so we plied her with nips of brandy to keep out the cold—she refused outright the clothes we had got, and stayed curled up in her rugs—and being a Russian girl, she was ready to drink all we offered her.

"If she's half-tight, so much the better," says I to East. "Distressing, of course, but she'll be less liable to give the game away if we run into trouble."

"It is terrible for her—to be subjected to this nightmare," says he. "But that was a noble lie you told, about her father—I wanted to shake your hand on that, old boy." And he wrung it then and there. "I still think I must be dreaming," says he. "This incredible country, and you and I—and this dear girl—fleeing for our lives! But we are nearly home, old fellow—a bare sixty miles to Arabat, and then eight hours at most will see us at Sevastopol, God willing. Will you pray with me, Flashman, for our deliverance?"

I wasn't crawling about in the snow, not for him or anyone, but I stood while he mumped away with his hands folded, beseeching the Lord that we might quit ourselves like men, or something equally useful, and then we climbed in and took our forty winks. Valla was dozing, and the brandy bottle was half-empty—if ever they start the Little White Ribboners in Russia, all the members will have to be boys, for they'll never get the women to take the pledge.

The rest did me little good. The scare we'd had from the wolves, and the perils ahead, had my nerves jangling like fiddle-strings, and after a bare hour of uneasy dozing I roused East and said we should be moving. The moon was up by now, so we should have light enough to ensure we didn't stray from the causeway; I took the driver's seat, and we slid away over the bridge and out on to the Arrow of Arabat.

For the first few miles it was quite wide, and as I kept to the eastern side there was a great expanse of hummocky snow to my right. But then the causeway gradually narrowed to perhaps half a mile, so that it was like driving along a very broad raised road, with the ground falling away sharply on either side to the snow-covered frozen waters of Azov and the Sivache lagoon; the salty charnel reek was awful, and even the horses didn't like it, tossing their heads and pulling awkwardly, so that I had to look sharp to manage them. We passed two empty post-stations, East and I exchanging at each one, and after about four hours he took the reins for what we hoped would be the last spell into Arabat.

I climbed into the back of the sled and made all the fastenings secure as we started off again, and was preparing to curl up on the back seat when Valla stirred sleepily in the darkness, murmuring "Harr-ee?" as she stretched restlessly in her pile of furs on the floor. I knelt down beside her and took her hand, but when I spoke to her she just mumbled and turned over; the laudanum and brandy still had her pretty well foxed, and there was no sense to be got out of her. It struck me she might be conscious enough to enjoy some company, though, so I slipped a hand beneath the furs and encountered warm, plump flesh; the touch of it sent the blood pumping in my head.

"Valla, my love," I whispered, just to be respectable; I could smell the sweet musky perfume of her skin, even over the brandy. I stroked her belly, and she moaned softly, and when I felt upwards and cupped her breast she turned towards me, her lips wet against my cheek. I was shaking as I put my mouth on hers, and then in a trice I was under the rugs, wallowing away like a sailor on shore leave, and half-drunk as she was she clung to me passionately. It was an astonishing business, for the furs were crackling with electricity, shocking me into unprecedented efforts— I thought I knew everything in the galloping line, but I'll swear there's no more alarming way of doing it than under a pile of skins in a sled skimming through the freezing Russian night; it's like performing on a bed of fire-crackers.

Engrossing as the novelty was, it was also exhausting, and I must have dozed off afterwards with Valla purring in her unconsciousness beside me. And then I became dimly conscious that the sled was slowing down, and gliding to a halt; I sat up, wondering what the blazes was wrong, buttoning myself hastily, and then I heard East jump down. I stuck my head out; he was standing by the sled, his head cocked, listening.

"Hush!" says he, sharply. "Do you hear anything?"

It crossed my mind that he'd overheard the heaving and crackling of my contortions with Valla, but his next words drove that idea out of my head, and implanted a new and disturbing one.

"Behind us," says he. "Listen!"

I scrambled out on to the snow, and we stood there, in the silent moonlight, straining our ears. At first there was nothing but the gentle sigh of the wind, the restless movement of the horses, and our own hearts thumping in the stillness—and then? Was there the tiniest murmur from somewhere back on the causeway, an indistinct but regular sound, softly up and down, up and down? I felt the hairs rise on my neck—it couldn't be wolves, not here, but what was it, then? We stared back along the causeway; it was very narrow now, only a couple of hundred yards across, but we had just come on to a stretch where it began to swerve gently towards the east, and it was difficult to make out anything in the gloom beyond the bend about a quarter of a mile behind us. Snow was falling gently, brushing our faces.

"I thought I heard..." Scud said slowly. "But perhaps I was wrong."

"Whatever it is, or isn't, there's no sense waiting here for it!" says I. "How far d'you reckon we are from Arabat?"

"Six miles, perhaps—surely not much more. Once there, we should be all right. According to that book of mine, there are little hills and gullies beyond the town, and we can lose ourselves in 'em if we want to, so..."

"The devil with dallying here, then!" cries I, in a fine stew. "Why the deuce are we wasting time, man? Let's be off from this blasted place, where there's *nowhere* to hide! Up on the box with you!"

"You're right, of course," says he. "I just...Hark, though! what's that?"

I listened, gulping—and there *was* a sound, a sound that I knew all too well. Very faintly, somewhere behind us, there was a gentle but now distinct drumming, and a tiny tinkling with it. There were horsemen on the causeway!

"Quick!" I shouted. "They're after us! Hurry, man—move those horses!"

He tumbled up on to the box, and as I swung myself on to the runner-mounting he cracked his whip and we slid forward across the snow. I clung to the side of the sled, peering back fearfully through the thin snow-fall, trying to make out if anything was showing beyond the bend in the causeway. We increased speed, and with the hiss of the runners it was impossible to listen for that frightening tell-tale sound.

"It may be just other travellers some distance back!" cries Scud from the box. "No one could be pursuing us!"

"Travellers at this time of night?" says I. "For God's sake, man, hurry those beasts!"

We were gathering speed now, cracking along at a good clip, and I was just about to swing myself under the cover—but I paused for another look back along the causeway, and what I saw nearly made me loose my hold. Very dimly through the falling flakes, I could just make out the causeway bend, and there, moving out on to the straight on this side of it, was a dark, indistinct mass —too big and irregular to be anything like a sled. And then the moonlight caught a score of twinkling slivers in the gloom, and I yelled at East in panic:

"It's cavalry—horsemen! They're after us, man!"

At the same time they must have seen us, for a muffled cry reached my ears, and now I could see the mass was indeed made up of separate pieces—a whole troop of them, coming on at a steady hand-gallop, and even as I watched they lengthened their stride, closing the distance. East was flogging at the horses, and the sled swayed and shuddered as we tore along—were they gaining on us? I clung there, trying to measure the distance, but I couldn't be sure; perhaps terror was colouring my judgment, making me see what I wanted to see, but so far as I could judge it looked as though we were holding our own for the moment.

"Faster!" I bawled to East. "Faster, man, or they'll have us!"

If only the bloody ass hadn't halted to listen—if only we hadn't wasted that precious hour dozing at Yenitchi! I couldn't begin to guess who these people were, or how they had got after us—but there they were, scudding along behind as fast as they could ride —four hundred yards, five hundred? Maybe five or more—I couldn't see whether they were hussars or dragoons or what, but I had a feeling they were heavies. Pray God they might be! I swung under the covers and threw myself on to the back seat, peering out through the window-flap. No, they weren't closing the distance—not yet. They were fanned out on the causeway as far as they could—good riding, that, for in column the rear files would have been ploughing into the churned snow of the men in front. Trust Russian cavalry to know about that.

But if they weren't gaining, they weren't dropping back, either. There was nothing in it—it's a queer thing, but where a horseman can easily overhaul a coach, or even a racing phaeton, a good sled on firm snow is another matter entirely. A horse with a load on his back makes heavy weather in snow, but unladen they can spank a sled along at nearly full gallop.

But how long could our beasts keep up their present pace? They were far from fresh—on the other hand, our pursuers didn't look too chipper, either. I watched them, my heart in my mouth, through the falling snow—was it getting thicker? By God, it was! If it really set in, and we could hold them as far as Arabat, we might be able to lose them—and even as the thought crossed my mind I felt the pace of the sled slacken just a little. I stared back at the distant horsemen, my throat dry, fixing on the centre man until my eyes ached and he seemed to be swimming mistily before me. He was just a vague blur—no, I could make out the shape of his head now—they were gaining, ever so little, but still gaining, creeping gradually up behind, yard by yard.

I couldn't stand it. I plunged to the side of the sled, stuck my head out, and bawled at East.

"They're closing, you fool! Faster! Can't you stir those bloody cattle!"

He shot a glance over his shoulder, cracked on the reins, and cried:

"It's no go . . . horses are almost played out! Can't . . . We're too heavy! Throw out some weight . . . the food . . . anything!"

I looked back; they were certainly gaining now, for the pale blobs of their faces were dimly visible even through the driving snow. They couldn't be much more than two hundred yards away, and one of 'em was shouting; I could just catch the voice, but not the words.

"Damn you!" I roared. "Russian bastards!" And fell back into the sled, scrabbling for our supplies, to hurl them out and lighten the sled. It was ridiculous—a few loaves and a couple of bottles— but out they went anyway, and not a scrap of difference did it make. The cover? If I let it go, would that help—it would cut down the wind resistance at least. I struggled with the buckles, stiff with the cold as they were, bruising my fingers and swearing feebly. There were eight of them, two to each side, and I just had the wit to undo the rear ones first, and the front ones last, whereupon the whole thing flew off, billowing away before it flopped on the snow. Perhaps it helped a trifle, but nothing like enough—they were still closing, almost imperceptibly, but closing nonetheless.

I groaned and cursed, while the freezing wind whipped at me, casting about for anything else to jettison. The furs? We'd freeze without them, and Valla didn't have a stitch—Valla! For an instant even I was appalled—but only for an instant. There was eight stone of her if there was an ounce—her loss would lighten us splendidly! And that wasn't all—they'd be bound to check, at least, if she came bouncing over the back. Gallant Russian gentle-men, after all, don't abandon naked girls in the snow. It would gain us seconds, anyway, and the loss of weight would surely do the rest.

I stooped over her, fighting to balance myself in the rocking sled. She was still unconscious, wrapped in her furs, looking truly lovely with her silver hair shining in the moonlight, murmuring a little in her half-drunken sleep. I heaved her upright, keeping the fur round her as best I could, and dragged her to the back seat. She nestled against me, and even in that moment of panic I found myself kissing her goodbye—well, it seemed the least I could do. Her lips were chill, with the snow driving past us in the wind; there'll be more than your lips cold in a moment, thinks I. At least her eyes were shut, and our pursuers would see to her before she froze.

"Good-bye, little one," says I. "Sleep tight," and I slipped my arm beneath her legs and bundled her over the back in one clean movement; there was a flash of white limbs as the furs fell away from her, and then she was sprawling on the snow behind us. The sled leaped forward as though a brake had been released, East yelled with alarm, and I could guess he was clinging to the reins for dear life; I gazed back at the receding dark blur where the fur lay beside Valla in the snow. She was invisible in the white confusion, but I saw the riders suddenly swerve out from the centre, a thin shout reached me, and then the leader and his immediate flankers were reining up, the riders on the wings were checking, too, but then they came on, rot them, while a little knot of the centre men halted and gathered, and I saw a couple of them swinging down from their saddles before they were lost in the snowy night.

And the dozen or so riders from the wings were losing ground, too! The lightened sled was fairly racing along. I yelled with delight, tossing my hands in the air, and scrambled forward, over the front of the sled, heaving myself up beside East on the box.

"On, Scud, on!" I shouted. "We're leaving 'em! We'll beat them yet!"

"What was it?" he cried. "What did you do? What did you throw out?"

"Useless baggage!" shouts I. "Never mind, man! Drive for your life!"

He shouted at the beasts, snapping the reins, and then cries:

"What baggage? We had none!" He glanced over his shoulder, at where the horsemen were dim shapes now in the distance, and his eyes fell on the sled. "Is Valla all—" and then he positively screamed. "Valla! Valla! My God!" He reeled in his seat, and I had to grab the reins as they slipped from his fingers. "You—you—no, you couldn't! Flashman, you . . ."

"Hold on, you infernal fool!" I yelled. "It's too late now!" He made a grab at the reins, and I had to sweep him back by main force, as I clutched the ribbons in one hand. "Stop it, damn you, or you'll have us sunk as well!"

"Rein up!" he bawled, struggling with me. "Rein up—must go back! My God, Valla! You filthy, inhuman brute—oh, God!"

"You idiot!" I shouted, lunging with all my weight to keep him off. "It was her or all of us!" Divine inspiration seized me. "Have you forgotten what we're doing, curse you? We've got to get to Raglan, with our news! If we don't—what about Ignatieff and his cursed plans? By heaven, East, I don't forget my duty, even if you do, and I tell you I'd heave a thousand Russian sluts into the snow for my country's sake!" And ten thousand for my own, but that's no matter. "Don't you see—it was that or be captured? And we've got to get through—whatever the cost!"

It stopped him struggling for the reins, at any rate; I felt him go limp beside me, and then he was sobbing like a man in torment, feebly beating with his fist against his temple.

"Oh, my God! How could you—oh, little Valla! I'd have gone —gladly! Oh, she'll die—freezing in that horrible waste!"

"Stop that damned babbling!" says I, stern duty personified. "Do you think I wouldn't have gone myself? And if I had, and some accident had then happened to you, where would our mission have been? While we're both free we double our hope of success." I snapped the reins, blinking against the driving snow as we sped along, and then stole a glance behind—nothing but whirling snow over the empty causeway; our pursuers were lost in the distance, but they'd still be there; we daren't check for an instant.

East was clinging to the box as we rocked along, a man stricken. He kept repeating Valla's name over and over again, and groaning. 'Oh, it's too much! Too high a price—God, have you no pity, Flashman? Are you made of stone?"

"Where my duty's concerned—aye!" cries I, in a fine patriotic fever. "You may thank God for it! If you'd had your way, we'd have died with Pencherjevsky, or be getting sabred to bits back yonder—and would that have served our country?" I decided a little manly rave would do no harm—not that I gave a damn what East thought, but it would keep him quiet, and stop him doing anything rash even now. "My God, East! Have you any notion what this night's work has cost me? D'you think it won't haunt me forever? D'you think I...I have no heart?" I dashed my knuckles across my eyes in a fine gesture. "Anyway, it's odds she'll be all right—they're her people, after all, and they'll wrap her up nice as ninepence."

He heaved a great shuddering breath. "Oh, I pray to God it may be so! But the horror of that moment—it's no good, Flashman—I'm not like you! I have not the iron will—I am not of your metal!"

You're right there, boy, thinks I, turning again to look back.

Still nothing, and then through the dimness ahead there was a faint glimmer of light, growing to a cluster, and the causeway was narrowing to nothing more than a dyke, so that I had to slow the sled for fear we should pitch down the banks to the frozen sea. There was a big square fort looming up on our right, and a straggle of buildings on the left, whence the lights came; between the road ran clear on to broad snowfields.

I snapped the whip, calling to the horses, and we drove through, never heeding a voice that called to us from the fort wall overhead. The horsemen might well have closed on us with our slowing down for the dyke, and there wasn't a second to spare. We scudded across the snowfield, casting anxious glances behind; the ground was becoming broken ahead, with little mounds and valleys, and stunted undergrowth—once into that, with the light snow still falling to blot out our tracks, we could twist away and lose them for certain.

"Bravo!" cries I, "we're almost there!" Behind us, Arabat and its fort were fading into the dark; the glimmer of the lights was diminishing as we breasted the first gentle slope and made for a broad gully in the rising ground. We sped silently into it, the sled rocking on the uneven surface; I reined in gently as we went down the reverse slope—and then the lead horse stumbled, whinnying, and came slithering down, the near-side beast swerved sharply, wrenching the reins from my hands, the sled slewed horribly, struck something with a fearful jar, East went flying over the side, and I was hurled headlong forward. I went somersaulting through the air, roaring, felt my back strike the rump of the near-side horse, and then I was plunging into the snow. I landed on my back, and there above me was the sled, hanging poised: I screamed and flung up my hands to save my head. The sled came lumbering over, slowly almost, on top of me, a fiery pain shot through my left side, a crushing weight was across my chest; I shrieked again, and then it settled, pinning me in the snow like a beetle on a card.

I beat at it with my fists, and tried to heave up, but its weight and the agony in my side stopped me—there was a rib gone for sure, if nothing worse. One of the horses was floundering about in the snow, neighing madly, and then I heard East's voice:

"Flashman! Flashman, are you all right?"

"I'm pinned!" I cried. "The sled—get the damned thing off me! Ah, God, my back's broken!"

He came blundering through the snow, and knelt beside me. He put his shoulder to the sled, heaving for all he was worth, but he might as well have tried to shift St Paul's. It didn't give so much as an inch.

"Get it off!" I groaned. "It's killing me—oh, Christ! Push, damn you—are you made of jelly?"

"I can't!" he whispered, straining away. "It won't ... budge. Ah!" And he fell back, panting.

"Rot you, it's crushing my guts out!" I cried. "Oh, God— I know my spine's gone—I can feel it! I'm—"

"Silence!" he hissed, and I could see he was listening, staring back towards Arabat. "Oh, no! Flashman—they're coming! I can hear the horsemen on the snow!" He flung himself at the sled, pushing futilely. "Oh, give me strength, God, please! Please!" He strove, thrusting at the sled, and groaning: "I can't ... I can't shift it! Oh, God, what shall I do?"

"Push, or dig, or anything, curse you!" I cried. "Get me loose, for God's sake! What are you doing, man? What is it?" For he was standing up now, staring back over the mouth of the gully towards Arabat; for half a minute he stood motionless, while I babbled and pawed at the wreck, and then he looked down at me, and his voice was steady.

"It's no go, old fellow. I know I can't move it. And they're coming. I can just see them, dimly—but they're heading this way." He dropped on one knee. "Flashman—I'm sorry. I'll have to leave you. I can hide—get away—reach Raglan. Oh, my dear comrade—if I could give my life, I would, but—"

"Rot you!" cries I. "My God, you can't leave me! Push the bloody thing—help me, man! I'm dying!"

"Oh, God!" he said. "This is agony! First Valla—now you! But I must get the news through—you know I must. You have shown me the way of duty, old chap—depend upon it, I shan't fail! And I'll tell them—when I get home! Tell them how you gave ... But I must go!"

"Scud," says I, babbling, "for the love of—"

"Hush," says he, clapping a hand over my lips. "Don't distress yourself—there's no time! I'll get there—one of the horses will serve, and if not—you remember the Big Side run by Brownsover, when we were boys? I finished, you know—I'll finish again, Flash, for your sake! They shan't catch me! Trust an old Rugby hare to distance a Russian pack—I will, and I'll hear you hallooing me on! I'll do it—for you, and for Valla—for both your sacrifices!"

"Damn Valla and you, too!" I squealed feebly. "You can't go! You can't leave me! Anyway, she's a bloody Russian! I'm British, you swine! Help me, Scud!"

But I don't think he so much as heard me. He bent forward, and kissed me on the forehead, and I felt one of his manly bloody tears on my brow. "Good-bye, dear old fellow," says he. "God bless you!"

And then he was ploughing away over the snow, to where the near-side horse was standing; he pulled the traces free of its head, and hurried off, pulling it along into the underbrush, with me bleating after him.

"Scud! For pity's sake, don't desert me! You can't—not your old school-fellow, you callous son-of-a-bitch! Please, stop, come back! I'm dying, damn you! I order you—I'm your superior officer! Scud! Please! Help me!"

But he was gone, and I was pinned, weeping, beneath that appalling weight, with the snow falling on my face, and the cold striking into my vitals. I would die, freezing horribly—unless they found me—oh, God, how would I die then? I struggled feebly, the pain lancing at my side, and then I heard the soft thumping of hooves on the snow, and a shout, and those cursed Russian voices, muffled from the mouth of the gully.

"*Paslusha-tyeh! Ah, tam—skorah!*"*

The jingle of harness was close now, and the pad of hooves —a horse neighed on the other side of the sled, and I squeezed my eyes shut, moaning. At any moment I expected to feel the agony of a lance-point skewering into my chest; then there was the snorting of a horse almost directly over my face, and I shrieked and opened my eyes. Two horsemen were sitting looking down on me, fur-wrapped figures with those stringy Cossack caps pulled down over their brows; fierce moustached faces peering at me.

* "Listen! Ah, there—quickly!"

"Help!" I croaked. "*Pamagityeh, pajalsta!*"*

One of them leaned forward. "*On syer-yaznuh ranyin*,"† says he, and they both laughed, as at a good joke. Then, to my horror, the speaker drew his *nagaika* from his saddle-bow, doubled it back, and leaned down over me.

"*Nyeh zashta*,"‡ says he, leering. His hand went up, I tried in vain to jerk my head aside, a searing pain seemed to cleave my skull, and then the dark sky rushed in on me.

* "Help, please!"
† "He is badly hurt."
‡ "Not at all."

8   I suppose my life has been full of
poetic justice—an expression customarily used by Holy Joes to
cloak the vindictive pleasure they feel when some enterprising
fellow fetches himself a cropper. They are the kind who'll say
unctuously that I was properly hoist with my own petard at
Arabat, and serve the bastard right. I'm inclined to agree; East
would never have abandoned me if I hadn't heaved Valla out of
the sled in the first place. He'd have stuck by me and the Christian
old school code, and let his military duty go hang. But my treatment of his beloved made it easy for him to forget the ties of
comradeship and brotherly love, and do his duty; all his pious
protestations about leaving me were really hypocritical moon-
shine, spouted out to salve his own conscience.

I know my Easts and Tom Browns, you see. They're never
happy unless their morality is being tried in the furnace, and
they can feel they're doing the right, Christian thing—and never
mind the consequences to anyone else. Selfish brutes. Damned
unreliable it makes 'em, too. On the other hand, you can always
count on me. I'd have got the news through to Raglan out of
pure cowardice and self-love, and to hell with East and Valla both;
but your pious Scud had to have a grudge to pay off before he'd
abandon me. Odd, ain't it? They'll do for us yet, with their
sentiment and morality.

In the meantime he had done for me, handsomely. If you're
one of the aforementioned who take satisfaction in seeing the
wicked go arse over tip into the pit which they have digged,
you'll relish the situation of old Flashy, a half-healed crack in his
head, a broken rib crudely strapped up with rawhide, lousy after a
week in a filthy cell under Fort Arabat, and with his belly muscles
fluttering in the presence of Captain Count Nicholas Pavlovitch
Ignatieff.

They had hauled me into the guard-room, and there he was,

the inevitable cigarette clamped between his teeth, those terrible hypnotic blue-brown eyes regarding me with no more emotion than a snake's. For a full minute he stared at me, the smoke escaping in tiny wreaths from his lips, and then without a change of expression he lashed me across the face with his gloves, back and forth, while I struggled feebly between my Cossacks guards, trying to duck my head from his blows.

"Don't!" I cried. "Don't, please! *Pajalsta!* I'm a prisoner! You've no right to . . . to treat me so! I'm a British officer . . . please! I'm wounded . . . for God's sake, stop!"

He gave me one last swipe, and then looked at his gloves, weighing them in his hand. Then, in that icy whisper, he said: "Burn those," and dropped them at the feet of the aide who stood beside him.

"You," he said to me, and his voice was all the more deadly for not bearing the slightest trace of heat or emotion, "plead for mercy. You need expect none. You are foresworn—a betrayer of the vilest kind. You were treated with every consideration, with kindness even, by a man who turned to you in his hour of need, laying on you the most solemn obligation to protect his daughter. You repaid him by abducting her, by trying to escape, and by abandoning her to her death. You . . ."

"It's a lie!" I shouted. "I didn't—it was an accident! She fell from the sled—it wasn't my fault! I was driving, I wasn't even with her!"

His reply to this was a gesture to the aide, who struck me with the gloves again.

"You are a liar," says Ignatieff. "The officer of the pursuing troop saw you. Pencherjevsky himself has told me how you and your comrade East left Starotorsk, how you basely seized the opportunity to escape . . ."

"It wasn't base . . . we'd given no parole . . . we had the right of any prisoners of war . . . in all honour . . ."

"You talk of honour," says he softly. "You thought to escape all censure, because you believed Pencherjevsky was doomed. Fortunately, he was not a *hetman* of Cossacks for nothing. He cut his way clear, and in spite of your unspeakable treatment of his daughter, she too survived."

"Thank God for that!" cries I. "Believe me, sir, you are quite mistaken. I intended no betrayal of the Count, and I swear I never mistreated his daughter—it was all an accident..."

"The only accident for you was the one that prevented your escaping. I promise you," he went on, in that level, sibilant voice, "that you will live to wish that sled had crushed your life out. For by your conduct, you understand, you have lost every right to be treated as an honourable man, or even as a common felon. You are beyond the law of nations, you are beyond mercy. One thing alone can mitigate your punishment."

He paused there, to let it sink in, and to take another cigarette. The aide lit it for him, while I waited, quaking and sweating.

"I require an answer to one question," says Ignatieff, "and you will supply it in your own language. Lie to me, or try to evade it, and I will have your tongue removed." His next words were in English. "*Why* did you try to escape?"

Terrified as I was, I daren't tell him the truth. I knew that if he learned that I'd found out about his expedition to India, it was all up with me.

"Because... because there was the opportunity... and there wasn't any dishonour in it. And we meant... ah, Miss Pencherjevsky no harm, I swear we didn't..."

"You lie. No one, in your situation, would have attempted such a foolhardy escape, let alone such a dishonourable one, without some pressing reason." The blue-brown eyes seemed to be boring into my brain. "I believe I know what it was—the only thing it could possibly be. And I assure you, in five minutes from now you will be dying, in excruciating agony, unless you can tell me what is meant by—" he paused, inhaling on his cigarette "—Item Seven." He let the smoke trickle down his nostrils. "If, by chance, you *are* unaware of what it means, you will die anyway."

There was nothing for it; I had to confess. I tried to speak, but my throat was dry. Then I stammered out hoarsely, in English:

"It's a plan... to invade India. Please, for God's sake, I found out about it by accident, I..."

"How did you discover it?"

I babbled it out, how we had eavesdropped in the gallery and heard him talking to the Tsar. "It was just by chance... I didn't mean to spy... it was East, and he said we must try to escape...

194

to get word to our people ... to warn them! I said it was dis-honourable, that we were bound as gentlemen ..."

"And Major East was with you, and overheard?"

"Yes, yes ... it was his notion, you see! I didn't like it ... and when he suggested we escape, when those beastly peasants attacked Starotorsk ... what could I do? But I swear we meant no harm, and ... and it's a lie that I mistreated Miss Pencherjevsky—I'll swear it, by my honour, on the Bible ..."

"Gag him," says Ignatieff. "Bring him to the courtyard. And bring a prisoner. Any one in the cells will do."

They stuffed a rag into my mouth, and bound it, stifling my pleas for mercy, for I was sure he was going to make away with me horribly, now that he had his information. They pinioned my wrists, and thrust me brutally out into the yard; it was freezing, and I had nothing but my shirt and breeches. I waited, trembling with cold and funk, until presently another Cossack appeared, driving in front of him a scared, dirty-looking peasant with fetters on his legs. Ignatieff, who had followed us out, and was pinching the paper of a cigarette, beckoned the Cossack.

"What was this fellow's offence?"

"Insubordination, Lord Count."

"Very good," says Ignatieff, and lit his cigarette.

Two more Cossacks appeared, carrying between them a curious bench, like a vaulting horse with very short legs and a flat top. The prisoner shrieked at the sight of it, and tried to run, but they dragged him to it, tearing off his clothes, and bound him on it face down, with thongs at his ankles, knees, waist and neck, so that he lay there, naked and immovable, but still screaming horribly.

Ignatieff beckoned one of the Cossacks, who held out to him a curious thick black coil, of what looked for all the world like shiny liquorice. Ignatieff hefted it in his hands, and then stepped in front of me and placed it over my head; I shuddered as it touched my shoulders, and was astonished by the weight of the thing. At a sign from Ignatieff the Cossack, grinning, drew it slowly off my shoulders, and I realized in horror as it slithered off like an obscene black snake that it was a huge whip, over twelve feet long, as thick as my arm at the butt and tapering to a point no thicker than a boot-lace.

"You will have heard of this," says Ignatieff softly. "It is called a *knout*. Its use is illegal. Watch."

The Cossack stood opposite the bench with its howling victim, took the *knout* in both hands, and swept it back over his shoulder so that its hideous lash trailed behind him in the snow. Then he struck.

I've seen floggings, and watched with fascination as a rule, but this was horrible, like nothing imaginable. That diabolical thing cut through the air with a noise like a steam whistle, so fast that you couldn't see it; there was a crack like a pistol-shot, a fearful, choked scream of agony, and then the Cossack was snaking it back for another blow.

"Wait," says Ignatieff, and to me: "Come here." They pushed me forward to the bench, the bile nearly choking me behind the gag; I didn't want to look, but they forced me. The wretched man's buttocks were cut clean across, as by a sabre, and the blood was pouring out.

"The drawing stroke," says Ignatieff. "Proceed."

Five more shrieking cuts, five more explosive cracks, five more razor gashes, and the snow beneath the bench was sodden with blood. The most horrible thing was that the victim was conscious still, making awful animal noises.

"Now observe," says Ignatieff, "the effect of a flat blow."

The Cossack struck a seventh time, but this time he didn't snap the *knout*, but let it fall smack across the patient's spine. There was a dreadful sound, like a wet cloth slapped on stone, but from the victim no cry at all. They unstrapped him, and as they lifted the bleeding wreck of his body from the bench, I saw it was hanging horribly limp in the middle.

"The killing stroke," said Ignatieff. "It is debatable how many of the drawing blows a man can endure, but with the flat stroke one is invariably fatal." He turned to look at me, and then at the blood-soaked bench, as though considering, while he smoked calmly. At last he dropped his cigarette in the snow.

"Bring him inside."

I was half-fainting with fear and shock when they dropped me sprawling in a chair, and Ignatieff sat down behind the table and waved them out. He lit himself another cigarette, and then said quietly:

"That was a demonstration, for your benefit. You see now what awaits you—except that when your turn comes I shall take the opportunity of ascertaining how many of the drawing strokes a vigorous and healthy man can suffer before he dies. Your one hope of escaping that fate lies in doing precisely as you are told —for I have a use for you. If I had not, you would be undergoing destruction by the *knout* at this moment."

He smoked in silence for a minute, never taking his eyes off me, and I watched him like a rabbit before a snake. Not only the hideous butchery I had watched, but the fact that he had condemned a poor devil to it *just to impress me*, appalled me utterly. And I knew I would do anything—anything, to escape that abomination.

"That you had somehow learned of Item Seven I already suspected," says Ignatieff at last. "Nothing else would have led you to flee. Accordingly, for the past week, we have proceeded on the assumption that intelligence of our expedition would reach Lord Raglan—and subsequently your government in London. We can now be certain that it has done so, since your companion, Major East, has not been recaptured. This betrayal is regrettable, but by no means disastrous. Indeed, it can be made to work to our advantage, for your authorities will suppose that they have seven months to prepare against the blow that is coming. They will be wrong. In four months from now our army will be advancing over the Khyber Pass, thirty thousand strong, with at least half as many Afghan allies eager to descend across the Indus. If every British soldier in India were sent to guard the frontier —which is impossible—it would not serve to stem our advance. No adequate help can arrive from England in time, and your troops will have a rebellious Indian population at their backs while we take them by the throat. Our agents are already at work, preparing that insurrection.

"You may wonder how it is possible to advance the moment of our attack by three months. It is simple. General Khruleff's original plan for an attack through the Syr Daria country to Afghanistan and India will be adhered to—our army had been preparing to take this route, which was abandoned only lately because of minor difficulties with native bandits and because the southern road, through Persia, offered a more secure and leisurely progress. The change of plan will thus be simple to effect, since the army is still poised for the northern route, and the arrangements for its transport by sea across Caspian and Aral can proceed immediately. This will ensure progress at twice the speed we could hope for if we went through Persia. And we will consolidate our position among the Syr Daria and Amu Daria tribesmen in passing."

I didn't doubt a word of it—not that I cared a patriotic damn. They could have India, China, and the whole bloody Orient for me, if only I could find a way out for myself.

"It is as well that you should know this," went on Ignatieff, "so that you may understand the part which I intend that you should play in it. A part for which you are providentially qualified. I know a great deal about you—so much, indeed, that you will be astonished at the extent of my knowledge. It is our policy to garner information, and I doubt," went on this cocky bastard, "whether any state in Europe can boast such extensive secret dossiers as we possess. I am especially aware of your activities in Afghanistan fourteen years ago—of your work, along with such agents as Burnes and Pottinger, among the Gilzais and other tribes. I know even of the exploit which earned you the extravagant nickname of 'Bloody Lance', of your dealings with Muhammed Akbar Khan, of your solitary survival of the disaster which befell the British Army*—a disaster in which, you may be unaware, our own intelligence service played some part."

Now, shaken and fearful as I was, one part of my mind was noting something from all this. Master Ignatieff might be a clever and devilish dangerous man, but he had at least one of the besetting weaknesses of youth: he was as vain as an Etonian duke, and it led him to commit the cardinal folly in a diplomatic man. He talked too much.

"It follows," says he, "that you can be of use to us in Afghanistan. It will be convenient, when our army arrives there, to have a British officer, of some small reputation in that country, to assist us in convincing the tribal leaders that the decay of British power is imminent, and that it will be in their interests to join in the conquest of India. They will not need much convincing, but

* See Flashman.

198

even so your betrayal will add to the impression our armed force will make."

For all his impassivity, I knew he was enjoying this; it was in the tilt of his cigarette, and the glitter in his gotch eye.

"It is possible, of course, that you will prefer death—even by the *knout*—to betrayal of your country. I doubt it, but I must take into consideration the facts which are to be found in your dossier. They tell me of a man brave to the point of recklessness, of proved resource, and of considerable intelligence. My own observation of you tends to contradict this—I do not judge you to be of heroic material, but I may be mistaken. Certainly your conduct at Balaclava, of which I have received eye-witness accounts, is of a piece with your dossier. It does not matter. If, when you have been taken to Afghanistan with our army, you decline to make what the Roman priests call a propaganda on our behalf, we shall derive what advantage we can from displaying you naked in an iron cage along the way. The *knouting* will take place when we arrive on Indian soil."

He had it all splendidly pat, this icy Muscovite bastard, and well pleased with himself he was, too. He pinched another cigarette between his fingers, thinking to himself to see if there was any other unpleasant detail he could rub into me, and deciding there wasn't, called to the Cossack guard.

"This man," says he, "is a dangerous and desperate criminal. He is to be chained wrist and ankle at once, and the keys are to be thrown away. He will accompany us to Rostov tomorrow, and if, while he is in your charge he should escape or die"—he paused, and when he went on it was as casually said as though he were confining them to barracks—"you will be *knouted* to death. And your families also. Take him away."

You may not credit it, but my feelings as they thrust me down into my underground pit, clamped chains on my wrists and ankles, and slammed the door on me, were of profound relief. For one thing, I was out of the presence of that evil madman with his leery optic—that may seem small enough, but you haven't been closeted with him, and I have. Point two, I was not only alive but due to be preserved in good health for at least four months—and I was old soldier enough to know that a lot can happen in that time. Point three, I wasn't going into the unknown: Afghanistan, ghastly place though it is, was a home county hunt to me, and if once I could get a yard start, I fancied I could survive the going a sight better than any Russian pursuers.

It was a mighty "if", of course, but funny things happen north of the Khyber—come to that, I wondered if Ignatieff and his brother-thugs knew exactly what they were tackling in taking an army through that country. We'd tried it, and God knew we were fitter to go to war than the Russians ever were, yet we'd come most horribly undone. I remembered my old sparring chums, the Gilzais and Baluchis and Khels and Afridis—and those fiends of Ghazis—and wondered if the Ruskis knew precisely the kind of folk they'd be relying on for safe-conduct and alliance.

They had their agents in Afghanistan, to be sure, and must have a shrewd notion of how things were; I wondered if they had secured their alliances in advance, perhaps with the King? And one thing was certain, the Afghans hated the British, and would join in an attack on India like Orangemen on the Twelfth. It would be all up with the Honourable East India Company then, and no bones about it.

Thinking about that, I could make a guess that if there was a point where the Russian force might run into trouble, it would be in the wild country that they must pass through before they reached Afghanistan. In my days at Kabul, Sekundar Burnes had told me a bit about it—of the independent Khanates at Bokhara and Samarkand and the Syr Daria country, where the Russians had even then been trying to extend their empire, and getting a bloody nose in the process. Fearsome bastards those northern tribes were, Tajiks and Uzbeks and the remnants of the great hordes, and from the little I'd heard from folk like Pencherjevsky, they were still fiercely resisting Russian encroachment. We'd had a few agents up that way ourselves, in my time, fellows like Burnes and Stoddart, trying to undermine Russian influence, but with our retreat from Afghanistan it was well out of our bailiwick now, and the Russians would no doubt eat up the tribes at their leisure. That's what Ignatieff had hinted, and I couldn't see the wild clans being able to stand up to an army of thirty thousand, with ten thousand Cossack cavalry and artillery trains and the rest of it.

No, setting aside a few minor rubs, this Russian expedition looked to me to be on a good firm wicket—but that mattered nothing as far as I was concerned. What I had to bide my time for was Afghanistan, and the moment when they brought me out of my blinkers to make what Ignatieff called a propaganda on Russia's behalf. That would be the moment to lift up mine eyes unto the hills, or the tall trees, or the nearest hole in the ground —anywhere at all, so long as it offered a refuge from Ignatieff. I didn't even think about the price of failure to escape—it was quite unthinkable.

You may think it strange, knowing me, that even in the hellish mess I found myself, with the shadow of horrible death hanging over me, I could think ahead so clearly. Well, it wasn't that I'd grown any braver as I got older—the reverse, if anything— but I'd learned, since my early days, that there's no point in wasting your wits and digestion blubbering over evil luck and folly and lost opportunities. I'll admit, when I thought how close I'd been to winning clear, I could have torn my hair—but there it was. However fearful my present predicament, however horrid the odds and dangers ahead, they'd get no better with being fretted over. It ain't always easy, if your knees knock as hard as mine, but you must remember the golden rule: when the game's going against you, stay calm—and cheat.

In this state of philosophic apprehension, then, I began my journey from Fort Arabat the following day—a journey such as I don't suppose any other Englishman has ever made. You can trace it on the map, all fifteen hundred miles of it, and your finger will go over places you never dreamed of, from the edge of civilization to the real back of beyond, over seas and deserts to mountains that perhaps nobody will ever climb, through towns and tribes that belong to the Arabian Nights rather than to the true story of a reluctant English gentleman (as the guide books would say) with two enormous scowling Cossacks brooding over him the whole way.

The first part of the journey was all too familiar, by sled back along the Arrow of Arabat, over the bridge at Yenitchi, and then east along that dreary winter coast to Taganrog, where the snow was already beginning to melt in the foul little streets, and the locals still appeared to be recovering from the excesses of the great winter fair at Rostov. Russians, in my experience, are part-drunk most of the time, but if there's a sober soul between the Black Sea and the Caspian for weeks after the Rostov *kermesse* he must be a Baptist hermit; Taganrog was littered with returned revellers. Rostov I don't much remember, or the famous river Don, but after that we took to *telegues*, and since the great Ignatieff was riding at the front of our little convoy of six vehicles, we made good speed. Too good for Flashy, bumping along uncomfortably on the straw in one of the middle wagons; my chains were beginning to be damned uncomfortable, and every jolt of those infernal *telegues* bruised my wrists and ankles. You may think fetters are no more than an inconvenience, but when every move you make means lifting a few pounds of steel, which chafes your flesh and jars your bones, and means you can never lie without their biting into you, they become a real torture. I pleaded to have them removed, if only for an hour or two, and got a kick in my half-mended rib for my pains.

Cossacks, of course, never wash (although they brush their coats daily with immense care) and I wasn't allowed to either, so by the time we were rolling east into the half-frozen steppe beyond Rostov I was filthy, bearded, tangled, and itchy beyond belief, stinking with the garlic of their awful food, and only praying that I wouldn't contract some foul disease from my noisome companions—for they even slept either side of me, with their *nagaikas* knotted into my chains. It ain't like a honeymoon at Baden, I can tell you.

There were four hundred miles of that interminable plain, getting worse as it went on; it took us about five days, as near as I remember, with the *telegues* going like blazes, and new horses at every post-house. The only good thing was that as we went the weather grew slightly warmer, until when we were entering the great salt flats of the Astrakhan, the snow vanished altogether, and you could even travel without your *tulup*.

Astrakhan city itself is a hell-hole. The land all about is as flat as the Wash country, and the town itself lies so low they have a great dyke all round to prevent the Volga washing it into the Caspian, or t'other way round. As you might expect, it's a plague spot; you can smell the pestilence in the air, and before we passed through the dyke Ignatieff ordered everyone to soak his face and hands with vinegar, as though that would do any good. Still, it was the nearest I came to making toilet the whole way.

Mark you, there was one good thing about Astrakhan: the women. Once you get over towards the Caspian the people are more slender and Asiatic than your native Russian, and some of those dark girls, with their big eyes and long straight noses and pouting lips had even me, in my unkempt misery, sitting up and dusting off my beard. But of course I never got near them; it was into the *kremlin* for Flash and his heavenly twins, and two nights in a steaming cell before they put us aboard a steamer for the trip across the Caspian.

It's a queer sea, that one, for it isn't above twenty feet deep, and consequently the boats are of shallow draught, and bucket about like canoes. I spewed most of the way, but the Cossacks, who'd never sailed before, were in a fearful way, vomiting and praying by turns. They never let go of me, though, and I realized with a growing sense of alarm that if these two watch-dogs were kept on me all the way to Kabul, I'd stand little chance of giving them the slip. Their terror of Ignatieff was if anything even greater than mine, and in the worst of the boat's heaving one of them was always clutching my ankle chains, even if he was rolling about the deck retching at the same time.

It was four days of misery before we began to steam through clusters of ugly, sandy little islands towards the port of Tishkandi, which was our destination. I'm told it isn't there any longer, and this is another strange thing about the Caspian—its coastline changes continually, almost like the Mississippi shores. One year there are islands, and next they have become hills on a peninsula, while a few miles away a huge stretch of coast will have changed into a lagoon.

Tishkandi's disappearance can have been no loss to anyone; it was a dirty collection of huts with a pier, and beyond it the ground climbed slowly through marshy salt flats to two hundred miles of arid, empty desert. You could call it steppe, I suppose, but it's dry, rocky heart-breaking country, fit only for camels and lizards.

"Ust-Yurt," says one of the officers, as he looked at it, and the very name sent my heart into my boots.

It's dangerous country, too. There was a squadron of lancers waiting for us when we landed, to guard us against the wild desert tribes, for this was beyond the Russian frontiers, in land where they were still just probing at the savage folk who chopped up their caravans and raided their outposts whenever they had the chance. When we made camp at night it was your proper little laager, with sangars at each corner, and sentries posted, and half a dozen lancers out riding herd. All very business-like, and not what I'd have expected from Ruskis, really. But this was their hard school, as I was to learn, like our North-west Frontier, where you either soldiered well or not at all.

It was five days through the desert, not too uncomfortable while we were moving, but freezing hellish at night, and the dromedaries with their native drivers must have covered the ground at a fair pace, forty miles a day or thereabouts. Once or twice we saw horsemen in the distance, on the low rocky *barchans*, and I heard for the first time names like "Kazak" and "Turka", but they kept a safe distance. On the last day, though, we saw more of them, much closer, and quite peaceable, for these were people of the Aral coast, and the Russians had them fairly well in order on that side of the sea. When I saw them near I had a strange sense of recognition—those swarthy faces, with here and there a hooked nose and a straggling moustache, the dirty puggarees swathed round the heads, and the open belted robes, took me back to Northern India and the Afghan hills. I found myself stealing a look at my Cossacks and the lancers, and even at Ignatieff riding with the other officers at the head of our caravan, and thinking to myself—these ain't your folk, my lads, but they're mighty close to some I used to know. It's a strange thing, to come through hundreds of miles of wilderness, from a foreign land and moving in the wrong direction, and suddenly find yourself sniffing the air and thinking, "home". If you're British, and have soldiered in India, you'll understand what I mean.

Late that afternoon we came through more salty flats to a long coastline of rollers sweeping in from a sea so blue that I found myself muttering through my beard "Thalassa or thalatta, the former or the latter?," it seemed so much like the ocean that old Arnold's Greeks had seen after their great march. And suddenly I could close my eyes and hear his voice droning away on a summer afternoon at Rugby, and smell the cut grass coming in through the open windows, and hear the fags at cricket outside, and from that I found myself dreaming of the smell of hay in the fields beyond Renfrew, and Elspeth's body warm and yielding, and the birds calling at dusk along the river, and the pony champing at the grass, and it was such a sweet, torturing longing that I groaned aloud, and when I opened my eyes the tears came, and there was a hideous Russian voice clacking "Aralskoe More!",* and bright Asian sunlight, and the chains galling my wrist and ankle-bones, and foreign flat faces all round, and I realized that my earlier thoughts of home had been an illusion, and this was alien, frightening land.

There was a big military camp on the shore, and a handy little steamer lying off, and while the rest of us waited Ignatieff was received with honours by a group of senior officers—and he only a captain, too. Of course, I'd realized before this that he was a big noise, but the way they danced attendance on him you'd have thought he was the Tsar's cousin. (Maybe he was, for all I know.)

They put us aboard the steamer that evening, and I was so tuckered out by the journey that I just slept where I lay down. And in the morning there was a coast ahead, with a great new wooden pier, and a huge river flowing down between low banks to the sea. As far as I could see the coast was covered with tents, and there was another steamer, and half a dozen big wooden transports, and one great warship, all riding at anchor between the pier and the river mouth. There were bugles sounding on the distant shore, and swarms of people everywhere, among the tents, on the pier, and on the ships, and a great hum of noise in the midst of which a military band was playing a rousing march; this is the army, I thought, or most of it, this is their Afghan expedition.

I asked one of the Russian sailors what the river might be, and he said: "Syr Daria," and then pointing to a great wooden stockaded fort on the rising land above the river, he added: "Fort Raim."[35] And then one of the Cossacks pushed him away, cursing, and told me to hold my tongue.

They landed us in lighters, and there was another delegation of smart uniforms to greet Ignatieff, and an orderly holding a horse for him, and all around tremendous bustle of unloading and

* "Aral Sea!"

ferrying from the ships, and gangs of orientals at work, with Russian non-coms bawling at them and swinging whips, and gear being stowed in the newly-built wooden sheds along the shore. I watched gun limbers being swung down from a derrick, and cursing, half-naked gangs hauling them away; the whole pier was piled with crates and bundles, and for all the world it looked like the levee at New Orleans, except that this was a temporary town of huts and tents and lean-to's. But there were just as many people, sweating and working in orderly chaos, and you could feel the excitement in the air.

Ignatieff came trotting down to where I was sitting between my Cossacks, and at a word they hauled me up and we set off at his heels through the confusion, up the long, gradual slope to the fort. It was farther off than I'd expected, about a mile, so that it stood well back from the camp, which was all spread out like a sand-table down the shore-line. As we neared the fort he stopped, and his orderly was pointing at the distant picket lines and identifying the various regiments—New Russian Dragoons, Romiantzoff's Grenadiers, Astrakhan Carabiniers, and Aral Hussars, I remember. Ignatieff saw me surveying the camp, and came over. He hadn't spoken to me since we left Arabat.

"You may look," says he, in that chilling murmur of his, "and reflect on what you see. The next Englishman to catch sight of them will be your sentry on the walls of Peshawar. And while you are observing, look yonder also, and see the fate of all who oppose the majesty of the Tsar."

I looked where he pointed, up the hill towards the fort, and my stomach turned over. To one side of the gateway was a series of wooden gallows, and from each one hung a human figure— although some of them were hard to recognize as human. A few hung by their arms, some by their ankles, one or two lucky ones by their necks. Some were wasted and blackened by exposure; at least one was still alive and stirring feebly. An awful carrion reek drifted down on the clear spring air.

"Unteachables," says Ignatieff. "Bandit scum and rebels of the Syr Daria who have been unreceptive to our sacred Russian imperial mission. Perhaps, when we have lined their river with sufficient of these examples, they will learn. It is the only way to impress recalcitrants. Do you not agree?"

He wheeled his horse, and we trailed up after him towards the fort. It was bigger, far bigger, than I'd expected, a good two hundred yards square, with timber ramparts twenty feet high, and at one end they were already replacing the timber with rough stone. The Russian eagle ensign was fluttering over the roofed gatehouse, there were grenadiers drawn up and saluting as Ignatieff cantered through, and I trudged in, clanking, to find myself on a vast parade, with good wooden barracks around the walls, troops drilling in the dusty square, and a row of two-storey administrative buildings down one side. It was a very proper fort, something like those of the American frontier in the 'seventies; there were even some small cottages which I guessed were officers' quarters.

Ignatieff was getting his usual welcome from a tubby chap who appeared to be the commandant; I wasn't interested in what they said, but I gathered the commandant was greatly excited, and was babbling some great news.

"Not both of them?" I heard Ignatieff say, and the other clapped his hands in great glee and said, yes, both, a fine treat for General Perovski and General Khruleff when they arrived.

"They will make a pretty pair of gallows, then," says Ignatieff. "You are to be congratulated, sir. Nothing could be a better omen for our march through Syr Daria."

"Ah, ha, excellent!" cries the tubby chap, rubbing his hands. "And that will not be long, eh? All is in train here, as you see, and the equipment arrives daily. But come, my dear Count, and refresh yourself."

They went off, leaving me feeling sick and hang-dog between my guards; the sight of those tortured bodies outside the stockade had brought back to me the full horror of my own situation. And I felt no better when there came presently a big, brute-faced sergeant of grenadiers, a coiled *nagaika* in his fist, to tell my Cossacks they could fall out, as he was taking me under his wing.

"Our necks depend on this fellow," says one of the Cossacks doubtfully, and the sergeant sneered, and scowled at me.

"My neck depends on what I've got in the cells already," growls he. "This offal is no more precious than my two birds. Be at peace; he shall join them in my most salubrious cell, from which even the lizards cannot escape. March him along!"

They escorted me to a corner on the landward side of the fort, down an alley between the wooden buildings, and to a short flight of stone steps leading down to an iron-shod door. The sergeant hauled back the massive bolts, thrust back the creaking door, and then reached up, grabbing me by my wrist-chains.

"In, *tut!*" he snarled, and yanked me headlong down into the cell. The door slammed, the bolts ground to, and I heard him guffawing brutally as their footsteps died away.

I lay there trembling on the dirty floor, just about done with fatigue and fear. At least it was dim and cool in here. And then I heard someone speaking in the cell, and raised my head; at first I could make nothing out in the faint light that came from a single window high in one wall, and then I started with astonishment, for suspended flat in the air in the middle of the cell, spread-eagled as though in flight, was the figure of a man. As my eyes grew accustomed to the dimness I drew in a shuddering breath, for now I could see that he was cruelly hung between four chains, one to each limb from the top corners of the room. More astonishing still, beneath his racked body, which hung about three feet from the floor, was crouched another figure, supporting the hanging man on his back, presumably to take the appalling strain of the chains from his wrists and ankles. It was the crouching man who was speaking, and to my surprise, his words were in Persian.

"It is a gift from God, brother," says he, speaking with difficulty. "A rather dirty gift, but human—if there is such a thing as a human Russian. At least, he is a prisoner, and if I speak politely to him I may persuade him to take my place for a while, and bear your intolerable body. I am too old for this, and you are heavier than Abu Hassan, the breaker of wind."

The hanging man, whose head was away from me, tried to lift it to look. His voice, when he spoke, was hoarse with pain, but what he said was, unbelievably, a joke.

"Let him . . . approach . . . then . . . and I pray . . . to God . . . that he has . . . fewer fleas . . . than you . . . Also . . . you are . . . a most . . . uncomfortable . . . support . . . God help . . . the woman . . . who shares . . . your bed."

"Here is thanks," says the crouching man, panting under the weight. "I bear him as though I were the Djinn of the Seven

Peaks, and he rails at me. You, *nasrani*,"* he addressed me: "If you understand God's language, come and help me to support this ingrate, this sinner. And when you are tired, we shall sit in comfort against the wall, and gloat over him. Or I may squat on his chest, to teach him gratitude. Come, Ruski, are we not all God's creatures?"

And even as he said it, his voice quavered, he staggered under the burden above him, and slumped forward unconscious on the floor.

* Christian.

9

The hanging man gave a sudden cry of anguish as his body took the full stretch of the chains; he hung there moaning and panting until, without really thinking, I scrambled forward and came up beneath him, bearing his trunk across my stooped back. His face was hanging backward beside my own, working with pain.

"God . . . thank you!" he gasped at last. "My limbs are on fire! But not for long—not for long—if God is kind." His voice came in a tortured whisper. "Who are you—a Ruski?"

"No," says I, "an Englishman, a prisoner of the Russians."

"You speak . . . our tongue . . . in God's name?"

"Yes," says I, "Hold still, curse you, or you'll slip!"

He groaned again: he was a devilish weight. And then: "Providence . . . works strangely," says he. "An *angliski* . . . here. Well, take heart, stranger . . . you may be . . . more fortunate . . . than you know."

I couldn't see that, not by any stretch, stuck in a lousy cell with some Asiatic nigger breaking my back. Indeed, I was regretting the impulse which had made me bear him up—who was he to me, after all, that I shouldn't let him dangle? But when you're in adversity it don't pay to antagonize your companions, at least until you know what's what, so I stayed unwillingly where I was, puffing and straining.

"Who . . . are you?" says he.

"Flashman. Colonel, British Army."

"I am Yakub Beg,"[36] whispers he, and even through his pain you could hear the pride in his voice. "Kush Begi, Khan of Khokand, and guardian of . . . the White Mosque. You are my . . . guest . . . sent to me . . . from heaven. Touch . . . on my knee . . . touch on my bosom . . . touch where you will."

I recognized the formal greeting of the hill folk, which wasn't appropriate in the circumstances.

"Can't touch anything but your arse at present," I told him, and I felt him shake—my God, he could even laugh, with the arms and legs being drawn out of him.

"It is a . . . good answer," says he. "You talk . . . like a Tajik. We laugh . . . in adversity. Now I tell you . . . Englishman . . . when I go hence . . . you go too."

I thought he was just babbling, of course. And then the other fellow, who had collapsed, groaned and sat up, and looked about him.

"Ah, God, I was weak," says he. "Yakub, my son and brother, forgive me. I am as an old wife with dropsy; my knees are as water."

Yakub Beg turned his face towards mine, and you must imagine his words punctuated by little gasps of pain.

"That ancient creature who grovels on the floor is Izzat Kutebar,"[37] says he. "A poor fellow of little substance and less wit, who raided one Ruski caravan too many and was taken, through his greed. So they made him 'swim upon land', as I am swimming now, and he might have hung here till he rotted—and welcome—but I was foolish enough to think of rescue, and scouted too close to this fort of Shaitan. So they took me, and placed me in his chains, as the more important prisoner of the two—for he is dirt, this feeble old Kutebar. He swung a good sword once, they say—God, it must have been in Timur's time!"

"By God!" cries Kutebar. "Did I lose Ak Mechet to the Ruskis? Was I whoring after the beauties of Bokhara when the beast Perovski massacred the men of Khokand with his grapeshot? No, by the pubic hairs of Rustum! I was swinging that good sword, laying the Muscovites in swathes along Syr Daria, while this fine fighting chief here was loafing in the bazaar with his darlings, saying 'Eyewallah, it is hot today, Give me to drink, Miriam, and put a cool hand on my forehead.' Come out from under him, *feringhee*, and let him swing for his pains."

"You see?" says Yakub Beg, craning his neck and trying to grin. "A dotard, flown with dreams. A *badawi zhazh-kayan** who talks as the wild sheep defecate, at random, everywhere. When you and I go hither, Flashman *bahadur*, we shall leave him, and even the Ruskis will take pity on such a dried-up husk, and employ

* A wild babbler.

211

him to clean their privies—those of the common soldiers, you understand, not the officers."

If I hadn't served long in Afghanistan, and learned the speech and ways of the Central Asian tribes, I suppose I'd have imagined that I was in a cell with a couple of madmen. But I knew this trick that they have of reviling those they respect most, in banter, of their love of irony and formal imagery, which is strong in Pushtu and even stronger in Persian, the loveliest of all languages.

"When you go hither!" scoffs Kutebar, climbing to his feet and peering at his friend. "When will that be? When Buzurg Khan remembers you? God forbid I should depend on the good-will of such a one. Or when Sahib Khan comes blundering against this place as you and he did two years ago, and lost two thousand men? Eyah! Why should they risk their necks for you—or me? We are not gold; once we are buried, who will dig us up?"

"My people will come," says Yakub Beg. "And *she* will not forget me."

"Put no faith in women, and as much in the Chinese," says Kutebar cryptically. "Better if this stranger and I try to surprise the guard, and cut our way out."

"And who will cut these chains?" says the other. "No, old one, put the foot of courage in the stirrup of patience. They will come, if not tonight, then tomorrow. Let us wait."

"And while you're waiting," says I, "put the shoulder of friendship beneath the backside of helplessness. Lend a hand, man, before I break in two."

Kutebar took my place again, exchanging insults with his friend, and I straightened up to take a look at Yakub Beg. He was a tall fellow, so far as I could judge, narrow waisted and big shouldered—for he was naked save for his loose *pyjamy* trousers —with great corded arm muscles. His wrists were horribly torn by his manacles, and while I sponged them with water from a *chatti** in the corner I examined his face. It was one of your strong hill figureheads, lean and long-jawed, but straight-nosed for once—he'd said he was a Tajik, which meant he was half-Persian. His head was shaved, Uzbek fashion, with a little scalp-lock to one side, and so was his face, except for a tuft of forked beard on his chin. A tough customer, by the look of him; one of

* Water-jug.

those genial mountain scoundrels who'll tell you merry stories while he stabs you in the guts just for the fun of hearing his knife-hilt bells jingle.

"You are an Englishman," says he, as I washed his wrists. "I knew one, once, long ago. At least I saw him, in Bokhara, the day they killed him. He was a man, that one—Khan Ali, with the fair beard. 'Embrace the faith,' they said. 'Why should I?' says he, 'since you have murdered my friend who forsook his church and became a Muslim. Ye have robbed; ye have killed; what do you want of me? And they said, 'Blood'. Says he: 'Then make an end.' And they killed him. I was only a youth, but I thought, when I go, if I am far from home, let me go like that one. He was a *ghazi*,* that Khan Ali."[38]

"Much good it did him," growled Kutebar, underneath. "For that matter, much good Bokhara ever did anyone. They would sell us to the Ruskis for a handful of millet. May their goats' milk turn to urine and their girls all breed Russian bastards—which they will do, no doubt, with alarming facility."

"You spoke of getting out of here," says I to Yakub Beg. "Is it possible? Will your friends attempt a rescue?"

"He has no friends," says Kutebar. "Except me, and see the pass I am brought to, propping up his useless trunk."

"They will come," says Yakub Beg, softly. He was pretty done, it seemed to me, with his eyes closed and his face ravaged with pain. "When the light fades, you two must leave me to hang —no, Izzat, it is an order. You and Flashman *bahadur* must rest, for when the Lady of the Great Horde comes over the wall the Ruskis will surely try to kill us before we can be rescued. You two must hold them, with your shoulders to the door."

"If we leave you to hang you will surely die," says Kutebar, gloomily. "What will I say to her then?" And suddenly he burst into a torrent of swearing, slightly muffled by his bent position. "These Russian apes! These scum of Muscovy! God smite them to the nethermost pit! Can they not give a man a clean death, instead of racking him apart by inches? Is this their civilizing empire? Is this the honour of the soldiers of the White Tsar? May God the compassionate and merciful rend the bowels from their bodies and—"

* Champion.

"Do you rest, old groaner," gasps Yakub, in obvious pain from the passionate heaving of his supporter. "Then you may rend them on your own account, and spare the All-wise the trouble. Lay them in swathes along Syr Daria—again."

And in spite of Kutebar's protests, Yakub Beg was adamant. When the light began to fade he insisted that we support him no longer, but let him hang at full stretch in his chains. I don't know how he endured it, for his muscles creaked, and he bit his lip until the blood ran over his cheek, while Kutebar wept like a child. He was a burly, grizzled old fellow, stout enough for all his lined face and the grey hairs on his cropped head, but the tears fairly coursed over his leathery cheeks and beard, and he damned the Russians as only an Oriental can. Finally he kissed the hanging man on the forehead, and clasped his chained hand, and came over to sit by me against the wall.

Now that I had a moment to think, I didn't know what to make of it all. My mind was in a whirl. When you have been tranquil for a while, as I had been at Starotorsk, and then dreadful things begin to happen to you, one after another, it all seems like a terrible nightmare; you have to force your mind to steady up and take it all in, and make yourself understand that it is happening. That flight through the snow with East and Valla—was it only four weeks ago? And since then I'd been harried half-way round the world, it seemed, from those freezing snowy steppes, across sea and desert, to this ghastly fort on the edge of nowhere, and here I was—Harry Flashman, rank of Colonel, 17th Lancers, aide-de-camp to Lord Raglan (God, this time last year I'd been playing pool in Piccadilly with little Willy)—here I was, in a cell with two Tajik-Persian bandits who talked a language[39] I hadn't heard in almost fifteen years, and lived in another world that had nothing to do with Raglan or Willy or Piccadilly or Starotorsk or —oh, aye, it had plenty to do with the swine Ignatieff. But they were talking of rescue and escape, as though it were sure to come, and they chained in a stinking dungeon—I had to grip hard to realize it. It might mean—it just might—that when I had least right to expect it, there was a chance of freedom, of throwing off the horrible fear of the death that Ignatieff had promised me. Freedom, and flight, and perhaps, at the end of it, safety?

I couldn't believe it. I'd seen the fort, and I'd seen the Russian host down on the shore. You'd need an army—and yet, these fellows were much the same as Afghans, and I knew *their* way of working. The sudden raid, the surprise attack, the mad hacking melee (I shuddered at the recollection), and then up and away before civilized troops have rubbed the sleep from their eyes. There were a thousand questions I wanted to ask Kutebar—but what was the use? They had probably just been talking to keep their spirits up. Nothing would happen; we were stuck, in the grip of the bear, and on that despairing conclusion I must have fallen asleep.

And nothing did happen. Dawn came, and three Russians with it bearing a dish of nauseating porridge; they jeered at us and then withdrew. Yakub Beg was half-conscious, swinging in his fetters, and through that interminable day Kutebar and I took turns to prop him up. I was on the point, once or twice, of rebelling at the work, which didn't seem worth it for all the slight relief it gave his tortured joints, but one look at Kutebar's face made me think better of it. Yakub Beg was too weak to joke now, or say much at all, and Kutebar and I just crouched or lay in silence, until evening came. Yakub Beg somehow dragged himself back to sense then, just long enough to order Kutebar hoarsely to let him swing, so that we should save our strength. My back was aching with the strain, and in spite of my depression and fears I went off to sleep almost at once, with that stark figure spread horribly overhead in the fading light, and Kutebar weeping softly beside me.

As so often happens, I dreamed of the last thing I'd seen before I went to sleep, only now it was I, not Yakub Beg, who was hanging in the chains, and someone (whom I knew to be my old enemy Rudi Starnberg) was painting my backside with boot blacking. My late father-in-law, old Morrison, was telling him to spread it thin, because it cost a thousand pounds a bottle, and Rudi said he had gallons of the stuff, and when it had all been applied they would get Narreeman, the Afghan dancing-girl, to ravish me and throw me out into the snow. Old Morrison said it was a capital idea, but he must go through my pockets first; his ugly, pouchy old face was leering down at me, and then slowly it changed into Narreeman's, painted and mask-like, and the dream became rather pleasant, for she was crawling all over me, and we were floating far, far up above the others, and I was roaring so lustfully that she put her long, slim fingers across my lips, cutting off my cries, and I tried to tear my face free as her grip grew tighter and tighter, strangling me, and I couldn't breathe; she was murmuring in my ear and her fingers were changing into a hairy paw—and suddenly I was awake, trembling and sweating, with Kutebar's hand clamped across my mouth, and his voice hissing me to silence.

It was still night, and the cold in the cell was bitter. Yakub Beg was hanging like a corpse in his chains, but I knew he was awake, for in the dimness I could see his head raised, listening. There wasn't a sound except Kutebar's hoarse breathing, and then, from somewhere outside, very faint, came a distant sighing noise, like a sleepy night-bird, dying away into nothing. Kutebar stiffened, and Yakub Beg's chains clinked as he turned and whispered:

"*Bhisti-sawad!** The sky-blue wolves are in the fold!"

Kutebar rose and moved over beneath the window. I heard him draw in his breath, and then, between his teeth, he made that same strange, muffled whistle—it's the kind of soft, low noise you sometimes think you hear at night, but don't regard, because you imagine it is coming from inside your own head. The Khokandians can make it travel up to a mile, and enemies in between don't even notice it. We waited, and sure enough, it came again, and right on its heels the bang of a musket, shattering the night.

There was a cry of alarm, another shot, and then a positive volley culminating in a thunderous roar of explosion, and the dim light from the window suddenly increased as with a lightning flash. And then a small war broke out, shots, and shrieks and Russian voices roaring, and above all the hideous din of yelling voices—the old Ghazi war-cry that had petrified me so often on the Kabul road.

"They have come!" croaked Yakub Beg. "It is Ko Dali's daughter! Quick, Izzat—the door!"

Kutebar was across the cell in a flash, roaring to me. We threw ourselves against the door, listening for the sounds of our guards.

"They have blown in the main gate with *barut*,"† cries Yakub Beg weakly. "Listen—the firing is all on the other side! Oh, my

* Heavenly!
† Gunpowder.

216

darling! Eyah! Kutebar, is she not a queen among women, a *najud*?* Hold fast the door, for when the Ruskis guess why she has come they will—"

Kutebar's shout of alarm cut him short. Above the tumult of shooting and yelling we heard a rush of feet, the bolts were rasping back, and a great weight heaved at the door on the other side. We strained against it, there was a roar in Russian, and then a concerted thrust from without. With our feet scrabbling for purchase on the rough floor we held them; they charged together and the door gave back, but we managed to heave it shut again, and then came the sound of a muffled shot, and a splinter flew from the door between our faces.

"*Bahnanas!*"† bawled Kutebar. "Monkeys without muscles! Can two weak prisoners hold you, then? Must you shoot, you bastard sons of filth?"

Another shot, close beside the other, and I threw myself sideways; I wasn't getting a bullet in my guts if I could help it. Kutebar gave a despairing cry as the door was forced in; he stumbled back into the cell, and there on the threshold was the big sergeant, torch in one hand and revolver in the other, and two men with bayoneted muskets at his heels.

"That one first!" bawls the sergeant, pointing at Yakub Beg. "Still, you!" he added to me, and I crouched back beside the door as he covered me. Kutebar was scrambling up beyond Yakub Beg; the two soldiers ignored him, one seizing Yakub Beg about the middle to steady him while the other raised his musket aloft to plunge the bayonet into the helpless body.

"Death to all Ruskis!" cries Yakub. "Greetings, Timur—"

But before the bayonet could come down Kutebar had launched himself at the soldier's legs; they fell in a thrashing tangle of limbs, Kutebar yelling blue murder, while the other soldier danced round them with his musket, trying to get a chance with his bayonet, and the sergeant bawled to them to keep clear and give him a shot.

Old dungeon-fighters like myself—and I've had a wealth of experience, from the vaults of Jotunberg, where I was sabre to sabre with Starnberg, to that Afghan prison where I let dear old

* A woman of intelligence and good shape.
† Apes.

Hudson take the strain—know that the thing to do on these occasions is find a nice dark corner and crawl into it. But out of sheer self-preservation I daren't—I knew that if I didn't take a hand Kutebar and Yakub would be dead inside a minute, and where would Cock Flashy be then, poor thing? The sergeant was within a yard of me, side on, revolver hand extended towards the wrestlers on the floor; there was two feet of heavy chain between my wrists, so with a silent frantic prayer I swung my hands sideways and over, lashing the doubled chain at his forearm with all my strength. He screamed and staggered, the gun dropping to the floor, and I went plunging after it, scrabbling madly. He fetched up beside me, but his arm must have been broken, for he tried to claw at me with his far hand, and couldn't reach; I grabbed the gun, stuck it in his face, and pulled the trigger—and the bloody thing was a single-action weapon, and wouldn't fire!

He floundered over me, trying to bite—and his breath was poisonous with garlic—while I wrestled with the hammer of the revolver. His sound hand was at my throat; I kicked and heaved to get him off, but his weight was terrific. I smashed at his face with the gun, and he released my throat and grabbed my wrist; he had a hold like a vice, but I'm strong, too, especially in the grip of fear, and with a huge heave I managed to get him half off me—and in that instant the soldier with the bayonet was towering over us, his weapon poised to drive down at my midriff.

There was nothing I could do but scream and try to roll away; it saved my life, for the sergeant must have felt me weaken, and with an animal snarl of triumph flung himself back on top of me —just as the bayonet came down to spit him clean between the shoulder blades. I'll never forget that engorged face, only inches from my own—the eyes starting, the mouth snapping open in agony, and the deafening scream that he let out. The soldier, yelling madly, hauled on his musket to free the bayonet; it came out of the writhing, kicking body just as I finally got the revolver cocked, and before he could make a second thrust I shot him through the body.

As luck had it, he fell on top of the sergeant, so there was Flashy, feverishly cocking the revolver again beneath a pile of his slain. The sergeant was dead, or dying, and being damned messy about it, retching blood all over me. I struggled as well as I could with my fettered hands, and had succeeded in freeing myself except for my feet—those damned fetters were tangled among the bodies—when Yakub shouted:

"Quickly, *angliski! Shoot!*"

The other soldier had broken free from Kutebar, and was in the act of seizing his fallen musket; I blazed away at him and missed —it's all too easy, I assure you—and he took the chance to break for the door. I snapped off another round at him, and hit him about the hip, I think, for he went hurtling into the wall. Before he could struggle up Kutebar was on him with the fallen musket, yelling some outlandish war-cry as he sank the bayonet to the locking-ring in the fellow's breast.

The cell was a shambles. Three dead men on the floor, all bleeding busily, the air thick with powder smoke, Kutebar brandishing his musket and inviting God to admire him, Yakub Beg exulting weakly and calling us to search the sergeant for his fetter keys, and myself counting the shots left in the revolver— two, in fact.

"The door!" Yakub was calling. "Make it fast, Izzat—then the keys, in God's name! My body is bursting!"

We found a key in the sergeant's pocket, and released Yakub's ankles, lowering him gently to the cell floor and propping him against the wall with his arms still chained to the corners above his head. He couldn't stand—I doubted if he'd have the use of his limbs inside a week—and when we tried to unlock his wrist-shackles the key didn't fit. While Izzat searched the dead man's clothes, fuming, I kept the door covered; the sounds of distant fighting were still proceeding merrily, and it seemed to me we'd have more Russian visitors before long. We were in a damned tight place until we could get Yakub fully released; Kutebar had changed his tack now, and was trying to batter open a link in the chain with his musket butt.

"Strike harder, feeble one!" Yakub encouraged him. "Has all your strength gone in killing one wounded Ruski?"

"Am I a blacksmith?" says Kutebar. "By the seven pools of Eblis, do I have iron teeth? I save your life—again—and all you can do is whine. We have been at work, this *feringhi* and I, while you swung comfortably—God, what a fool's labour is this!"

"Cease!" cries Yakub. "Watch the door!"

There were feet running, and voices; Kutebar took the other side from me, his bayonet poised, and I cocked the revolver. The feet stopped, and then a voice called "Yakub Beg?" and Kutebar flung up his hands with a crow of delight.

"Inshallah! There is good in the Chinese after all! Come in, little dogs, the work is done! Come and look on the bloody harvest of Kutebar!"

The door swung back, and before you could say Jack Robinson there were half a dozen of them in the cell—robed, bearded figures with grinning hawk faces and long knives—I never thought I'd be glad to see a Ghazi, and these were straight from that stable. They fell on Kutebar, embracing and slapping him, while the others either stopped short at sight of me or hurried on to Yakub Beg, slumped against the far wall. And foremost was a lithe black-clad figure, tight-turbaned round head and chin, with a flowing cloak—hardly more than a boy. He stooped over Yakub Beg, cursing softly, and then shouted shrilly to the tribesmen:

"Hack through those chains! Bear him up—gently—ah, God, my love, my love, what have they done to you?"

He was positively weeping, and then suddenly he was clasping the wounded man, smothering his cheeks with kisses, cupping the lolling head between his hands, murmuring endearments, and finally kissing him passionately on the mouth.

Well, the Pathans are like that, you know, and I wasn't surprised to find these near-relations of theirs similarly inclined to perversion; bad luck on the girls, I always think, but all the more skirt for chaps like me. Disgusting sight, though, this youth slobbering over him like that.

Our rescuers were eyeing me uncertainly, until Kutebar explained whose side I was on; then they all turned their attention to Oscar and Bosie. One of the tribesmen had hacked through Yakub's chains, and four of them were bearing him towards the door, while the black-clad boy flitted alongside, cursing them to be careful. Kutebar motioned me to the door, and I followed him up the steps, still clutching my revolver; the last of the tribesmen paused, even at that critical moment, to pass his knife carefully across the throats of the three dead Russians, and then joined us, giggling gleefully.

"The *hallal!*"* says he. "Is it not fitting, for the proper despatch of animals?"

"Blasphemer!" says Kutebar. "Is this a time for jest?"

The boy hissed at them, and they were silent. He had authority,
this little spring violet, and when he snapped a command they
jumped to it, hurrying along between the buildings, while he
brought up the rear, glancing back towards the sound of shooting
from the other side of the fort. There wasn't a Russian to be seen
where we were, but I wasn't surprised. I could see the game—a
sudden attack, with gunpowder and lots of noise, at the main gate,
to draw every Russian in that direction, while the lifting party
sneaked in through some rear bolt-hole. They were probably
inside before the attack began, marking the sentries and waiting
for the signal—but they hadn't bargained, apparently, for the
sergeant and his men having orders to kill Yakub Beg as soon as
a rescue was attempted. We'd been lucky there.

Suddenly we were under the main wall, and there were figures
on the cat-walk overhead; Yakub Beg's body, grotesquely limp,
was being hauled up, with the boy piping feverishly at them to be
easy with him. Not fifty feet away, to our left, muskets were
blazing from one of the guard towers, but they were shooting away
from us. Strong lean hands helped me as I scrambled clumsily at
a rope-ladder; voices in Persian were muttering around us in the
dark, robed figures were crouching at the embrasures, and then
we were sliding down the ropes on the outside, and I fell the last
ten feet, landing on top of the man beneath, who gave a brief
commentary on my parentage, future, and personal habits as only
a hillman can, and then called softly:

"All down, Silk One, including the clown Kutebar, your beloved the Atalik Ghazi, and this misbegotten pig of a *feringhi*
with the large feet."

"Go!" said the boy's voice from the top of the wall, and as they
thrust me forward in the dark a long keening wail broke out from
overhead; it was echoed somewhere along the wall, and even
above the sound of firing I heard it farther off still. I was stumbling
along in my chains, clutching at the hand of the man who led me.

"Where are we going?" says I. "Where are you taking me?"

"Ask questions in the council, infidel, not in the battle," says

* Ritual throat-cutting.

he. "Can you ride, you *feringhi* who speaks Persian? Here, Kutebar, he is your friend; do you take him, lest he fall on me again."

"Son of dirt and dung," says Kutebar, lumbering out of the dark. "Did he not assist me in slaying Ruskis, who would undoubtedly have cut our throats before your tardy arrival? What would the Silk One have said to you then, eh? A fine rescue, by God! The whores of Samarkand market could have done it better!"

I thought that a trifle hard, myself; it had been as neat a jail clearance, for my money, as heart could desire, and I doubt if ten minutes had passed since I'd woken with Kutebar's hand on my mouth. I'd killed one man, perhaps two, and their blood was still wet on my face—but I was free! Whoever these fine chaps were, they were taking me out of the clutches of that rascal Ignatieff and his beastly *knouts* and *nagaikas*—I was loose again, and living, and if my fetters were galling me and my joints aching with strain and fatigue, if my body was foul and fit to drop, my heart was singing. You've sold 'em again, old son, I thought; good for you—and these accommodating niggers, of course.

About half a mile from the fort there was a gully, with cypress trees, and horses stamping in the dark, and I just sat on the ground, limp and thankful, beside Kutebar, while he reviled our saviours genially. Presently the boy in black came slipping out of the shadows, kneeling beside us.

"I have sent Yakub away," says he. "It is far to the edge of the Red Sands. We wait here, for Sahib Khan and the others—God grant they have not lost too many!"

"To build the house, trees must fall," says Kutebar complacently. I agreed with him entirely, mind you. "And how is His Idleness, the Falcon on the Royal Wrist—God, my back is broken, bearing him up! How many days did I carry his moping carcase, in that filthy cell, with never a word of complaint from my patient lips? Has my labour been in vain?"

"He is well, God be thanked," says the boy, and then the furious little pansy began to snivel like a girl. "His poor limbs are torn and helpless—but he is strong, he will mend! He spoke to me, Kutebar! He told me how you—cared for him, and fought for him just now—you and the *feringhi* here. Oh, old hawk of the hills, how can I bless you enough?"

And the disgusting young lout flung his arms round Kutebar's neck, murmuring gratefully and kissing him, until the old fellow pushed him away—he was normal, at least.

"Shameless thing!" mutters he. "Respect my grey hairs! Is there no seemliness among you Chinese, then? Away, you bare-faced creature—practise your gratitude on this *angliski* if you must, but spare me!"

"Indeed I shall," says the youth, and turning to me, he put his hands on my shoulders. "You have saved my love, stranger; therefore you have my love, forever and all." He was a nauseatingly pretty one this, with his full lips and slanting Chinese eyes, and his pale, chiselled face framed by the black turban. The tears were still wet on his cheeks, and then to my disgust he leaned forward, plainly intending to kiss me, too.

"No thank'ee!" cries I. "No offence, my son, but I ain't one for your sort, if you don't mind ..."

But his arms were round my neck and his lips on mine before I could stop him—and then I felt two firm young breasts pressing against my chest, and there was no mistaking the womanliness of the soft cheek against mine. A female, bigad—leading a Ghazi storming-party on a neck-or-nothing venture like this! And such a female, by the feel of her. Well, of course, that put a different complexion on the thing entirely, and I suffered her to kiss away to her heart's content, and mine. What else could a gentleman do?

&10

There are some parts of my life that I'd be glad to relive any time—and some that I don't care to remember at all. But there aren't many that I look back on and have to pinch myself to believe that they really happened. The business of the Khokandian Horde of the Red Sands is one of these, and yet it's one of the few episodes in my career that I can verify from the history books if I want to. There are obscure works on Central Asia by anonymous surveyors and military writers,[40] and I can look in them and find the names and places— Yakub Beg, Izzat Kutebar and Katti Torah; Buzurg Khan and the Seven Khojas, the Great and Middle Hordes of the Black Sands and the Golden Road, the Sky-blue Wolves of the Hungry Steppe, Sahib Khan, and the remarkable girl they called the Silk One. You can trace them all, if you are curious, and learn how in those days they fought the Russians inch by inch from the Jaxartes to the Oxus, and if it reads to you like a mixture of Robin Hood and the Arabian Nights—well, I was there for part of it, and even I look back on it as some kind of frightening fairy-tale come true.

And when I've thumbed through the books and maps, and mumbled the names aloud as an old man does, looking out of my window at the cabs clopping past by the Park in twentieth-century London, and the governesses stepping demurely with their little charges (deuced smart, some of these governesses), I'll go and rummage until I've found that old clumsy German revolver that I took from the Russian sergeant under Fort Raim, and for a threadbare scarf of black silk with the star-flowers embroidered on it—and I can hear again Yakub's laughter ringing behind me, and Kutebar's boastful growling, and the thunder of a thousand hooves and the shouting of the turbanned Tajik riders that makes me shiver still. But most of all I smell the wraith of her perfume, and see those slanting black eyes—"Lick up the honey, stranger, and ask no questions." That was the best part.

On the night of the rescue from Fort Raim, of course, I knew next to nothing about them—except that they were obviously of the warlike tribes constantly warring with the Russians who were trying to invade their country and push the Tsar's dominions south to Afghanistan and east to the China border. It was a bloody, brutal business that, and the wild people—the Tajiks, the Kirgiz-Kazaks, the Khokandians, the Uzbeks and the rest— were being forced back up the Syr Daria into the Hungry Steppe and the Red Sands, harrying all the way, raiding the new Russian outposts and cutting up their caravans.

But they weren't just savages by any means. Behind them, far up the Syr Daria and the Amu Daria, were their great cities of Tashkent and Khokand and Samarkand and Bokhara, places that had been civilized when the Russians were running round bare-arsed—these were the spots that Moscow was really after, and which Ignatieff had boasted would be swept up in the victorious march to India. And leaders like Yakub and Kutebar were waging a desperate last-ditch fight to stop them in the no-man's-land east of the Aral Sea along the Syr Daria.

It was to the brink of that no-man's-land that they carried us on the night of our deliverance from Fort Raim—a punishing ride, hour after hour, through the dark and the silvery morning, over miles of desert and gully and parched steppe-land. They had managed to sever my ankle chain, so that I could back a horse, but I rode in an exhausted dream, only half-conscious of the robed figures flanking me, and when we finally halted I remember only arms supporting me, and the smell of camel-hair robes, and sinking on to a blessed softness to sleep forever.

It was a good place, that—an oasis deep in the Red Sands of the Kizil Kum, where the Russians still knew better than to venture. I remember waking there, to the sound of rippling water, and crawling out of the tent in bright sunlight, and blinking at a long valley, crowded with tents, and a little village of beautiful white houses on the valley side, with trees and grass, and women and children chattering, and Tajik riders everywhere, with their horses and camels—lean, ugly, bearded fellows, bandoliered and booted, and not the kind of company I care to keep, normally. But one of them sings out: "Salaam, *angliski!*" as he clattered by, and one of the women gave me bread and coffee, and all seemed very friendly.

Somewhere—I believe it's in my celebrated work, *Dawns and Departures of a Soldier's Life*—I've written a good deal about that valley, and the customs and manners of the tribesfolk, and what a little Paradise it seemed after what I'd been through. So it was, and some fellows would no doubt have been content to lie back, wallowing in their freedom, thanking Providence, and having a rest before thinking too hard about the future. That's not Flashy's way; given a moment's respite I have to be looking ahead to the next leap, and that very first morning, while the local smith was filing off my fetters in the presence of a grinning, admiring crowd, I was busy thinking, aye, so far so good, but where next? That Russian army at Fort Raim was still a long sight too close for comfort, and I wouldn't rest easy until I'd reached real safety—Berkeley Square, say, or a little ale-house that I know in Leicestershire.

Afghanistan looked the best bet—not that it's a place I'd ever venture into gladly, but there was no other way to India and my own people, and I figured that Yakub Beg would see me safe along that road, as a return for services rendered to him in our cell at Fort Raim. We jail-birds stick together, and he was obviously a man of power and influence—why, he was probably on dining-out terms with half the *badmashes** and cattle-thieves between here and Jallalabad, and if necessary he'd give me an escort; we could travel as horse-copers, or something, for with my Persian and Pushtu I'd have no difficulty passing as an Afghan. I'd done it before. And there would be no lousy Russians along the road just yet, thank God—and as my thoughts went bounding ahead it suddenly struck me, the magnificent realization—I was free, within reach of India, and I had Ignatieff's great secret plan of invasion! Oh, East might have taken it to Raglan, but that was nothing in the gorgeous dream that suddenly opened up before me—the renowned Flashy, last seen vanishing into the Russian army at Balaclava with boundless energy, now emerging in romantic disguise at Peshawar with the dreadful news for the British garrison.

"You might let the Governor-General know," I would tell my goggling audience, "that there's a Russian army of thirty thousand coming down through the Khyber shortly, with half Afghan-

* Ruffians.

istan in tow, and if he wants to save India he'd better get the army up here fairly smart. Yes, there's no doubt of it—got it from the Tsar's secret cabinet. They probably know in London by now—fellow called East got out through the Crimea, I believe —I'd been wounded, you see, and told him to clear out and get the news through at any price. So he left me—well, you take your choice, don't you? Friendship or duty?—anyway, it don't signify. I'm here, with the news, and it's here we'll have to stop 'em. How did I get here? Ha-ha, my dear chap, if I told you, it wouldn't make you any wiser. Half-way across Russia, through Astrakhan, over the Aral Sea (Caspian, too, as a matter of fact) and across the Hindu Kush—old country to me, of course. Rough trip? No-o, not what I'd call rough, really—be glad when these fetter-marks have healed up, though—Russian jailers, I don't mind telling you, have a lot to learn from English chambermaids, what? Yes, I assure you, I am Flashman—yes, *the* Flashman, if you like. Now, do be a good fellow and get it on the telegraph to Calcutta, won't you? Oh, and you might ask them to forward my apologies to Lord Raglan that I wasn't able to re-join him at Balaclava, owing to being unavoidably detained. Now, I'd give anything for a bath, and a pair of silk socks and a hairbrush, if you don't mind. . . ."

Gad, the Press would be full of it. Hero of Afghanistan, and now Saviour of India—assuming the damned place *was* saved. Still, I'd have done my bit, and East's scuttle through the snow would look puny by comparison. I'd give him a careful pat on the back, of course, pointing out that he'd only done his duty, even if it did mean sacrificing his old chum. "Really, I think that in spite of everything, I had the easier part," I would say gravely. "I didn't have that kind of choice to make, you see." Modest, off-hand, self-deprecatory—if I played it properly, I'd get a knight-hood out of it.

And all I had to do to realize that splendid prospect was have a chat with Yakub Beg, as soon as he had recovered from his ordeal, point out that the Russians were our mutual enemies and I was duty bound to get to India at once, thank him for his hos-pitality, and be off with his blessing and assistance. Not to waste time, I broached the thing that afternoon to Izzat Kutebar, when he invited me to share a dish of *kefir* with him in the neighbouring tent where he was recovering, noisily, from his captivity and escape.

"Eat, and thank Providence for such delights as this, which you infidels call ambrosia," says he, while one of his women put the dish of honey-coloured curds before me. "The secret of its preparation was specially given by God to Abraham himself. Personally, I prefer it even to a Tashkent melon—and you know the proverb runs that the Caliph of the Faithful would give ten pearl-breasted beauties from his hareem for a single melon of Tashkent. Myself, I would give five, perhaps, or six, if the melon were a big one." He wiped his beard. "And you would go to Afghanistan, then, and to your folk in India? It can be arranged —we owe you a debt, Flashman *bahadur*, Yakub and I and all our people. As you owe one to us, for your own deliverance," he added gently.

I protested my undying gratitude at once, and he nodded gravely.

"Between warriors let a word of thanks be like a heart-beat —a small thing, hardly heard, but it suffices," says he, and then grinned sheepishly. "What do I say? The truth is, we all owe our chief debt to that wild witch, Ko Dali's daughter. She whom they call the Silk One." He shook his head. "God protect me from a wayward child, and a wanton that goes bare-faced. There will be no holding her in after this—or curbing Yakub Beg's infatuation with her, either. And yet, my friend, would you and I be sitting here, eating this fine *kefir*, but for her?"

"Who is she?" I asked, for I'd seen—and felt—just enough of that remarkable female last night to be thoroughly intrigued. She'd have been a phenomenon anywhere, but in a Muslim country, where women are kept firmly in their place, and never dream of intruding in men's work, her apparent authority had astounded me. "Do you know, Izzat, last night until she . . . er, kissed me—I was sure she was a man."

"So Ko Dali must have thought, when the fierce little bitch came yelping into the world," says he. "Who is Ko Dali?—a Chinese war lord, who had the good taste to take a Khokandian wife, and the ill luck to father the Silk One. He governs in Kashgar, a Chinese city of East Turkestan a thousand miles east of here, below the Issik Kul and the Seven Rivers Country. Would to God he could govern his daughter as well—so should we be spared much shame, for is it not deplorable to have a woman who struts like a khan among us, and leads such enterprises as that which freed you and me last night? Am I, Kutebar, to hold up my head and say: 'A woman brought me forth of Fort Raim jail'? Aye, laugh, you old cow," he bellowed at the ancient serving-woman, who had been listening and cackling. "You daughter of shame, is this respect? You take her side, all you wicked sluts, and rejoice to see us men put down. The trouble with the Silk One," he went on to me, "is that she is always right. A scandal, but there it is. Who can fathom the ways of Allah, who lets such things happen?"

"Well," says I, "it happened among the Ruskis, you know, Kutebar. They had an empress—why, in my own country, we are ruled by a queen."

"So I have heard," says he, "but you are infidels. Besides, does your Sultana, Vik Taria, go unveiled? Does she plan raid and ambush? No, by the black tomb of Timur, I'll wager she does not."

"Not that I've heard, lately," I admitted. "But this Silk One—where does she come from? What's her name, anyway?"

"Who knows? She is Ko Dali's daughter. And she came, on a day—it would be two years ago, after the Ruskis had built that devil's house, Fort Raim, and were sending their soldiers east of the Aral, in breach of all treaty and promise, to take our country and enslave our people. We were fighting them, as we are fighting still, Yakub and I and the other chiefs—and then she was among us, with her shameless bare face and bold talk and a dozen Chinese devil-fighters attending on her. It was a troubled time, with the world upside down, and we scratching with our fingernails to hold the Ruskis back by foray and ambuscade; in such disorders, anything is possible, even a woman fighting-chief. And Yakub saw her, and. . . ." He spread his hands. "She is beautiful, as the lily at morning—and clever, it is not to be denied. Doubtless they will marry, some day, if Yakub's wife will let him—she lives at Julek, on the river. But he is no fool, my Yakub—perhaps he loves this female hawk, perhaps not, but he is ambitious, and he seeks such a kingdom for himself as Kashgar. Who knows, when Ko Dali dies, if Yakub finds the throne of Khokand beyond his reach, he may look to Ko Dali's daughter to help him wrest Kashgar province from the Chinese. He has spoken of it, and she sits, devouring him with those black Mongolian eyes of hers. It is said," he went on confidentially, "that she devours other men also, and that it was for her scandalous habits that the governor of Fort Raim, Engmann the Ruski—may wild hogs mate above his grave!—had her head shaved when she was taken last year, after the fall of Ak Mechet. They say—"

"They lie!" screeched the old woman, who had been listening. "In their jealousy they throw dirt on her, the pretty Silk One!"

"Will you raise your head, mother of discord and ruiner of good food?" says Izzat. "They shaved her scalp, I say, which is why she goes with a turban about her always—for she has kept it shaved, and vowed to do so until she has Engmann's own head on a plate at her feet. God, the perversity of women! But what can one do about her? She is worth ten heads in the council, she can ride like a Kazak, and is as brave as . . . as . . . as I am, by God! If Yakub and Buzurg Khan of Khokand—and I, of course—hold these Russian swine back from our country, it will be because she has the gift of seeing their weaknesses, and showing us how they may be confounded. She is touched by God, I believe —which is why our men admit her, and heed her—and turn their heads aside lest they meet her eye. All save Yakub Beg, who has ever championed her, and fears nothing."

"And you say she'll make him a king one day, and be his queen? An extraordinary girl, indeed. Meanwhile she helps you fight the Ruskis."

"She helps not me, by God! She may help Yakub, who fights as chief of the Tajiks and military governor under Buzurg Khan, who rules in Khokand. They fight for their state, for all the Kirgiz-Kazak people, against an invader. But I, Izzat Kutebar, fight for myself and my own band. I am no statesman, I am no governor or princeling. I need no throne but my saddle. I," says this old ruffian, with immense pride, "am a bandit, as my fathers were. For upwards of thirty years—since I first ambushed the Bokhara caravan, in fact—I have robbed the Russians. Let me wear the robe of pride over the breastplate of distinction, for I have taken more loot and cut more throats of theirs since they put their thieving noses east of the Blue Lake* than any—"

* The Aral Sea.

"And a chit of a girl had to lift you from Fort Raim prison," cries the crone, busy among her pots. "Was it an earthquake they had in Samarkand last year—nay, it was Timur turning in his grave for the credit of the men of Syr Daria! Heh-heh!"

". . . and it is as a bandit that I fight the Ruskis," says he, ignoring the interruption. "Shall I not be free to rob, in my own country? Is that not as just a cause as Yakub's, who fights for *his* people's freedom, or Buzurg's, who fights for *his* throne and *his* fine palace and revenue and dancing-women? Or Sahib Khan, who fights to avenge the slaughter of *his* family at Ak Mechet? Each to his own cause, I say. But you shall see for yourself, when we go to greet Yakub tonight—aye, and you shall see the Silk One, too, and judge what manner of thing she is. God keep me from the marriage-bed of such a demon, and when I find Paradise, may my *houris* not come from China."

So that evening, when I had bathed, trimmed my beard, and had the filthy rags of my captivity replaced by shirt, *pyjamy* trousers, and soft Persian boots, Kutebar took me through the crowded camp, with everyone saluting him as he strutted by, with his beard oiled and his silver-crusted belt and broad gold medal worn over his fine green coat, and the children crowding about him for the sweets which he carried for them. A robber he might be, but I never saw a man better liked—mind you, I liked him myself, and the thought struck me that he and Pencherjevsky and old Scarlett would have got on like a house on fire. I could see them all three hunting in Rutland together, chasing poachers, damning the government, and knocking the necks off bottles at four in the morning.

We climbed up to the white houses of the village, and Izzat led me through a low archway into a little garden where there was a fountain and an open pillared pavilion such as you might find in Aladdin's pantomime. It was a lovely little place, shaded by trees in the warm evening, with birds murmuring in the branches, the first stars beginning to peep in the dark blue sky overhead, and some flute-like instrument playing softly beyond the wall. It's strange, but the reality of the East is always far beyond anything the romantic poets and artists can create in imitation.

Yakub Beg was lying on a pile of cushions beneath the pavilion, bare-headed and clad only in his *pyjamys*, so that his shoulders could be massaged by a stout woman who was working at them with warmed oil. He was tired and hollow-eyed still, but his lean face lit up at the sight of us—I suppose he was a bit of a demon king, with his forked beard and skull-lock, and that rare thing in Central Asia, which they say is a legacy of Alexander's Greek mercenaries—the bright blue eyes of the European. And he had the happiest smile, I think, that ever I saw on a human face. You only had to see it to understand why the Syr Daria tribes carried on their hopeless struggle against the Russians; fools will always follow the Yakub Begs of this world.

He greeted me eagerly, and presented me to Sahib Khan, his lieutenant, of whom I remember nothing except that he was unusually tall, with moustaches that fell below his chin; I was trying not to look too pointedly at the third member of the group, who was lounging on the cushions near Yakub, playing with a tiny Persian kitten on her lap. Now that I saw her in full light, I had a little difficulty in recognizing the excitable, passionate creature I had taken for a boy only the night before; Ko Dali's daughter this evening was a very self-possessed, consciously feminine young woman indeed—of course, girls are like that, squealing one minute, all assured dignity the next. She was dressed in the tight-wrapped white trousers the Tajik women wear, with curled Persian slippers on her dainty feet, and any illusion of boyishness was dispelled by the roundness of the cloth-of-silver blouse beneath her short embroidered jacket. Round her head she wore a pale pink turban, very tight, framing a striking young face as pale as alabaster—you'll think me susceptible, but I found her incredibly fetching, with her slanting almond eyes (the only Chinese thing about her), the slightly-protruding milk-white teeth which showed as she teased and laughed at the kitten, the determined little chin, and the fine straight nose that looked as though it had been chiselled out of marble. Not as perfectly beautiful as Montez, perhaps, but with the lithe, graceful gift of movement, that hint of action in the dark, unfathomable eyes which —aye, well, well. As Yakub Beg was saying:

"Izzat tells me you are eager to rejoin your own people in India, Flashman *bahadur*. Before we discuss that, I wish to make a small token sign of my gratitude to you for . . . well, for my life, no less. There are perhaps half a dozen people in the world who have saved Yakub Beg at one time or another—three of them you see here...."

"More fool us," growls Kutebar. "A thankless task, friends."

"... but you are the first *feringhi* to render me that service. So"—he gave that frank impulsive grin, and ducked his shaven head—"if you are willing, and will do me the great honour to accept...."

I wondered what was coming, and caught my breath when, at a signal from Sahib Khan, a servant brought in a tray on which were four articles—a little bowl containing salt, another in which an ember of wood burned smokily, a small square of earth with a shred of rank grass attaching to it, and a plain, wave-bladed Persian dagger with the snake-and-hare design on its blade. I knew what this meant, and it took me aback, for it's the ultimate honour a hillman can do to you: Yakub Beg wanted to make me his blood brother. And while you could say I had saved his life —still, it was big medicine, on such short acquaintance.

However, I knew the formula, for I'd been blood brother to young Ilderim of Mogala years before, so I followed him in tasting the salt, and passing my hand over the fire and the earth, and then laying it beside his on the knife while he said, and I repeated:

"By earth, and salt, and fire; by hilt and blade; and in the name of God in whatever tongue men call Him, I am thy brother in blood henceforth. May He curse me and consign me to the pit forever, if I fail thee, my friend."

Funny thing—I don't hold with oaths, much, and I'm not by nature a truthful man, but on the three occasions that I've sworn blood brotherhood it has seemed a more solemn thing than swearing on the Bible. Arnold was right; I'm damned beyond a doubt.

Yakub Beg had some difficulty, his shoulders were still crippled, and Sahib Khan had to lift his hand to the tray for him. And then he had to carry both his hands round my neck as I stooped for the formal embrace, after which Kutebar and Ko Dali's daughter and Sahib Khan murmured their applause, and we drank hot black coffee with lemon essence and opium, sweetened with sherbet.

And then the serious business began. I had to recite, at Yakub Beg's request, my own recent history, and how I had come into the hands of the Russians. So I told them, in brief, much of what I've written here, from my capture at Balaclava to my arrival in Fort Raim—leaving out the discreditable bits, of course, but telling them what they wanted to hear most, which was why there was a great Russian army assembling at Fort Raim, for the march to India. They listened intently, the men only occasionally exploding in a "Bismillah!" or "Eyah!", with a hand-clap by way of emphasis, and the woman silent, fondling the kitten and watching me with those thoughtful, almond eyes. And when I had done, Yakub Beg began to laugh—so loud and hearty that he hurt his torn muscles.

"So much for pride, then! Oh, Khokand, what a little thing you are, and how insignificant your people in the sight of the great world! We had thought, in our folly, that this great army was for *us*, that the White Tsar was sending his best to trample us flat—and we are just to be licked up in the bygoing, like a mosquito brushed from the hunter's eye when he sights his quarry. And the Great Bear marches on India, does he?" He shook his head. "Can your people stop him at the Khyber gate?"

"Perhaps," says I, "if I get word to them in time."

"In three weeks you might be in Peshawar," says he, thoughtfully. "Not that it will profit us here. The word is that the Ruskis will begin their advance up Syr Daria within two weeks, which means we have a month of life left to us. And then—" he made a weary little gesture. "Tashkent and Khokand will go; Perovski will drink his tea in the serai by Samarkand bazaar, and his horses will water in the See-ah stream. The Cossacks will ride over the Black Sands and the Red." He smiled wryly. "You British may save India, but who shall save us? The wise men were right: 'We are lost when Russia drinks the waters of Jaxartes'. They have been tasting them this four years, but now they will sup them dry."

There was silence, the men sitting glum, while the Silk One toyed with her cat, and from time to time gave me a slow, disturbing glance.

"Well," says I, helpfully, "perhaps you can make some sort of . . . accommodation with them. Terms, don't you know."

"Terms?" says Yakub. "Have you made terms with a wolf lately, Englishman? Shall I tell you the kind of terms they make?

234

When this scum Perovski brought his soldiers and big guns to my city of Ak Mechet two years ago, invading our soil for no better reason than that he wished to steal it, what did he tell Mahomed Wali, who ruled in my absence?" His voice was still steady, but his eyes were shining. "He said: 'Russia comes not for a day, not for a year, but forever'. Those were his terms. And when Wali's people fought for the town, even the women and children throwing their *kissiaks** against the guns, and held until there was no food left, and the swords were all broken, and the little powder gone, and the walls blown in, and only the citadel remained, Wali said: 'It is enough. We will surrender'. And Perovski tore up the offer of surrender and said: 'We will take the citadel with our bayonets'. And they did. Two hundred of our folk they mowed down with grape, even the old and young. That is the honour of a Russian soldier; that is the peace of the White Tsar."[41]

"My wife and children died in Ak Mechet, beneath the White Mosque," says Sahib Khan. "They did not even know who the Russians were. My little son clapped his hands before the battle, to see so many pretty uniforms, and the guns all in a row."

They were silent again, and I sat uncomfortably, until Yakub Beg says:

"So you see, there will be no terms. Those of us whom they do not kill, they will enslave: they have said as much. They will sweep us clean, from Persia to Balkash and the Roof of the World. How can we prevent them? I took seven thousand men against Ak Mechet two winters since, and saw them routed; I went again with twice as many, and saw my thousands slain. The Russians lost eighteen killed. Oh, if it were sabre to sabre, horse to horse, man to man, I would not shirk the odds—but against their artillery, their rifles, what can our riders do?"

"Fight," growls Kutebar. "So it is the last fight, let it be one they will remember. A month, you say? In that time we can run the horse-tail banner to Kashgar and back; we can raise every Muslim fighting-man from Turgai to the Killer-of-Hindus,† from Khorassan to the Tarm Desert." His voice rose steadily from a growl to a shout. "When the Chinese slew the Kalmucks in the

---

* Hard dung balls used as missiles.
† Hindu Kush range.

old time, what was the answer given to the faint hearts: 'Turn east, west, north, south, there you shall find the Kirgiz'. Why should we lie down to a handful of strangers? They have arms, they have horses—so have we. If they come in their thousands, these infidels, have we not the Great Horde of the far steppes, the people of the Blue Wolf,[42] to join our *jihad*?* We may not win, but by God, we can make them understand that the ghosts of Timur and Chinghiz Khan still ride these plains; we can mark every yard of the Syr Daria with a Russian corpse; we can make them buy this country at a price that will cause the Tsar to count his change in the Kremlin palace!"

Sahib Khan chimed in again: "So runs the proverb: 'While the gun-barrel lies in its stock, and the blade is unbroken'. It will be all that is left to us, Yakub."

Yakub Beg sighed, and then smiled at me. He was one of your spirited rascals who can never be glum for more than a moment. "It may be. If they overrun us, I shall not live to see it; I'll make young bones somewhere up by Ak Mechet. You understand, Flashman *bahadur*, we may buy you a little time here, in Syr Daria—no more. Your red soldiers may avenge us, but only God can help us."

"And He has a habit of choosing the winning side, which will not be ours," says Kutebar. "Well, I'm overdue for Paradise; may I find it by a short cut and a bloody one."

Ko Dali's daughter spoke for the first time, and I was surprised how high and yet husky her voice was—the kind that makes you think of French satin sofas, with the blinds down and purple wall-paper. She was lying prone now, tickling the kitten's belly and murmuring to it.

"Do you hear them, little tiger, these great strong men? How they enjoy their despair! They reckon the odds, and find them heavy, and since fighting is so much easier than thinking they put the scowl of resignation on the face of stupidity, and swear most horribly." Her voice whined in grotesque mimicry. " 'By the bowels of Rustum, we shall give them a battle to remember—hand me my scimitar, Gamal, it is in the woodshed. Aye, we shall make such-and-such a slaughter, and if we are all blown to the ends of Eblis—may God protect the valorous!—we shall at least be blown

* Holy war.

236

like men. Eyewallah, brothers, it is God's will; we shall have done our best'. This is how the wise warriors talk, furry little sister—which is why we women weep and children go hungry. But never fear—when the Russians have killed them all, I shall find myself a great, strong Cossack, and you shall have a lusty Russian tom, and we shall live on oranges and honey and cream forever."

Yakub Beg just laughed, and silenced Kutebar's angry growl. "She never said a word that was not worth listening to. Well, Silk One, what must we do to be saved?"

Ko Dali's daughter rolled the kitten over. "Fight them now, before they have moved, while they have their backs to the sea. Take all your horsemen, suddenly, and scatter them on the beach."

"Oh, cage the wind, girl!" cries Kutebar. "They have thirty thousand muskets, one-third of them Cossack cavalry. Where can we raise half that number?"

"Send to Buzurg Khan to help you. At need, ask aid from Bokhara."

"Bokhara is lukewarm," says Yakub Beg. "They are the last to whom we can turn for help."

The girl shrugged. "When the Jew grows poor, he looks to his old accounts. Well, then, you must do it alone."

"How, woman? I have not the gift of human multiplication; they outnumber us."

"But their ammunition has not yet come—this much we know from your spies at Fort Raim. So the odds are none so great— three to one at most. With such valiant sabres as Kutebar here, the thing should be easy."

"Devil take your impudence!" cries Kutebar. "I could not assemble ten thousand swords within a week, and by then their powder and cartridge ships will have arrived."

"Then you should have assembled them before this," was the tart rejoinder.

"Heaven lighten your understanding, you perverse Chinese bitch! How could I, when I was rotting in jail?"

"That was clever," says she, "that was sound preparation, indeed. Hey, puss-puss-puss, are they not shrewd, these big strong fellows?"

"If there were a hope of a surprise attack on their camp succeeding, I should have ordered it," says Yakub Beg. "To stop them here, before their advance has begun. . . ." He looked at me. "That would solve your need as well as ours, Englishman. But I see no way. Their powder ships will arrive in a week, and three days, perhaps four thereafter, they will be moving up Syr Daria. If something is to be done, it must be done soon."

"Ask her, then," says Kutebar sarcastically. "Is she not waiting to be asked? To her, it will be easy."

"If it were easy, even you would have thought of it by now," says the girl. "Let me think of it instead." She rose, picking up her cat, stroking it and smiling as she nuzzled it. "Shall we think, little cruelty? And when we have thought, we shall tell them, and they will slap their knees and cry: 'Mashallah, but how simple! It leaps to the eye! A child could have conceived it.' And they will smile on us, and perhaps throw us a little jumagi,* or a sweetmeat, for which we shall be humbly thankful. Come, butcher of little mice."

And without so much as a glance at us, she sauntered off, with those tight white pants stirring provocatively, and Izzat cursing under his breath.

"Ko Dali should have whipped the demons out of that baggage before she grew teeth! But then, what do the Chinese know of education? If she were mine, by death, would I not discipline her?"

"You would not dare, father of wind and grey whiskers," says Yakub genially. "So let her think—and if nothing comes of it, you may have the laugh of her."

"A bitter laugh it will be, then," says Kutebar. "By Shaitan, it will be the last laugh we have."

Now their discussion had been all very well, no doubt, but it was of no great interest to me whether they got themselves cut up by the Russians now or a month hence. The main thing was to get Flashy on his way to India, and I made bold to raise the subject again. But Yakub Beg disappointed me.

"You shall go, surely, but a few days will make no difference. By then we shall have made a resolve here, and it were best your chiefs in India knew what it was. So they may be the better

* Pocket-money.

238

prepared. In the meantime, Flashman *bahadur*, blood brother, take your ease among us."

I couldn't object to that, and for three days I loafed about, wandering through the camp, observing the great coming and going of couriers, and the arrival each day of fresh bands of horsemen. They were coming in from all parts of the Red Sands, and beyond, from as far as the Black Sands below Khiva, and Zarafshan and the Bokhara border—Uzbeks with their flat yellow faces and scalp-locks, lean, swarthy Tajiks and slit-eyed Mongols, terrible-looking folk with their long swords and bandy legs— until there must have been close on five thousand riders in that valley alone. But when you thought of these wild hordes pitted against artillery and disciplined riflemen, you saw how hopeless the business was; it would take more than the Silk One to think them out of this.

An extraordinary young woman that—weeping passionately over Yakub's wounds on the night of the rescue, but in council with the men as composed (and bossy) as a Mayfair mama. A walking temptation, too, to a warm-blooded chap like me, so I kept well clear of her in those three days. She might be just the ticket for a wet week-end, but she was also Yakub Beg's intended—and that apart, I'm bound to confess that there was something about the cut of her shapely little jib that made me just a mite uneasy. I'm wary of strong, clever women, however beddable they may be, and Ko Dali's daughter was strong and too clever for comfort. As I was to find out to my cost—God, when I think what that Chinese-minded mort got me into!

I spent my time, as I say, loafing, and getting more impatient and edgy by the hour. I wanted to get away for India, and every day that passed brought nearer the moment when those Russian brutes (with Ignatieff well to the fore, no doubt) came pouring up the Syr Daria valley from Fort Raim, guns, Cossacks, foot and all, and spread like a tide over the Khokand country. I wanted to be well away before that happened, bearing the glad tidings to India and reaping the credit; Yakub Beg and his hairy fellows could fight the Russians how they liked, for although I'll own I'd conceived an affection for him and his Tajiks and Uzbeks, and wished them no harm, it was all one to me how *they* fared, so long as I was safely out of it. But Yakub still seemed uncertain how to prepare for the fight that was coming; he'd tried his over-lord, Buzurg Khan, for help, and got little out of him, and egged on by Kutebar, he was coming round to the Silk One's notion of one mad slash at the enemy before they had got under way from Fort Raim with their magazines full. It was a doomed enter-prise, of course, but he figured he'd do them more damage on the beach than when they were upcountry on the march; good luck, thinks I, just give me a horse and an escort first, and I'll bless your enterprise as I wave farewell.

And it would have fallen out like that, too, but for the infernal ingenuity of that kitten-tickling besom—Kutebar was right: Ko Dali should have whaled the wickedness out of her years ago.

It was the fourth day, and I was lounging in the camp's little market, improving my Persian by learning the ninety-nine names of God (only the Bactrian camels know the hundredth, which is why they look so deuced superior) from an Astrabad caravan-guard-turned-murderer, when Kutebar came in a great bustle to take me to Yakub Beg at once. I went, thinking no evil, and found him in the pavilion with Sahib Khan and one or two others, squatting round their coffee table. Ko Dali's daughter was lounging apart, listening and saying nothing, feeding her kitten with sweet jelly. Yakub, whose limbs had mended to the point where he could move with only a little stiffness, was wound up like a fiddle-string with excitement; he was smiling gleefully as he touched my hand in greeting and motioned me to sit.

"News, Flashman *bahadur*! The Ruski powder boats come to-morrow. They have loaded at Tokmak, the *Obrucheff* steamer and the *Mikhail*, and by evening they will be at anchor off Syr Daria's mouth, with every grain of powder, every cartridge, every pack for the artillery in their holds! The next day their cargoes will be dispersed through the Ruski host, who at the moment have a bare twenty rounds to each musket." He rubbed his hands joyfully. "You see what it means, *angliski*? God has put them in our hands—may his name be ever blessed!"

I didn't see what he was driving at, until Sahib Khan en-lightened me.

"If those two powder boats can be destroyed," says he, "there will be no Ruski army on the Syr Daria this year. They will be a bear without claws."

"And there will be no advance on India this year, either!" cries Yakub. "What do you say to that, Flashman!"

It was big news, certainly, and their logic was flawless—so far as it went: without their main munitions, the Russians couldn't march. From my detached point of view, there was only one small question to ask.

"Can you do it?"

He looked at me, grinning, and something in that happy bandit face started the alarms rumbling in my lower innards.

"That you shall tell us," says he. "Indeed, God has sent you here. Listen, now. What I have told you is sure information; every slave who labours on that beach at Fort Raim, unloading and piling baggage for those Ruski filth, is a man or a woman of our people—so that not a word is spoken in that camp, not a deed done, not a sentry relieves himself, but we know of it. We know to the last peck of rice, to the last horse-shoe, what supplies already lie on that beach, and we know, too, that when the powder-ships anchor off Fort Raim, they will be ringed about with guard-boats, so that not even a fish can swim through. So we cannot hope to mine or burn them by storm or surprise."

Well, that dished him, it seemed to me, but on he went, happily disposing of another possibility.

"Nor could we hope to drag the lightest of the few poor cannon we have to some place within shot of the ships. What then remains?" He smiled triumphantly and produced from his breast a roll of papers, written in Russian; it looked like a list.

"Did I not say we were well served for spies? This is a manifest of stores and equipment already landed, and lying beneath the awnings and in the sheds. My careful Silk One"—he bowed in her direction—"has had them interpreted, and has found an item of vast interest. It says—now listen, and bless the name of your own people, from whom this gift comes—it says: 'Twenty stands of British rocket artillery; two hundred boxes of cases.'"

He stopped, staring eagerly at me, and I was aware that they were all waiting expectantly.

"Congreves?" says I. "Well, what—"

"What is the range of such rockets?" asked Yakub Beg.

"Why—about two miles." I knew a bit about Congreves from my time at Woolwich. "Not accurate at that distance, of course;

if you want to make good practice, then half a mile, three-quarters, but—"

"The ships will not be above half a mile from the shore," says he, softly. "And these rockets, from what I have heard, are fiercely combustible—like Greek fire! If one of them were to strike the upperworks of the steamer, or the wooden hull of the *Mikhail*—"

"We would have the finest explosion this side of Shaitan's lowest pit!" exulted Kutebar, thumping the table.

"And then—a Russian army without powder, with cannon that would be so much useless lumber, with soldiers armed for nothing better than a day's hunting!" cries Yakub. "They will be an army *bahla dar!*"*

For the life of me, I couldn't understand all this excitement.

"Forgive me," says I. "But the Ruskis have these rockets—you don't. And if you're thinking of stealing some of 'em, I'm sorry, Yakub, but you're eating green corn. D'ye know how much a single Congreve rocket-head weighs, without its stick? Thirty-two pounds. And the stick is fifteen feet long—*and* before you can fire one you have to have the firing-frame, which is solid steel weighing God knows what, with iron half-pipes. Oh, I daresay friend Kutebar here has some pretty thieves in his fighting-tail, but they couldn't hope to lug this kind of gear out from under the Russians' noses—not unseen. Dammit, you'd need a mule-train. And if, by some miracle, you did get hold of a frame and rockets, where would you find a firing-point close enough? For that matter, at two miles —maximum range, trained at fifty-five degrees—why, you could blaze away all night and never score a hit!"

I suddenly stopped talking. I'd been expecting to see their faces fall, but Yakub was grinning broader by the second, Kutebar was nodding grimly, even Sahib Khan was smiling.

"What's the joke, then?" says I. "You can't do it, you see."

"We do not need to do it," says Yakub, looking like a happy crocodile. "Tell me: these things are like great sky-rockets, are they not? How long would it take unskilled men—handless creatures like the ancient Kutebar, for example—to prepare and fire one?"

"To erect the frame?—oh, two minutes, for artillerymen. Ten

* Literally, "wearing hunting gloves in one's belt", i.e. unarmed.

242

times as long, probably, for your lot. Adjust the aim, light the fuse, and off she goes—but dammit, what's the use of this to you?"

"Yallah!" cries he, clapping his hands delightedly. "I should call you *saped-pa*—white foot, the bringer of good luck and good news, for what you have just told us is the sweetest tidings I have heard this summer." He reached over and slapped my knee. "Have no fear—we do not intend to steal a rocket, although it was my first thought. But, as you have pointed out, it would be impossible; this much we had realised. But my Silk One, whose mind is like the puzzles of her father's people, intricately simple, has found a way. Tell him, Kutebar."

"We cannot beat the Ruskis, even if we launch our whole power, five or six thousand riders, upon their beach camp and Fort Raim," says the old bandit. "They must drive us back with slaughter in the end. But"—he wagged a finger like an eagle's talon under my nose—"we can storm their camp by night, in one place, where these *feringhi* ra-kets are lying—and that is hard by the pier, in a little go-down.* This our people have already told us. It will be a strange thing if, descending out of the night past Fort Raim like a thunderbolt, we cannot hold fifty yards of beach for an hour, facing both ways. And in our midst, we shall set up this ra-ket device, and while our riders hold the enemy at bay, our gunners can launch this fire of Eblis against the Ruski powder ships. They will be in fair range, not half a mile—and in such weather, with timbers as dry as sand, will not one ra-ket striking home be sufficient to burn them to Jehannum?"

"Why—yes, I suppose so—those Congreves burn like hell. But, man," I protested, "you'll never get off that beach alive—any of you! They'll ring your storming party in, and cut it down by inches—there are thirty thousand of them, remember? Even if you do succeed in blowing their ships to kingdom come, you'll lose—I don't know, a thousand, two thousand swords doing it."

"We shall have saved our country, too," says Yakub Beg, quietly. "And your India, Flashman *bahadur*. Like enough many will die on that beach—but better to save Khokand for a year, or perhaps even for a generation, and die like men, than see our country trampled by these beasts before the autumn comes." He paused. "We have counted the odds and the cost, and I ask your

* Warehouse.

advice, as a soldier of experience, not on the matter of holding the beach and fighting off the Ruskis, for that is an affair we know better than you, but only as to these rockets. From what you have told us, I see that it can be done. Silk One"—he turned towards her, smiling and touching his brow—"I salute your woman's wit —again."

I looked at her with my skin crawling. She'd schemed up this desperate, doomed nonsense, in which thousands of men were going to be cut up, and there she sat, dusting her kitten's whiskers. Mind you, I didn't doubt, when I thought of the thing, that they could bring it off, given decent luck. Five thousand sabres, with the likes of Kutebar roaring about in the dark, could create havoc in that Russian camp, and probably secure a beachhead just long enough for them to turn the Russians' own rockets on the powder ships. And I knew any fool could lay and fire a Congreve. But afterwards? I thought of the shambles of that beach in the dark —and those rows of gallows outside Fort Raim.

And yet, there they sat, those madmen, looking as pleased as if they were going to a birthday party, Yakub Beg calling for coffee and sherbet, Kutebar's evil old face wreathed in happy smiles. Well, it was no concern of mine, if they wanted to throw their lives away—and if they did succeed in crippling the Russian invasion before it had even started, so much the better. It would be glad news to bring into Peshawar—by jove, I might even hint that I'd engineered the whole thing: if I didn't, the Press probably would. "British Officer's Extraordinary Adventure. Russian Plot Foiled by His Ingenuity. Tribal Life in the Khokand. Colonel Flashman's Remarkable Narrative." Yes, a few helpings of that would go down well ... Elspeth would be in raptures ... I'd be the lion of the day yet again. . . .

And then Yakub Beg's voice broke in on my day-dreams.

"Who shall say there is such a thing as chance?" he was exulting. "All is as God directs. He sends the Ruski powder ships. He sends the means of their destruction. And"—he reached out to pass me my coffee cup—"best of all, he sends you, blood brother, without whom all would be naught."

You may think that until now I'd been slow on the uptake— that I should have seen the danger signal as soon as this lunatic mentioned Congreve rockets. But I'd been so taken aback by the scheme, and had it so fixed in my mind that I had no part in it, anyway, that the fearful implication behind his last words came like a douche of cold water. I nearly dropped my coffee cup.

"Naught?" I echoed. "What d'you mean?"

"Who among us would have the skill or knowledge to make use of these rockets of yours?" says he. "I said you were sent by God. A British officer, who knows how these things are employed, who can ensure success where our bungling fingers would..."

"You mean you expect me to fire these bloody things for you?" I was so appalled that I said it in English, and he looked at me in bewilderment. Stammering, and no doubt going red in the face, I blundered back into Persian.

"Look, Yakub Beg—I'm sorry, but it cannot be. You know I must go to India, to carry the news of this Russian invasion... this army...I can't risk such news going astray...it's my bounden duty, you see..."

"But there will be no invasion," says he, contentedly. "We will see to that."

"But if we—you—I mean, if it doesn't work?" I cried. "I can't take the risk! I mean—it's not that I don't wish to help you— I would if I could, of course. But if I were killed, and the Russians marched in spite of your idiotic—I mean, your daring scheme, they would catch my people unprepared!"

"Rest assured," says he, "the news will go to Peshawar. I pledge my honour, just as I pledge my people to fight these Ruskis tooth and nail from here to the Killer-of-Hindus. But we will stop them *here*—" and he struck the ground beside him. "I know it! And your soldiers in India will be prepared, for a blow that never comes. For we will not fail. The Silk One's plan is sound. Is she not the *najud*?"

And the grinning ape bowed again in her direction, pleased as Punch.

By George, this was desperate. I didn't know what to say. He was bent on dragging me into certain destruction, and I had to weasel out somehow—but at the same time I daren't let them see the truth, which was that the whole mad scheme terrified me out of my wits. That might well be fatal—you've no idea what those folk are like, and if Yakub Beg thought I was letting him down . . . well, one thing I could be sure of: there'd be no excursion train ordered up to take me to the coral strand in a hurry.

"Yakub, my friend," says I. "Think but a moment. I would ask nothing better than to ride with you and Kutebar on this affair. I have my own score to settle with these Ruski pigs, believe me. And if I could add one asper in the scale of success, I would be with you heart and soul. But I am no artilleryman. I know something of these rockets, but nothing to the purpose. Any fool can aim them, and fire them—Kutebar can do it as easily as he breaks wind—" that got them laughing, as I intended it should. "And I have my duty, which is to my country. I, and I alone, must take that news—who else would be believed? Don't you see—you may do this thing without me?"

"Not as surely," says he. "How could we? An artilleryman you may not be, but you are a soldier, with those little skills that mean the difference between success and failure. You know this— and think, blood brother, whether we stand or fall, when those ships flame like the rising sun and sink into destruction, we will have shattered the threat to your folk and mine! We will have lit a fire that will singe the Kremlin wall! By God, what a dawn that will be!"

Just the glitter in those eyes, the joyful madness on that hawk face, sent my spirits into my boots. Normally I'll talk myself hoarse in my skin's interest, and grovel all the way to Caesar's throne, but in that moment I knew it would be no use. You see, even with the saliva pumping into my mouth, I knew that his reasoning was right—ask Raglan or the Duke or Napoleon: they'd have weighed it and said that I should stay. And it's no use trying to defeat an Oriental's logic—let alone one who has the fire in his guts. I tried a little more, as far as I dared, and then let it lie, while the coffee went round again, and Kutebar speculated gloatingly on how many Russians he would kill, and Yakub sat with his hand on my shoulder, praising God and giving thanks for the opportunity to confound the politics of the Tsar. And the cause of it all, that slant-eyed witch in the tight trousers, said nothing at all, but sauntered across to a bird cage hanging on the pavilion trellis, murmuring and pursing her lips to the nightingale to coax it to sing.

I sat pretty quiet myself, feverishly trying to plot a way out of this, and getting nowhere. The others got down to the details of the business, and I had to take part and try to look happy about it. I must say, looking back, they had it well schemed out: they would take five thousand riders, under Yakub and Kutebar and Sahib Khan, each commanding a division, and just go hell for leather past Fort Raim at four in the morning, driving down to the beach and cutting off the pier. Sahib Khan's lot would secure the northern flank beyond the pier, facing the Syr Daria mouth; Yakub would take the south side, fronting the main beach, and their forces would join up at the landward end of the pier, presenting a ring of fire and steel against the Russian counter-attacks. Kutebar's detachment would be inside the ring, in reserve, and shielding the firing party—here they looked at me with reverent eyes, and I managed an offhand grin that any dentist would have recognized first go.

The rockets and stands were in a go-down, Kutebar had said; they would have their spies—the impressed labourers who slept on the beach—on hand to guide us to them. And then, while all hell was breaking loose around us, the intrepid Flashy and his assistants would set the infernal things up and blaze away at the powder ships. And when the great Guy Fawkes explosion occurred—supposing that it did—we would take to the sea; it was half a mile across Syr Daria mouth, and Katti Torah—a horrible little person with yellow teeth and a squint, who was one of the council that night—would be waiting on the other side to cover all who could escape that way. Well, it was at least a glimmer of hope; I'd swum the Mississippi in my time.*

But the more I considered the thing, the more appalling it looked. Indeed, my mind was already running on a different tack entirely: if I could get a horse tonight, and ride for it—anywhere, but south towards Persia for preference, where they wouldn't expect me to go—could I make a clean getaway? Anywhere else, I'd have chanced it, but south was pure desert—for that matter, it was all bloody wilderness, on every side—and if I didn't lose myself and perish horribly, I'd be run down for certain. And blood brother or not, I couldn't see Yakub Beg condoning desertion. Even the beach and the rockets offered a little hope—it couldn't

* See *Flash for Freedom!*

be worse than Balaclava, surely? (God, what a fearful thought that was.) So I looked as steady as I could, while those grinning wolves chuckled over their plan, and when the Silk One broke silence to announce that she personally would go with Kutebar's detachment, and assist with the rockets, I even managed to join in the hum of approval, and say how jolly it would be to have her along. One thing tribulation teaches you, and that is to wear the mask when there's nothing else for it. She gave me a thoughtful glance, and then went back to her nightingale.

As you can guess, I slept fitfully that night. Here I was again, with my essentials trapped in the mangle, and devil a thing to do but grin and bear it—but it was such madness, I kept swearing to myself as I thumped the pillow. Once on a day I'd have wept, or even prayed, but not now; I'd never had any good from either in the past. I could only sweat and hope—I'd come through so much, so often, perhaps my luck would hold again. One thing I was sure of—the first man into the water tomorrow night was going to be H. Flashman, and no bones about it.

I loafed about my tent, worrying, next morning, while the camp hummed around me—you never saw so many happy faces at the prospect of impending dissolution. How many of them would be alive next day? Not that I cared—I'd have seen 'em all dead and damned if only I could come off safe. My guts were beginning to churn in earnest as the hours went by, and finally I was in such a sweat I couldn't stand it any longer. I decided to go up to the pavilion and have a last shot at talking some sense into Yakub Beg—I didn't know what I could say, but if the worst came to the worst I might even chance a flat refusal to have any-thing to do with his mad venture, and see what he would do about it. In this desperate frame of mind I made my way up through the village, which was quiet with everyone being down in the camp below, went through the little archway and past the screen to the garden—and there was Ko Dali's daughter, alone, sitting by the fountain, trailing her fingers in the water, with that damned kitten watching the ripples.

In spite of my fearful preoccupations—which were entirely her fault, in the first place—I felt the old Adam stir at the sight of her. She was wearing a close-fitting white robe with a gold-embroidered border, and her shapely little bare feet peeping out beneath it; round her head was the inevitable turban, also of white. She looked like Sheherazade in the caliph's garden, and didn't she know it, just?

"Yakub is not here," says she, before I'd even had time to state my business. "He has ridden out with the others to talk with Buzurg Khan; perhaps by evening he will have returned." She stroked the kitten. "Will you wait?"

It was an invitation if ever I heard one—and I'm used to them. But it was unexpected, and as I've said, I was something wary of this young woman. So I hesitated, while she watched me, smiling with her lips closed, and I was just on the point of making my apology and withdrawing, when she leaned down to the kitten and said:

"Why do you suppose such a tall fellow is so afraid, little sister? Can you tell? No? He would be wise not to let Yakub Beg know it—for it would be a great shame to the Atalik Ghazi to find fear in his blood brother."

I don't know when I've been taken more aback. I stood astonished as she went on, with her face close to the kitten's:

"We knew it the first night, at Fort Raim—you remember I told you? We felt it even in his mouth. And we both saw it, last night, when Yakub Beg pressed him into our venture—the others did not, for he dissembles well, this *angliski*. But we knew, you and I, little terror of the larder. We saw the fear in his eyes when he tried to persuade them. We see it now." She picked the kitten up and nuzzled it against her cheek. "What are we to make of him, then?"

"Well, I'm damned!" I was beginning, and took a stride forward, red in the face, and stopped.

"Now he is angry, as well as frightened," says she, pretending to whisper in the brute's ear. "Is that not fine? We have stirred him to rage, which is one of the seven forbidden sins he feels against us. Yes, pretty tiger, he feels another one as well. Which one? Come, little foolish, that is easy—no, not envy, why should he envy us? Ah, you have guessed it, you wanton of the night walls, you trifler in *jimai najaiz*.* Is it not scandalous? But be at ease—we are safe from him. For does he not fear?"

Kutebar was undoubtedly right—this one should have had the mischief tanned out of her when she was knee-high. I stood there,

* Illicit love.

wattling, no doubt, and trying to think of a cutting retort—but interrupting a conversation between a woman and a cat ain't as easy as it might seem. One tends to look a fool.

"You think it a pity, scourge of the milk bowls? Well . . . there it is. If lechery cannot cast out fear, what then? What does he fear, you ask? Oh, so many things—death, as all men do. That is no matter, so that they do not cross the line from 'will' to 'will not'. But he fears also Yakub Beg, which is wisdom—although Yakub Beg is far away, and we are quite alone here. So . . . still he wavers, although desire struggles with fear in him. Which will triumph, do you suppose? Is it not exciting, little trollop of the willow-trees? Are your male cats so timorous? Do they fear even to sit beside you?"

I wasn't standing for that, anyway—besides, I was becoming decidedly interested. I came round the fountain and sat down on the grass. And, damme, the kitten popped its face round her head and miaowed at me.

"There, brave little sister!" She cuddled it, turned to look at me out of those slanting black eyes, and returned to her conversation. "Would you protect your mistress, then? Eyah, it is not necessary —for what will he do? He will gnaw his lip, while his mouth grows dry with fear and desire—he will think. Oh, such thoughts —there is no protection against them. Do you not feel them touching us, embracing us, enfolding us, burning us with their passion? Alas, it is only an illusion—and like to remain one, so great is his fear."

I've seduced—and been seduced—in some odd ways, but never before with a kitten pressed into service as pimp. She was right, of course—I was scared, not only of Yakub Beg, but of her: she knew too much, this one, for any man's comfort, and if I knew anything at all it wasn't just for love of my brawny frame and bonny black whiskers that she was taunting me into attempting her. There was something else—but with that slim white shape tantalizing me within arm's length, and that murmuring voice, and the drift of her perfume, subtle and sweet as a garden flower, I didn't care. I reached out—and hesitated, sweating lustfully. My God, I wanted her, but—

"And now he pants, and trembles, and fears to touch, my furry sweet. Like the little boys at the confectioner's stall, or a beardless

youth biting his nails outside a brothel, and he such a fine, strong
—nothing of a man. He—"

"Damn you!" roars I, "and damn your Yakub Beg! Come here!"

And I grabbed her round the body, one hand on her breast,
the other on her belly, and pulled her roughly to me. She came
without resistance, her head back, and those almond eyes looking
up at me, her lips parted; I was shaking as I brought my mouth
down on them, and pulled the robe from her shoulders, gripping
her sharp-pointed breasts in my hands. She lay quivering against
me for a moment, and then pulled free, pushing the kitten gently
aside with her foot.

"Go find a mouse, little idleness. Will you occupy your mistress
all day with silly chatter?"

And then she turned towards me, pushing me back and down
with her hands on my chest, and sliding astride of me while her
tongue flickered out against my lips and then my eyelids and
cheeks and into my ear. I grappled her, yammering lustfully, as
she shrugged off the robe and began working nimbly at my girdle
—and no sooner had we set to partners and commenced heaving
passionately away, than up comes that damned kitten beside my
head, and Ko Dali's daughter had to pause and lift her face to
blow at it.

"Does no one pay heed to you, then? Fie, selfish little inquisi-
tive! Can your mistress not have a moment to pleasure herself
with an *angliski*—a thing she has never done before?" And they
purred at each other while I was going mad—I've never been
more mortified in my life.

"I shall tell you all about it later," said she, which is an
astonishing thing to hear, when you're at grips.

"Never mind telling the blasted cat!" I roared, straining at her.
"Dammit, if you're going to tell anyone, tell me!"

"Ah," says she, sitting back. "You are like the Chinese—you
wish to talk as well? Then here is a topic of conversation." And
she reached up and suddenly plucked off her turban, and there she
was, shaved like a Buddhist monk, staring mischievously down at
me.

"Good God!" I croaked. "You're bald!"

"Did you not know? It is my vow. Does it make me—" she
stirred her rump deliciously "—less desirable?"

"My God, no!" I cried, and fell to again with a will, but every time I became properly engrossed, she would stop to chide the cat, which kept loafing around miaowing, until I was near crazy, with that naked alabaster beauty squirming athwart my hawse, as the sailors say, and nothing to be done satisfactorily until she had left off talking and come back to work. And once she nearly unmanned me completely by stopping short, glancing up, and crying "Yakub!" and I let out a frantic yelp and near as anything heaved her into the fountain as I strained my head round to look at the archway and see—nothing. But before I could remonstrate, or swipe her head off, she was writhing and plunging away again, moaning with her eyes half-closed, and this time, for a wonder, the thing went on uninterrupted until we were lying gasping and exhausted, in each other's arms—and the kitten was there again, purring censoriously in my ear.

By then I was too blissfully sated to care. A teasing, wicked-minded sprite she might be, but Ko Dali's daughter had nothing to learn about killing a chap with kindness, and one of my fondest recollections is of lying there ruined in the warmth of that little garden, with the leaves rustling overhead, watching her slip into her robe and turban again, sleek and satisfied as the kitten which she picked up and cuddled against her cheek. (If only the English dowagers of my acquaintance could know what I'm remembering when I see them pick up their gross fat tabbies in the drawing-room. "Ah, General Flashman has gone to sleep again, poor dear old thing. How contented he looks. Ssh-hh.")

Presently she got up and went off, returning with a little tray on which there were cups of sherbet, and two big bowls of *kefir* —just the thing after a hot encounter, when you're feeling well and contented, and wondering vaguely whether you ought not to slide out before the man of the house comes back, and deciding the devil with him. It was good *kefir*, too—strangely sweet, with a musky flavour that I couldn't place, and as I spooned it down gratefully she sat watching me, with those mysterious dark eyes, and murmuring to her kitten as it played with her fingers.

"Did cruel mistress neglect her darling?" says she. "Ah, do not scold—do I reproach you when you come home with your ears scratched and your fur bedraggled? Do I pester you with impertinent questions? Mmm? Oh, shameless—it is not proper to ask, in his presence. Besides, some little evil bird might hear, and talk . . . and what then? What of me—and Yakub Beg—and fine dreams of a throne in Kashgar some day? Ah, indeed. And what of our fine *angliski*? It would go hard with all of us, if certain things were known, but hardest of all with him . . ."

"Capital *kefir*, this," says I, cleaning round the bowl. "Any more?"

She gave me another helping, and went on whispering to the cat—taking care that I could hear.

"Why did we permit him to make love, then? Oh, such a question! Because of his fine shape and handsome head, you think, and the promise of a great *baz-baz**—oh, whiskered little harlot, have you no blushes? What—because he was fearful, and we women know that nothing so drives out a man's fear as passion and delight with a beautiful darling? That is an old wisdom, true —is it the poet Firdausi who says 'The making of life in the shadow of death is the blissful oblivion . . .'?"

"Stuff and nonsense, beautiful darling," says I, wolfing away. "The poet Flashman says that a good gallop needs no philosophic excuse. You're a lusty little baggage, young Silk One, and that's all about it. Here, leave that animal a moment, and give us a kiss."

"You enjoy your kefir?" says she.

"The blazes with the *kefir*," says I, putting down my spoon. "Here a minute, and I'll show you."

She nuzzled the kitten, watching me thoughtfully. "And if Yakub should return?"

"Blazes with him, too. Come here, can't you?"

But she slipped quickly out of harm's way, and stood slim and white and graceful, cradling the kitten and smiling at it.

"You were right, curious tiny leopard—you and Firdausi both. He is much braver now—and he is so very strong, with his great powerful arms and thighs, like the black djinn in the story of es-Sinbad of the sea—he is no longer safe with delicate ladies such as we. He might harm us." And with that mocking smile she went quickly round the fountain, before I could stop her. "Tell me, *angliski*," she said, looking back, but not stopping. "You who speak Persian and know so much of our country—have you ever heard of the Old Man of the Mountains?"

* An indelicate synonym for virility.

"No, by jove, I don't think I have," says I. "Come back and tell me about him."

"After tonight—when the work has been done," says she, teasing. "Perhaps then I shall tell you."

"But I want to know now."

"Be content," says she. "You are a different man from the fearful fellow who came here seeking Yakub an hour ago. Remember the Persian saying: 'Lick up the honey, stranger, and ask no questions'."

And then she was gone, leaving me grinning foolishly after her, and cursing her perversity in a good-humoured way. But, do you know, she was right? I couldn't account for it, but for some reason I felt full of buck and appetite and great good humour, and I couldn't even remember feeling doubts or fears or anything much—of course, I knew there was nothing like a good lively female for putting a chap in trim, as her man Firdausi had apparently pointed out. Clever lads, these Persian poets. But I couldn't recall ever feeling so much the better for it—a new man, in fact, as she'd said.

☙11

Now, you who know me may find what I've just written, and what I am about to tell you, extremely strange, coming from me at such a time. But as I've said before, there's nothing in these memoirs that isn't gospel true, and you must just take my word for it. My memory's clear, even if my understanding isn't always perfect, and I'm in no doubt of what happened on that day, or on the night that followed.

I went striding back down to the valley, then, singing "A-hunting we will go", if I remember rightly, and was just in time to see Yakub and Kutebar return from their meeting with Buzurg Khan in a fine rage: the overlord had refused to risk any of his people in what he, the shirking recreant, regarded as a lost hope. I couldn't believe such poltroonery, myself, and said so, loudly. But there it was: the business was up to us and our five thousand sabres, and when Yakub jumped on a pile of camel bales in the valley market, and told the mob it was do or die by themselves for the honour of Old Khokand, and explained how we were going to assault the beach that night and blow up the powder-ships, the whole splendid crowd rose to him as a man. There was just a sea of faces, yellow and brown, slit-eyed and hook-nosed, bald-pated and scalp-locked or turbanned and hairy, all yelling and laughing and waving their sabres, with the wilder spirits cracking off their pistols and racing their ponies round the outskirts of the crowd in an ecstasy of excitement, churning up the dust and whooping like Arapahoes.

And when Kutebar, to a storm of applause, took his place beside Yakub, and thundered in his huge voice: "North, south, east, and west—where shall you find the Kirgiz? By the silver hand of Alexander, they are *here!*" the whole place exploded in wild cheering, and they crowded round the two leaders, promising ten Russian dead for every one of ours, and I thought, why not give 'em a bit of civilized comfort, too, so I jumped up myself, roaring "Hear, hear!", and when they stopped to listen I gave it to them, straight and manly.

"That's the spirit, you fellows!" I told them. "I second what these two fine associates of mine have told you, and have only this to add. We're going to blow these bloody Russians from Hell to Huddersfield—and I'm the chap who can do it, let me tell you! So I shall detain you no longer, my good friends—and Tajiks, and niggers, and what-not—but only ask you to be upstanding and give a rousing British cheer for the honour of the dear old Schoolhouse—hip, hip, hip, hurrah!"

And didn't they cheer, too? Best speech I ever made, I remember thinking, and Yakub clapped me on the back, grinning all over, and said by the beard of Mohammed, if we had proposed a march on Moscow every man-jack would have been in his saddle that minute, riding west. I believed him, too, and said it was a damned good idea, but he said no, the powder ships were enough for just now, and I must take pains to instruct the band of assistants whom he'd told off to help me with the rockets when we got to the beach.

So I got them together—and Ko Dali's daughter was there, too, lovely girl and so attentive, all in black, now, shirt, *pyjamys*, boots and turban, very business-like. And I lectured them about Congreves—it was remarkable how well I remembered each detail about assembling the firing-frame and half-pipes, and adjusting the range-screws and everything; the excellent fellows took it all in, spitting and exclaiming with excitement, and you could see that even if they weren't the kind to get elected to the Royal Society for their mechanical aptitude, their hearts were in the right place. I tried to get Ko Dali's daughter aside afterwards for some special instruction, but she excused herself, so I went off to the grindstone merchant to get a sabre sharpened, and got Kutebar to find me a few rounds for my German revolver.

"The only thing that irks me," I told him, "is that we are going to be stuck in some stuffy go-down, blazing away with rockets, while Yakub and the others have got the best of the evening. Damn it, Izzat, I want to put this steel across a few Ruski necks —there's a wall-eyed rascal called Ignatieff, now, have I told you about him? Two rounds from this pop-gun into his midriff, and then a foot of sabre through his throat—that's all he needs. By gad, I'm thirsty tonight, I tell you."

"It is a good thirst," says he approvingly. "But think, *angliski*, of the countless hundreds infidel pigs—your pardon, when I say infidels, I mean Ruskis—whom we shall send to the bottom of Aral with these fine ra-kets. Is that not worthy work for a warrior?"

"Oh, I daresay," I grumbled. "But it ain't the same as jamming a sword in their guts and watching 'em wriggle. That's my sort, now. I say, have I ever told you about Balaclava?"

I didn't know when I'd felt so blood-lusty, and it got worse as the evening wore on. By the time we saddled up I was full of hate against a vague figure who was Ignatieff in a Cossack hat with the Tsar's eagle across the front of his shirt; I wanted to settle him, gorily and painfully, and all the way on our ride across the Kizil Kum in the gathering dark I was dreaming fine nightmares in which I despatched him. But from time to time I felt quite jolly, too, and sang a few snatches of "The Leather Bottel" and "John Peel" and other popular favourites, while the riders grinned and nudged each other, and Kutebar muttered that I was surely bewitched. And all the way the Silk One rode knee to knee with me —not so close that I could give her a squeeze, unfortunately, and silent most of the time, although she seemed to be watching me closely. Well, what girl doesn't—especially when she's just had her first taste of Flashy? I recalled it fondly, and promised myself I would continue her education, for she deserved it, the dear child —but not until I'd satisfied my yearning for slaughter of Russians. That was the main thing, and by the time we had trotted silently into the scrubby wood that lies a bare half-mile from Fort Raim, I was fairly dribbling to be at them.

It took a good hour in the cold dark to bring all the riders quietly into the safety of the wood, each man holding his horse's nostrils or blanketing its head, while I fidgeted with impatience. It was the waiting that infuriated me, when we could have been down on the beach killing Russians, and I spoke pretty sharp to Yakub Beg about it when he emerged out of the shadows, very brave in spiked helmet and red cloak, to say that we should move when the moon hid behind the cloud bank.

"Come along, come along, come along," says I. "What are we about, then? The brutes'll be sounding reveille in a moment."

"Patience, blood brother," says he, giving me a puzzled look, and then a grin. "You shall have your rockets at their throats presently. God keep you. Kutebar, preserve that worthless carcase if you can, and you, beloved Silk One—" he reached out and pressed her head to his breast, whispering to her. Bully for some, thinks I: wonder if you can do it on a trotting horse? Have to try some time—and then Yakub was calling softly into the dark:

"In the name of God and the Son of God! Kirgiz, Uzbek, Tajik, Kalmuk, Turka—remember Ak Mechet! The morning rides behind us!" And he made that strange, moaning Khokand whistle, and with a great rumbling growl and a drumming of hooves the whole horde went surging forward beneath the trees and out on to the empty steppe towards Fort Raim.

If I'd been a sentry on those walls I'd have had apoplexy. One moment an empty steppe, and the next it was thick with mounted men, pouring down on the fort; we must have covered quarter of a mile before the first shot cracked, and then we were tearing at full tilt towards the gap between fort and river, with the shouts of alarm sounding from the walls, and musketry popping, and then with one voice the yell of the Ghazi war-cry burst from the riders (one voice, in fact, was crying "Tally-ho! Ha-ha!"), five thousand mad creatures thundering down the long slope with the glittering sea far ahead, and the ships riding silent and huge on the water, and on to the cluttered beach, with men scattering in panic as we swept in among the great piles of bales, sabring and shooting, leaping crazily in the gloom over the boxes and low shelters, Yakub's contingent streaming out to the left among the sheds and go-downs, while our party and Sahib Khan's drove for the pier.

God, what a chaos it was! I was galloping like a dervish at Kutebar's heels, roaring "Hark forrard! Ha-ha, you bloody foreigners, Flashy's here!", careering through the narrow spaces between the sheds, with the muskets banging off to our left, startled sleepers crying out, and everyone yelling like be-damned. As we burst headlong onto the last stretch of open beach, and swerved past the landward end of the pier, some stout Russian was bawling and letting fly with a pistol; I left off singing "Rule, Britannia" to take a shot at him, but missed, and there ahead someone was waving a torch and calling, and suddenly there were dark figures all around us, clutching at our bridles, almost pulling us from the saddles towards a big go-down on the north side of the pier.

I was in capital fettle as I strode into the go-down, which was full of half-naked natives with torches, all in a ferment of excitement.

"Now, then, my likely lads," cries I, "where are these Congreves, eh? Look alive, boys, we haven't got all night, you know."

"Here is the devil-fire, oh slayer of thousands," says someone, and there sure enough was a huge pile of boxes, and in the smoky torchlight I could see the broad arrow, and make out the old familiar lettering on them: "Royal Small Arms Factory. Handle with Extreme Care. Explosives. Danger. This side up."

"And how the deuce did this lot get here, d'ye suppose?" says I to Kutebar. "Depend upon it, some greasy bastard in Birmingham with a pocketful of dollars could tell us. Right-o, you fellows, break 'em out, break 'em out!" And as they set to with a will, I gave them another chorus of "John Peel" and strode to the sea end of the go-down, which of course was open, and surveyed the bay.

Ko Dali's daughter was at my elbow, with a chattering nigger pointing out which ship was which. There were two steamers, the farther one being the *Obrucheff*, three vessels with masts, of which the *Mikhail* was farthest north, and a ketch, all riding under the moon on the glassy sea, pretty as paint.

"That's the ticket for soup!" says I. "We'll have 'em sunk in half a jiffy. How are you, my dear—I say, that's a fetching rig you're wearing!" And I gave her a squeeze for luck, but she wriggled free.

"The firing-frame, *angliski*—you must direct them," says she, and I turned reluctantly from surveying the bay and listening to the war that was breaking out along the beach—hell of a din of shooting and yelling, and it stirred my blood to action. I strode in among the toilers, saw the firing-frame broken from its crate, and showed them where to position it, at the very lip of the go-down, just above the small boats and barges which were rocking gently at their moorings on the water six feet below our feet.

Putting up the frame was simple—it's just an iron fence, you see, with supports both sides, and half-pipes running from the ground behind to the top of the fence, to take the rockets. I've never known my fingers so nimble as I tightened the screws and adjusted the half-pipes in their sockets; everyone else seemed slow by comparison, and I cursed them good-naturedly and finally left Ko Dali's daughter to see to the final adjustments while I went off to examine the rockets.

They had them broken out by now, the dull grey three-foot metal cylinders with their conical heads—I swore when I saw that, as I'd feared, they were the old pattern, without fins and needing the fifteen-foot sticks.[43] Sure enough, there were the sticks, in long canvas bundles; I called for one, and set to work to fit it into a rocket head, but the thing was corroded to blazes.

"Now blast these Brummagem robbers!" cries I. "This is too bad —see how British workmanship gets a bad name! At this rate the Yankees will be streets ahead of us. Break out another box!"

"Burst it open! off with the lid, sons of idleness!" bawls Kutebar, fuming with impatience. "If it was Russian gold within, you'd have them open fast enough!"

"They will open in God's time, father of all wisdom," says one of the riders. "See, there they lie, like the silver fish of See-ah— are they not pretty to behold?"

"Prettier yet when they strike those Ruski ships of Eblis!" roars Kutebar. "Bring me a stick that I may arm one of these things! What science is here! Wisdom beyond that of the great astronomer of Samarkand has gone to the making of these fine instruments. I salute you, Flashman *bahadur*, and the genius of your infidel professors of Anglistan. See, there it stands, ready to blow the sons of pigs straight up Shaitan's backside!" And he flourished the stick, with the rockethead secured—upside down, which made me laugh immoderately.

I was interrupted by the Silk One, tugging urgently at my sleeve, imploring me to hurry—I couldn't see what all the fuss was, for I was enjoying things thoroughly. The battle was going great guns outside, with a steady crackle of gunfire, but no regular volleys, which meant, as I pointed out, that the Ruskis hadn't come to order yet.

"Lots of time, darling," I soothed her. "Now, how's the frame? Very creditable, very handy, you fellows—well done. Right-ho, Izzat, let's have some of those rockets along here, sharp now! Mustn't keep ladies waiting, what?" And I took a slap at her tight little backside—I don't know when I've felt so full of beans.

It was a fine, sweaty confusion in the go-down as they dragged the rockets down to the firing-frame, and I egged 'em on, and showed them how to lay a rocket in the half-pipe—no corrosion there, thank God, I noted, and the Silk One fairly twitched with impatience—strange girl, she was, tense as a telegraph wire at moments like this, but all composure when she was at home—while I lectured her on the importance of unrusted surfaces, so that the rockets flew straight.

"In God's name, *angliski!*" cries Kutebar. "Let us be about it! See the *Mikhail* yonder, with enough munitions aboard to blow the Aral dry—for the love of women, let us fire on her!"

"All right, old fellow," says I. "Let's see how we stand." I squinted along the half-pipe, which was at full elevation. "Give us a box beneath the pipe, to lift her. So—steady." I adjusted the ranging-screw, and now the great conical head of the rocket was pointing just over her main-mast. "That's about it. Right, give me a slow-match, someone."

Suddenly there wasn't a sound in the go-down, apart from me whistling to myself as I took a last squint along the rocket and glanced round to see that everything was ready. I can see them still—the eager, bearded hawk-faces, the glistening half-naked bodies running sweat in the stuffy go-down, even Kutebar with his mouth hanging open, quiet for once, Ko Dali's daughter with her face chalk-white and her eyes fixed on me. I gave her a wink.

"Stand clear, boys and girls," I sang out. "Papa's going to light the blue touch-paper and retire immediately!" And in that instant before I touched the match to the firing-vent, I had a sudden vivid memory of November the Fifth, with the frosty ground and the dark, and little boys chattering and giggling and the girls covering their ears, and the red eye of the rocket smouldering in the black, and the white fizz of sparks, and the chorus of admiring "oohs" and "aahs" as the rocket bursts overhead—and it was something like that now, if you like, except that here the fizzing was like a locomotive funnel belching sparks, filling the go-down with acrid, reeking smoke, while the firing-frame shuddered, and then with an almighty whoosh like an express tearing by the Congreve went rushing away into the night, clouds of smoke and fire gushing from its tail, and the boys and girls cried "By Shaitan!" and "Istagfarullah!", and Papa skipped nimbly aside roaring "Take that, you sons of bitches!" And we all stood gaping as it soared into the night like a comet, reached the top of its arc, dipped towards the *Mikhail*—and vanished miles on the wrong side of it.

"Bad luck, dammit! Hard lines! Right, you fellows, let's have another!" And laughing heartily, I had another box shoved under the pipe to level it out. We let fly again, but this time the rocket must have been faulty, for it swerved away crazily into the night, weaving to and fro before plunging into the water a bare three hundred yards out with a tremendous hiss and cloud of steam. We tried three more, and all fell short, so we adjusted the range slightly, and the sixth rocket flew straight and true, like a great scarlet lance searching for its target; we watched it pass between the masts of the *Mikhail*, and howled with disappointment. But now at least we had the range, so I ordered all the pipes loaded, and we touched off the whole battery at once.

It was indescribable, and great fun—like a volcano erupting under your feet, and a dense choking fog filling the go-down; the men clinging to steady the firing-frame were almost torn from their feet, the rush of the launching Congreves was deafening, and for a moment we were all staggering about, weeping and coughing in that filthy smoke. It was a full minute before the reek had cleared sufficiently to see how our shots had fared, and then Kutebar was flinging himself into the air and rushing to embrace me.

"Ya'allahah! Wonder of God! Look—look yonder, Flashman! Look at the blessed sight! Is it not glorious—see, see how they burn!"

And he was right—the *Mikhail* was hit! There was a red ball of fire clinging to her timbers just below the rail amidships, and even as we watched there was a climbing lick of flame—and over to the right, by some freakish chance, the ketch had been hit, too: there was a fire on her deck, and she was slewing round at anchor. All about me they were dancing and yelling and clapping hands, like school girls when Popular Penelope has won the sewing prize.

All except Ko Dali's daughter. While Kutebar was roaring and I was chanting "For we are jolly good fellows," she was barking shrill commands at the men on the frame, having them swivel the pipes round for a shot at the *Obrucheff*—trust women to interfere, thinks I, and strode over.

"Now then, my dear, what's this?" says I, pretty short. "I'll decide when we leave off shooting at our targets, if you don't mind. You, there—"

"We have hit one, *angliski*—it is time for the other." She rapped it out, and I was aware that her face was strained, and her eyes seemed to be searching mine anxiously. "There is no time to waste—listen to the firing! In a few moments they will have broken through Yakub's line and be upon us!"

You know, I'd been so taken up with our target practice, I'd almost forgotten about the fighting that was going on outside. But she was right; it was fiercer than ever, and getting closer. And she was probably right about the *Mikhail*, too—with any luck that fire aboard her would do the business.

"You're a clever girl, Silk One, so you are," says I. "Right-ho, bonny boys, heave away!" And I flung my weight on the frame, chanting "Yo-ho", while the gleeful niggers dragged up more rockets—they were loving this as much as I was, grinning and yelling and inviting God and each other to admire the havoc we had wrought.

"Aye, now for the steamer!" shouts Kutebar. "Hasten, Flashman *bahadur*! Fling the fire of God upon them, the spawn of Muscovy! Aye, we shall burn you here, and Eblis will consume your souls thereafter, you thieves, you disturbers, you dunghill sons of whores and shameless women!"

It wasn't quite as easy as that. Perhaps we'd been lucky with the *Mikhail*, but I fired twenty single rockets at the *Obrucheff* and never came near enough to singe her cable—they snaked over her, or flew wide, or hit the water short, until the smoky trails of their passing blended into a fine mist across the bay; the go-down was a scorching inferno of choking smoke in which we shouted and swore hoarsely as we wrestled sticks and canisters into pipes that were so hot we had to douse them with water after every shot. My good humour didn't survive the twentieth miss; I raged and swore and kicked the nearest nigger—I was aware, too, that as we laboured the sounds of battle outside were drawing closer still, and I was in half a mind to leave these infernal rockets that wouldn't fly straight, and pitch into the fighting on the beach. It was like hell, outside and in, and to add to my fury one of the ships in the bay was firing at us now; the pillar of cloud from the go-down must have made a perfect target, and the rocket trails had long since advertised to everyone on that beach exactly what was going on. The smack of musket balls on the roof and walls was continuous—although I didn't know it then, detachments of Russian cavalry had tried three times to drive through the lumbered beach in phalanx to reach the go-down and silence us, and Yakub's riders had halted them each time with desperate courage. The ring round our position was contracting all the time as the Khokandian riders fell back; once a shot from the sea pitched right in front of the go-down, showering us with spray, another howled overhead like a banshee, and a third crashed into the pier alongside us.

"Damn you!" I roared, shaking my fist. "Come ashore, you swine, and I'll show you!" I seemed to be seeing everything through a red mist, with a terrible, consuming rage swelling up inside me; I was swearing incoherently, I know, as we dragged another rocket into the reeking pipe; half-blinded with smoke and sweat and fury I touched it off, and this time it seemed to drop just short of the *Obrucheff*—and then, by God, I saw that the ship was moving; they must have got steam up in her at last, and she was veering round slowly, her stern-wheel churning as she prepared to draw out from the shore.

"Ah, God, she will escape!" It was Ko Dali's daughter, shrill beside me. "Quickly, quickly, *angliski*! Try again, with all the rockets! Kutebar, all of you, load them all together before she has gone too far!"

"Cowardly rascals!" I hollered. "Turn tail, will you? Why don't you stand and fight, you measly hounds? Load 'em up, you idle bastards, there!" And savagely I flung myself among them as they hauled up the five rockets—one of 'em was still half off its stick, I remember, with a little nigger still wrestling to fix it home even as the man with the match was touching the fuse. I crammed the burning remnant of my match against a vent, and even as the trail of sparks shot out the whole go-down seemed to stand on end, I felt myself falling, something hit me a great crack on the head, and my ears were full of cannonading that went on and on until the pain of it seemed to be bursting my brain before blackness came.

I've reckoned since that I must have been unconscious for only a few minutes, but for all I knew when I opened my eyes it might have been hours. What had happened was that a cannon shot had hit the go-down roof just as the rockets went off, and a falling slat had knocked me endways; when I came to the first thing I saw was the firing-frame in ruins, with a beam across it, and I remember thinking, ah well, no more Guy Fawkes night until next year. Beyond it, through the smoke, I could see the *Mikhail*, burning quite nicely now, but not exploding, which I thought strange; the ketch was well alight, too, but the *Obrucheff* was under way, with smoke pouring from her funnel and her wheel thrashing great guns. There was a glow near her stern, too, and I found myself wondering, in a confused way, if one of the last salvo had got home. "Serve you right, you Russian scoundrels," I muttered, and tried to pull myself up, but I couldn't; all the strength had gone from my limbs.

But the strangest thing was, that my head seemed to have floated loose from my shoulders, and I couldn't seem to focus properly on things around me. The great berserk rage that had possessed me only a moment since seemed to have gone, and I felt quite tranquil, and dreamy—it wasn't unpleasant, really, for I felt that nothing much mattered, and there was no pain or anxiety, or even inclination to do anything, but just lie there, resting body and brain together.

And yet I have a pretty clear recollection of what was happening around me, although none of it was important at the time. There were folk crawling about the go-down, among the smoke and wreckage, and Kutebar was thundering away blasphemously, and then Ko Dali's daughter was kneeling beside me, trying to raise my head, which was apparently swollen as big as a house. Outside, the fight was raging, and among the shots and yells I could hear the actual clash of steel—it didn't excite me now, though, or even interest me. And then Yakub Beg was there, his helmet gone, one arm limp with a great bloodied gash near the shoulder, and a naked sabre in his good hand. Strange, thinks I, you ought to be out on the beach, killing Russians; what the deuce are you doing here?

"Away!" he was shouting. "Away—take to the water!" And he dropped his sabre and took Ko Dali's daughter by the shoulder. "Quickly, Silk One—it is done! They have driven us in! Swim for it, beloved—and Kutebar! Get them into the sea, Izzat! There are only moments left!"

Ko Dali's daughter was saying something that I couldn't catch, and Yakub was shaking his head.

"Sahib Khan can hold them with his Immortals—but only for minutes. Get you gone—and take the Englishman. Do as I tell you, girl! Yes, yes, I will come—did I not say Sahib Khan is staying?"

"And you will leave him?" Her voice seemed faint and far away.

"Aye, I will leave him. Khokand can spare him, but it cannot spare me; he knows it, and so do I. And he seeks his wife and little ones. Now, in God's name, get out quickly!"

She didn't hesitate, but rose, and two of the others half-dragged, half-carried me to the mouth of the go-down. I was so dazed I don't think it even crossed my mind that I was in no case to swim; it didn't matter, anyway, for some clever lads were cutting loose the lighter that swung under the edge of the go-down, and men were tumbling into it. I remember a fierce altercation was going on between Yakub Beg and Kutebar, the latter protesting that he wanted to stay and fight it out with Sahib Khan and the others, and Yakub more or less thrusting him down into the lighter with his sound arm, and then jumping in himself. I was aware that one wall of the go-down was burning, and in the glare and the smoke I caught a glimpse of a swirling mass of figures at the doors, and I think I even made out a Cossack, laying about him with a sabre, before someone tumbled down on top of me and knocked me flat on the floor of the lighter.

Somehow they must have poled the thing off, for when I had recovered my breath and pulled myself up to the low gunwale, we were about twenty yards from the go-down, and drifting away from the pier as the eddy from the river mouth, I suppose, caught the lighter and tugged it out to sea. I had only a momentary sight of the interior of the go-down, looking for all the world like a mine-shaft, with the figures of miners hewing away in it, and then I saw a brilliant light suddenly glowing on its floor, growing in intensity, and then the rush-rush-rush sound of the Congreves as the flames from the burning wall reached them, and I just had sense enough to duck my head below the gunwale before the whole place dissolved in a blinding light— but strangely enough, without any great roar of explosion, just the rushing noise of a huge whirlwind. There were screams and oaths from the lighter all around me, but when I raised my head there was just one huge flame where the go-down had been, and the pier beside it was burning at its landward end, and the glare was so fierce that beyond there was nothing to be seen.

I just lay, with my cheek on the thwart, wondering if the eddy would carry us out of range before they started shooting at us, and thinking how calm and pleasant it was to be drifting along here, after all the hellish work in the go-down. I still wasn't feeling any sense of urgency, or anything beyond a detached, dreamy interest, and I can't say even now whether we were fired on or not, for I suddenly became aware that Ko Dali's daughter was crouched down beside me at the gunwale, staring back, and people were pressed close about us, and I thought, this is a splendid opportunity to squeeze that lovely little rump of hers. There it was, just nicely curved within a foot of me, so I took a handful and kneaded away contentedly, and she never even noticed—or if she did, she didn't mind. But I think she was too preoccupied with the inferno we had left behind us; so were the others, craning and muttering as we drifted over the dark water. It's queer, but in my memory that drifting and bum-fondling seems to have gone on for the deuce of a long time—I suppose I was immensely preoccupied with it, and a capital thing, too. But some other things I remember: the flames of the go-down and pier seen at a distance, and a wounded man groaning near me in the press of bodies; Ko Dali's daughter speaking to Yakub Beg, and Kutebar saying something which involved an oath to do with a camel; and a water-skin being pressed against my lips, and the warm, brackish water making me choke and cough. And Yakub Beg saying that the *Mikhail* was burning to a wreck, but the *Obrucheff* had got away, so our work was only half-done, but better half-done than not done at all, and Kutebar growling that, by God, it was all very well for those who had been loafing about on the beach, building sand-castles, to talk, but if Yakub and his saunterers had been in the go-down, where the real business was . . .

And pat on his words the sun was suddenly in the sky—or so it seemed, for the whole place, the lighter, the sea around, and sky itself, were suddenly as bright as day, and it seemed to me that the lighter was no longer drifting, but racing over the water, and then came the most tremendous thundering crash of sound I've ever heard, reverberating over the sea, making the head sing and shudder with the deafening boom of it, and as I tried to put up my hands to my ears to shut out the pain, I heard Kutebar's frantic yell:

"The *Obrucheff!* She has gone—gone to the pit of damnation! Now whose work is half-done? By God!—it is done, it is done, it is done! A thousand times done! Ya, Yakub—is it not done? Now the praise to Him and to the foreign professors!"

℘12

More than two thousand Khokandians were killed in the battle of Fort Raim, which shows you what a clever lad Buzurg Khan was to keep out of it. The rest escaped, some by cutting their way eastward off the beach, some by swimming the Syr Daria mouth, and a favoured few travelling in style, by boat and lighter. How many Russians died, no one knows, but Yakub Beg later estimated about three thousand. So it was a good deal bigger than many battles that are household words, but it happened a long way away, and the Russians doubtless tried to forget it, so I suppose only the Khokandians remember it now.

It achieved their purpose, anyhow, for it destroyed the Russian munition ships, and prevented the army marching that year. Which saved British India for as long as I've lived—and preserved Khokand's freedom for a few years more, before the Tsar's soldiers came and stamped it flat in the 'sixties. I imagine the Khokandians thought the respite was worth while, and the two thousand lives well lost—what the two thousand would say, of course, is another matter, but since they went to fight of their own free will (so far as any soldier ever does), I suppose they would support the majority.

Myself, I haven't changed my opinion since I came back to my senses two days afterwards, back in the valley in Kizil Kum. I remember nothing of our lighter being hauled from the water by Katti Torah's rescue party, or of the journey back through the desert, for by that time I was in the finest hallucinatory delirium since the first Reform Bill, and I came out of it gradually and painfully. The terrible thing was that I remembered the battle very clearly, and my own incredible behaviour—I knew I'd gone bawling about like a Viking in drink, seeking sorrow and raving heroically in murderous rage, but I couldn't for the life of me understand why. It had been utterly against nature, instinct and judgement—and I knew it hadn't been booze, because I hadn't had any, and anyway the liquor hasn't been distilled that can make me oblivious of self-preservation. It appalled me, for what security does a right-thinking coward have, if he loses his sense of panic?

At first I thought my memory of that night's work must be playing me false, but the admiring congratulations I got from Yakub Beg and Kutebar (who called me "Ghazi", of all things) soon put paid to that notion. So I must have been temporarily deranged—but why? The obvious explanation, for some reason, never occurred to me—and yet I knew Ko Dali's daughter was at the bottom of it somehow, so I sought her out first thing when I had emerged weak and shaky from my brief convalescence. I was too upset to beat about the bush, and although she played the cool arch tart at first, and pretended not to understand what I was talking about, I went at it so hard that at last she told me —not to put my mind at rest, you may be sure, but probably because she knew that the only fun to be had from a secret lies in betraying it, especially if it makes someone wriggle.

"You remember I spoke to you about the Old Man of the Mountains, of whom you had never heard?"

"What's he got to do with me rushing about like a lunatic?"

"He lived many years ago, in Persia, beyond the Two Seas and the Salt Desert. He was the master of the mad fighting-men— the *hasheesheen*—who nerved themselves to murder and die by drinking the *hasheesh* drug—what the Indians call *bhang*. It is prepared in many ways, for many purposes—it can be so concocted that it will drive a man to any lengths of hatred and courage—and other passions."

And she said it as calm as a virgin discussing flower arrangement, sitting there gravely cross-legged on a *charpai** in a corner of her garden, with her vile kitten gorging itself on a saucer of milk beside her. I stared at her astounded.

"The *hasheesheen*—you mean the Assassins?⁴⁴ Great God, woman, d'you mean to say you filled me with an infernal drug, that sent me clean barmy?"

"It was in your *kefir*," says she, lightly. "Drink, little tiger, there is more if you need it."

"But . . . but . . ." I was almost gobbling. "What the devil for?"

* Bed platform.

270

"Because you were afraid. Because I knew, from the moment I first saw you, that fear rules you, and that in the test, it will always master you." The beautiful face was quite impassive, the voice level. "And I could not allow that to happen. If you had proved a coward that night, when all depended on you, we would have been lost—Yakub's enterprise would have failed, and Khokand with it. I would do—anything, rather than see him fail. So I drugged you—has it done any harm, in the end?"

"I never heard of such infernal impudence in my life!" I stormed. By George, I was angry, and resentful, and bursting with it. "Blast you, I might have got myself killed!"

She suddenly laughed, showing those pretty teeth. "You are sometimes an honest man, *angliski!* Is he not, puss? And he does wrong to rage and abuse us—for is he not alive? And if he had turned coward, where would he have been?"

A sound argument, as I've realized since, but it didn't do much to quieten me just then. I detested her in that moment, as only a coward can when he hears the truth to his face, and I didn't have to look far to see how to vent my spite on her.

"If I'm honest, it's more than you are. All this fine talk of not failing your precious Yakub Beg—we know how much that's worth! You pretend to be devoted to him—but it doesn't stop you coupling like a bitch in heat with the first chap that comes along. Hah! That shows how much you care for him!"

She didn't even blush, but smiled down at the kitten, and stroked it. "Perhaps it does, eh, puss? But the *angliski* would not be pleased if we said as much. But then—"

"Stop talking to the blasted cat! Speak plain, can't you?"

"If it pleases you. Listen *angliski*, I do not mock—now, and I do not seek to put shame on you. It is no sin to be fearful, any more than it is a sin to be one-legged or red-haired. All men fear —even Yakub and Kutebar and all of them. To conquer fear, some need love, and some hate, and some greed, and some even— *hasheesh*. I understand your anger—but consider, is it not all for the best? You are here, which is what matters most to you—and no one but I knows what fears are in your heart. And that I knew from the beginning. So—" she smiled, and I remember it still as a winning smile, curse her. "'Lick up the honey, stranger, and ask no questions'."

And that was all I could get from her—but somewhere in it I detected a tiny mite of consolation. I've got my pride in one direction, you know—or had then. So before I left her, I asked the question:

"Why did you goad me into making love to you?"

"Call that a drug, too, if you will—to make certain you ate my *kefir*."

"Just that, eh? Lot of trouble, you Chinese girls go to."

She laughed aloud at that, and gave a little pout. "And I had never met an *angliski* before, you remember. Say I was curious."

"May I ask if your curiosity was satisfied?"

"Ah, you ask too much, *angliski*. That is one tale I tell only to my kitten."

I daresay I've no cause to remember her with much affection, but I do, like the old fool I am. As indeed I do all my girls, now that they're at a safe distance. Perhaps she was right, and I owed it to her that I'd come out with a whole skin—but that was blind luck, and anyway, she had plunged me into the stew in the first place. But it's all by now, and I have only to hold that faded flower scarf that she gave me as a parting gift, and I'm back in the bright garden behind the ranges, looking into those black almond eyes, and feeling the sun's warmth and those soft lips against my cheek, and—aye, but she knew too much, the Silk One. Kutebar was decidedly right.

Still, I had no cause for complaint, once I'd recovered from the shock of realizing that I'd fought a do-or-die action by means of a bellyful of some disgusting Oriental potion. I've often wondered since, if chaps like Chinese Gordon and Bobs and Custer *always* went about feeling the way I did that night—not knowing what fear was? It would account for a lot, you know. But God help anyone who's born that way; I'm sorry for 'em. You can't know real peace of mind, I think, unless you've got a windy streak in you.

But I didn't think too long about it just then. The danger was past, all right, I was safe out of the Russians' reach, and among friendly folk who thought I was the best thing to come their way since Tamburlaine—but I'd no wish to linger. When I took stock of what I'd been through in the past year, from the hell of Balaclava and the snow-sodden nightmare of Russia, with its wolves and knouts and barbarous swine like Ignatieff, to the shocking perils of Fort Raim and the go-down (I shudder to this day at the mention of Guy Fawkes), I had only one notion in my head: India, and a hero's welcome, no doubt, and after that home, and the sounds of London and Leicestershire, and the comfort of clubs and taverns and English bed-clothes and buttered toast, and above all my beautiful blonde Elspeth—who didn't have the wit to converse with kittens, and could be relied on not to lace my kidneys and bacon with opium. By God, though, I wondered if Cardigan had been mooching round in my absence—unless he'd got himself killed, with luck? For that matter, was the war over, or what? Decidedly I must get back to civilization quickly.

Yakub Beg was deuced good about it—as well he might have been, considering the risks I'd run on his behalf—and after a tremendous feast in the Kizil Kum valley, at which we celebrated the Russians' confusion, and the salvation of Khokand—oh, and India, too—we set out for Khiva, where he was moving his folk out of reach of Russian reprisals. From there we went east to Samarkand, where he had promised to arrange for some Afghan pals of his to convoy me over the mountains and through Afghanistan to Peshawar. I wasn't looking forward, much, to that part of the journey, but our trip to Samarkand was like a holiday outing. It was clear air and good horses, with Kutebar and Yakub snarling happily at each other, and Ko Dali's daughter, though I never entirely trusted that leery glint in her eye, was as cheerful and friendly as you could wish. I tried to board her at Khiva, but the caravanserai was too crowded, and on the Samarkand road there wasn't the opportunity, which was a pity. I'd have liked another tussle with her, but Yakub Beg was too much with us.

He was a strange, mad, mystic-cheery fellow, that one. I don't know how much he knew, or what Ko Dali's daughter told him, but for some reason he talked to me a good deal on our journey —about Khokand, and whether the British would help him maintain its independence, and his ambitions to found a state of his own, and always his talk would turn to the Silk One, and Kashgar, far over the deserts and mountains, where even the Russians could never reach. The very last words he said to me were on that score.

We had passed the night in Samarkand, in the little serai near the market, under the huge turquoise walls of the biggest mosque in the world, and in the morning they rode out with me and my new escort a little way on the southern road. It was thronged with folk—bustling crowds of Uzbeks in their black caps, and big-nosed hillmen with their crafty faces, and veiled women, and long lines of camels with their jingling bells shuffling up the yellow dust, and porters staggering under great bales, and children underfoot, and everywhere the babbling of twenty different languages. Yakub and I were riding ahead, talking, and we stopped at a little river running under the road to water our beasts.

"The stream of See-ah," says Yakub, laughing. "Did I say the Ruskis would water their horses in it this autumn? I was wrong —thanks to you—and to my silk girl and Kutebar and the others. They will not come yet, to spoil all this"—and he gestured round at the crowds streaming by—"or come at all, if I can help it. And if they do—well, there is still Kashgar, and a free place in the hills."

" 'Where the wicked cease from troubling,' eh," says I, because it seemed appropriate.

"Is that an English saying?" he asked.

"I think it's a hymn." If I remember rightly, we used to sing it in chapel at Rugby before the miscreants of the day got flogged.

"All holy songs are made of dreams," says he. "And this is a great place for dreams, such as mine. You know where we are, Englishman?" He pointed along the dusty track, which wound in and out of the little sand-hills, and then ran like a yellow ribbon across the plain before it forked towards the great white barrier of the Afghan mountains. "This is the great Pathway of Expectation, as the hill people say, where you may realize your hopes just by hoping them. The Chinese call it the Baghdad Highway, and the Persians and Hindus know it as the Silk Trail, but we call it the Golden Road." And he quoted a verse which, with considerable trouble, I've turned into rhyming English:

> To learn the age-old lesson day by day:
> It is not in the bright arrival planned,
> But in the dreams men dream along the way,
> They find the Golden Road to Samarkand.

"Very pretty," says I. "Make it up yourself?"

He laughed. "No—it's an old song, perhaps Firdausi or Omar. Anyway, it will take me to Kashgar—if I live long enough. But here are the others, and here we say farewell. You were my guest, sent to me from heaven: touch upon my hand in parting."

So we shook, and then the others arrived, and Kutebar was gripping me by the shoulders in his great bear-hug and shouting: "God be with you, Flashman—and my compliments to the scientists and doctors in Anglistan." And Ko Dali's daughter approached demurely to give me the gift of her scarf and kiss me gently on the lips—and just for an instant the minx's tongue was half-way down my throat before she withdrew, looking like St Cecilia. Yakub Beg shook hands again and wheeled his horse.

"Goodbye, blood brother. Think of us in England. Come and visit us in Kashgar some day—or better still, find a Kashgar of your own!"

And then they were thundering away back on the Samarkand road, cloaks flying, and Kutebar turning in the saddle to give me a wave and a roar. And it's odd—but for a moment I felt lonely, and wondered if I should miss them. It was a deeply-felt sentimental mood which lasted for at least a quarter of a second, and has never returned, I'm happy to say. As to Kashgar, and Yakub's invitation—well, if I could get guaranteed passports from the Tsar, and the Empress of China, and every hill-chief between Astrakhan and Lake Baikal, and a private Pullman car the whole way with running buffet, bar, and waitresses in constant attendance—I might think quite hard about it before declining. I've too many vivid memories of Central Asia; at my time of life Scarborough is far enough east for me.

It was strange, though, to go back into Afghanistan again, with my escort—heaven knows where Yakub had got 'em from, but one look at their wolfish faces and well-stuffed cartridge belts reassured me that this was one party that no right-minded badmash would dream of attacking. It took us a week over the Hindu-Killer, and another couple of days through the hills to Kabul—and suddenly there was the old Bala Hissar again, and I sat in disbelief looking across to the overgrown orchards where Elphy Bey's cantonment had been, so many years ago, and the Kabul River, and the hillside where Akbar had spread his carpet and McNaghten had died—I could close my eyes and almost hear the drums of the 44th beating "Yankee Doodle" and old Lady Sale berating some unfortunate bearer for brewing tea before the water was *thoroughly* boiling.

I even took a turn up by the ruined Residency, and found my heart beating faster as I looked at the bullet-pocked walls, and marked the window where Broadfoot had tumbled to his death —and from there I turned and tried to find the spot where the Ghazis had set on me and the Burnes brothers, but I couldn't find it.

It was strange—everything the same and yet different. I stood looking round at the close-packed houses, and wondered in which one Gul Shah had tried to murder me with his infernal snakes— and at that I found myself shivering and hurrying back to the market where my escort were waiting: sometimes ghosts can hover in too close for comfort. I didn't want to linger in Kabul any longer, and to the astonishment of my escort I insisted that we journey on to Peshawar by the north bank of the Kabul River although, as the leader pointed out, there was a fine road by way of Boothak and Jallalabad to the south.

"There are serais, huzoor," says he, "and all comfort for us and our beasts—this way is broken country, where we must lie out by night in the cold. Truly, the south road is better."

"My son," says I, "when you were a *chotah wallah** gurgling your mother's milk, I travelled that south road, and I didn't like it one little bit. So we'll stick to the river, if you don't mind."

"Aye-ee!" says he, grinning with his jagged teeth. "Perchance you owe money to someone in Jallalabad?"

"No," says I, "not money. Lead on, friend of all travellers—to the river."

So that way we went, and cold it was by night, but I didn't have nightmares, waking or sleeping, all the way to the Khyber and the winding road down to Peshawar, where I said goodbye to my escort and rode under the arch where Avitabile used to hang the Gilzais, and so into the presence of a young whipper-snapper of a Company ensign.

"A very good day to you, old boy," says I. "I'm Flashman."

He was a fishy-looking, fresh young lad with a peeling nose, and he goggled at me, going red.

* Little fellow.

"Sergeant!" he squeaks. "What's this beastly-looking nigger doing on the office verandah?" For I was attired *à la* Kizil Kum still, in cloak and *pyjamys* and puggaree, with a bigger beard than Dr Grace.

"Not at all," says I, affably, "I'm English—a British officer, in fact. Name of Flashman—Colonel Flashman, 17th Lancers, but slightly detached for the moment. I've just come from—up yonder, at considerable personal expense, and I'd like to see someone in authority. Your commanding officer will do."

"It's a madman!" cries he. "Sergeant, stand by!"

And would you believe it, it took me half an hour before I could convince him not to throw me in the lock-up, and he summoned a peevish-looking captain, who listened, nodding irritably while I explained who and what I was.

"Very good," says he. "You've come from Afghanistan?"

"By way of Afghanistan, yes. But—"

"Very good. This is a customs post, among other things. Have you anything to declare?"

(The end of the fourth packet of the Flashman Papers).

Appendix I: Balaclava

So much has been written about this battle, by its survivors, by journalists and historians, and even by propagandists and poets, that it is hardly necessary to say more than that Flashman's account, while it adds certain graphic details that have not been recorded hitherto, agrees substantially with other eyewitness descriptions. Much of what he says of the actual charge of the Light Brigade, for example, may be verified by comparison with the accounts of those who survived the action, such as Paget, Trooper Farquharson, Captain Morgan, Cardigan, and others.

But the great controversy of Balaclava, which will probably never be settled satisfactorily, is why the Light Brigade attacked the battery at all. Experts and amateurs of history alike, who have read Russell, Kinglake, Woodham-Smith, Fortescue and a host of others, and who are familiar with the points of view of Raglan, Lucan, and Cardigan, may decide for themselves whether Flashman casts valuable light on the subject or not. Many believe that Raglan and Airey were principally at fault for issuing an imprecise order, that Nolan's excitement in transmitting it to Lucan led to the final fatal confusion, and that neither Cardigan nor Lucan can be fairly blamed for what followed. These are conclusions with which Flashman himself would obviously not disagree. The whole question hinges dramatically on the moment when Nolan made his wild gesture (down the valley? towards the redoubts? how great was the angle of difference anyway? did he say "*our* guns" or "*your* guns" or what?) and if he was at fault, he paid the highest price for it. So too, perhaps, did Raglan; he died in the Crimea, like the six hundred sabres, and if there was a blunder, it was buried with them.

Appendix II: Yakub Beg and Izzat Kutebar

Yakub (Yakoob) Beg, who became the greatest chief in Central Asia and the leading resistance fighter against Russian imperialism, was born in Piskent in 1820. He was one of the Persian–Tajik people, and a descendant of Tamerlaine the Great (Timur)—Flashman's description of him corresponds closely to the reconstruction of features recently made from Timur's skull by the Russian expert, Professor Gerasimov.

In 1845 Yakub became chamberlain to the Khan of Khokand, and then Pansad Bashi (commander of 500). He was made Kush Begi (military commander) and Governor of Ak Mechet, an important fortress on the Syr Daria, in 1847, and in the same year married a girl from Julek, a river town; she is described as "a Kipchak lady of the Golden Horde". Yakub was active in raiding the new Russian outposts on the Aral coast, and after the fall of Ak Metchet in 1853 he made strenuous efforts to retake it from the Russians, without success.

After the Russian invasion, Yakub eventually turned his attention to making his own state in Kashgar. In 1865, as commander-in-chief to the decadent Buzurg Khan, he took Kashgar, then dispossessed his own overlord, and assumed the throne himself as Amir and Atalik Ghazi; in this same year he married "the beautiful daughter of Ko Dali, an officer in the Chinese army", by whom he had several children.

As ruler of Kashgar and East Turkestan, Yakub Beg was the most powerful monarch of Central Asia. He remained a bitter enemy of Russia and a close friend of the British, whose envoys were received in Kashgar, where a British–Kashgari commercial treaty was concluded in 1874. It was Russia's fear that he would eventually unite all the Muslims of Central Asia in a holy war against the Tsar, but in 1876 Kashgar was attacked by China, and Yakub was driven out; he was assassinated on May 1, 1877, by Hakim Khan, a son of Buzurg Khan.

His biographer has described Yakub Beg as "a great man born centuries too late". Certainly, as a nationalist leader and resistance fighter he was unique in his time and country, for "alone in Central Asia he remained free", and he fought his campaigns and ruled his independent state without wealth or any large following; his great gifts, according to contemporaries, were a keen intelligence, a winning and handsome appearance, and a refusal to be panicked—he also seems to have had a sense of timing, as witness the neatness with which he betrayed Buzurg Khan.

Anywhere else in the world he would probably be remembered as William Wallace, Hereward, and Crazy Horse are remembered, but not in modern Russia. In Tashkent recently I asked an educated Russian what kind of place Yakub Beg occupied in local history: his name was not even known. (See D. C. Boulger's *Yakoob Beg*, 1878.)

Izzat Kutebar, brigand, rebel, and guerrilla leader, was a Kirgiz, born probably in 1800. He first robbed the Bokhara caravan in 1822, and was at his height as a raider and scourge of the Russians in the 1840s. They eventually persuaded him to suspend his bandit activities, and rewarded him with a gold medal (see page 231), but he cut loose again in the early fifties, was captured in 1854, escaped or was released, raised a revolt, and lived as a rebel in the Ust-Yurt until 1858, when he finally surrendered to Count Ignatieff and made his peace with Russia.

Notes

1. Possibly because of the war scare, as Flashman suggests, there was a craze for growing moustaches, in addition to beards and whiskers, in the early months of 1854. Another fashion among the young men was for brilliantly-coloured shirts with grotesque designs, skulls, snakes, flowers, and the like. Both fads bore an interesting resemblance to modern "hippy" fashions," not least in the reactions they provoked: Bank of England clerks were expressly forbidden to join "the moustache movement", as it was called.

2. The "eunuchs". The open-range musketry target in use at this time consisted of the usual concentric circles, but with a naked human figure in the centre; the bull was a black disc discreetly placed below the figure's waist-line.

3. Although Britain was not formally at war until March 28, 1854, the preparations for conflict had been going on for many weeks amid growing popular determination for a showdown with Russia. The Scots (3rd) Guards had embarked a month earlier, and Palmerston, the Home Secretary, and Sir James Graham, First Lord of the Admiralty, made their jingoistic Reform Club speeches on March 7. These were brilliantly parodied by *Punch* ("Shomeshay we're norrawar. Norrawar! Hash-ha! No! Norrawar! Noshexactly awar. But...") But while the war fever was strong in Britain it was not as universal as Flashman suggests; there was an active peace movement, and anti-war sentiments could be passionate. For an extreme but interesting view, see J. McQueen's *The War: who's to blame?* (1854).

4. The play was almost certainly Balzac's "The Married Unmarried", which caused a minor controversy.

5. Shell-out, skittle pool, go-back, etc. The rules of these early variations on pool (and forerunners of snooker) are to be found in "Captain Crawley's" standard Victorian work, *Billiards*, which is a mine of practical information and billiards lore, and contains much information on pool-room sharks and swindles. Joe Bennet was a champion player of the time. A jenny is a difficult in-off shot to the middle pocket, usually with the object ball close to the side-cushion; a pair of breeches is a simultaneous in-off and pot red in the top pockets.

6. Sir William Molesworth's Commons committee met in March, 1854, to consider small arms production. Lord Paget was among the members, and Lt-Col. Sam Colt, the American inventor of the Colt revolver, was among those who gave evidence.

7. Quite apart from the popular criticism he had been receiving for allegedly meddling in State affairs, Prince Albert's zeal for designing military clothing attracted considerable ridicule in the spring of 1854. In fact, judging from contemporary sketches, the so-called "Albert Bonnet" for the Guards was a sensible, if ugly, multi-purpose forage cap. But there was growing controversy at this time about British uniforms—the traditional tight stocks and collars being a principal target—and any suggestions from H.R.H. were, as usual, unwelcome.

8. The main bombardment of Odessa by British ships took place on April 22, but without doing great damage.

9. "Villikins and his Dinah" was the hit song of 1854.

10. From this, and one later reference, it seems obvious that Flashman was particularly impressed by a *Punch* cartoon, published shortly after Balaclava, showing a stout British father brandishing a poker with patriotic zeal in the morning-room as he reads news of the Charge of the Light Brigade.

11. The Cabinet did meet at Pembroke Lodge, Richmond, on the evening of June 28, 1854, and agreed on important orders to be sent to Lord Raglan for the invasion of the Crimea. "Agreed" may be too strong a word, since most of the Cabinet were asleep during the meeting, and were not fully aware of what orders were being sent; they woke up once, when someone knocked over a chair, and then dozed off again. The authority for this is no less than A. W. Kinglake, the great Crimea historian, who devotes a separate appendix to the incident in his massive history of the war, *The Invasion of the Crimea*. Kinglake was obviously uneasy about disclosing that the Cabinet had taken the vital decision of the war while in a state of torpor, and speculated about the possibility "of a narcotic substance having been taken by some mischance" in their food. He was too tactful or charitable to mention the obvious conclusion, which is that they had had too much to drink.

12. Flashman's account of this important meeting between Raglan and Sir George Brown is largely corroborated by Brown's own version in Kinglake. Both Newcastle's despatch and his personal note to Raglan were definite on the need to besiege Sevastopol, while leaving the final responsibility with Raglan and his French colleagues.

13. Mrs Duberly, wife of an officer of the 8th Hussars, and an old friend of Flashman's (see *Flash for Freedom!*), left a vivid journal of her experiences in the Crimea, including the incident described here, when she boarded a transport "wrapped up in an old hat and shawl . . . an extraordinary figure" to avoid detection by Lord Lucan. (See E. E. P. Tisdall's *Mrs Duberly's Campaigns*.)

14. "The policeman at Herne Bay". This mythical policeman was a humorous by-word of the time.

15. It is interesting to note that William Howard Russell, in his original despatch to *The Times*, made the mistake of reporting that the High-landers were involved in the attack on the Redoubt, but corrected this in later despatches. His histories of the Crimea are the work of a brilliant newspaperman, and even those who question his criticism of Raglan and other British leaders (see Colonel Adye's *The Crimean War*) acknowledge the quality of his reporting. Anyone interested in verifying Flashman's statements cannot do better than refer to Russell, or to Kinglake, who was also an eye-witness. Incidentally, Flashman's account of the Alma action is extremely accurate, especially where Lord Raglan's movements are concerned, but his memory has surely played him false in a slightly earlier passage when he suggests that the Russian gunners fired on the army at the start of its march down the Crimea coast: this took place some hours later.

16. For an account of this incident, see Russell's *The War from the landing at Gallipoli to the death of Lord Raglan* (1855).

17. Generally Flashman disagrees with other eye-witnesses no more than they disagree among themselves, and these discrepancies are minor ones. For example, some authorities suggest that the Highlanders fired three volleys against the Russian cavalry, not two, and at fairly long range (E. H. Nolan actually says that there was properly speaking "no cavalry charge upon the Highlanders", but this is not borne out by others). Again, as to casualties in the Heavy Brigade charge, Flashman saw comparatively few, but Trooper Farquharson of the 4th Light

Dragoons, who rode over the ground immediately afterwards, "saw dozens . . . with the ugliest gashes about their heads and faces." (See R. S. Farquharson, *Reminiscences of Crimean Campaigning*).

18. The original pencilled order, scribbled by Airey, is still preserved. It reads: "Lord Raglan wishes the Cavalry to advance rapidly to the front, follow the Enemy & try to prevent the Enemy carrying away the guns. Troop Horse Attily may accompany. French Cavalry is on yr left. Immediate." As to what verbal instructions may have been added, there is no certainty, but one of the rumours which later arose (see H. Moyse-Bartlett's *Louis Edward Nolan*) was that Nolan had been told to tell Lucan to act on the *defensive*, but had passed on the vital word as *offensive*.

19. It is one of the true curiosities of the charge of the Light Brigade that Lord George Paget rode into action smoking a cheroot—obviously the one which Flashman gave him—and did not actually draw his sabre until the moment of entering the battery, when his orderly, Parkes, advised him to do so. Paget's coolness, which as much as anything saved the remnants of the Light Brigade, was notorious; Trooper Farquharson, who rode with him in the charge, recalled how earlier in the battle Paget was hit by a shell splinter, and reacted only by telling his orderly to collect it as a souvenir.

20. The recklessness of the British cavalry charge so amazed the Russians that Liprandi's immediate conclusion was that the Light Brigade must have been drunk. (See Cecil Woodham-Smith's *The Reason Why*, and Kinglake.)

21. Whatever may be said of his opinions, Flashman's information about the plight of the Russian serfs in the 1850s is entirely accurate, and is borne out by several other contemporary authorities. The best of these are perhaps Baron von Haxthausen, whose *The Russian Empire* appeared in 1856, and Shirley Brooks's *The Russians of the South* (1854). They also corroborate his descriptions of Russian life in general, as does *The Englishwoman in Russia*, by "a Lady ten years resident in that country", published in 1855. *Savage and Civilised Russia*, by "W.R." (1877), is an informative work; two largely political tracts by S. Stepniak, *Russia under the Tsars* (1885) and *The Russian Peasantry* (1888), contain useful material and interesting bias; and the *Memoirs* of the celebrated Russian radical, Alexander Herzen (1812–70), give an illuminating insight into the serf mentality. Like Flashman, he observed how his family's land serfs "somehow succeed in not believing in their complete slavery", and contrasted this with the plight of the house serfs who, although they were paid wages, had their existence destroyed and poisoned by "the terrible consciousness of serfdom".

22. Captain Count Nicholas Pavlovitch Ignatieff was later to become one of Russia's most brilliant agents in the Far East. He served in China, undertook daring missions into Central Asia, and was also for a time military attaché in London. There is evidence that early in the Crimean War he was serving on the Baltic, and this must have been shortly before his encounter with Flashman. He was twenty-two at this time.

23. For confirmation, and other details of Harry East's military career, see *Tom Brown at Oxford*, by Thomas Hughes (1861).

24. The commander of Prince Vigenstein's Hussars in 1837 was, in fact, Colonel Pencherjevsky.

25. If anything, Flashman's description of the punishments meted out to Russian serfs by their owners appears to be on the mild side. The works cited earlier in these notes contain examples of fearful cruelty and the carelessness with which extraordinary penalties were some-

times imposed—Alexander Herzen gives instances of atrocities, and also recalls the psychological misery caused when his father, a nobleman, ordered a village patriarch's beard to be shaved off. Turgenev the novelist, another nobleman who saw serfdom at first hand, described how his mother banished two young serfs to Siberia because they failed to bow to her in passing—and how they came to bid her farewell before leaving for exile. (See A. Yarmolinsky's *Turgenev the Man*.)

26. It was a folk-saying—and may still be—that one could tell a true Russian by that fact that he would go with his neck open and unprotected, even in the coldest weather.

27. It is interesting that Pencherjevsky had heard of Marx at this time, for although the great revolutionary had already gained an international notoriety, his influence was not to be felt in Russia for many years. Non-Communist agitators were, however, highly active in the country, and no doubt to the Count they all looked alike.

28. Flashman seems to suggest that this incident took place in February, 1855. If it did, then Tsar Nicholas I had only weeks, and possibly days, to live: he died on March 2 in St Petersburg, after influenza which had lasted about a fortnight. There is no evidence that he visited the south in the closing weeks of his life; on the other hand Flashman's account seems highly circumstantial. Possibly he has confused the dates, and Nicholas came to Starotorsk earlier than February. However, anyone scenting a mystery here may note that while the Tsar died on March 2, he was last seen *in public* on February 22 at an infantry review. (See E. H. Nolan's *History of the War against Russia*.)

29. The Khruleff and Duhamel plans were only two in a long list of proposed Russian invasions of British India. As far back as 1801 Tsar Paul, hoping to replace British rule by his own, agreed to a joint Franco-Russian invasion through Afghanistan (Napoleon was at that time in Egypt, and the French Government were to pave the invaders' way by sending "rare objects" to be "distributed with tact" among native chiefs on the line of march.) The Russian part of the expedition actually got under way, but with the death of the Tsar and the British victory at Copenhagen the scheme was abandoned.

General Duhamel's plan for an invasion through Persia was first put to the Tsar in 1854, and was followed in early 1855 by General Khruleff's proposed Afghan-Khyber expedition. The details of the two plans, as given by Flashman, correspond almost exactly with the versions subsequently published as a result of British intelligence work (see *Russia's March to India*, published anonymously by an Indian Army officer in 1894). Indeed, at various points in Flashman's account Ignatieff repeats passages from Duhamel and Khruleff almost verbatim.

30. The "soul tax" was simply a tax on each male, of 86 silver kopecks annually (see J. Blum's *Lord and Peasant in Russia*). If a serf died, his family had to continue to pay the tax until he was officially declared dead at the next census. Blocking the family stove was a common inducement to pay.

31. It is probably mere coincidence, but one of V. I. Lenin's immediate ancestors bore the surname Blank.

32. ". . . with his belt at the last hole". Obviously a corpulent Cossack, or one near retiring age. It was a rule that the Cossacks wore belts of a standard length, and were not permitted to grow stouter than the belt allowed.

33. Leaking Russian stoves could be highly poisonous. At least three British officers were killed by fumes ("smothered in charcoal") at Balaclava in the first week of January 1855. (See General Gordon's letters from the Crimea, Jan. 3–8, 1855.)

34. The serf rising at Starotorsk may have astonished Flashman, but such rebellions were exceedingly common (as he himself remarks elsewhere in his narrative). More than 700 such revolts took place in Russia during the thirty years of Nicholas I's reign.

35. Fort Raim was built on the Syr Daria (the Jaxartes) in 1847, the year after Russia's first occupation on the Aral coast, and was immediately raided by Yakub Beg. The Russian policy of expansion followed the fort's establishment, and their armed expeditions eastward began in 1852 and 1853.

36. Yakub Beg (1820–77), fighting leader of the Tajiks, chamberlain to the Khan of Khokand, warlord of the Syr Daria, etc. (See Appendix II.)

37. Izzat Kutebar, bandit, guerrilla fighter, so-called "Rob Roy of the Steppe". (See Appendix II.)

38. "Khan Ali" was Captain Arthur Conolly, a British agent executed at Bokhara in 1842, along with another Briton, Colonel Charles Stoddart. They had been kept in terrible conditions in the Shah's dungeons, but Conolly was told his life would be spared if he became a Muslim, as Stoddart had done. He refused—his words quoted by an eye-witness were: "Do your work."

39. The language would not be pure Persian, as Flashman suggests, but the Tajik dialect of that language—the Tajiks, being of Persian origin, considered themselves a cut above other Central Asians, and clung to their traditional language and customs.

40. Presumably such works as *England and Russia in Central Asia* (1879), *Central Asian Portraits* (1880), by D. C. Boulger, and *Caravan Journeys and Wanderings*, by J. P. Ferrier. These, and companion volumes, give in addition to biographical details an account of the occupation of the Eastern lands by Russia, which had its origins in the agreement of 1760, when the Kirgiz-Kazak peoples, under their khan, Sultan Abdul Faiz, became nominal subjects of the Tsar, receiving his protection in return for their promise to safeguard the Russian caravans. Neither side kept its bargain.

41. The Russian expansion into Central Asia in the middle of the last century, which swallowed up all the independent countries and khanates east of the Caspian as far as China and south to Afghanistan, was conducted with considerable brutality. The massacre at Ak Mechet (the White Mosque), by General Perovski, on August 8, 1853, took place as Yakub Beg describes it, but it was surpassed by such atrocities as Denghil Tepe, in the Kara Kum, in 1879, when the Tekke women and children, attempting to escape from the position which their menfolk were holding, were deliberately shot down by Lomakin's troops. In this, as in other places, the Russian commanders made it clear that they were not interested in receiving surrenders.

It is customary nowadays for Russians to refer to this expansion as "Tsarist imperialism"; however, it will be noted that while the much-abused Western colonial powers have now largely divested themselves of their empires, the modern Russian Communist state retains an iron grip on the extensive colonies in Central Asia which the old Russian empire acquired.

42. The Mongols were said to be descended from a sky-blue wolf. Flashman's Khokandian friends seem to have used the term rather loosely, possibly because many of them were part Mongol by descent. Incidentally, much of Kutebar's speech at this point is almost word for word with a rallying-call heard in the Syr Daria country at the time of the Russian advance.

43. The military rockets devised by Sir William Congreve were used in the War of 1812, and those described by Flashman were obviously similar to this early pattern, which continued in use for many years.

The Congreve was a gigantic sky-rocket, consisting of an iron cylinder four inches in diameter and over a yard long, packed with powder and attached to a fifteen-foot stick. It was fired from a slanting trough or tube, and travelled with a tremendous noise and a great trail of smoke and sparks, exploding on impact. Although they could fly two miles, the rockets were extremely erratic, and throughout the first half of the nineteenth century frequent modifications were made, including William Hale's spinning rocket, and the grooved and finned rocket, which could be fired without a stick.

44. The secret society of Assassins, founded in Persia in the eleventh century by Hassan el Sabbah, "the Old Man of the Mountains", were notorious for their policy of secret murder and their addiction to the hashish drug from which they took their name. At their height they operated from hill strongholds, mostly in Persia and Syria, and were active against the Crusaders before being dispersed by the Mongol invasion of Hulagu Khan in the thirteenth century. Traces of the sect exist today in the Middle East.